TRIUMPH
OF THE
SPIRIT

TRIUMPH OF THE SPIRIT

David Pilarski

TRIUMPH OF THE SPIRIT

iUniverse books may be ordered through booksellers or by contacting:

iUniverse LLC
1663 Liberty Drive
Bloomington, IN 47403
www.iuniverse.com
1-800-Authors (1-800-288-4677)

ISBN: 978-1-4759-5857-7 (sc)
ISBN: 978-1-4759-5859-1 (hc)
ISBN: 978-1-4759-5858-4 (e)

Printed in the United States of America

iUniverse rev. date: 07/11/2014

For the four most amazing souls
I am divinely blessed to have in this life

Otherwise known as my children
Adam, Amanda, Alyssa and Alexander

Because of you I know the true nature
of unconditional love

CHAPTER 1

DISCOVERY

In spite of being eighteen years old and in his final week of high school, Matthew had never seen the ocean. The furthest from Indiana he had ever ventured from was Kentucky, and that had just been a weekend trip. He had liked Kentucky because it was somewhere different from where he grew up, and he had little experience of anything else. What he knew was Indiana. He knew the way it looked, the way it smelled, the way people acted. He knew the flat, open land that stretched out endlessly in every direction with the occasional barn or silo that erupted into the void of vertical space above the crops. Most especially, he knew his grandfather's farm, an eighty-acre piece of land in northern Indiana where he had spent the best times of his childhood. He knew how to have fun on the farm and also how to work on it. As a young child, Matthew learned the single most important chore was ensuring the horses had enough hay to eat during the cold winter months. This unfortunately meant physically taxing work during the hottest months of the summer from June to August baling hay, which Matthew knew how to do since he was old enough to climb up onto a tractor seat.

As a physical specimen, Matthew was quite an impressive young man. He stood six feet, four inches tall and had a dark complexion, taking after his father's Italian heritage, with a lean muscular build from all of his years of weight training from football and basketball. The young man has dark brown eyes and extremely thick, black hair that was always well trimmed just above the ear and parted to the right. He often wondered how he grew so tall given the heights of his parents. David, his father,

1

was also a lean fellow, since he was an avid runner, but barely stood six feet tall. Matthew's mother, Ann, stood five feet five inches. She, too, was a fit runner with hazel eyes and light brown, shoulder-length hair that she consistently maintained at the hair salon. Matthew always towered over her during family photos, and he never missed the opportunity to tease her about it. He especially enjoyed it when he could spot a gray hair on the top of her head from his elevated vantage point to which her response was always to pull it out before anyone else noticed.

Like a typical teenager, Matthew had dated a few girls throughout high school. The relationships varied in duration and how they ended. Some of them he broke off and others they initiated. The longest running one was about a year long that started midway through his junior year. Although it was mutual, it still hurt nonetheless when they broke up. As a result, Matthew decided to take a break from dating and remain unattached. He learned one key thing from his experiences thus far at the ripe old age of eighteen—he couldn't stand excessive drama. Being a smart, handsome, good guy afforded him the opportunity to attract a lot of girls who were interested in him, but he found that he was looking for something that kept eluding him. The physical chemistry was an important element at first because of the spark of attraction. But over time, Matthew kept hoping for someone who shared his passions and dreamed of bigger things for the future, and ultimately that's where things would begin to fizzle over time with anyone he became involved with. It wasn't a good or bad thing, it was just an inner pull that he felt. There was a woman out there who would be a great match. All he had to do was find her. He hoped that beginning anew in college with a whole new set of girls from all over the country would provide the answer for his search. Matthew began counting down the days because college was only a few short months away now and his excitement grew at the prospects for a whole new life.

He had been given early admission into The University of Notre Dame, thereby fulfilling his life-long dream, not to mention his father's expectations. David had graduated from

Notre Dame, so nothing else was ever seriously considered for Matthew. He didn't mind though, because he loved everything about it—the beauty of the campus, the legendary football team, the "mystique" . . . something you couldn't really grasp unless you had experienced it. Growing up only an hour away, he had already spent a great deal of time there. He and his father attended several football and basketball games each year, including pep rallies, tailgates and endless walks around the ivy-covered buildings. He and his entire family would go to campus at least once each summer. They would feed the ducks on St. Mary's lake, light a candle at the Grotto, attend Mass at the Basilica of the Sacred Heart, and of course spend hundreds of dollars on merchandise at the Bookstore. Yes, the spirit of Notre Dame had long been a part of him. When he was on campus, he felt a deep sense of something sacred. He couldn't name it or adequately describe it, but it moved him whenever he was there. David was a deeply devout Catholic, and Matthew had always fashioned his spiritual practices after him. It just seemed a lot simpler. You go to Mass, and you're all set. He loved the feeling of knowing he had done exactly what was expected of him on Sunday morning. Then you go through your upcoming week and come back again the next Sunday. It all fit so nicely in the tidy organization of his life which he often took great comfort in.

His parents, being devout Catholics, were the main reason he never went by the name Matt, because they wanted him to retain the strong Biblical ties to his name. Of course, there was also his paternal Italian grandmother who influenced the outcome of his name. His grandma immigrated to the United States as a young girl and was about as old school as you could get, right down to her broken English accent. She could cook like no one's business, which explained Matthew's love for Italian food. His grandmother had a heart of gold and exuded so much love for her four children and nineteen grandchildren. Matthew had been very close to her right up to her death at the age of ninety-seven. He still missed her. Even though she barely stood five feet tall, you didn't mess with her because she was the stereotypical loving, but strong-willed tough Italian woman. Being a deeply religious person of strong faith, she loved the name Matthew and was the one who suggested it to his parents upon his birth. In the end, he didn't mind though, because he grew accustomed to it at such an early age that the shortened version didn't sound right. Now, he actually preferred going by Matthew.

He studied frantically during high school, taking all honors classes and acing them, because he knew that academic success was the key to being admitted into the University. He also played football, basketball and trumpet in the band to round out his resume. From all of this, Matthew knew his place in the world—a straight-A honors student, athlete, good son, "church-goer." He was the kid who went next door after a big snowfall and shoveled elderly Mrs. Seuss's driveway without being asked and without accepting any payment beyond a nice cup of hot cocoa with little marshmallows. He was as "All American" as you could get, and he was comfortable in this role. It had been somehow preordained that this was who he would be. He never considered being anything else. This was his spot in the world, created for him. Anything else might not fit him as well, and the notion of deviating from it actually scared him. But yet, he had this nagging feeling at the core of his being since he was a young boy. In spite of the comfortable life and roles he played, he felt a pull in another direction, a desire for something more.

Now a young adult, Matthew's assistance was all the more valuable to his grandfather during hay baling season; that's what Matthew was doing on the day everything changed, baling hay on a hot, humid day in early June. The sky was a deep blue, and the sound of the tree leaves blowing in the strong breeze on the outskirts of the alfalfa field were drowned out by the constant hum of the farm tractor. The sound of leaves blowing in the wind and the sound of the tractor were things that Matthew knew very well and gave him great comfort. This was the day, however, when the line between what he knew and what he could not even imagine became forever blurred.

It was Matthew's turn to drive the tractor as it pulled the baler across the hay field, which had been cut the day before. He'd always loved to drive the tractor. When he was small, Matthew's father would let him sit between his legs and steer, while David worked the pedals with his long legs. The very smell of the gasoline and the sound of the roaring engine still ignited a sense of excitement in the young man because of the power he had felt as a kid at the helm of the mighty machine. It seemed silly now that he could drive a car, but the thought of driving a tractor still invigorated him. Maybe it was not so much the tractor as it was the memory of sitting between his father's legs, feeling safe and secure, knowing there was someone there bigger than you to take the wheel if you were headed toward trouble. So often in life, how we desire to know that someone is there to help steer us in the right direction when we may turn astray. Matthew knew he could always count on his dad.

The mid-nineties temperature was perfect for baling hay. Matthew learned long ago that the alfalfa needs to be perfectly dry in order to be formed into rectangular bales and stored in the hay barn as winter feed for the horses. Also there that day, the day when everything changed, were Matthew's uncles, Bud and Don. The three brothers had been running the farm for as long as Matthew could remember. That's what you did in Indiana. If your father needed his farm run, you ran it. You didn't ever stop to consider there might be an alternative, because you just did what was expected of you. That's how it was with Matthew. He was expected to bale hay so bale hay he did. He had never really considered whether he liked it, and surely no one else had ever considered this either. Why would a parent give his child a choice he himself had never been given? Too many options could compromise the system. Deep inside the private world of Matthew's mind, however, the awareness did exist that he didn't actually care for baling hay. It was hot, sticky, very physically demanding and usually took up his entire weekend.

Suddenly, a loud whistle pierced Matthew's thoughts as his father signaled him to pull over for a water break, and he began to turn the tractor in response. As Matthew turned the tractor toward the edge of the field and turned off the engine, a streak of light whizzed by. Caught in Matthew's peripheral vision, he instinctively turned toward the streak, only to see a small plume of white smoke billowing in the air in the adjacent corn field. Startled, Matthew quickly turned back toward his dad and uncles to see if they had seen it. Their backs were turned and were casually passing around the jug of water. Sweat dripped from their foreheads as they were solely focused on replenishing the water their bodies had lost over hours of intense work. They clearly hadn't seen anything. Matthew felt a slight twinge of fear. He did not like knowing that he was the only one who had witnessed this strange sight. Then it occurred to him that he must have been seeing things. He quickly looked back to see if the smoke was still there. He thought he saw a faint trail. Maybe it was something else. Maybe it was the sun playing tricks on his weary, sweat-filled, allergy-irritated eyes. The temporarily lost feeling in his legs slowly returned. It wasn't until he took a deep breath that he realized he had been holding his breath. He shook his head to dislodge the image and tried to erase the entire event from his mind.

With still shaky legs, he climbed down off his high perch. Matthew wore faded and torn blue jeans and a white T-shirt. The jeans were meant to protect your legs from the scratchy hay while the white shirt deflected the heat from the sun. When his feet hit the ground, he relaxed into the comfort of the solid Indiana soil beneath him. Security returned as his father handed him the cold jug of water.

"Looks like the rain they predicted this afternoon is going to hold off until tonight," declared David. "We shouldn't have any problems finishing the field by five or six o'clock."

Matthew looked around at his dad and uncles. Nothing seemed out of the ordinary. Yet Matthew couldn't get the image out of his mind. Surely, he had been imagining it. He had seen his fair share of bad science fiction movies. It seemed like something so typical of a predictable B-movie. Even knowing this, he couldn't let it go. Although he was a bit frightened, Matthew realized that he wanted it to be real. He wanted something amazing to happen to him. Nothing amazing had ever happened to him. Sometimes, he felt the urge to break free from his pre-defined roles and move into a completely new direction, to live for himself and not for others' expectations of him. These are things that he sometimes fancied but not for very long as he never expected such thoughts could ever come to fruition. He didn't exactly know what this other existence would look like. He just somehow knew that in the grand scheme of life, we are far more than what appears on the surface. But what if somehow this strange event could lead to something out of this ordinary life? He realized that he needed to know.

"Did any of you happen to see a strange streak of light or cloud of dust and smoke hovering above the plowed corn field?" Matthew inquired as he turned his head in that general direction and motioned with his right arm.

They all looked at him as though he suddenly grew another head. Politely, they all turned in that direction. Even Matthew saw nothing now.

"No, son," replied David as he gave Matthew a quizzical look. "I think we all had an eye on the water cooler since we've been baking in this hot sun for a few hours. What did you see?"

Good, ol' Dad. That's why Matthew loved his dad more than life itself. He felt safe with his father. His dad would never tease him. David was a good man and incredibly devoted to his family. Matthew had always wanted to be like his father. He had never seen any fun in teasing other kids or making them feel inferior. Matthew was kind-hearted and compassionate like David.

"I'm not sure," Matthew responded. "I'm going to run over there to see what it might have been."

He hadn't planned on running over there, but perhaps, it was his dad's kindness that laid a safe foundation for him to take this risk. What did he have to lose anyway? Maybe there was something there after all. When he really thought about it, he was quite sure he had seen something.

"Go ahead," Don said as he stood up to place the water jug back into the red cooler beneath the shade of a tree. "We'll get started again, and you can catch up to us once we circle back around."

"I'll take over driving the tractor," offered Bud without hesitation.

Driving the tractor was a nice diversion from the physical demands of baling hay, since all you needed to do was to sit and drive as the tractor pulled the baler behind it while the crew stacked the bales on a wagon. That's why they all took turns. With that, David and Don climbed back onto the wagon, and Bud started the engine as they set off to resume their job.

Matthew set out in the direction where he had seen the streak of light and cloud of dust. Inexplicably, the fear had disappeared probably because he wasn't expecting to find anything. If he did find something, it would probably have a perfectly logical explanation. Maybe it had been a flare, or a very sophisticated radio control plane. It was probably something that could be traced back to some kids. Matthew learned at a young age that most trouble in Indiana could be traced back to kids just messing around.

Just sixty or so yards away from their watering tree, Matthew found something that threw him off guard. There in the dirt, he saw a small trench that stretched some two hundred yards. This was unexpected. The fear suddenly returned, and he felt the familiar paralyzing coldness rush through his arms and legs. He stood frozen. His mind began to race, not only thinking what it could be but also what he should do. Should he turn back and call for his dad? They would never hear him over the roar of the tractor. As he stood there immobilized, he studied the trench. It was as though something fell from the sky, struck the earth and left a trail as it slowed upon impact. The trench ran several feet wide at the apparent point of impact but gradually narrowed. As he continued to study it, Matthew knew what he had to do. He must walk forward and find the end of the trail. He had to know what made this trench. It was likely nothing to fear. It was probably something perfectly logical. Although, he couldn't imagine how a radio-controlled plane could crash with such an impact and make such a large hole in the ground. As he tentatively walked forward, he tried to imagine what it could possibly be. He allowed himself to consider the possibility that it wasn't something logical at all. His first thought was of a small piece of meteorite that had fallen to the earth. This sent a chill up his spine and a nervous flutter in his stomach. He had always loved space as it reminded him of the vastness of the universe. It appealed to his sense of that something "more" beyond merely existing on this planet. Finding the meteorite would be a dream come true for him. It seemed impossible that something so important could ever happen to him, something that significant right here and now on his grandfather's Indiana farm.

Drenched in sweat, Matthew finally reached what appeared to be the end of the trench. Peering down a good, six feet, he hoped to see a fragment of space rock at the bottom. His thoughts immediately turned to a small meteorite that was discovered in Antarctica a few years ago that NASA announced had most likely originated from Mars more than sixteen million years ago. What Matthew found even more exciting, was that scientists found what they believed to be fossilized evidence of microscopic organisms within the meteorite. The existence of life outside earth, either now or even in the past, had always fascinated the young man from Indiana. As all of these thoughts swirled in his mind, he forgot to be afraid, jumped down into the trench and began kicking dirt in a brushing motion with his right foot. Suddenly, he caught a glimpse of something shiny after a minute or two of digging. He stopped and the fear quickly returned.

Shiny? Matthew thought. *A meteorite wouldn't be shiny. Would it? What is this thing?*

He once again contemplated getting his dad, but his fear was overshadowed by a curiosity and a thrill he could not contain. Impulsively, he knelt down to brush away the earth, which still partially covered his newfound treasure. As he lowered his hand toward the ground, Matthew felt an intense heat emanating from the object.

This thrilled him as it furthered his meteorite theory from plausible to probable. He recalled past science lessons of how objects entering the earth's atmosphere must endure incredible heat. Matthew knew he couldn't touch it right then, so he decided to pour some water on his find to expedite the cooling process. He climbed out of the pit and headed back to the shade tree beneath which their water supply was stored. Matthew's mind raced as fast as his legs propelled him toward the water jug, his excitement growing. He fantasized of how the news would get out.

"Indiana Farm Kid Finds Meteorite," the headline would read.

He would be famous. CNN would come and do a story. He would be interviewed on the Today Show. The people at NASA would want him to convey all the details of his discovery. This would surely be a new beginning for him and feed his desire for that "something more."

Returning to the mysterious object, Matthew carried out his plan and poured cold water over it. Immediately, steam rose out of the trench. Thinking it would most likely take several hours to cool down, Matthew decided to go back to baling hay and return at the end of the day to retrieve it. He was sure he had been gone much too long. His dad was a kind and patient man, but taking a break while others worked was something you didn't do. He knew he had to get back to work, but he was anxious to update his dad on his discovery. If he went back and told him immediately, would he stop the day's work? Would they all come rushing over and make a big fuss? What if they didn't? What if they thought this wasn't a big deal? What if it wasn't important enough to stop baling hay? These possibilities crushed Matthew's spirit, because this was the biggest thing that ever happened to him. He couldn't live with his uncles belittling it by not immediately running right over to check it out. Matthew decided to play it safe and wait until they stopped for the day to tell his dad. This would also give the thing plenty of time to cool down.

As he started back, Matthew continued to indulge himself by considering that perhaps he had really found something significant. He began to contemplate how many millions of miles or even millions of years this potential meteorite traveled before reaching its ultimate destination on his grandfather's farm. This intrigued Matthew immensely. His dad had given him a telescope for his eleventh birthday, and he spent hours gazing at the vastness of the stars in space. He thrilled with the infinite possibilities this vista represented which would inevitably always give him goose bumps. He could barely comprehend what life would be like outside of Indiana let alone other realities that might exist on a distant planet millions of miles from Earth. He loved to imagine that other life forms existed on these far off planets. This was probably why he enjoyed science fiction movies so much. And now to think that his own life was actually beginning to mimic one! Although he surely knew this was science and not fiction. A genuine, bona fide meteorite was what this was. Although one curious point continued to nag at him. How could, what presumably may be a rock, have a shine to it? He remembered reading that meteorites could have some metallic properties, but could it have enough surface metal to shine? His curiosity grew as he became more anxious to return to his find.

The rest of the day went much quicker than Matthew would have imagined as he kept quiet about his find, especially since his father and uncles didn't ask, given they were feverishly attempting to finish the hay field before the rain storm rolled in. He was so lost in thought over his meteorite and the exciting destiny awaiting him that his mind was barely aware of the taxing physical work his body performed in the intense heat. About 6:30 in the evening, the group finally finished baling the last of the alfalfa.

"Looks like we made it in the nick of time," Don noted as he assumed command of the tractor and turned it in the direction of the barn.

The sky had darkened in the distance, and they could begin to hear faint rolling thunder and see a few flashes of lightning within the dark clouds.

"I'll meet you back at the farm house," Matthew noted anxiously.

"Where are you going, son?" asked David.

At that moment, Matthew realized that not even his dad had asked him if he found anything earlier. Clearly, he had dismissed Matthew's claim to have seen something. He couldn't wait to prove him wrong; Matthew felt it was truly an extraordinary find.

"I just have to get something," Matthew answered, slightly angry. Matthew's aggravation over their apparent disregard seeped into his response.

"Get what?" David inquired with a slightly disapproving tone in response to his son's unusual hint of disrespectfulness.

"Remember when I thought I saw something out of the corner of my eye in the plowed corn field, just before our water break?" Matthew reminded his father.

"Oh, right," David responded now recalling the incident which occurred a few hours before. "What was it?"

"I'm not sure, but I'm going to get it and bring it home for us to take a look at, if that's okay with you," Matthew asked with respectfulness returning to his voice.

"Okay. That's fine," David commented. "But, better hurry. This looks like it's going to be a whopper of a thunder storm!"

With that, Matthew hopped down from the hay wagon being pulled behind the tractor and started to run excitedly in the direction of the trench. Although he started out in a light jog, the anticipation grew, causing him to run faster. By the time Matthew reached the trench, he found himself out of breath. As he collected himself, his fear also dissipated. Matthew jumped down into the trench and began to brush away the dirt using his gloved hands. Soon, he had managed to remove the remaining dirt. His movements became slower and more deliberate in order to concentrate his efforts in gently uncovering the object lodged in the earth.

As he brushed away the last of the brown soil, Matthew found it difficult to decipher what he had uncovered. It was like nothing he had ever seen and certainly nothing like what he had expected. The object was oval and appeared completely made of metal. Its surface was smooth and possessed a deep golden, metallic shine. Confused, he dug beneath it and began to scoop the oval object out of the dirt. As he released it from its earthly cradle, he couldn't believe how heavy it was. It was shaped like a large egg that was roughly two feet in length and weighed at least twenty pounds. Even through his work gloves, Matthew could feel that it was still quite warm. He stood there in the bottom of the trench, mesmerized as he held and stared at it in disbelief. His mind reached for something to wrap this new experience in to produce a sense of order and comfort, but there was nothing there. This thing he now held would have to create a new place in his understanding, and this was unsettling. How would he make sense of it? He was comforted when he realized he would tell his father. His father would help him understand it all. He would know what to do. After all, his dad is a science teacher.

Matthew was suddenly jolted from his reverie by the increasing intensity of the rain which had gone unnoticed until now. Placing the object on the ground, he removed his shirt and spread it completely out on the dirt, leaving his muscular upper body exposed to the elements.

With his shirt now lying on the ground, Matthew picked the object back up and gently placed it in the middle of his shirt. Bringing all four corners together, he hoisted his makeshift carrying sack and began to run back to the farmhouse driveway where his car awaited. By the time he reached his vehicle, the rain was coming down in sheets as the thunder and lightning intensified. One seldom feels smaller next to Mother Nature than during a thunderstorm while standing unprotected outside in an open field. Matthew placed his small sack on the ground and frantically fished for his keys as he finally wiggled them out of his denim pocket. After unlocking the door, Matthew laid the object carefully on the back seat and then hurriedly opened the driver's side door and slid behind the wheel. Now safe within the shelter of his vehicle, Matthew noticed his shoulders aching from the day's work. Just as he was about to put his car into drive, David pulled up next to him in his own red, four-door sedan.

"Did you find what you were looking for?" yelled his father over the noise of the pouring rain.

"Yeah, Dad, I did!" Matthew replied enthusiastically. "I want to show it to you when we get home, okay?"

David gave an affirmative nod and drove off down the long driveway leading from the farm house to the main road. Matthew put his small, two-door silver Chevy with black cloth interior into gear and followed his father home. The thought of showing his dad this important discovery filled him with excitement but also an unfamiliar dread. He was anxious to share it with his dad, yet something inside him wanted to keep it all to himself. This would allow him to continue fantasizing over the significance of his find.

Fifteen minutes later, they pulled into the driveway of their two-story, colonial-style brick home. David drove right into the garage next to his wife's minivan and left the overhead door open so Matthew could run quickly inside to escape the rain. Matthew pulled up directly behind his father's car. As soon as he put the gear into park, Matthew reached around to the back seat, grabbed the mysterious object, which was still wrapped in his drenched, dirty white T-shirt, and ran into the garage. David glanced at the bundle his son was carrying into the garage.

"What on earth?" he asked with genuine interest.

"Remember when I told you I saw a flash of light and smoke?" Matthew asked.

His father nodded.

"This is what I found," Matthew exclaimed. "I can't figure out what it is. I thought it might be a meteorite."

Matthew paused a moment to read his dad's expression.

"It seems too shiny and smooth though," Matthew continued. "Hold it, and feel how heavy it is."

He removed the object from his shirt and transferred it to his father's outstretched arms.

"Wow," David commented as he gently lifted the object up and down in mid-air to gauge its relative weight and density.

"It's still warm, too," Matthew added.

David then transferred the item back to his son.

"Let's go inside, change out of these wet clothes and take a closer look," David instructed.

Matthew was pleased with his father's reaction. He could tell that his dad shared his belief that this was something important. Matthew had always appreciated being the son of a science teacher. His dad had a genuine curiosity about the world around him and looked at things very analytically. He knew he would help him make sense of this. When they walked into the kitchen, Matthew's mom, Ann, greeted them.

"Hi, guys!" she said, kissing them each on the cheek. "Wow! You're drenched." She then noticed the oval object Matthew was carrying into their home. "What is that, Matthew?" Ann asked.

"I have no idea," he responded. "But we're going to try and figure that out."

"You're not going to set that on the kitchen table, are you?" she asked.

Matthew had planned on it, but apparently not, after Ann's comment.

"Where should I set it?" he asked compliantly but mildly annoyed.

"Well, what on earth is it?" Ann inquired again seemingly more concerned with the impact it would have on the order of her house than its scientific significance.

"I already told you I don't know," Matthew repeated. "I found it out in a field while we were baling hay. Judging from the trench it left when it hit the field, it must have come from somewhere in space."

"From space?!" she replied with shock.

Now his mom seemed intrigued.

"Matthew, what are you talking about?" Ann asked while wearing a look of confusion.

David intervened.

"Listen, we're going to go up, shower and get changed," he stated. "Would you mind warming up our dinner, honey? Then we'll try to look at this thing more closely."

With that, David took the oval object from Matthew, set it carefully on the kitchen floor and guided his son upstairs. Matthew looked back at his treasure while being physically turned by his dad to the kitchen staircase leading to the second floor. Oddly, Matthew felt he couldn't leave the object there by itself. However, the two men disappeared upstairs without further remark.

Ann, left alone in the kitchen with the strange object, knelt down to take a closer look. She gazed at it, becoming transfixed in the process. Time seemed to stand still as she was completely mesmerized. Her mind and body became relaxed, and she had no awareness of the passage of time. David and Matthew then reappeared in the kitchen, clean and dry.

"Mom," Matthew called, jolting her back to the moment.

She blinked and turned slowly toward him.

David looked around searchingly, hoping for something to eat. Ann noticed and stood. She headed to the fridge and pulled out the leftover dinner to commence the warming process.

"Sorry," she said apologetically. "I just . . . I don't know what happened. I was looking at this thing and . . ." Her voice trailed off, but it went unnoticed.

By this time, Matthew and David were both on the floor examining the strange, shiny object. David stood and disappeared into the den only to return a moment later with a large magnifying glass and a microscope. Ignoring Ann's earlier plea, he hoisted it up onto the kitchen table, grabbed a pocketknife from the junk drawer, and sat down at the table. While peering into the magnifying glass, David proceeded to scrape the blade of the knife across the surface of the object in an attempt to collect a sample. Much to everyone's surprise, however, none of the surface material scraped off. David repeated the procedure as Matthew watched in awe, but the result was the same. In a last attempt, David placed the tip of the knife directly on top of the object and applied a great deal of pressure while again sliding the knife across the surface. Suddenly, the tip of the knife broke off, and the three stared in disbelief.

"What is this thing made of?" David asked. "I have never seen anything like this before."

Matthew felt his excitement once again mounting. He was becoming increasingly convinced that this was something of major importance. He could hardly wait to see what his dad would do next.

"I should have at least scratched the surface, but it did absolutely nothing," David said disbelievingly.

He rolled the object slowly across the table back and forth, searching for any kind of markings which might indicate who had made it, or at least establish it was, in fact, man-made. Unfortunately, there were no letters or markings of any kind. David turned to Matthew with great interest.

"Where did you first see this thing again?" he asked as he looked up at his son sitting to his left at the table.

Ignoring the annoyance at being dismissed earlier, Matthew replied, "I saw a streak of light out of the corner of my eye while I was driving the tractor this afternoon," he began. "Remember when I ran over to the corn field to check it out? I saw a trench, and at the bottom I found this."

"So it came from the sky?" Ann asked.

"I think it did, mom," Matthew replied although he wasn't entirely certain.

He didn't say what he was feeling, that he *hoped* it came from the sky. Matthew was still afraid of looking like a fool. The last thing he wanted to be was some kid who got all carried away just to find out it was nothing. Still, there were certain facts you could not ignore.

"The thing is, it was really hot when I found it," Matthew offered in hopes it would aid their understanding.

"Maybe an airplane dropped it, or it fell from a satellite or something," suggested Ann.

"Really hot?" David asked in search of more clarity.

"Yeah," Matthew replied. "I couldn't even touch it for several hours after it hit the ground and sat in the trench."

David sat back in his chair and rubbed his chin with his right hand. His facial expression clearly conveyed the depth of his concentration on deciding the next course of action.

"I'm thinking we call NASA," David declared.

There, that's it! thought Matthew. Hi dad had uttered the one word he had been thinking all day—*NASA*. Matthew could hardly contain his excitement.

"Let's eat!" David then stated most matter-of-factly.

Let's eat?! Matthew repeated in his mind. *How the hell could he be thinking of food at this moment? Does Dad not understand how important this object could be to my life or to the lives of our entire family?!*

Matthew's annoyance vanished almost instantly when he suddenly became aware of the irresistible aroma of his mom's lasagna. After he had finished eating, Matthew glanced at the clock on the kitchen wall. It was only 9:35, but after filling his stomach, the exhaustion that lay beneath the surface of excitement raised its weary head. He admittedly was beat. He said goodnight to his parents and headed upstairs. After removing his contacts and brushing his teeth, he crawled slowly into bed wearing only a pair of comfortable exercise shorts. His muscles were already tightening up, which was their way of complaining about the demanding work they had performed all day. He just started to get comfortable when he heard a knock on the door. His sister Samantha peeked into his room. Unlike Matthew, Samantha was of lighter complexion with thick, long flowing blond hair. She, too, was in high school but two years behind her older brother.

"Matthew?" she said, checking to see if Matthew had fallen asleep yet.

"Yeah, what is it?" Matthew replied. He realized he had not seen her or their seventh grade sister, Katie, since arriving home. "Where were you?" he asked, not waiting for her answer.

"I was in my room studying for a big test tomorrow," she responded. "What on earth is that thing down in the kitchen?"

"Not sure," he said in return. "I found it in one of the fields on the farm." He then proceeded to relay the details to Samantha. "Dad is going to call NASA tomorrow," Matthew concluded, saving the best for last.

"That's unbelievable," she responded obviously impressed. "What do you think they will do?"

At this point, Matthew realized his eyes were closed and he wasn't even looking in his sister's direction.

"I'm really tired, Sam," he stated. "Do you mind if we talk about it more tomorrow?"

Quite used to taking his hints and feeling satisfied that Matthew had shared something so important with her, Samantha said goodnight and left the room.

Even though he was exhausted, his mind was racing with the prospect of sharing his discovery with someone at NASA the next day. He tried to keep his fantasies in check, but it was challenging. In spite of himself, he was soon imagining what everyone at school would say when they heard about his discovery. No one from his little town had ever attained any sort of notoriety. The only kids who sometimes stood out in his high school were the athletes. Matthew was a good athlete, but he knew his future had nothing to do with sports. Some kids had received scholarships from local colleges to play football or basketball. Matthew had always felt that sports were something to be left behind in high school, so he never considered pursuing them beyond graduation. They were fun and all, but he had always been a stronger student, and his parents had made sure he understood that academics were the key to a successful future. With only one week left in his high school career, his thoughts then turned to his future at Notre Dame. He planned on being a straight-A student in college, although he secretly worried it would be much more difficult. But now he had an ace in the hole. Having discovered a meteor while still in high school would certainly propel him onto the fast track in his studies of science. When he got to Notre Dame in the fall, surely his reputation would precede him. Maybe he would be asked to speak in all the science classes. He would come in and give a presentation on what he had found and what NASA was doing with it now. The faculty would want to ask him questions, and they would hang on his every word. College would be just the beginning for him. Between Notre Dame and his involvement at NASA, he was sure to have a bright future. Perhaps this is the "more" he felt tugging at his spirit.

Although he had been exhausted when he climbed into bed, sleep seemed a distant reality. Propelled by his desire to see his discovery again, he climbed out of bed and headed down into the kitchen. It wasn't until he saw it again that he became aware that he had actually *missed* it. He picked it up and carried it back up to his bedroom. He turned on his desk lamp and his computer. He would browse the internet in hopes of finding some clues. He went right to nasa.gov.

On the home page, he began scanning his options. However, the tiredness, which had eluded him only moments before, seemed to be engulfing him. It became more and more difficult to focus, and his eyes started to blur. He felt the soreness from baling hay settle into his shoulders and back. Even though he was an avid weight lifter, he had used muscles today that normally didn't work so hard. He performed a search of NASA sites and facilities and found the Glenn Research Center in Cleveland, Ohio. This appeared to be the nearest one. He jotted down the phone number and decided he would contact them tomorrow in hopes that they could at least steer him to the proper department.

Despite the desire to continue his research, Matthew had to surrender to the will of his body and rest. Leaving the object on his desk, he turned off the lamp and logged off the computer. He took one step toward his bed and collapsed face-down onto his mattress. Turning onto his left side to face the object, Matthew rested his head on his pillow and looked one last time at his find before falling fast asleep.

CHAPTER 2

FIRST OF MANY

Matthew awoke suddenly and became immediately aware of how uncomfortable he was. The bed was incredibly hard, and something scratched at his face. When he opened his eyes, he realized he wasn't in his bed at all. His first sight was that of the brilliant, blue sky with an occasional white, fluffy cloud moving slowly across it. As he became more fully awake, Matthew realized he was lying on the ground, and the source of the scratchy discomfort were long, thick blades of green grass. He sat up bewildered and in total disbelief. The young man looked around and struggled to make sense of his surroundings. He realized he was in an open field with tall grass and sporadic purple wildflowers. It was oppressively warm, but there was a strong wind providing some relief from the heat. Matthew was overcome with confusion. The last thing he remembered was falling asleep in his bed.

"Where am I?" he demanded aloud, not knowing exactly whom he was addressing. His first thought was his grandfather's farm, but there was no field there such as this, and the landscape was altogether unfamiliar. Suddenly, he heard voices in the distance. Matthew slowly stood up and looked directly behind him. Just beyond a small tree line, there was another adjacent field where he saw some movement. Matthew focused more intently and saw at least two men on horseback and a number of people working in the field. He had absolutely no idea where he was or how he had gotten there.

He decided to walk over to the neighboring field in an attempt to stumble upon something familiar. His last conscious act that he could recall was turning off his computer and crawling into bed. He reached the tree line and walked through it until he had an open view of the next field. As he walked, Matthew noticed the vegetation changing. The field was covered with green spiny plants with very unique white fuzzy flowers. Matthew bent down to get a closer look. He had never seen such a plant, but when he reached out and touched the flower, it had the consistency of a cotton ball. It suddenly dawned on him that these were indeed cotton plants. Matthew straightened and resumed walking as bewildered as before about how he had come to be in this place.

As he approached the workers in the field, he noticed that the two horsemen looked to be of Caucasian descent and the field workers of African descent. He also noticed their clothing was rather strange as well. The male workers donned white, long-sleeved button-down shirts that hung loosely on their bodies and long pants cut off at the calf. The women were wearing long, brown dresses with aprons and red scarves tied around their heads. They were apparently harvesting the cotton off the plants and placing it into baskets on the ground beside them. Matthew's mind flashed to the hay baler and he wondered why these people weren't employing a more automated system of picking the cotton. Maybe this was a small farmer who couldn't afford fancy equipment and hired migrant workers instead. One of the women workers stood to stretch her back, no doubt strained from hunching over the plants. Matthew then turned his attention to the two white horsemen. They were also dressed in strange clothing, wearing similar white shirts, brown cowboy style boots and hats. He also noticed a most surprising item dangling down from their saddles. They each had a whip, which added to his confused state of mind. Matthew finally reached one of the workers and stopped.

"Excuse me," Matthew said politely while simultaneously trying to suppress his panicked feeling. "Can you tell me where I am?"

He was sure it sounded like a ridiculous question and felt a little foolish asking it, but it was after all, the burning inquiry of the moment. The worker not only had no response, but did not even stand up to greet him. Matthew bent down to get at eye level and repeated the question but was again met with no response of any kind. He stood and walked over to the next closest person and tapped him on the shoulder from behind.

"Excuse me, I seem to be lost," he said.

This time the male worker stopped, looked behind him and brushed his hand across the same shoulder Matthew tapped as though swatting away a fly.

What the hell? Matthew thought.

Even if they didn't speak English, they should have at least acknowledged him. It was as though they had not even seen him. He walked over to one of the horsemen and again attempted to politely address his request, but he not only ignored Matthew's question, he didn't even acknowledge his existence. Matthew glanced over to the other horseman who was a good forty yards away. His heart leapt when he realized the man made direct eye contact with him, but it was short lived when the horseman quickly gave his steed a swift kick and trotted off. Matthew knew that man had seen him and was frustrated that he had ridden off so quickly. No one else here seemed to be able to see him. The fear he fought to suppress suddenly overcame him.

Where am I? he thought. Then the questions stormed through his mind.

Why was he standing here with these strange people, none of whom would acknowledge him? Where was his bed, his room, and his home? More than anything, he wanted to get out of here. Panic began to rise within him. He jumped in front of the male worker and screamed.

"Hey! Hey!" Matthew yelled in desperation. "Look at me! Can't you see me? Where am I? What's going on?!"

Not surprisingly, the man looked right past Matthew. He was frightened and felt completely out of control. Matthew had no idea where he was, how he had gotten there, or why he had become invisible. Then he heard one of the men on horseback speak.

"Finish up your baskets and bring 'em over to the gin-house for the final weighin' of the day," the man called out to the workers.

Evening appeared to be imminent as the sun began to set in the horizon. A bell began ringing in the distance. The workers complied with the horseman's request and filled each of their baskets over the course of the next few minutes. Once completely full, each worker picked up his or her basket and began to walk silently to a large, barn-like building about a half mile off in the distance. In the absence of any other possible option, Matthew decided to walk along with the group. There were about twenty of them, and they were all completely oblivious to Matthew's presence. He had never before experienced the impotence of being invisible. He felt trapped, hopeless and terrified. As a means of comforting himself, Matthew told himself that this thing, this dream or whatever it was, could not last forever. Eventually he would be back in his bedroom and would just have to endure it until then. He would just follow the group until this ended, which he continued to tell himself, would be only moments from now. It seemed that since no one could see him, no harm could come to him. His mind quickly jumped to the horseman who made direct eye contact. If he could indeed see him, why hadn't he offered to help? Of course, he really did not know if he was a friend or foe. With that thought, Matthew suddenly felt safer being invisible. He hoped he wouldn't come across that man again. It didn't occur to him that if one person could see him, maybe there were others who could as well.

As they walked along, they eventually reached a dirt road at the very edge of the cotton field. On the other side of the road was another large, open field. The road seemed to lead to a group of buildings, which appeared to be their intended destination. Just fifty yards away, Matthew noticed a single log pole with a dangling sign blowing in the breeze. He quickly jogged over to the pole in order to get a better view of the sign.

Terra Nor Plantation
Since 1749
Virginia's Pride Cotton Plantation

"Virginia?" Matthew mumbled under his breath. "How could I possibly be in Virginia? 1749? This farm is over two hundred and fifty years old!"

Matthew glanced back toward the farm and noticed the group was lined up outside a building, which he could only guess was the gin-house. He quickly caught up with them, feeling less vulnerable blending into the mass of humanity than standing alone. He reached the outskirts of the yard and quickly looked around at the different buildings. To the left of the road, there was the gin-house and another barn structure, which smelled as though it housed some animals, an all-too-familiar odor to Matthew from the countless hours he spent on his grandfather's farm. To the right of the road, there were several small, crude wooden homes, which apparently housed the field hands. The dirt road continued beyond all of these structures and gently curved around another tree line to a large white building another half a mile away. Matthew focused his vision and noticed the building had huge white pillars, a red brick porch, and fourteen windows across the entire front of the home. This whole scene definitely had the makings of a southern plantation, straight out of his mother's favorite movie, "Gone with the Wind." Surely, there would be a phone in the big house. Abandoning his desire to stay with the crowd, his new goal was to reach that house and find some means of communication. He would call home and get some answers. He did not stop to consider what those answers could possibly be, but at the moment, the promise of speaking to his parents was the only thing keeping him going.

As Matthew continued along the dirt road past the gin-house, he came upon a man reading a piece of paper. The man took no notice of him but continued to read the paper. Curiosity got the best of Matthew, so he went behind the man and read over his shoulder. Shock and terror ran through Matthew's blood as he read.

> *To Be Sold and Let by Public Auction*
> *On Monday the 18ᵗʰ of June, 1859*
> *Male and Female*
> **SLAVES**
> *Also for sale at Eleven O'clock*
> *Fine Rice, Gram, Paddy, Books, Needles, Pins, Ribbons*
> *County Courthouse*
> *Richmond, Virginia*

Matthew felt dizzy and was suddenly overcome with nausea. He knelt to the ground and placed his head between his knees. After a few moments, he gathered himself and looked up. The man had walked away but left the paper lying on the ground right next to him. A strong gust of wind carried the paper away as Matthew watched it scurry across the ground and eventually lodge itself against the branches of a nearby bush. He didn't know what to think, what to do or where to turn for help.

Panic stricken and feeling the need to find shade from the intense heat, Matthew stood and ran over to the first little home he came upon in hopes of finding someone or something to wake him from this delirious state. He quickly reached the first little hut and went inside. It had one room with a dirt floor. There were no beds but only three planks of wood resting on the ground. There was a crude fireplace and an empty basin in one corner with a few cooking pots and pans neatly stacked inside. There was no phone, no TV, no radio, no bathroom, obviously no electricity. As Matthew wondered how anyone could live under these conditions, a towering large man walked through the door followed by a woman and a young boy who could not be any older than sixteen. Seeing this family unit made him long for his own. Matthew said nothing in hopes they might notice him on their own accord, but as he expected, they didn't acknowledge his presence.

"Benny, go tend the garden before mama gets supper for us," said the man who was obviously the father of this small family.

"Yes, sir," replied the boy obediently as he turned and walked back out the door.

"Carrie, I gots word from Big George," the man continued once his son left the hut. "There's a group from the Connor's Plantation plannin' to go tonight after dark."

"Tonight?" responded Carrie in protest, obviously troubled by the news. "But Thomas, we don't gots enough dried food yet. I thoughts we was goin' to leave in a month."

Thomas was not deterred.

"George says we can meets up with 'em three miles down the James River," he continued. "Moses herself arrangin' this trip. We can't wait. This the best chance we gots to go north and frees ourselves. Besides, I heards there mights be a slave auction happin' soon. With the master's poor crop this year, he can't keep feedin' all us much longer. He goin' to have to sell some of us."

A chill overcame Carrie as she gave Thomas a panic-stricken look. Flashes of a day four years ago came back to her. Their master had sold five of his slaves that day and one of them was a twelve-year-old girl. Carrie watched in agony as the overseers pulled the girl from her mother's last embrace, never knowing if they might someday see each other again. That image of their hands slowly slipping away from one another until they were separated still haunted Carrie. The screams of the parents and child ripped away from each other still echoed in her mind to this day. She now knew they had no choice but to leave tonight and make do as best they could.

Matthew stood in the corner frozen with disbelief. Clearly, he was witnessing a scene from a different time. He had no idea how he had gotten here. All that mattered to him now was getting out and going home. The idea of being trapped here was beyond fathomable. His mind was racing as to how he could escape but was completely void of any ideas. He suddenly realized how similar his predicament was to that of these people. Except at least they had each other, he thought with self-pity.

Thomas walked toward his wife and embraced her lovingly.

"This the day our ma, pa and grandparents been dreamin' for us," Thomas proclaimed. "Most of alls, this what we wants for Benny. He smart and can have a different life in the north. It's time we gives him what he deserves. His own free life!"

Carrie slowly looked up at Thomas and gave him a reassuring smile.

Several hours seemingly had passed since Matthew had mysteriously been transported to this strange place, and darkness was beginning to settle on the plantation. Benny had returned from working in their small garden, and the family was sitting down to eat what Matthew assumed would be their final meal here. It was a meager feast comprised of rice, corn and beans.

Matthew decided to slip out of the hut and explore the big house, hoping a clue would emerge, giving him some indication as to what was going on and the slim possibility of finding a phone. He walked outside navigating his way back to the main home through the growing darkness as evening approached. When he arrived, Matthew knocked at the door out of habit from polite, Midwestern manners, but no one answered, so he opened it and entered the home uninvited. He couldn't shake the feeling of breaking and entering, but he told himself he had no choice. He hadn't asked to be in this position, and all he could do now is try to find a way out of here.

The foyer of the house was huge and Matthew immediately noticed the spiral staircase leading to the upstairs hallway balcony.

"Gone with the Wind for sure," Matthew whispered to himself almost amused at the predictable absurdity of it all.

There was no one in sight, but he soon heard voices coming from somewhere on the first floor. He stepped inside the grand foyer and began to make his way through the house, searching for the source of the conversation. The house itself was amazing. The ceilings were much higher than that of his Indiana home, and the banister woodwork was beautiful. He successfully navigated through a series of hallways and rooms until he finally reached what appeared to be the kitchen. He pushed open the swinging door and walked inside. There were two black women wearing stained white dresses feverishly tending a multitude of pots boiling on the stove. Sweat visibly dripped through the red bandanas tightly tied across their foreheads.

"Excuse me!" Matthew said forcefully as he decided to try again, hoping that whatever had turned him invisible had somehow turned him back. "Can you hear me? Can you see me?"

The young man got his answer when neither woman looked in his direction but continued to focus on their task at hand. Matthew was just about to resume exploring the house when he heard another voice just outside the back door of the kitchen. He briskly walked outside and saw a man hunched over on one knee busily moving his hands on the ground. Matthew walked up and tapped him on the shoulder.

"Excuse me sir," he said, no longer even expecting a response. "Can you hear me?"

Matthew walked around in front of the man and saw him raise a hatchet and swiftly bring it down onto an old stump. Matthew peered through the darkness and saw the man holding a decapitated chicken by both feet, and Matthew suddenly became ill again. He felt the intense need to get away from there as quickly as possible and began to run around to the front of the house in full sprint. He ran to the small house of Thomas, Carrie and Benny. The familial love and affection he had felt there had given him a small sense of connectedness in this unending nightmare.

When he reached his new sanctuary, he found the family quietly packing some food and a few meager belongings. They said not a word as they completed the process and began to walk carefully in a single file out the door of their small home. Matthew could feel the nervous energy dancing between them as they embarked on this terrifying journey. He could not contemplate what unknown fate awaited them if they were to be caught.

As Matthew contemplated that possibility, he remembered the whips dangling from the white horsemen's saddles.

For lack of any other viable option, Matthew decided to join them on their journey. Being apparently invisible, he believed he was safe from the threat of the overseers. It also occurred to him that even if he was spotted with the group, he was neither black nor a slave and really had no reason to hide. The idea of him hiding struck him as strange since he could not get any one to see him no matter how hard he tried. Hiding seemed to be the only thing he was capable of doing at this moment. If only he could transfer his invisibility to the fleeing slaves.

The four quickly ran through the field the slaves had tended just a few hours before, guided only by the dim light of the half-moon above. They came upon the line of trees which separated the two largest fields of the plantation. Once they cleared the tree line, they were in an open field of wild flowers. Further ahead, Matthew could make out what appeared to be a much denser brush of trees on the edge of the wildflower field. This must be the forest cover the family was targeting to make their dangerous attempt at escape. They ran through the darkness for what seemed like a half an hour when they came upon a river. Matthew surmised they must have covered a few miles during that time.

"Let's stops here and rest," suggested Thomas.

All four parties bent low to the ground to catch their breath and tried to stay out of sight as much as possible. Matthew saw nothing but the whites of their eyes, within which, he could see their fear. He speculated that they now began to comprehend the severity of the offense they had chosen to commit. He was struck by the reality that it was too late to turn back now. They had escaped the confines of the plantation, and that was the first step. Whether or not they ever made it to freedom was still a huge uncertainty, but they had run away nonetheless and if caught, would be severely punished. Matthew's own current state of despair seemed to temporarily drift away as he once again contemplated the fate of this family. They were risking their lives and their family unity by fleeing the plantation. They risked everything for one singular purpose—the hope of a free life in the north. After a few minutes of catching their breath, Thomas whispered to his wife and child their next steps.

"We only gots a ways to go up the shore before we reach the meetin' point," he stated with an encouraging tone.

"What's the meetin' point?" asked Carrie as she slumped over to grasp her knees from exhaustion and catch her breath.

"It's a giant old oaks tree on the shore of the river with a wooden swing hangin' down from one of its branches," replied Thomas. "Someone from Moses' group is awaitin' to help us cross the river."

Matthew wondered who Moses was.

After too brief a rest, they resumed their journey with a brisk walk. Thomas was leading the way, Benny behind him, then Carrie and Matthew, unbeknownst to them, bringing up the rear. It occurred to Matthew as they walked that he was getting further and further away from the plantation and may not be able to find his way back. He considered the possibility that he would need to leave this nightmare at the exact same point from which he had entered. Maybe there was some kind of a portal or something in that field where he could somehow access his own space and time. He suddenly was filled with regret for coming along. He should have stayed right there in that field, in the exact spot he had awakened. Maybe if he had stayed there, he would already be back in his own bed, in his own room and in his own time.

He did not have long to wallow in regret and fear. Thomas suddenly stopped in his tracks and silently stood for a moment as the rest of the group followed his lead. Matthew snapped out of his torment when he realized the cause of the delay. He could hear something in the distance causing his blood to run cold—dogs. Somewhere behind them, dogs were barking.

"Run!" Thomas yelled.

They all quickly ran as fast as they could up the shore. Carrie stumbled and fell but Thomas quickly lifted her up. The barking grew louder as the dogs drew closer, and then they heard voices.

The overseers! Matthew thought with a ball of stress suddenly forming within his stomach.

The dogs were on their scent. It was only a matter of time before they would catch up to them. Matthew had to remind himself that he was safe. He was first of all, invisible and second, a free white man. He again wished either of those conditions applied to Thomas, Carrie and Benny.

Thomas suddenly stopped when he knew what must be done. With that realization, came a darkness that swept across his soul by what it meant but he could not allow himself to be consumed by it. They were on a mission and he had to see it through to the end for his wife and child.

"You both listen to me now!" Thomas urgently whispered. "Keeps goin' ups the shore. We don't gots much time before they catches us. I'm goin' back to distract the dogs and you two keep runnin'. Keep runnin' and runnin' and don't stop for nothin'. Run till you's free! Don't never looks back! Get to the meetin' point!"

"No, Pa! We won't leaves you!" protested Benny with desperation and fear in his voice.

"That's right!" added Carrie, her voice cracking from emotion. "We's a family, we sticks together!"

"You both listens to me," Thomas began again. "They gonna whip us bad if they catches us. Benny too, and then they probably gonna sells us to different masters to keep us apart. There's no goin' back now. We ain't got a choice! Do as I tells ya!"

Thomas placed both hands on Benny's shoulder and looked in his son's eyes.

"Son, you's the man of the family now," Thomas said with as much strength as he could muster. "I wants ya to take your mama and gets cross that river and don't stop. I want my boy to be's a free man!"

Matthew could hear Benny sobbing as he spoke. "I loves you, Pa," Benny said, barely able to say the words.

"I loves you, too, boy," Thomas replied with deep sorrow while hugging his son. He struggled to hold back tears and keep himself together in order to remain strong for his family. Benny buried his head deep into his father's muscular chest where he always felt safe, where he always felt loved.

Thomas tried to summon a strength and resolve deep within he knew was needed now for his wife and child. He kissed Benny on the forehead and gave him a reassuring smile as he paused one final moment to look deep into his son's big, brown eyes. Thomas wished he could convey to his son all of his wisdom and knowledge in these final moments. He wanted to somehow transfer everything he wanted to say throughout Benny's life as though he were always going to be there over the course of the next several decades. But alas, Thomas knew this was the end, and a sinking feeling befell his heart. Time stood still for a few seconds as Thomas felt a sense of peace surrounding his next course of action. He never felt more connected to his son than at this very moment. He knew that all would be okay with his wife and child. He somehow knew they would make it and his sacrifice was worth their freedom.

"I so proud of ya, son," Thomas said, as the tears now freely flowed down both their faces.

"Oh, Pa," Benny said clinging to his father.

Thomas released his son from their embrace and turned to Carrie who looked at him with tear-filled, loving eyes. They both knew this was the only course of action they must take in order to provide Benny the best life possible and break the twine of slavery that had bound their family for generations.

"I can't says goodbye," Carrie said, barely able to speak as the tears streamed down her face.

Thomas looked deeply into his wife's beautiful, hazel eyes.

"You knows my heart is yours," Thomas said as he held Carrie tightly. "Always has been. You mades me so happy. You deserves to be free, and I wants that for ya both even if I can't be there's which ya." Thomas paused a moment to collect himself in order to summon the strength to speak the final words to his wife whom he loved with all his heart.

"I'd rather wanders the Earth as a ghost, my love, than pass through the gates of heaven withouts ya," Thomas said with immense clarity, purpose, and love.

"Oh, Thomas," Carrie responded as she lifted her left hand and gently caressed Thomas' right cheek.

Thomas, who towered over his wife, bent down one final time to kiss her on the lips, a ritual he had done so many times over these past two decades, but none with so much meaning.

Their final kiss.

Thomas made it count as their passionate embrace filled his soul. It also reassured him the importance of the personal sacrifice he was about to make.

To save his family.

They all swiftly embraced and kissed each other one final time. Each had tears of love and sorrow freely flowing as they knew this would likely be the last moment they would ever share together again as a family. Thomas lifted his head and listened again for the sounds of their pursuers who were drawing even closer. They were almost out of time, and Thomas knew he had to act right now.

"Now, go!" he said with great urgency. "Son, you takes care of your mama. I loves you both more than the stars in the sky. Ain't nothin' ever gonna change that."

Thomas turned and ran back down the shore in the opposite direction in hopes he could run their captors off course and buy his family some time. He never looked back for he knew the pain he felt in his heart would be magnified all the more. He couldn't possibly bear seeing them stand there in their own sorrow as they watched him disappear. He couldn't risk any delays or become swept away by his own pain that may neutralize him, because now every second mattered. He had to remain strong. He had to be their rock just as he has been for their entire lives.

Unconditional love. No power greater in the Universe.

Matthew stood there with tears in his eyes and a huge lump in his throat. *What can I do?!* He thought. Helplessness settled in as an overwhelming wave of panic began to consume him. He yelled out in frustration. "God damn it!" he screamed. "What can I do to help them?! Jesus!"

Carrie and Benny took one more futile look backward through the darkness to catch a final glimpse of Thomas before he disappeared and then began running again as quickly as they could. Matthew couldn't take watching this family being ripped apart, unable to control the well of emotion churning within. The tears welling within his eyes now began flowing down his face.

"It can't end this way!" Matthew yelled in disbelief. "This isn't happening! Christ! This can't be happening." Then Matthew realized that he could possibly do something to help them.

"No! Thomas, wait!" Matthew pleaded as he ran after him. "Let *me* go, Thomas! Let me take your place! Let me distract them!" The panic and pain in his voice was palpable.

Matthew was suddenly startled by a shrill alarm. He quickly sat up and opened his eyes. His focus was dazed at best, as he tried to get his bearings. After a few moments, he realized he was back in the comforts of his bedroom. He was sweating, and his sheets were drenched, but he was actually in his own bed. There was no sign of Thomas, Benny or Carrie. He was safe and overcome with relief that the horrible separation had been just a dream. Thomas was safe. They were all safe. It had all been a dream unlike any he ever had.

"Rise and shine, sleepy head," said his mom as she walked down the hall passing Matthew's doorway.

Matthew looked up and smiled with immense relief. He was filled with a peace and contentment never before associated with the simple pleasure of waking up in his own room. He jumped out of bed, still trembling and flipped on his computer. Still caught between the two realities, he searched the word, "Moses," and in doing so, several Biblical references appeared. He quickly scrolled through them until he found one that referred to slavery.

Matthew highlighted the text and clicked on it. A picture of a black woman appeared in the upper right hand corner of the screen with the name Harriet Tubman beneath it. Matthew's eyes flickered back and forth as he read the article. He soon learned that Harriet Tubman was a former slave who escaped to the north to freedom only to return to help other slaves escape. A network of other sympathizers across the country formed what was called the Underground Railroad. Matthew began to recall what he had learned in Mr. Smithburn's middle school history class. He went on to read that Ms. Tubman was sometimes referred to as "Moses" by slaves as a title of her importance in freeing as many of them as possible.

Matthew was baffled as to why his subconscious mind had reached into his memory and hijacked a character from eighth grade history to appear in his dream. What's next? Eli Whitney and his cotton gin?

At least it was just a dream. That was too much drama for him. He was still haunted by the all-too-real emotions he just experienced. Thankfully, Matthew was now standing there in his own reality, in his bedroom safe and sound. Yet, he was still experiencing the fear of being caught by the overseers or the dogs. He was weak with sorrow at the thought of Benny and Carrie being separated from Thomas forever. And what would become of Thomas? Would he be killed? He seemed to remember hearing that sometimes slaves who had attempted to run away would have their feet or legs cut off to prevent them from ever running again. He then marveled at Thomas' bravery. Matthew believed if he had been born a slave, he would have died a slave, confident he lacked the courage to ever risk running away. What gave Thomas such courage? Not to mention the completely selfless act of running back *toward* their pursuers to sacrifice himself so that his wife and son would know freedom. Who would do that? But yet the second he posed the question, the answer rang loudly in his own mind and heart. His own father would do the same for him, his siblings and his mother—that much he knew for sure. The giving, kind, selfless, and protective, paternal love Matthew has always known from David now took on a much deeper meaning and appreciation. It was something Matthew would certainly never take for granted—unconditional love. This experience also made him realize how important it is to tell the ones we love so dearly how much we appreciate them and how we feel because we truly don't know what lies ahead in life.

Matthew was extremely happy that things were back to normal, and he could begin the first day of his last week of high school. It wasn't until he glanced over to his monitor that he noticed the shiny object he found yesterday in his grandfather's field. Preoccupied by his dream, Matthew had completely forgotten about his treasure. His heart jumped in anticipation as he remembered about the phone call he and his dad would be making to NASA today. After getting himself ready for school, Matthew grabbed the paper with the NASA phone number and ran downstairs.

David and Ann were sitting at the kitchen table finishing breakfast. Impulsively, he bent down and kissed them each on the cheek, thinking of the turmoil of the family in his dream.

"Good morning!" he said enthusiastically.

"Well, thank you," said his mother, completely taken off guard.

Not one to dwell on the spontaneous show of affection, Matthew immediately asked his dad, "When are you going to call NASA, Dad? I wrote down the number of a research center in Cleveland."

Matthew was not prepared for the look of befuddlement on his father's face.

"NASA?" David asked as his coffee cup paused half-way to his mouth.

"Yeah, NASA," Matthew repeated. "You said you'd call them, remember?" Surely his dad couldn't have been that tired last night that he had forgotten the plan.

"Why would I call NASA, son?" David questioned.

Matthew felt his patience wane, and it clearly showed in his tone of voice. "The thing I found in the field yesterday," Matthew reminded his father. "You remember, right?"

Mathew's facial expression clearly gave no hint of any such recollection.

"Matthew, what did you find?" he asked, trying not to upset his son who obviously had a lot riding on this NASA call.

Matthew gave a frustrated-teenager sigh.

"Dad, yesterday in the field at Grandpa's farm," Matthew began. "I found that shiny, oval object. We think it might be some kind of meteorite, remember?"

"Meteorite?" David repeated. "Matthew, if you found a meteorite yesterday, this is the first I've heard about it."

Matthew stood before them in total silence for a few moments, completely perplexed by his father's ignorance of the events that transpired these past twelve hours. His parents silently stared back.

"It's in my room. I'll show you," Matthew stated with slight desperation.

"Son, I'd love to see it when I get home," David said as he stood and headed for the door. "I'm already late. I really have to run. We'll talk about this when I get home."

Matthew noticed his mom and dad exchange a non-verbal "he's obviously crazy" type of look.

"You already know about it," Matthew stated again. "The oval object I discovered in the plowed corn field next to where we were baling hay."

"Tell ya what, sport," David said, trying to appease his son. "As soon as we both get home, you show me your oval thing okay?"

With that, David placed his coffee cup down on the kitchen table and made his way to the door. He kissed Ann, said goodbye, stepped into the garage and left for work. Matthew then turned to his mother in hopes that she didn't suffer the same temporary amnesia on the topic as his father.

"Mom?" Matthew said questioningly. "You remember, don't you?"

"Are you feeling okay, honey?" she asked while walking over and placing her right hand on his forehead. "You don't seem to have a fever."

"I feel totally fine!" Matthew replied curtly. "You don't remember anything?"

Before Ann could answer, Samantha ran down the backstairs to the kitchen in a rush.

"Matthew, we'd better get going or we'll be late," she announced impatiently.

Then Matthew realized that his sister had seen the oval as well last night, just before he went to sleep.

"Sam!" he said with renewed excitement, hoping he would receive a validating response. "You saw it!"

"Saw what?" she asked while walking toward the garage door.

Not her too! Matthew thought, beginning to feel completely exasperated.

"The oval, God damn it!" Matthew yelled in frustration.

Ann gave Matthew a disapproving look for his language.

"Whatever," Sam replied. "Let's go, because I can't be late for exams."

Defeated, Matthew walked out the front door with his sister, and they both got into his car. He started the engine and backed down the driveway. As Matthew applied the brake to engage in forward drive when they reached the street, he paused and glanced back to his bedroom window in the front of the house.

What is that thing? he thought to himself.

"Come on, space cadet," blurted Samantha. "Let's go!"

"Oh, sorry," Matthew said as he was suddenly whisked back to reality and finally drove off to school.

The eighteen-year-old boy from Indiana, who had never seen the ocean, was about to ride one incredible wave.

CHAPTER 3

DREAM OR REALITY

Matthew found himself totally distracted the entire day at school. Concentrating was an impossible chore as his thoughts were pre-occupied by the oval object, the intense dream, and the fact his family had mysteriously forgotten the events of the night before. The plight of the slave family from his dream haunted him throughout the day. Why couldn't he shake it? It wasn't real. The feelings he had experienced upon awakening had barely subsided as the day progressed. The scene played repeatedly in his mind, and he found himself mysteriously consumed with a desire to understand as much as possible about this period of history. When the final bell rang, he surprised himself by heading directly to the classroom of Mr. Fisher, his senior year American History teacher.

When he arrived at the classroom, Matthew found him packing up his room in preparation for summer. There were numerous boxes strewn about as Mr. Fisher filled them with various posters, books and knick knacks used to decorate his classroom.

"Hi, Mr. Fisher," Matthew said as he greeted one of his favorite teachers.

"Well, hello Matthew," responded Mr. Fisher. "To what do I owe the pleasure of an after-school visit?"

"I had a question that I wanted to ask you about a certain person from history," Matthew replied feeling a little self-conscious but cutting right to the chase.

The look on Mr. Fisher's face was a combination of surprise and skepticism. "Uh huh," the teacher said cautiously. "Let me get this straight. You've come into my room on the last week of school after school hours, mind you, to ask me a question on American history? Oh, and I almost forgot, a graduating senior, no less."

Matthew was a little surprised by Mr. Fisher's response, but he merely nodded his head.

"Okay, Matthew," Mr. Fisher began. "You're a good kid, but where are your buddies? I'm guessing they asked you to distract me as they planned some kind of end-of-the-year prank. I've been teaching twenty-eight years, son, and you've got to get up pretty early in the morning to fool me. I've practically seen it all." Mr. Fisher walked past Matthew into the hallway and glanced cautiously around.

"No, sir," Matthew said reassuringly. "It's nothing like that at all. I know it seems a bit odd to be asking, but I had a bizarre dream last night about Harriet Tubman and wanted to learn more about her."

The mere mention of her name apparently was enough to shift his teacher's mood and instantly remove his guardedness. "Ah, yes," Mr. Fisher confirmed. "'Moses' as she was known among the slave community."

"Yes, exactly!" Matthew said excitedly. "When was she alive and actually helped slaves escape to the North?"

"Well, it started in the mid-1800s and continued for several years," Mr. Fisher replied. "I actually have a book about her and some of the slaves she helped escape. As I recall, I think it even has a picture or two of her, if you would like to see it. She was known for her work as a 'conductor' with the Underground Railroad."

Mr. Fisher walked over to his desk where there were several books piled neatly into three stacks logistically placed next to an empty box waiting to be packed into storage for the summer. He fanned the first stack out in order to reveal their covers, at which point he pulled the fifth book from the top and began to walk toward Matthew who was patiently standing in the doorway.

"Tell you what," said Mr. Fisher. "Why don't you borrow this for the summer and have your sister return it to me in the fall."

"Thanks a lot, Mr. Fisher," replied Matthew. "I just want to glance through it, if you don't mind, for the next day or two and return it before the end of the week, if that's ok."

"Keep it for as little or long as you like, Matthew," replied Mr. Fisher. "I'm always excited when any student of mine wants to learn just for fun. By the way, you already have an 'A' in my class, so your motivation isn't for some kind of extra credit, is it?"

"No, sir," Matthew answered. "Not at all. Like I said, I had a bizarre dream last night and the characters kept referring to Moses."

"That must have been some dream, Matthew," noted his teacher.

"You have no idea," Matthew replied. "Thanks again."

Matthew took the book from Mr. Fisher's hand and placed it into his backpack. After securing the information for his little research project, Matthew walked to the school parking lot and started the drive home. All the while, his thoughts and emotions continued to be consumed by the events of the night before. Matthew quickly realized that he had forgotten Samantha but then remembered his sister had an after-school meeting for the football cheerleading squad the upcoming fall.

Matthew pulled into the driveway of his home and started to push the garage door button. Without even noticing, he glanced in the direction of his bedroom window as his thoughts drifted to the oval that lay upon his bedroom desk.

What are you? he thought.

Matthew was relieved to find the garage empty. He could really use a little home-alone time. He grabbed his backpack resting on the front passenger seat, opened the driver's side door and pulled himself out of the car. Matthew immediately noticed the soreness in his hamstrings and lower back from the physical work of baling hay the day before. As he walked into the house placing his back pack on the kitchen table, he noticed a note hanging from the refrigerator.

Matthew,

Dad and I had to run some errands. There's a frozen dinner in the freezer you can microwave.

Love,
Mom

Matthew rummaged through the freezer until he found the turkey dinner. He placed the tray in the microwave and pushed the three-minute button to commence the cooking process. Matthew then turned his attention to his back pack and walked over to the kitchen table to retrieve the history book. He pulled the book out and sat down at the table as he waited for the ring of the microwave signaling his food was ready.

Matthew immediately opened the book toward the back and began fanning through the pages with his left thumb. As he slowly flipped through the book, a full-page black and white photo caught his eye, and he immediately retreated backwards a few pages in order to study it more closely. It was a group photo consisting of six African Americans arranged in two rows of three people. The front row people were kneeling while the back row stood. At the bottom of the picture, a brief caption described the photo.

> Small group of former slaves assisted by Harriet Tubman
> (center back row) estimated early 1860's. Photo taken at
> some unknown location in upstate New York.

Matthew was struck by the mere fact not a single person in the photo was smiling. They all had a somber look, and Matthew pondered the difficulties of the road they traveled to freedom, especially after the intensity of his dream. Matthew's attention turned to the five other individuals besides Harriet Tubman and made a stunning discovery. His eyes focused intently upon the two individuals standing to the immediate left of Ms. Tubman in the back row. It was a woman and a young man. It was unmistakable. There standing next to Harriet Tubman were Carrie and Benny.

Matthew placed the book face down on the table in a state of utter disbelief and slowly slid it away from himself.

"How?" he said aloud. "How could this even be possible?!"

Matthew stood up quickly, walked to the kitchen sink and turned on the faucet. Almost in desperation, he splashed some cool water on his face in an attempt to wake himself up, clear his vision or otherwise jar him into making sense of it all.

At that moment, the microwave chimed, and his turkey dinner was ready. Matthew turned his focus to the appliance thinking that maybe some food in his stomach would snap him out of this apparent delusional state. He opened the microwave door, pulled out the warm tray and sat down at the table. Matthew refused to gaze upon the photo again until he had finished his meal.

After devouring the last morsel of food, Matthew slowly stood, placed the tray in the kitchen trash and walked back to the open book lying face down upon the table. He hovered next to the table, momentarily uncertain what to do next until he finally summoned the courage to pick the book up again and look at the picture. As expected, consuming a barely palatable, frozen dinner didn't change anything. The haunting characters of his past night's dream were staring back at him in this *real* photo from history. Matthew was overcome with dizziness and his legs were unable to sustain the weight of his body as he stumbled back into one of the kitchen table chairs.

What should I do? He thought. *Who can I tell? Will they even believe me?*

Countless thoughts raced through his mind.

"I'm really losing it," Matthew said aloud. The empty house he had welcomed now became a source of fear and anxiety. He felt completely alone. He longed to be able to share the picture with someone, but no one else had experienced his dream. This astounding coincidence would never be appreciated by anyone but him. It was truly his own alternate reality.

Then something flashed into his mind that seemed to bridge the lonely river between him and the rest of the world.

The oval object.

Matthew stood up and quickly walked up the back kitchen stairs. There was a deliberate purpose to his gait as he skipped every other step upwards until he approached his bedroom.

Matthew stood at the entry way and fixed his eyes on the object resting on his desk in the precise position he had left it. He paused only a moment and then slowly approached his find and sat down at his desk chair. The metallic golden finish seemed brighter than he recalled. Matthew reached out and touched it with his right hand and quickly discovered something unexpected.

It was still emitting heat.

It had certainly cooled from the moment he first discovered it within the trench, but oddly enough, it was still quite warm. Not too warm to the touch, however, as Matthew gently ran his right hand over the flawlessly smooth surface.

What now? he thought.

Matthew stood back up again and walked over to his bedroom window facing the front of the house. He hoped some fresh air would clear his mind. As he gazed out the window, he realized it was an especially breezy day. The leaves on the large oak tree directly outside Matthew's window were moving swiftly as they danced to the silent music of the wind. The rustling noise of the leaves had always been a comfort to Matthew even as a little boy. He particularly enjoyed it on warm starry summer nights as he drifted off to sleep dreaming of being an astronaut.

Suddenly, the wind paused, and the leaves slowed to a calm sway. Watching the slow movement of the leaves became almost mesmerizing until Matthew's attention was drawn to a *single* leaf. It wasn't unlike any other of the hundreds, if not thousands, of leaves adorning the giant tree, but the difference now was in his power of observation. Matthew was seeing the unnaturally enhanced details of the leaf with only his natural eyesight. This leaf must have been at least eight feet from his window, yet

Matthew saw details as if looking through binoculars. He studied the intricate system of veins and the incredibly deep green color, never looking as rich as in it did in that precise moment. Matthew has seen oak leaves countless times during his eighteen years of life, and yet, it was as though he was truly seeing their beauty for the first time now. The sudden appreciation took his breath away.

Suddenly, magnification increased again, and Matthew saw even more details. This leaf was an aggregation of thousands of cells intricately connected to one another resulting in the formation of a unit serving the life-gathering purpose of an enormous organism. The chlorophyll substance, which gave the leaf its green hue, actually became visible! Matthew's eyes then adjusted back to the entirety of the leaf at which point he detected a glow emitting from the leaf. The glow intensified until the colors had disappeared, and all that remained was a bright white light whose shape was in the silhouette of an oak leaf.

As quickly as it began, Matthew's vision suddenly returned to normal. This incredible experience, however, did not come without a side effect as he stumbled backwards dizzy and disoriented. Fortunately, Matthew's backward momentum was disrupted by his bed as he clumsily fell onto his mattress. The room was spinning as he stared at the ceiling of his bedroom. Matthew's stomach began to churn as nausea crept into his body. Instinctively, Matthew closed his eyes and began to take slow, deep and deliberate breathes.

After a minute or two of this exercise, Matthew's stomach calmed, and his dizziness subsided. Although he was feeling better, Matthew became acutely aware of another development. As he lay on his back, Matthew found it next to impossible to move his appendages. His arms and legs felt as though they were made of lead. He had experienced moments of severe exhaustion and fatigue, especially during the late summer months when football resumed and his coach required two practices each day in ninety-plus degree heat. His current weakness, however, was much more intense as he tried to lift his arms, legs and even his head, but it was to no avail.

All Matthew could think of next was to call for help, but his lips struggled to form the word. He then surrendered to the next signal his body was sending.

Sleep.

The last thing he remembered was the image of his ceiling fan fading out of sight as his eyelids slowly closed.

CHAPTER 4

OUT OF THIS WORLD

Matthew woke up startled. His bed was shaking violently as he quickly sat up attempting to remember where and when he was, and how he came to be in his bed. Completely disoriented, Matthew stood and looked out the window, noticing the darkness which had set in but with one noticeable difference. It was completely dark.

The entire world around him had become devoid of light. The street lamps, which normally illuminated the neighborhood, were not emitting their usual soft soothing light. There were no lights aglow within his neighbor's windows. In fact, Matthew couldn't even see any homes as his eyes attempted to penetrate the blackness. He then glanced skyward and immediately noticed the absence of any stars gleaming from their heavenly perch.

His attention quickly turned again, however, back to the original cause of his disrupted sleep. It wasn't only his bed shaking violently but his entire bedroom. In fact, Matthew surmised that the problem was pervasive through the entire house as he struggled to keep his feet beneath the shaking floor. His only thought was that perhaps Indiana was experiencing what would surely be its first significant earthquake, and the power had been knocked out as a result. Matthew recalled learning somewhere that when confined within a building during an earthquake, one should seek safety directly beneath a doorway. He never knew how accurate or true such advice was, but rather than hesitate, he began walking in the direction of his bedroom door. He felt his way through the darkness as he approached the entryway.

When he was within arm's length, he was startled when the door automatically opened. Instead of swinging open in its usual fashion, it retreated within the wall itself. Matthew's startled reaction didn't last long as his mind granted him mercy with a single thought: another dream. None of this was real, therefore nothing should be feared.

His relief was disrupted when he realized there was light emitting from the hallway. Matthew felt compelled to investigate. He stepped into the doorway and noticed the light was to his immediate right according to his peripheral vision. It was flashing red at the end of the hallway where usually the back stairway to the kitchen would be located. Immediately beneath this red flashing light was another door. By this time, the shaking had calmed a bit but Matthew barely noticed due to his recent discoveries. He, then, called out to his parents.

"Mom?! Dad?!"

He began to walk toward the door at the end of the hall and noticed a slight upward incline. A floodgate of thoughts and memories of the past twenty four hours rushed Matthew's mind.

He was baling hay with his father and uncles.

The oval dropped from the sky.

The intense slave dream.

The shocking discovery of the underground railroad photo with Carrie and Benny.

The bizarre visual of the oak tree leaf and the ensuing collapse onto his bed.

Matthew paused his ascent up the hallway, closed his eyes, took a deep breath and braced himself with each arm against the opposite walls.

"Wake up!" he yelled to himself in hopes of disrupting this current dream and return everything to normal.

He opened his eyes, but much to his dismay, he found his predicament unchanged.

"Okaaaay," Matthew said to himself. "Looks like I need to keep walking until something wakes me up."

He struggled to maneuver himself toward the mysterious door, pausing periodically during more violent periods of turbulence to brace himself. Matthew came within a few feet of the door only to notice that it lacked a key component: a door knob.

"Naturally," he stated with amusement.

Looking all over for some kind of mechanism to open the door, Matthew finally decided to reach out with his right hand and touch it. His brief moment of levity quickly dissipated as his hand came to within a few inches of the door, causing it to open in the same fashion as his bedroom door.

Dream or not, nothing could have prepared Matthew for what he saw. Instead of the expected staircase or even his kitchen, he saw what appeared to be the cock pit of an airplane, but the view from the observation windows displayed an incredible sight. To Matthew's left, a planet swirling in blue and white hues was prominently outlined in the window. He immediately presumed it was Earth.

I must be on one of the US space shuttles, Matthew thought, grasping for a logical explanation.

Matthew could make out spots of cloud cover hovering within the atmosphere as well as land masses and oceans from his present vantage point. Before he could further study this heavenly view, however, his attention was diverted by the loudness in the cockpit. Matthew heard a shrill, beeping noise. No doubt it was some kind of alarm to warn the crew that something was very wrong. The severity of the vibrations increased as he now realized the culprit behind their unstable condition was turbulence.

Matthew's eyes glimpsed various instrument panels with readouts, switches, buttons and flashing lights of various colors. Four uniformed crew members in light blue jump suits were frantically adjusting the instrument panels, attempting to rectify the immediate threat.

"This is just a dream, this is just a dream, this is just a dream, and I'm not part of this mess," Matthew repeated in a self-comforting attempt to suppress the brewing well of panic. He closed his eyes and took a deep breath.

"This would make one helluva simulation ride at an amusement park," he said aloud trying to use humor to diffuse his fear.

Suddenly the ship took a sharp turn to the left, catching him off balance. He fell swiftly to the floor, striking his left temple on the armrest of the nearby captain's chair. Slightly disoriented from the blow to the head, Matthew rolled onto his left side and reached up to the chair immediately behind him. He hoisted his body up and scrambled to buckle the harness before he could be thrown from his perch. After securing the straps over his shoulders and waist, he immediately felt the throbbing pain from his injury. He gently rubbed his left temple in an attempt to both sooth his wound and assess if he was bleeding. Fortunately, there was no evidence of blood, but he could barely touch the area without flinching.

How could I be feeling pain? he thought.

At that moment, Matthew heard one of the crew members speak.

"Base 292, come in! Base 292 come in! We have entered into some kind of gravitational anomaly above the planet's atmosphere, and we are unable to compensate! This is Captain Logan, please come in!"

Realizing that his efforts appeared to be in vain, the captain turned his attention toward his crew.

"Stevens! Initiate delta sequence 560!"

"Acknowledged!" answered the man to the captain's immediate right.

Suddenly the shipped lunged forward, and the turbulence worsened as Matthew was violently thrown about in his seat, despite being harnessed into the chair.

"Disengage now, or the ship will tear itself apart!" blurted the captain. "We have no choice. Prepare for emergency landing!"

Matthew momentarily forgot his pain as his attention turned to the drama now unfolding. A red-tinted shield began to lower just outside the ship covering the observation windows, but the scene outside was still visible. Matthew then noticed a fifth crewmember seated dead center to the cockpit struggling with some control mechanism. He presumed it must be the pilot of this vessel.

Matthew engaged in a death grip onto the armrest of his seat as he was suddenly jerked to the left while the ship began to shake violently from the stress of entering the planet's atmosphere. The pilot continued to wrestle with the steering control attempting to steady the ship during its frenzied descent. Matthew heard one of the other crewmembers shout, "Five hundred degrees and one hundred fifty thousand feet!"

A few moments later the crew member yelled out again, "One hundred thousand feet!"

Then fifty, twenty and ten until it was evident they were about to crash at any moment.

"Brace for impact!" warned the captain.

Matthew wondered if it was possible to die in a dream. With one more violent lunge forward, the ship clearly struck the surface and began to slide. Vegetation was striking the windows at an alarming rate.

"Reversing thrusters!" yelled the pilot.

As violently as they lunged forward, Matthew was immediately thrust backward in his chair, unable to move from the G forces at play. After a minute or two, the pilot eased off the thrusters, and they eventually slowed to a halt. There was complete silence as an eerie stillness settled within the ship. The captain then turned his attention to the well-being of his crew.

"Is everyone alright?!" he asked.

They each uttered an affirmative response after which Captain Logan turned his attention back to their unfortunate predicament. "Stevens, take Thomas outside, and perform a visual inspection of the ship," Logan quickly ordered, not allowing his crew to become overwhelmed by their misfortune. "Murphy, initiate a diagnostic of all navigational systems and life support."

Logan then pulled some kind of radio device from the right armrest of his chair.

"Base 292," he began. "This is the shuttle, Centurion. Come in!"

Pausing for a few moments in hopes of a response, his efforts only yielded a static air wave. Matthew then sensed the unease among the crew as they looked at each other with dread.

Logan then pressed a button on the left armrest of his chair, and a panel slid open. He reached into the compartment and pulled out what looked like a microphone.

"Captain's Log," Logan said. "This is Captain Logan of the shuttle, Centurion. We encountered some kind of gravitational anomaly above Planet 317 within the Orion System. It is May 17, 2311."

The captain then continued with a description of the details leading to their crash landing with the technical readouts of key ship systems. Matthew, however, did not hear anything after the words, "Orion System" and "May 17, 2311." Matthew's gaze slowly moved to the observation window as his brain unsuccessfully attempted to process this new reality.

"No," he said aloud to himself in a disbelieving tone. "This can't be possible. This is a dream, and I'm going to wake up any moment."

Matthew then had a memory flash from his Virginia cotton farm dream in which no one was able to see, hear, or interact with him in any way.

Eager but doubtful, Matthew slowly unbuckled his harness straps and stood up to test his theory. He began walking over to Logan who was still seated in his chair. Matthew noted that his uniform was adorned with special markings in the shape of a crescent moon on the tops of both shoulders. He could only assume these were indicative of his status as captain of the ship. Logan appeared to be middle-aged, perhaps in his mid-forties. He had a brown, receding hair line and was very slim and fit. Given the situation, he had a stern look upon his face. Approaching the captain's chair from behind, Matthew spoke.

"Hello," Matthew said timidly at first.

Logan did not respond.

"Hello!" Matthew repeated more forcefully. "Captain, Sir. Can you hear me? Can you see me?"

He reached out with his right hand and touched Logan's right shoulder. Logan clicked off his microphone and slowly swiveled his chair in Matthew's direction. Matthew suddenly developed a fist-sized lump in his throat and butterflies fluttered in his stomach. His heart felt like it would pound out of his chest. Logan had stopped directly in front of the young stowaway and appeared to be looking straight at Matthew.

"Are you ready?" Captain Logan asked.

Matthew stood frozen in place. He struggled to move his lips to respond to the question levied in his direction. Before Matthew could utter a sound, an answer came from directly behind him.

"Yes sir," replied the one called Stevens.

Matthew quickly turned his head and realized that Captain Logan was addressing his crew member and not him. He was clearly just as invisible among the space crew as he had been among the slaves. His heart immediately slowed and he found that he could move again. A wave of relief swept over him but was followed by a twinge of disappointment. Momentarily stumbling, Matthew retreated back to his seat and sat down. He took a few deep breaths and then leaned forward to place his head between his knees in order to thwart the onset of nausea he felt rising. After riding out the physical and emotional stress placed upon his body, Matthew sat up and made a confident declaration. "It's just another dream," he said aloud.

Matthew unconsciously reached up and ran his hand through his hair. It was a self-soothing gesture he has always done since he was a child. But unlike countless other times he had unknowingly performed this ritual, he felt a sharp pain. The throbbing of his left temple jolted him back to the present reality. Matthew wondered again if one is supposed to feel pain in a dream state. After all, isn't that why you are put to sleep during a surgery so you can be oblivious to any pain?

Matthew then looked up and was startled by Stevens and Murphy who had donned black, bulky space suits. They were moving into the next phase of carrying out their captain's orders as they gathered their equipment and proceeded toward the back of the cockpit. Matthew fervently wished that somewhere on the other side of that door awaited the peace and familiar comfort of his home.

"I'll disengage the hatch locks once you've entered the compression chamber," announced a yet unidentified crewmember busily working at his station.

On an impulse, Matthew leapt from his seat to follow the two crew members embarking on a journey into this seemingly unknown world. He followed Murphy and Stevens toward the back of the shuttle where one of them then accessed a number-key control panel on the wall. After entering a code sequence, a divider began to descend from the ceiling and Matthew quickly moved toward his comrades to ensure he was on the "right" side of the divider.

A small whoosh of air then filled the chamber, and a hatch began to open from the top of the ceiling. The automatic door slowly descended until it rested upon the ground leaving a convenient walking platform for them to gradually exit the ship and make contact with the planet.

Matthew was in such a state of awe and wonder, he didn't notice that Stevens and Murphy began walking down the platform before it had fully descended to the ground leaving him behind at the entrance of the hatch. The crew members did not take any time to sightsee as they went about their work activating the instruments in their hands and scan the area around the ship.

"All clear," chirped Murphy.

"I do not detect any sentient life forms within one hundred meters of the ship and no detectible traces of harmful elements in the atmosphere," noted Murphy.

"Affirmative," responded Stevens. "I get the same reading."

They both then placed their hand-held instruments on the ground and reached up to their space helmets in order to disengage them from their suits.

"It'll be a lot easier to inspect the ship without these bulky things on," one of them proclaimed.

Matthew was still at the back of the ship staring out into this new world, attempting to process the sights his eyes took in. It was a beautiful environment, rich with vegetation he had never before seen. This dream was now giving Matthew a thrill he had not felt in the previous one. Considering his fascination with space, this experience, real or not, was immensely exciting.

The ship had apparently come to rest in a grassy field approximately one hundred feet away from a ravine that sloped steeply downward. Matthew stepped forward but immediately shielded his eyes from the immensely bright light as he tried to peer further out into the environment. At that moment, he glanced skyward and realized the extreme brightness was due to the fact that there were two sources of light.

"Amazing," he said aloud in fascination. "Two suns."

Matthew closed his eyes momentarily as a reprieve from the intense solar rays and took in a deep breath, his other senses kicking into high gear. He felt the warmth upon his face, a wonderful swirling wind blowing around his body, the sounds of grass and leaves swaying about, and an incredibly sweet odor detected from his calming breaths. He felt an easy joy slowly sweep through his body. Senses he continuously took for granted now became all the more important in enhancing this incredible experience.

Matthew opened his eyes again only to notice the explosion of color as he better adjusted to the intensity of daylight on this planet. The grassy field appeared to be waist-high and was performing a unique dance as the wind commanded its every move, but the color of the grass was not green but a deep purple with yellow tips at the end. Depending upon the direction the wind was blowing, sections of the field flashed a brilliant yellow while others a deep purple.

Matthew's gaze moved beyond the colorful show as an entirely new phenomenon caught his attention. Hundreds of leaves, or so it seemed, were swiftly being carried across the grassy knoll. Instead of randomly floating above the ground, the leaves swirled in a funnel of air, resembling a snake-like creature twisting up and down suspended in mid-air yet moving at an incredibly fast pace. A myriad of colors were displayed as the "sky snake" of leaves twisted and turned in the turbulent air. Shades of green, red, yellow and blue wove a tapestry of color as the leaves danced in unison.

Matthew then heard the discussion of the two crew members assessing the damage to their vessel. Reluctantly pulled back into the reality of the situation, Matthew's dazed wonder faded away, and he descended the ramp until his feet touched the planet's surface.

Stepping off the ramp, he turned to his immediate right to follow the sounds of the crew members. Approaching the front of the ship, Matthew was startled by its size. It was far wider and longer than he would have guessed from within the cramped quarters of the cockpit. Surprisingly, the wingspan of the vessel was much smaller than he would expect and appeared almost stubby relative to the size of the long fuselage. Continuing to study the ship as he walked along side it, Matthew noticed it was mostly white in color, with thousands of rivets affixing the exterior hull material to its shell. Matthew then noticed the words "US TT 117-4 Centurion, Commissioned April 19, 2302." Matthew found the two crewmen assessing the ship's condition.

"Looks like we found the problem with the Captain's communications," noted Murphy.

"What is it?" asked Stevens.

"I ran a quick diagnostic scan on the communication disk array and found some misalignment in the transmitter cones," answered Murphy.

"That explains why he couldn't get a message out, but at least it's reparable," confirmed Stevens. "Looks like we'd better deal with that first, since it's going to take at least an hour to re-align."

As the two men continued to discuss the repairs, Matthew saw another crew member emerge from the ship wearing the standard light blue jump suit. The new person turned toward Matthew and his comrades but stopped twenty feet away and simply stared in their direction. In fact, it was almost as though he was looking exclusively at Matthew.

"I've been fooled before," said Matthew aloud as he met the gaze of this previously unnoticed member of the crew.

Matthew then noticed out of the corner of his eye that Murphy and Stevens had moved around to the other side of the ship. Matthew turned his head to locate them, but they had moved out of sight. Matthew moved about ten paces away from the ship in an attempt to determine if there was any chance the newcomer noticed him. He studied the man's face, particularly his eyes, very closely to see if he turned his head or shifted his gaze in response to Matthew's change in position. The crewman continued to stare straight ahead with no detectable shift in head or eye movement.

"Thought so," Matthew proclaimed. "You're just like all the rest of the characters in these bizarre dreams of mine."

Or was he?

Suddenly, Matthew realized that he had seen this man before. *The cotton farm dream,* he recalled.

"You were there, on the horse," Matthew said to the man who was only standing a few feet away. "You looked right at me! I know you did!"

Before Matthew could fathom this unlikely realization, the man turned his head, looked directly into Matthew's eyes, and smiled. It took a moment for Matthew to register what just happened.

"You can see me?" Matthew whispered, feeling a little trepidation.

Unexpectedly, the man turned and ran.

"Hey, hey!" Matthew yelled. "Wait, you can see me? I need to talk to you!"

Matthew immediately ran after him, desperate to make contact with anyone who could explain what has been going on. The man reached the back of the ship and ran up the ramp back into the vessel.

"Wait, please!" Matthew yelled as he ran.

Seconds later, Matthew reached the ramp and darted into the ship after him. As he reached the top, he paused to find his target. Matthew could see the man running through a corridor of the ship towards the bridge. He resumed his pursuit but only managed a few more steps before he plunged face first into a clear and previously unnoticed glass wall.

Matthew's body was flung backwards onto the deck of the ship. Another blow to the head left him flat on his back in a daze. He felt the wave of pain sweep down from his forehead all along the front of his entire body. Unable to keep his eyes open any longer, Matthew succumbed to his pain and exhaustion and closed his eyes.

CHAPTER 5

GUIDE

"Maaathew. Maaathew."

Matthew heard a soft voice crawl through the thick darkness toward him and then became aware of a gentle touch on his forehead.

"Honey, are you alright?" asked his mother softly, trying not to startle her son.

He slowly opened his eyes to his mother's concerned face. He was once again completely disoriented as he wearily sat up in his bed. Slowly, the relief of finding himself back in his own reality settled in him.

"I was sleeping?" Matthew asked hoping for a reassuring answer.

Ann felt his forehead again.

"I don't think you have a fever," she said, but it clearly brought her no comfort.

"I was surprised to find you asleep, and I had such a hard time waking you," Ann explained. "Are you feeling okay, Matthew?"

"What time is it?" Matthew asked ignoring her question.

"It's about 7:30 at night," she answered. "How long were you asleep?"

"I'm not sure," replied Matthew. "I microwaved one of the frozen turkey dinners and came up to my room after I ate. It was probably about 4:30 or 5:00. I just got so sleepy and couldn't stay awake."

"Seriously, do you feel okay?" Ann persisted.

"Yeah, I think so," he answered. "I just felt so tired. I think I'll just go into the bathroom and get myself ready for bed. I'm still feeling groggy."

"Alright," Ann said. "If you need anything, let Dad or I know, and we can bring it up to you."

"Thanks, Mom," Matthew responded gratefully.

"Good night, honey," Ann said as she leaned over and kissed him on the cheek.

In response, he reached up and gave his mother a quick hug which she reciprocated.

"You sure you're okay?" she asked once more.

Matthew just smiled weakly and sighed. They both knew something was going on, but neither one had any idea what it was. She slowly pulled away and left the bedroom, pausing just for a moment at the doorway to take one last look at her son to reassure herself.

Matthew sat all the way up in his bed, turned to place his feet on the floor but remained seated at the edge of the bed. Attempting to shake off his tiredness, Matthew took some deep breaths and forced himself to open his eyes as wide as possible while simultaneously retracing the sequence of events which led him to this precise moment.

Another bizarre dream, Matthew thought while shaking his head.

The wind was once again blowing the leaves of the great oak tree outside his bedroom window triggering his memory.

The leaf, he thought. *I was staring at the leaf before I blacked out.*

Matthew then remembered turning to view the object, at which point he became overwhelmed with exhaustion and collapsed onto his bed before falling asleep.

"That guy," Matthew pondered aloud. "I know he could see and hear me in this last dream. He was the same man on the horse who looked straight at me in my slave dream."

Matthew glanced back again toward his desk where the object lay innocently. He was afraid to look at it too long.

"I'm going to take you somewhere where someone can run some tests and figure out what the hell you are," Matthew proclaimed speaking to the oval as though this inanimate object were an intelligent living thing.

Exhaustion still wearing on him, Matthew concluded that his quest to solve the mystery of the oval would continue tomorrow after he was fully rested and more alert. He slowly stood, paused to stretch for a moment by arching his back and extending his arms fully. He then carefully walked to the bathroom to commence his bed time ritual.

Matthew flipped on the bathroom light and took his usual position in front of the medicine cabinet containing all of his toiletries. As his eyes finally recovered from his afternoon slumber and adjusted to the brightness of the light, Matthew reached for the cabinet door. It was at that moment he first noticed the mark on his left temple in the bathroom mirror. A red discoloration peered from beneath his bangs.

"What the hell?" he blurted in disbelief.

He reached up with left hand to brush away his hair and examine the mark more closely. As he gently touched the cherry red mark with his index finger, a sudden streak of pain pierced his temple. Not only was a bruise beginning to visibly form but it was genuinely painful to the touch. Matthew then remembered the fall he suffered in his dream as the spacecraft crash-landed on the strange planet.

"This is impossible!" Matthew said. "It was just a dream. This can't be real."

But there Matthew stood, staring at this apparent remnant from his afternoon dream. His mind and heart began to race feverishly as he sought for a logical explanation. He felt himself break out into a cold sweat. Suddenly feeling dizzy, Matthew stumbled backwards until his back hit the wall with a thud. He slowly slid down until he sat on the cold tile floor with his knees bent. His head visible in the mirror attached to the door to his left, Matthew sat staring at the red mark on his temple for several minutes unable to move. His eyes then focused on the golden knob of the vanity drawer as he struggled not to succumb to a mindless state. Shocked and confused, he attempted to calm himself yet again by closing his eyes and taking two deep breaths.

I must have fallen from my bed and hit my head during the dream, Matthew proclaimed as he desperately clung to any plausible explanation. *I must have hit it on the floor or maybe the corner of my desk.*

Feeling compelled to accept this, Matthew decided to move on and continue his routine as he hoisted himself off the floor. He was also grateful that his mother hadn't noticed since his room was too dark and her worry would have gone overboard. Not to mention the fact, he wouldn't have been able to explain it.

"None of this can be real, none of this can be happening," he repeated to himself in a reassuring manner. "I simply fell out of bed."

Matthew reached inside the medicine cabinet which revealed an assortment of razors, creams and medicine bottles. He selected a bottle of aspirin and took two caplets in hopes the painkiller would provide him some temporary relief and a more restful slumber. After brushing his teeth and changing into his long, black sleeping shorts and a clean, white V-neck, Matthew was ready for bed. As he walked out of the bathroom, Matthew flipped on his ceiling fan to create a cool, calming breeze. Climbing into his bed and resting his head on the soft pillow, Matthew lay on his back mesmerized by the swift movement of the fan.

"It was only a dream, it was only a dream, it was only a dream," he whispered to himself. "I just fell out of my bed."

Struggling to get any more words out, Matthew again found himself overcome by sleep. His eyes became very heavy and slowly closed as the image of his ceiling fan faded. Matthew then heard his name being called from a distance.

"Matthew," called an unfamiliar male voice.

"Matthew," he said again. "Open your eyes, and sit up."

The voice was beginning to draw nearer and clearer.

Matthew slowly opened his eyes but instinctively squinted as a bright light was shining directly down upon his bed. He gradually sat up while shielding his eyes with his right hand.

"That's better," said the stranger.

"Who's there?" responded Matthew. "Who are you? Show yourself!"

Matthew impatiently spun around to the left side of his bed and scrambled to his feet. The source of light provided a spotlight of about four feet in diameter around his bed. Beyond his small island of light, however, there was total darkness. Matthew was unable to see anything but heard footsteps approach in the darkness.

"Who's there?!" Matthew yelled out again as he felt the walls of panic close in on him.

"Don't be frightened, Matthew," responded the voice. "I'm here to help you."

Sensing he was no longer in his room, or anywhere near his family, Matthew demanded, "Where am I, and what have you done with my family?!"

"They are safe and in the same place you left them," the voice replied calmly.

"Left them? I didn't leave them anywhere!" Matthew retorted angrily.

A Caucasian man about six feet tall slowly emerged from the blackness just behind where Matthew stood next to his bed. He was wearing a black, long-sleeved collarless shirt made of a silky material. His pants were a solid black color as well and appeared to be made of a cotton weave unlike anything he had ever seen. Matthew turned sharply to fix his gaze firmly upon the mysterious man. Within a few seconds, however, Matthew's feelings of angst were quickly replaced by bewilderment.

"You?" Matthew said disbelievingly.

It was him. The same man perched upon a horse from his slave dream and the very same person he had unsuccessfully chased into the crashed spacecraft.

"Hello, Matthew," the man said as he walked to the end of the bed and rested his forearms upon the wood footboard.

This must be another bizarre dream, Matthew thought to himself.

He slowly sat down on the edge of his bed and placed his head between his knees while initiating deep calming breaths. Matthew then looked up again at his unknown visitor.

"I'm still here," the man said wearing a bit of a smirk. "Matthew, my apologies for my poor manners. It's terribly rude of me to know so much about you and yet you are at a disadvantage, not knowing me at all."

He moved slightly to the left side of the footboard and extended his right hand to Matthew.

"My name is Samuel," the man said, introducing himself.

Matthew slowly stood and walked to the foot of his bed. Although he was a bit leery, his friendly Midwestern upbringing prevented him from doing anything but accept the handshake. His fear gave way to relief as he inexplicably sensed he was safe in Samuel's presence.

"Nice, firm grip. I appreciate that in a man," Samuel stated.

Matthew more carefully studied Samuel. His hair was black, peppered with some white around his temples. His eyes were brown and his skin was of a darker, almost Mediterranean complexion. Now being in closer proximity, Matthew could see Samuel was fairly tall, just slightly shorter than himself.

"You know what?" Matthew noted with a confident tone. "I don't believe you are real. I've just had the two most intense dreams of my life, and you appeared in both of them. They were just dreams, so I'm sure this one is too. I'm guessing we're in for some sort of big emotional and physically threatening drama. Then just when we're on the verge of some big development, I'll wake up shaken and confused but find myself back in my own room. So maybe we could just skip the big chase scene this time. I'll sit here quietly and safely on this bed and wait for my mom or dad to wake me up."

"Hmm," pondered Samuel as he glanced downward and stroked his chin with left hand. He patiently tolerated Matthew's rambling.

"I suppose that's one point of view, but you fail to remember, Matthew, two critical factors which seem to contradict your theory," noted Samuel.

"What would those be?" Matthew said a little sarcastically.

"Don't you recall the picture of Carrie and Benny?" Samuel asked. "Don't you remember noticing the bruise on your temple from your unfortunate fall? Didn't both those things happen when you were awake?"

The confident expression on Matthew's face quickly faded into one of shock from the immediate recollection of events. Matthew's eyes glazed over as he sat down on the edge of his bed with a far off look, struggling to find a counter argument to his apparent flawed thinking.

"Don't you want to learn the secret of the oval object?" Samuel asked knowing full well the reaction he would invoke.

Astonished, Matthew then shot him a hard look.

"How do you know about the oval?!" he asked.

"I can explain that later, but you must first know The Oval is precisely why I am here," Samuel replied. "To help you unlock the object."

"Unlock it? How?" Matthew inquired.

It didn't really appear locked to Matthew. All he wanted to do was turn it over to NASA and stop having these dreams, to resume his normal existence as a teenager about to embark on his next stage of life but with added excitement from the accolades of his discovery.

Samuel wore a serious expression as he leaned both arms on the foot of Matthew's bed.

"Matthew, you have the ability to do so much," he stated passionately. "Your potential is immense, and I'm here to give you a glimpse into the future. A glimpse into a world where seeming realities will be challenged. It will be only then that you will have the insight into unlocking The Oval and take a huge step into your growth and evolution."

Matthew began to chuckle.

"Look, you have the wrong guy," Matthew began. "That all sounds a bit intense. I don't even know what you're talking about. My growth and evolution? Come on. Give me a break!"

"Don't play dumb with me and deny that which you feel within yourself, Matthew," Samuel challenged. "That 'aw-shucks' Indiana farm boy routine doesn't fool me for a minute. I know you much better than that."

Matthew was surprised. How could Samuel know him? Of course he was beginning to learn that anything was possible in these dreams. What surprised him most was that Samuel was right. Matthew knew he was much more than his public persona, but no one had ever called him on it before. He knew his part and played it well. He never pushed himself beyond the script, although, he secretly kept wishing and dreaming for more.

Apparently, Samuel was the new director of the show now. Matthew knew himself to be smart; his grades were proof of that. He knew he was a good kid, capable of anything he set his mind to. But up until this point in his life, he preferred to deal in reality. He was not comfortable pushing himself outside of his pre-determined parameters, despite his deeply suppressed desires. His old paradigm of thinking drove his preparation in contacting NASA, getting this thing registered as a meteor, have his picture in the newspaper, and go on to claim his spot as a new scientific prodigy. That was the only step he wanted to take in his evolution. He laughed again.

"Was there something specific I said that you find amusing?" Samuel inquired.

"Look," Matthew began. "I think I'm ready to wake up now."

Matthew began to retreat back into the familiar after flirting with new ideas that dangerously challenged his status quo. He reclined back down in the bed and closed his eyes.

"I'm just going to go to sleep, so I can wake up back in my room," he succinctly stated.

Determined to turn this into something he could understand, Matthew focused for a moment on the familiar feeling of his blue quilted comforter that his Aunt Jane made for him when he was twelve. He slowly ran his hands back and forth with palms down on the soft quilt in a self-soothing motion.

Samuel, who apparently expected some resistance, calmly replayed his card.

"Feel your forehead," he suggested.

Matthew reached up and felt the small bump, producing a twinge of pain.

"I fell out of my bed," he said as his remained closed. "Besides, I'm dreaming now anyway."

"No, you didn't fall out of your bed, and you know it," Samuel said as he slowly walked to the left side of Matthew's bed.

Matthew knew Samuel was right. He had never believed the lie he told himself for one second. It occurred to Matthew at that moment how right his parents had always been about one key value they instilled within their children: When you are honest with yourself, you truly can't lie to yourself.

He also knew for a fact that he had seen Benny and Carrie's picture. There was no explaining all this away. Matthew was silent for a moment as he contemplated where to take his line of thinking next.

"This is the first time that I have ever had a tour guide for one of my dreams," Matthew stated amusingly while opening his eyes and sitting up.

Samuel smiled in response. Matthew once again could not deny the ease and comfort he felt in Samuel's presence.

"I'm curious, though, why is it that you decided to reveal yourself now, in this dream?" Matthew inquired as he made direct eye contact with Samuel. "Why didn't you talk to me in my first two dreams?"

"Actually Matthew, that's a very good question," Samuel said encouragingly. "Where I come from, I am known as a Dream Sequencer. Almost like a dream monitor, if you will. But, we can't start there. We can talk about that more in due time."

Where he comes from? Matthew thought as he immediately pondered what that even meant.

"Are you ready to begin?" Samuel asked.

Matthew sobered quickly as he thought of the irony of being trapped within his own dream, trapped within his mind while his body lay asleep in the comfort of his home. Or so he was thinking and hoping.

"Seeing that I'm not doing anything or going anywhere at the moment, what choice do I have, Samuel?" Matthew surmised logically. "As soon as I wake up, though, I'm going to turn that thing over to some scientific group, so they can study it."

"Matthew, who said you're not already awake?" Samuel challenged with a wide smile on his face.

CHAPTER 6

FIRST STEPS

"Ok, Matthew. Step around to the foot of your bed with me," Samuel instructed.

Obligingly, Matthew walked over to the end of the bed where Samuel stood. A twinge of fear suddenly gripped him.

Am I really going to do this? Matthew thought.

"Your journey begins with a test," explained Samuel. "A bit of a challenge, in fact."

"A test? What kind of test?" inquired Matthew, starting to panic.

"There is a small chest with a key that opens it," Samuel noted. "You must find them both and use the key to open the chest. Very simple really."

"What's inside the chest?" Matthew anxiously asked. "The secret to The Oval?"

"First things, first, Matthew, as I need you to trust me," replied Samuel.

He turned to directly face the young man and placed his hands on Matthew's shoulders while looking directly into his eyes. "I want you to close your eyes and take a deep breath," Samuel began. "I need you to totally relax and clear your mind."

Matthew immediately felt a surge of nervousness in response to Samuel's instruction. Whenever someone told him to clear his mind, that command had always been his mind's cue to begin racing.

That's just great! Matthew mused to himself. He would fail this first test and get kicked out of Samuel's dream adventure program. He suddenly wondered if Samuel could read his thoughts.

"Something funny?" asked Samuel noticing the slight smile on his pupil's face.

"It's just that I've never been good at clearing my mind," Matthew replied.

Samuel reached up with his right hand and gently touched Matthew's forehead with his palm. Strangely, his touch immediately helped Matthew relax, and begin breathing deeply. Samuel spoke in a slow, soothing voice. "Good, Matthew," Samuel encouraged. "Now, let all of your worries, questions and uncertainties melt away. I want you to count to ten with your eyes closed, but don't just say the numbers. I need you to visualize each number from one to ten slowly and deliberately while maintaining your relaxed breathing. Once you reach ten, you will open your eyes, and your search will begin."

Samuel then lifted his hand from Matthew and took a few steps backwards. Matthew became more relaxed. His mind became a blank white canvas. He then began the counting process aloud and visualized each number.

"One," Matthew gently spoke as a large black number one filled the white empty space in his mind. As he continued counting, Matthew felt himself disengage from his current surroundings.

"Ten," Matthew concluded.

A few seconds before Matthew opened his eyes, his hearing and smell were already being bombarded with input. Matthew heard birds chirping, insects buzzing and detected a damp, musty odor in the air. An unexpected twist revealed itself as Matthew slowly opened his eyes.

His bed was gone, as was Samuel. Matthew was standing in a dense tropical jungle that appeared so real that he immediately began to perspire from the heat and humidity.

"Samuel!" Matthew yelled out. "Are you out there?"

"Don't forget the goal of this test," said his guide booming through the jungle.

"Oh, right," Matthew said sarcastically. "I'm supposed to find some chest and the key that will open it. But why a jungle?"

No answer came as Samuel had apparently left Matthew alone to embark on his adventure. As tempting as it was, Matthew guessed that standing in one safe spot wasn't the way to find the key and chest. He would have to take a risk by moving out of his comfort zone, which clearly he had been forced to do anyway. Remaining stationary in a new situation didn't exactly seem to be a good course of action. After all, without movement, how would one get anywhere at all?

Reluctantly, he began to walk through the dense jungle pondering where he had been transported and why Samuel couldn't have at least created an easier walking path through all of the vegetation. As he walked along, he heard many unfamiliar sounds of life in the jungle. He constantly scanned the lush vegetation, on the lookout for any possible menacing creatures. His heart raced in anticipation of something unexpected jumping into his path. After what seemed to be about fifteen to twenty minutes of uneasy walking, Matthew stopped to catch his breath and wipe the sweat from his brow. Reaching down to dab his forehead with the bottom of his white T shirt, he realized the intensity of the heat as his clothing was drenched in perspiration.

He paused a moment to take in the amazing site. The plants, which surrounded him at ground level, appeared to be some type of fern. A few leaves were waist high as Matthew reached down with his right hand to grasp one between his index finger and thumb. While holding the plant, Matthew ran his fingers across the top of the leaf with his left hand. It was very smooth yet had quite a sturdy quality about it, as though it had been laminated in a plastic coating. Matthew was startled as a huge, hairy black spider suddenly darted out from beneath the leaf. He quickly released the plant and jumped back several feet.

Matthew then looked skyward and saw a canopy of life. The trees, which provided shade from the intense sunlight, towered above him. He could see the interwoven connectivity of vines and limbs. Each tree was a separate entity but also an intricate part of a larger living organism.

Then Matthew noticed some of the creatures who called the tree tops home. A large parrot was perched about twenty feet above the ground on the branch of a tree approximately five feet from where he stood. It was a brilliant red color with blue wing tips and a plume of purple feathers protruding from the top of its head. Matthew lost himself for a moment while admiring its beauty. Detecting a disturbance within the immediate environment, the parrot suddenly took flight, at which point Matthew noticed a small brown monkey swing into view, landing on the same branch previously occupied by the tropical bird. The monkey's pending arrival had scared off the parrot as it conformed to the pecking order of this unique habitat. Amidst the orchestral chirps, buzzing and occasional howling sounds flying about the jungle, Matthew attempted to absorb the myriad of animals responsible for the increased decibel levels in his new environment.

"At least my subconscious mind has a great imagination for details," declared Matthew aloud. Then he recalled the doubt and confusion Samuel introduced in Matthew's previous attempts to explain away all these events. "At least that's what I hope this is, just a dream," he said with uncertainty.

Matthew took one last glance at the canopy, putting an end to his reverie and getting back to the task at hand of finding the chest and key. Matthew started to walk but was uncertain as to which direction he should go. Suddenly, he caught a glimpse of a falling object in his right peripheral vision. It happened so quickly that all he could ascertain was that a blurry, brown object had fallen from the trees.

Matthew quickly turned his head to identify the object, but it had disappeared beneath the vegetation cover of the jungle floor. Within another second or two, Matthew heard the object strike the ground with a loud thump. Although unseen to Matthew, he heard the ground-dwelling creatures respond to the unexpected intruder as they scurried away. Having a good idea of its whereabouts, Matthew turned toward the direction of the brown blur that fell from the sky. After approximately ten feet or so, he discovered the object resting upon a flattened patch of ferns and other plants. To his great surprise, Matthew realized it was a light brown monkey. It was not moving nor breathing. Matthew immediately looked up toward the branch where he had just seen the monkey, but it was now unoccupied. He presumed that it was the same little monkey he had observed just moments before. He glanced back toward the tangled creature that had most unfortunately fallen to its doom. Just as Matthew was about to step over the pathetic little thing to resume his search, his eye caught a small object protruding from just beneath one of its long thin arms. Not especially interested in touching the animal, Matthew looked around his feet for something to lift the arm and reveal the unnatural item extending from the monkey's body. He found a stick and using it as a lever, Matthew lifted the arm of the monkey and moved it enough to fully expose the object. It was a tubular shaft with a stream of feathers cut neatly in three groups just as Matthew has seen at the end of an arrow from his days as a Boy Scout practicing archery. It was no more than three or four inches in length. Matthew reached down and grabbed the end of the shaft, carefully avoiding contact with the carcass, and pulled it out from underneath the animal. A sharp needle protruded from the end that had impaled the monkey.

A dart? Matthew thought to himself. He looked again to the treetops uncertain what to think or even do next.

Suddenly catching sight of movement amidst the ferns approximately twenty feet away, Matthew was startled by yet another turn of events. In a matter of seconds, he realized that he wasn't alone. His eyes took a moment to adjust to the image standing there before him to his immediate left. It appeared to be a male jungle native. Judging from his appearance, Matthew could only conclude that the man had a primitive existence within this habitat. He appeared to be much shorter than Matthew's six-foot, four-inch frame but very lean and muscular. His skin was a very dark brown, and his nose was adorned with a gold ornamental hoop piercing through both nostrils as it hung down just above his lips. The native displayed an elaborate headpiece that contained plumes of feathers of all types and colors which Matthew presumed was a sign of his hunting prowess. He also wore a chest plate apparently made of small bamboo, but most disturbingly, the intruder was wearing a necklace of small primate skulls strung together and prominently displayed around his neck. The last thing Matthew noticed was a long tubular stick the native held in his left hand. Matthew froze in fear, as did his new visitor.

"Umm, hello," Matthew quietly spoke.

The expression on the native's face shifted from surprise to one of sheer confusion. Matthew glanced down to his left hand where he held the dart extracted from the monkey.

"Hunting, I see," Matthew said in an attempt to placate the man with his calm, cool conversation. He thought he would at least try to converse with the man, even if he didn't understand what he was saying.

"Is this dinner?" Matthew asked as he motioned to the ground in the direction of the monkey. The thought of eating that thing made Matthew feel sick to his stomach.

The native said nothing as his gaze moved away from Matthew's face toward the hand which held the dart, and then shifted to the monkey lying motionless on the ground.

"My name is Matthew," he offered, for lack of any other reasonable conversation starter. In an effort to ease the tension, Matthew extended his right hand in a gesture of peace. The man, startled by Matthew's inexplicable motion, quickly changed posture from a passive stance to a defensive squat as he shifted his tubular pole to an apparent attack position.

In that instant, Matthew realized that the pole was the weapon from which the man launched his deadly darts, and the native must have felt compelled to defend himself.

"No! It's ok!" Matthew said desperately raising both hands in surrender. "I mean you no harm. Please lower your dart gun.

"Samuel!" Matthew yelled. "A little help here would be nice!"

Reacting to the changed intonation and volume of Matthew's voice, the native reached down into a pouch dangling around his waist and pulled out another dart.

"Oh shit!" Matthew said, under his breath as panic began to well up inside him.

He realized he had to make a split second decision and followed the only instinct that came to him in that moment. He rushed his apparent attacker, sprinting at full speed as though the native were an opposing quarterback. Matthew had executed this instinctive action countless times during his high school football career as a defensive end for his team. He reached the jungle native just as he raised the dart gun to his lips. Matthew then lowered his shoulder just before impact and hit the native in the stomach while wrapping his arms around the would-be attacker's waist. Using his momentum and summoning the strength within his arms and legs, Matthew lifted the jungle man off his feet, which sent him backward slamming into the ground.

It was a perfect tackle.

The native was momentarily stunned as he lay on his back. The problem Matthew now faced was what to do next. Deciding not to linger about and wait for the native's next move, Matthew took advantage of the jungle man's disorientation and leapt over him bursting into a sprinter's run.

The jungle man shook off his disoriented state and lifted himself off the ground. Matthew heard a shrill cry behind him as he ran. *Some kind of battle sound,* he thought to himself. A few moments later, he realized his situation had grown dire. The cry emitted from the dart-bearing man was a battle call to his fellow natives. Matthew could hear them in the distance joining in the pursuit.

Fearing for his life, the rush of adrenaline easily launched him into a faster sprint. His plan was to put as much distance between himself and his pursuers as quickly as possible. He ran with no specific direction only slowing occasionally upon encountering a tree or to slap away a tropical plant hanging in his path. Aware that he was successful in distancing himself from his pursuers,

Matthew then decided to change direction to further lose the natives. He quickly took a hard left, drawing on a strength and resolve within himself to pick up speed despite the burning sensation now present within his lungs.

It seemed he had been running forever when he felt as though his lungs were about to burst. Matthew had no choice but to stop and catch his breath. He fell to his knees, trying to resist the desire to completely collapse on the ground. Matthew attempted to gain control of his breathing and heart rate. Perspiration dripped from every pore of his body as he again noticed that the hot humid tropical conditions were to blame for his deteriorating physical condition. After a few minutes, Matthew hoisted himself off the ground but remained hunched over as he rested his hands on his knees to take a few more deep breaths. Moments passed until Matthew was able to stand upright again. He then quickly knelt back down in order to remain undetected after temporarily forgetting the cause of his flight.

Matthew stayed still for several minutes, unsure if it was safe to move. It became apparent that he was successful in his escape when he could no longer hear his pursing attackers. Having been lost in the recent turn of events, Matthew's mind now cleared, and a single word popped into his consciousness:

Samuel.

"What the hell is going on?" Matthew whispered to himself.

He so desperately wanted to call out to his guide for help but thought better of it due to the unknown whereabouts of the jungle natives. Still kneeling, Matthew had no idea what his next move would be in his search for the chest and key. Once again, he decided not moving wasn't an acceptable option and decided to more carefully and quietly continue his search. Matthew slowly stood and looked around in a three-hundred sixty degree radius to ensure that his pursuers were nowhere in the immediate area. Just as he was about to take his first steps, Matthew heard a low rumbling noise immediately behind him. It sounded like a growl. He slowly turned, careful not to make any sudden movements. His eyes frantically searched for the source of the noise. Matthew could not detect anything in the immediate area amidst the dense jungle vegetation, but after a few moments, his eyes locked onto the culprit. The creature was difficult to locate given its natural camouflage. Matthew could only make out the head of the beast protruding slightly from the bushes approximately fifteen feet directly in front of him.

It was a tiger, and Matthew's heart rate immediately escalated again as he felt his entire chest throbbing in response. "This just gets better and better," he said aloud.

Yet again, Matthew wished he could summon help from his new-found guide, Samuel. Worried that any such attempt would startle the tiger or give away his position to the natives, Matthew stood quietly contemplating how he would remove himself from this precarious situation. He was not given the opportunity to think for very long, however, as Matthew noticed the animal began to crouch lower to the ground. It was obvious to Matthew that the mighty cat was preparing to lunge.

"Here we go again!" Matthew blurted as he turned and sprung into another run.

Matthew pondered the odds of outrunning a tiger, but his thoughts were interrupted as he heard the cat emit a mighty and bone chilling roar behind him, which produced another burst of adrenaline. He could hear the tiger getting closer as Matthew realized he was only a minute or two away from certain capture. He finally let out a blood curdling call for help.

"SAMUEL!!!" he yelled in desperation.

Just then, he noticed what appeared to be a clearing ahead and a vine dangling from a very large tree. Within seconds, Matthew leapt up and grabbed hold of the vine and began to climb. His momentum caused him to swing several feet forward, making the climb even more challenging. Matthew glanced down to check his progress as he continued to feverishly climb higher and higher. As he looked down, he realized the tree was located on the edge of a cliff, and Matthew now found himself suspended eighty feet above a blue body of water. The forward motion of the swinging vine momentarily paused, then began to swing back toward the edge of the cliff. Standing there on its hind legs with his massive front paws stretched high on the tree was the mighty tiger, patiently awaiting his prey's return.

Matthew quickly realized that his efforts to scale the vine would be futile, as the height did not provide a safe enough escape from his predator, whom he figured possessed an unnatural leaping ability. He had only a few seconds to make a decision on his next move. Matthew let go of the vine and began to plunge toward the blue pool of water beneath him.

"Oh shit!" Matthew yelled as gravity had him speeding toward the earth. Just before impact, Matthew had a horrifying thought: *Is this water deep enough to cushion my fall?*

At the last possible moment, Matthew took one big gasp of air. As he hit the water, the sudden change in temperature caused Matthew's body to shiver uncontrollably. His momentum slowed instantly as he sank deeper into the water. After a few seconds, Matthew gathered his wits about him and started to swim. Sensing no injury to his body, Matthew began to kick his legs and paddle his arms up toward the surface. His ascent seemed to take much longer than expected. Aiming for the source of light above him, Matthew started to feel the burn in his lungs as he swam more frantically toward oxygen. Finally reaching the surface, Matthew gasped for air as he gratefully emerged from the water.

Matthew's disorientation waned as he filled his lungs with air. After catching his breath, he attempted to get his bearings by looking in all directions while treading water. After a few moments, he spotted the shore about fifteen to twenty yards away. Feeling strong enough, he headed toward land. His pace was slow and laborious as his body struggled to comply. He continued to push himself until he could touch the bottom and slowly walked up the slope of the shoreline.

At last, he made it out of the water and collapsed face first onto the sand, completely exhausted. Too tired now to even consider the possibility of another threat, he melted into the warm, scratchy sand. Taking very deep and deliberate breaths, he gradually regained control over his breathing and his heart rate slowed down. He then summoned all his strength to flip himself onto his back. Matthew stared at the sky above and for the first time, noticed the perfect brilliant blue color. Matthew firmly planted the palms of his hands in the ground as he slowly sat up. Now facing the body of water, Matthew looked behind him toward the endless jungle and felt a wave of relief as it appeared he was safe for now. Then he experienced a rush of thoughts as it all came back to him. The Oval, Samuel, the key, the chest and these bizarre dreams flooded his mind. This dream was the most physically taxing one yet. When would he awaken? What did Samuel mean, when he asked if he was sure that he was dreaming? Does Samuel know that Matthew was definitely not dreaming?

After a few more minutes of rest and contemplation, Matthew hoisted himself up to his feet. Still standing at the water's edge, he looked to his left and right along the shore searching for any clues to guide him. Matthew then looked into the dense jungle but nothing unique or obvious appeared within his line of vision. Frustration and hopelessness crept into Matthew at which point there was but one more course of action to take.

"SAMMMUUELLLL!" Matthew yelled at the top of his lungs as he cared not who or what may hear him.

So he had failed the test. He didn't even care anymore. Any test that runs the risk of death by poison dart or tiger mauling wasn't worth passing. It wasn't even worth taking. This was the first test he had ever failed, and it didn't feel good. Even though he was really getting pissed at Samuel for devising such a difficult, impossible test, it still troubled Matthew to fail. He did not fail tests. He didn't fail at anything.

Until now.

And yet, maybe somehow there was still a way. He paused a moment or two but received no response to his cry for help.

"How am I supposed to find this chest and key?" Matthew lamented aloud as his voice rose, hoping Samuel could hear his frustration. "This is an impossible test!"

Finally, Matthew received an answer from his guide.

"Matthew, you are wasting time," Samuel said from some unknown location. "What are you doing?"

Matthew looked up toward the sky and all around the area as he could hear Samuel's echoing voice but could not physically see him.

"Wasting time?!" Matthew retorted. "Where have you been all this time? What's with the radio silence? I could have used some help over the past thirty minutes or so. Do you have any idea what I've been through? If you answer yes, you're damn lucky I can't see you for me to plant my fist in your mouth!"

"Matthew, I am going to help you through your quest, but I need you to listen to my direction," Samuel responded, completely unmoved by Matthew's rants. "Can you do that?"

Feeling relief from finally establishing contact with his guide, Matthew annoyingly replied, "Yes."

"Good," replied Samuel "The first thing you must do is calm yourself, so close your eyes, take four deep breathes and say the word 'Om' with each exhale."

"What?!" Matthew protested. "I'm in a jungle surrounded by life-threatening predators and God only knows what else, and you want me to meditate or something? What kind of a dream guide are you?"

Once again, Samuel was unaffected by Matthew's frustration.

"Matthew, I realize that is how you are conditioned to respond to challenges, through knee jerk reactions," Samuel began. "But now I am teaching you a new way, a way that will give you greater results than you ever imagined. But you have to trust me. First you must turn inward, center yourself and rely on your own creative power. All action will come forth from there. Are you ready to try my way now? Are you ready to trust me?"

Samuel patiently waited for Matthew to come around.

Matthew considered what Samuel said. Something about the calm confidence in his voice and his demeanor inspired Matthew to trust him in spite of his desire to punch him in the face for putting him through all this. He might as well try it, given that he now stood in a jungle talking to some invisible dream guide. Clearly all bets were off for any sense of normalcy.

Matthew agreed. "Alright," he said shortly.

"Okay, Matthew, close your eyes, take four deep breaths and repeat the word 'om' with each exhale," Samuel instructed once again.

Matthew awkwardly complied and found to his surprise that he immediately began to relax. He was about to open his eyes when Samuel provided the second instruction.

"Now, keep your eyes closed, Matthew, and I want you to visualize the chest in your mind," he said.

Tentatively beginning to believe in this mumbo jumbo approach, Matthew complied once again. He had to fight the temptation to open his eyes and instead attempted to form a picture in his mind's eye of this secret chest. To Matthew's surprise, a small brown chest suddenly appeared in his mind. It was roughly two feet wide with a rounded top. Two leather straps draped over the top which fastened to corresponding buckles affixed to the base. In the middle of the chest, perfectly centered in between the leather straps, Matthew could clearly see a key hole.

"Do you have an image in your mind now, Matthew?" asked Samuel.

"Yes," replied Matthew. "I can see it."

"Excellent," Samuel said encouragingly. "Now I want you to slowly open your eyes, and the path to the chest will be revealed."

Although that seemed utterly impossible, Matthew slowly opened his eyes as instructed. At first, his environment remained unchanged as he saw the now familiar view of the dense jungle vegetation before him. He felt himself deflate with disappointment, but he intuitively knew he couldn't follow that feeling. He commanded himself to believe something would happen. After a few seconds, an amazing transformation took place before Matthew's eyes. Some of the jungle plants and trees began to fade away. There appeared to be a pattern to the disappearance, as the fading vegetation gave way to a path leading through the jungle.

The perfectly straight path ended about thirty feet away from where he stood along the shore. At the end of it, Matthew could see a small brown object on the jungle floor.

It was a chest. In fact, it was the exact chest Matthew had visualized just seconds before. Matthew stood in utter amazement at how little effort it actually took to find it. He rubbed his eyes to make sure what he was seeing was real.

"Wow," Matthew said with disbelief. "How did you do that?"

"I didn't do it, Matthew," Samuel corrected. "You did. Now all that is left is the key, and then you can walk over to the chest and open it."

"Oh right," responded Matthew, who had forgotten about that important missing element he still needed to complete the task at hand. "What should I do next?"

"Matthew, I want you to turn around and look into the water," Samuel directed.

Matthew complied and walked closer to the water's edge and looked down. He saw his reflection staring back at him.

"All I see is my reflection," noted Matthew.

"Look again, but before doing so, I want you first to close your eyes again and visualize the key you are searching for," Samuel instructed. "Think of every detail, including how it feels as you hold it."

Matthew, thrilled with the success he had with the chest, was eager to try this magic trick again. He closed his eyes and tried to visualize the object, noting every detail including the cold metal surface within his grasp. As he gained a picture in his mind, Matthew slowly opened his eyes and gazed once again into the blue water. As his eyes adjusted to the bright shimmering light reflecting from the water, Matthew focused all of his attention at scanning the sandy bottom for the elusive object.

Then he spotted something. It was just beneath the reflection of his right hand in the water. Upon closer inspection, Matthew quickly realized that it wasn't resting beneath the water but actually in the reflection of his hand. Matthew then glanced down to his right hand and there, contained within its grasp, was the key he had just imagined. It was a large, golden key with two teeth designed to turn the locking tumblers of an old chest. The metal texture was cold and smooth just as he had visualized moments ago.

Matthew paused momentarily in disbelief but then swiftly turned away from the water and headed up the path leading back to the chest. He took each step with a commanding purpose. Matthew noticed that as he drew closer, his body grew more excited at the prospect of solving the mystery of The Oval, and his pace quickened. Within moments, Matthew was upon the chest. He knelt down and inserted the golden key into the key hole and turned it in a clockwise direction. He heard a distinctive click that could only mean he was successful. Leaving the key still in the hole, Matthew proceeded to unbuckle the leather straps.

The decisive moment was now upon him. Matthew took a deep breath and lifted the top which swung up and backward on its hinges. Uncertain what he might find, Matthew's mind began to formulate various possibilities. Could it be an electronic device that activated The Oval? Could it be yet another key that somehow would open the object?

When he leaned over to see what treasure lay within, he discovered an ordinary hand mirror, just like the one his mother uses to look at the back of her hair. In fact, it appeared to be an exact replica of his mother's mirror. It was circular in shape with a plastic-coated, black handle and frame. He had seen her use it a million times. His mother's mirror. He picked it up and looked into it and saw his own confused face staring back at him.

"Samuel," prompted Matthew. "What is this, my mom's mirror? I thought I was going to discover the secret to unlocking The Oval inside this chest."

"You have," answered Samuel who was now standing directly behind Matthew.

Puzzled, Matthew stood and spun around to face his guide. Then he noticed that the jungle scene had completely disappeared, and he had been somehow transported back to the original spot where he and Samuel had first met. They were standing next to

Matthew's bed again illuminated in a small island of light with the unending darkness beyond.

Matthew was still holding the mirror in his hand. Comforted by Samuel's reappearance, he looked Samuel directly in the eye and repeated his question.

"Why is it that the chest only had this mirror in it?" Matthew repeated. "How is this supposed to help me unlock the mystery of The Oval?"

"Look into the mirror again and tell me what you see," Samuel instructed.

Matthew complied as he focused intently upon the mirror only to find that it contained merely his own reflection.

"It's just my reflection, Samuel," Matthew replied in exhausted frustration.

"So, the answer to your question is that you see yourself?" Samuel asked very succinctly.

"Yeah, okay, I see myself," responded Matthew, still not really appreciating the symbolism.

"So Matthew, then do you not suppose that the answer to unlocking the secret of The Oval is, in fact, you?" Samuel noted.

"I don't understand," Matthew admitted.

"Matthew, I want you to let go of every pre-conceived notion in your mind and open yourself up to a new possibility," Samuel began to explain. "I am hoping that you can appreciate the critical lesson of the adventure you just experienced. Where did you find the key?"

"In my hand, but I have no idea how it got there," Matthew noted with disbelief.

Samuel remained silent as Matthew thought for a moment.

"I was so relieved and excited that I didn't take any time to think about how it got there," Matthew explained. "I had just been through so much. With the hair-raising things that led me to that point, I just wanted to take that key and immediately open the chest."

"Indeed," said Samuel. "Matthew, your experience should give you a fundamental but crucial insight."

"What's that?" Matthew asked, not aware of any crucial insights.

"You were holding the key all along," Samuel stated. "You just had to realize you already possessed it. Through visualizing, you allowed that image of the key to merge with the reality of what you desired and perceive. Once you did that, you held the real key. In effect, the key jumped from your mind into your hand."

Matthew pondered that a moment. "Is that what visualization is?" he asked with a sense of wonder. "Bringing something from your mind into actual physical reality?"

"It certainly can be," replied Samuel. "I think you can now attest to that."

Matthew was blown away, but Samuel had more to say. "Once you called the key forth from your imagination into your reality, you then held the power to unlock the chest," Samuel concluded.

Matthew slowly nodded.

"And what were you hoping to find inside the chest?" Samuel inquired, knowing full well Matthew's response.

"Something that would explain or reveal the mystery of The Oval," answered Matthew. "What it is or where it came from and what is its purpose, if any."

"So you found a mirror within which reflected back to you the answer to your question," Samuel stated.

"So I am that 'thing' to solve the mystery and answer my own question?" Matthew asked thoughtfully as he began to slowly understand.

"PRECISELY, Matthew!" Samuel said excitedly. "You are the key to unlocking your own potential which will solve the mystery of The Oval. You not only held the key to open the chest, but you ARE the key! That's why the key appeared in your hand as your desire to find it and open the chest was brought forth from within yourself."

Matthew was momentarily taken aback. On one level, it seemed to make sense, but on another, his intellect couldn't wrap itself around this mind-blowing possibility. It went well beyond anything he ever would have imagined within the confines of his traditional life of logic and order.

"I'm not sure if I buy that," retorted Matthew after a few moments of reflection and letting doubt get the better of him momentarily. "Before we get into that, though, I have one question for you."

"Yes?" replied Samuel sensing the sudden shift in his pupil's demeanor.

"Why the hell did you send me into a jungle, have me be chased by poison dart-shooting natives and hunted by a man-eating tiger, from which the only escape, mind you, was a death-defying plunge into a lake from a cliff?" Matthew demanded. "Why didn't you just tell me?!"

"Interesting, yes," Samuel replied. "I am so glad you asked, as it is yet another crucial realization in your quest to unlock The Oval. The truth is, my friend, I didn't do any of that, Matthew. You chose it for yourself."

Completely shocked by Samuel's answer, Matthew replied indignantly, "Yeah. Right!"

"Do you remember what I first told you about finding the secret of The Oval?" prompted Samuel.

"You said something about a small challenge or test in finding a chest and the key to open it," answered Matthew. "When I opened my eyes, you were gone, and I found myself in this tropical jungle not knowing where to even begin looking. It was all uphill from there."

"Matthew, I never intended for you to have such challenges," noted Samuel. "Those obstacles were placed before you by your own mind."

"Bullshit!" Matthew refuted. "Why would I do that to myself?"

"Because the second you heard the words 'challenge' or 'test,' your mind immediately began to conjure up an elaborate setting that would be worthy of such a quest," Samuel explained. "It placed before you all of these obstacles and twists in making the achievement of your goal all the more difficult. You just didn't realize it until it had already happened!"

Matthew listened intently but still struggled to fully comprehend Samuel's hypothesis.

"So I created my own little video game of challenges to overcome, in order to pass the test and find the key," Matthew summarized.

"Yes, my friend," replied Samuel who was clearly charmed by Matthew's translation.

"But why would I make it so hard?" Matthew inquired.

"Why, indeed," repeated Samuel smiling like the cat who had eaten the proverbial canary. "Maybe because at the time, you had no idea you were creating all these hardships for yourself. It happens all the time. In fact Matthew, did you notice how your adventure actually increased in difficulty as you went along?"

"Did it ever!" responded Matthew.

Samuel gave an affirmative nod.

"Therein lies the other lesson you need to take away from this experience, Matthew," Samuel stated more intensely. "The notion of CONTROL. Things turned from bad to worse in the blink of an eye, because you lost control of your mind and your corresponding thoughts, which then led to severe emotional responses. Once things started getting a little hairy, your imagination ran away from you and conjured up even more intense possibilities until the whole thing seemed impossible and hopeless at which point you called out for my help. Once you asked me for assistance, I was able to simply calm your mind and help you to truly focus on the task at hand. The effortless nature of revealing the chest and the key, which you held all along, was your own doing through the channeling of your mind and spirit."

Matthew was speechless. He would never have drawn such a conclusion, but admittedly, Samuel's words were beginning to make some sense. He didn't fully understand it intellectually, because his mind wanted to grasp to the familiar, clinging to his old paradigms of thinking. The understanding that seemed to be taking hold was doing so at a much deeper level, almost like intuition.

"Of course you could have done it that way from the beginning, but I find that's rarely the case when someone is introduced to this for the very first time," Samuel explained.

Matthew let it all sink in. What Samuel was saying was intriguing. Matthew liked considering the potential path of just simply visualizing the key and chest from the beginning and foregoing the life-threatening encounters. To allow the path to unfold as you desire or intend.

Matthew turned away from Samuel and looked out at the darkness that surrounded him.

"Samuel, what is all of this?" Matthew asked sweeping his left hand through the darkness that was beyond the little island of light.

"It represents your next choice, Matthew," responded Samuel. "I have been sent here to guide you on your journey, but you must consciously choose to leave the familiar and step into the unknown."

Matthew peered in vain into the blackness before them.

"So by stepping into the darkness, you will teach me how I am the alleged key to unlocking The Oval?" Matthew inquired.

"That's right," replied Samuel. "But this is only a choice you can make, and if you do decide to take this step with me, you must commit yourself to letting go of your old perceptions of reality and open your mind and soul to possibilities you have yet to even imagine. Can you do that?"

Matthew paused for a moment. It seemed to him that his mind and spirit were now being opened for him. It was as though a force so much bigger than him was at play, leading him through the most intense and amazing experiences of his life. Maybe if he took an active role in the process, he would shorten the paths to get there. Whatever was going on, he suddenly became overwhelmed with the urge to move forward, to wade into deep, uncharted waters that would expand across a limitless sea.

"Yes, I believe I can," Matthew replied.

"I thought that would be your answer, Matthew," Samuel responded with an approving smile.

Samuel then took three steps into the darkness where he completely disappeared from sight. Matthew watched as an arm and outreached hand re-appeared into the light, inviting him forward.

Matthew remained still, fully visible within the light, standing next to his comfy, old familiar bed. He fought the twinge of fear to stay in his comfort zone. Before grasping Samuel's hand and taking his first steps, Matthew glanced one last time at his bed. He then asked his guide another question.

"Samuel, is this real or am I dreaming?" he asked.

"Like I said Matthew, let go and open your mind," Samuel replied. Samuel felt the excitement grow within him by the young man's choice. He knew all too well, however, that it wasn't just Matthew's mind that would be opened to new possibilities. There was something far greater at stake, but that was Samuel's burden to carry, at least for the moment.

Nervous, anxious and excited, Matthew took the leap of faith as he grabbed hold of Samuel's hand and stepped into the darkness, disappearing from sight.

CHAPTER 7

BREAKING FREE

Matthew's heart rate escalated as he stepped into the unknown darkness, unsure of what he might see or find on the other side. Samuel released his hand as Matthew became fully engulfed by this new environment. Having only taken a few steps, Matthew looked back to find the island of light and his comfortable old bed looking miles away. His familiar world seemed so distant and small as the few steps he took warped him far away. He chilled with the awareness that it would take an extreme effort to reverse his progress and return to his comfort zone, and yet, his true desire was driving him forward.

He turned back around to face his guide and take in the new surroundings. Matthew expected not to be able to see due to the striking darkness he had seen from the outside just moments ago while standing next to his bed. The reality, however, was quite surprising as a soft glow of twilight provided enough illumination to clearly see his guide.

"I'm proud of you, Matthew," commented Samuel. "How do you feel?"

"A little freaked out, to be honest," replied Matthew. Not wanting to dwell on his trepidation, the young man pushed forward. "Now what?" he asked.

Samuel turned to walk directly in front of Matthew and placed his hands on Matthew's shoulders. "Your next lesson," Samuel answered very matter of fact. "Are you ready?"

"As ready as I'll ever be," Matthew replied. The cliché was the only possible answer he could come up with at that moment.

"Although I wish I had some clue as to what I should be ready for," Matthew said with great curiosity.

"Let me show you," Samuel responded.

Samuel then moved to Matthew's right side revealing an object that now appeared on the floor behind the location where his guide previously stood. Matthew was uncertain if it had always been there and he just now noticed it or if Samuel somehow magically made it appear. Based upon his current circumstances and the crazy sequence of events thus far, Matthew wouldn't be surprised if it was the latter.

It was a large circular ring emitting a brilliant white light along its edges. The circumference was large enough for Matthew to lie down in and encompass his six-foot, four-inch frame. Samuel then stepped within the ring, activating some kind of mechanism as Matthew heard a low hum emitting from the ring itself. He quickly assumed that stepping within the ring activated its power source.

"Come," said Samuel, motioning Matthew to step into the ring.

Matthew stepped toward Samuel and onto the platform. From the center of the ring, a series of circular lights began to flash in an outward direction beneath their feet. The pattern of lights resembled that of a rock tossed within the center of a pond generating a series of ripples that extended outward until they disappeared upon reaching the shoreline. Matthew had no idea what to expect next.

"Is this thing going to scramble my atoms or something?" he asked with a concerned tone.

Samuel let out a short chuckle, amused by Matthew's comment. "Matthew, this will be our transport on your personal journey," his guide explained.

Matthew dubiously looked down at the floor and the ring around them. "You mean I am going to travel somewhere in this thing?"

"That's right," Samuel answered.

Matthew quickly remembered his pledge to open his mind and reminded himself that nothing made any sense anymore. The best he could do is go with it and try not to be alarmed. There was only one question he had to address before they embarked on the next step. "Samuel, will I be safe?" Matthew asked.

Samuel looked deeply and kindly into Matthew's eyes. "Center yourself, Matthew, and you will always find safety and peace there," he replied.

Before Matthew could voice a complaint to his guide for not completely answering his question, the ring began to lift off the ground.

Here we go, Matthew thought, trying to find comfort in Samuel's re-assuring tone and resist the urge to jump off.

"What is this thing?" Matthew asked.

"I told you Matthew, it's our transport," repeated Samuel. "It's a hover craft that will allow us to surf the threads across space-time."

Matthew looked at Samuel incredulously before deciding to make light of the absurdity of the situation. "Oh, alright," commented Matthew in a nonchalant tone. "Why didn't you just say so in the first place?"

Samuel let out a loud, booming laugh "That's one of the things I really like about you, Matthew," noted Samuel. "You have a great sense of humor even amidst stressful or uncertain situations."

Matthew couldn't help but be flattered by the compliment. He actually liked that about himself too.

They were a good twelve feet or more off the ground when their floating disc began to move forward. Samuel then waved his right hand in the direction of his feet and a rod emerged from within the floor of the disc. The rod rose up and stopped abruptly as soon as it reached the height of Samuel's waist. The tip revealed some kind of large marble ball that spun uncontrollably in place. It was smooth in texture and contained interconnected white lines woven into a deep blue backdrop. Samuel reached out and grasped the ball in his left hand.

"Let me guess," Matthew began. "A steering wheel?"

"Precisely, my boy!" Samuel replied with a bright smile.

Their disc then began to pick up speed, and Matthew took a moment to take in the surroundings as he felt the rush of wind lift the bangs of his hair. There was an eerie silence within this foreign place. The only audible noise Matthew detected came from the low hum emitted by their hovering platform and the breeze from their forward motion. It was still difficult to observe much beyond their transport due to the dim lighting, but he saw that they were approaching an object high above them in the distance. Matthew attempted to focus on their destination. Samuel was silent as he operated the steering device. As they drew closer and higher up, Matthew gained a better appreciation of its large size despite still being several hundred feet above them yet. He looked down to gauge their ascension thus far, but it was to no avail. They were either too high, the conditions too dark or a combination of both as Matthew was unable to fully ascertain their position.

"Hold on," blurted Samuel suddenly as he broke the silence.

Looking around at the complete lack of framework to their transportation vehicle, Matthew demanded, "Hold on to what?!" Instinctively, he reached out and grabbed the only thing available—Samuel.

With Matthew grasping Samuel's right shoulder, they quickly slowed to a complete stop, and within a split second, they resumed motion but this time heading straight up. Unlike the gradual ascension of an elevator, they shot up with tremendous speed. Matthew felt his stomach drop.

"Samuuueeellll!!" Matthew yelled in protest to this unexpected thrill ride.

"Relax, Matthew," Samuel said attempting to comfort the young man. "We're here."

Their transport came to a stop at their target destination. They hovered before the very object which had first appeared in the background of a black tapestry just moments ago. The object was enormous. Matthew quickly concluded that his house could easily fit inside its parameters. Matthew's mouth hung open, and his eyes widened. Never before has he seen such a strange anomaly. It was oval in shape, at least, at times it took an oval shape. It was not made of a solid substance and almost appeared two dimensional. A golden light highlighted the outer rim of the oval, and its center appeared liquid in form. It was as though an ocean of glistening white light ebbed and flowed in a vertical position totally contained within the golden rim of this oval ring. Its shape was in constant fluctuation, the likes of which Matthew could only liken to his experience as a child when blowing bubbles with his siblings. Each bubble, as it floated, would bend and sway in a similar fashion. The larger the bubble, the more challenging it was to maintain a perfect shape. Matthew then noticed yet another unusual characteristic. He could FEEL it.

The ring was emitting energy as though it had a presence or self-awareness. Its power made Matthew's hair on the back of his neck stand up.

"What is this?" Matthew softly spoke while soaking in his visual and physical observations.

"It's a portal, Matthew," replied Samuel.

"A portal?" Matthew responded. "A portal to what?"

"Not a portal to what!" answered Samuel with a heightened sense of excitement. "But a portal to WHEN and WHERE."

"Ooookaaay," Matthew said cautiously. "We're going to enter that thing, aren't we?"

"Yes," stated Samuel succinctly.

"I had a feeling you were going to say that," Matthew responded. "And what exactly will we find on the other side?"

"Your next lesson," Samuel answered with a hint of a smile. "Have I steered you wrong yet?"

"I'm not exactly sure," retorted Matthew. "Considering you have apparently steered me into a BLOB!"

Samuel let out another booming laugh while simultaneously engaging their hover craft, moving them forward directly into the floating "blob" of energy. They entered slowly and disappeared within the white, glistening liquid energy as it completely engulfed them. Matthew's eyes were blinded momentarily by the intensity of light. After approximately thirty seconds, he could then see the white light bending and swaying, at which point they emerged on the other side of the energy portal.

Matthew then saw yet another amazing site: a labyrinth of golden energy beams intertwining at various points. These energy ribbons were woven together into an elaborate pattern where the connecting points contained miniature gateways similar to the one through which they just passed.

"What is all this?" Matthew asked, filled with a sense of awe and wonder he had never before experienced.

"We just entered into the master portal that allows us to see and access the golden energy signatures of past, present and future events," replied Samuel. "But never mind that now. You will be able to appreciate this more later. Right now, you need to focus on the next step of your journey."

"I've almost forgotten about why we are here," admitted Matthew, completely mesmerized by the scene before him. His heart was overwhelmed with so many emotions that it was difficult to process. Fear, anxiety and excitement all bombarded his entire being. The closest thing he could liken this experience to was riding a roller coaster but at an unimaginable level of intensity.

Samuel then engaged their flying disc yet again. He selected an apparent entry point at the end of an energy wave and began to "ride" along its surface. They passed several connections all around them, but their speed accelerated so quickly, making it difficult for Matthew to observe any details. They moved up and down the curvature of the energy ribbon as it bent toward the left and moved swiftly downward. Matthew responded once again by grasping the shoulder of his tour guide to steady himself.

Within a few moments, they slowed upon arriving at an apparent pre-determined connection. Similar to the master gateway, their hover craft guided them into the smaller version of this portal. They disappeared within the fluctuating white, liquid energy, floating and glistening within the circular boundaries of the gateway.

Once again, Matthew was temporarily blinded by the intensity of the light, but it quickly faded as they emerged on the other end. Matthew was immediately struck by the intensity of color. He could see green, brown and blue but they appeared blurred, as though the objects were being stretched.

"Don't worry," Samuel began, knowing full well what Matthew was experiencing. "Your eyes will adjust from entering the gateway."

Samuel was right as the distortion quickly improved, and Matthew could tell that the lines of color he was seeing belonged to the water of a river that they were levitating above as well as the surrounding trees and plants along its bank. Matthew was struck by a sense of familiarity. He looked all around him in an effort to unlock his memory. Approximately two hundred yards directly ahead of them, Matthew caught sight of three people standing in the shallow bank of the river.

Samuel engaged their transport so they sped along the river, quickly arriving at the location where the three people stood. Standing there motionless were Benny, Carrie and the patriarch of the family, Thomas.

Matthew was overcome by dizziness from the sudden and overwhelming rush of emotion. It was as though Samuel had transported Matthew back to the precise moment when he awoke from his dream of the slave family attempting to break free from their captivity. Matthew stumbled downward to his knees on the hovering platform attempting to regain composure and fully process the scene before them. He dropped his head into his hands and took deep breaths to counteract the sudden stress placed upon his body.

"Are you alright?" asked Samuel.

"I know this place," replied Matthew. "I was here before in my first dream."

"I know, Matthew," confirmed Samuel. "That's why we are here."

As Matthew's heart rate returned to normal and the dizziness subsided, he slowly stood again. They were at the precise moment where Carrie and her husband embraced for the last time before he sacrificed his own freedom, and likely his own life, for the sake of his family's escape to the North. Matthew then realized the obvious peculiarity he had previously overlooked due to the shocking realization of his surroundings. The African-American family was completely still. The couple was embracing, but Benny had not moved a muscle.

"Why aren't they moving?" Matthew inquired.

"Because, Matthew, we are merely visiting and observing this ripple in space and time," responded Samuel. "The portal through which we passed enabled us to ride along that energy ribbon and guided us back to this precise moment. Think of it like pausing a movie, where we can watch more closely the details within this sequence of events."

"This really happened, didn't it?" asked Matthew, apparently catching on. "This is a real story whose characters are as real as you and me."

"You remember the photo you discovered within the book your history teacher gave you?" answered Samuel with a question.

"Yes," replied Matthew. "Wait, how do you know that anyway? That didn't happen when I was dreaming."

"I know a great deal about you, Matthew, including many of your thoughts and experiences you have brought with you to this precise moment," replied Samuel.

Matthew wasn't sure how to process this ability Samuel possessed, but he knew that at that moment, raiding his thoughts and emotions felt like an incredible invasion of privacy.

"What does this have to do with solving the mystery of The Oval?" Matthew asked. "How is this even possible?"

"Matthew, you accepted the one condition on this journey you have chosen to take, remember?" reminded Samuel. "You must keep an open mind and spirit as you let go of any pre-conceived notions of reality or what you deem possible or impossible."

Samuel then stepped down from the platform of their transport vehicle and onto the surface of the water. He casually walked along, drawing closer to the slave family and then paused, looking back at the transport where Matthew still stood.

"Come," he prompted Matthew as he motioned with his left arm.

Dumbfounded yet again, Matthew was frozen in disbelief.

"Come, it's alright," Samuel said again with a slight smile. "It's time for you to take the next step in your journey."

Summoning the necessary courage, Matthew slowly walked to the edge of their small circular haven of transportation and looked downward. He then took a deep breath and extended his right leg outward as he took his first step. As soon as his foot touched the surface of the river, Matthew immediately fell into the water. He scrambled to his feet and stood within the knee deep body of water completely soaked.

"What the hell?!" Matthew shouted as his heart rate escalated from the plunge.

"You took your first step!" Samuel encouragingly noted. "Very good."

"You know what I mean!" snapped Matthew. "Why did you walk on the water while I stepped off and took a swim?"

"I have one word for you, Matthew," exclaimed Samuel. "Doubt. Your mind focused on the impossible, infusing doubt, which in turn, created the only reality you believed could happen. We will get into that later, but now we must talk about why we're here."

Matthew, now dripping wet, walked over to join Samuel who was standing directly next to the hugging couple.

"What are they doing?" asked Samuel.

"They're hugging," Matthew immediately replied with annoyance lingering in his voice.

"Matthew, try to look beyond the obvious," Samuel stated. "What are they really doing here at this location in this very moment?"

"They are trying to escape to the North through the Underground Railroad," answered Matthew. "They knew that the cotton farmer who owned them might be forced to start selling some slaves which could break up their family."

"Yes, go on," prompted Samuel. "What is it that you suppose they really wanted in the depth of their souls?"

Matthew took a few steps around the hugging couple and studied Thomas's face more closely, staring into his eyes. He felt he had just caught a glimpse into Thomas' soul, sending a slight chill up his spine.

"Matthew, I want you to place both your hands on the backs of the couple," Samuel instructed. "One on Carrie and one on Thomas."

Matthew looked back at Samuel with great confusion.

"What?" Matthew questioned. "Why?"

"Just trust me, Matthew, because you are about to gain insights you never thought possible," Samuel replied.

Matthew was intrigued and decided not to further question Samuel as he slowly raised both arms toward the backs of the embraced couple. He hesitated briefly in fear of what might happen. Samuel sensed Matthew's anxiety and tried to provide some reassurance.

"It's okay, Matthew," Samuel said. "This is going to help you better understand the depth of my question and ultimately the answer as well."

Matthew glanced at Samuel who gave an encouraging nod. He took a deep breath and moved his hands forward the remaining few inches until he was touching the back of each person. Matthew then noticed a small, circular white light begin to glow in between the eyes of both Carrie and Thomas. It grew increasingly brighter until Matthew's view became completely engulfed by the white light.

Then it struck.

Matthew suddenly became consumed by the most intense emotions. He felt and saw images spanning the life experiences of both Carrie and Thomas almost simultaneously. He saw them as children, adolescents, and young adults. He felt their fear, excitement, frustrations and dreams throughout their important life events. Matthew could see brief images of their physical beings while also simultaneously feeling their emotional states as well. It was as though he was not only witnessing but experiencing all the moments in their lives that shaped them as adults, partners and parents. It was similar to fast-forwarding a movie but with the incredible distinction of being completely immersed inside the characters. The events flashed by so quickly that the lights and images streamed across his consciousness in a blur while Matthew felt all of their corresponding emotions. It was completely unreal, but Matthew suddenly realized a common thread throughout their lives: pain.

The bondage of slavery that bound them and their ancestors their entire lives ate away at their souls. A way of life they had always known but with dreams of liberation that could not come soon enough. It was a feeling of pure entrapment with hope a faint awareness. Matthew sensed sheer desperation that would define the willingness of a human being to do anything to change what seemed to be forever fixed in time.

The stream of emotions was so palpable that Matthew began to almost lose himself. He became more entangled in this web spun by Carrie and Thomas over numerous decades of life that they shared. The life events of both streamed across Matthew's view at a maddening pace. Suddenly, a scene slowed, and Matthew witnessed it in real time.

A black man was facing a tall wooden post with his hands bound above his head. A strong breeze blew his torn shirt exposing his bare back. A circle of people gathered around to watch the spectacle, most of whom appeared to be slaves as well. A white man stood holding a whip in his right hand.

"This is what happens to you when you disobey!" the white man shouted.

He suddenly raised the whip and brought it down harshly onto the back of the man secured to the post. The black man let out a muffled scream. Matthew could tell that the slave was attempting to hold back the extreme pain inflicted upon him.

Matthew stood in horrified disbelief. He suddenly sensed someone's thoughts and feelings within the gathered crowd. Matthew walked along trying to hone in on the person whom he was being drawn to so powerfully. He then found the source. It was a young boy whom Matthew thought couldn't be more than eleven or twelve years of age. The boy stood watching with tears streaming down his face.

"This ain't gonna ever happens to my kids," thought the boy.

Matthew realized the boy was the son of the man being punished, forced to watch his father endure such pain. Matthew instinctively knew the boy was Thomas as a child.

As quickly as the image slowed, it sped away again among the stream of scenes that continued to encompass his immersion experience. It was as though Matthew was being force-fed a lifetime of events and emotions that spanned the existence of two human beings. Two people whom he did not know. Two people who came from a different time and place. Another scene then came into focus.

Matthew was in a cotton field with a small group of slaves harvesting the crop. He could see Carrie and Thomas working within twenty feet of each other. Then two of the white plantation workers quickly rode up on horses toward them. Matthew immediately sensed the couple's distress at their sudden appearance. One of the men rode up to Carrie and grabbed her brown dress from behind and hoisted her up onto his horse. Matthew instantly felt Carrie's shock and then the ensuing panic from the couple simultaneously as they both realized what this abduction of Carrie would certainly lead to . . . the two white men planned on having their way with her.

Matthew fell to his knees as the infusion of adrenaline from both people consumed him. Carrie was yelling and crying out to Thomas in sheer terror as they galloped off.

"No!" Thomas screamed out as he dropped his cotton basket and immediately went in pursuit of the riders.

Matthew did not need to run to catch up with them, for the scene moved with the couple as Matthew remained motionless on his knees trying to process the event and corresponding emotions of both people. It was all so overwhelming. Matthew felt Thomas's pounding heart as though it was about to burst through his chest. The slave was fueled by the intense need to protect his wife and the terror of what was happening. His only goal was to reach Carrie in time to save her. Thomas ran as quickly as he could to reach the adjacent field where the two men had taken her, and Matthew felt the anger well within him with each stride.

Matthew's view of the scene then shifted to where he could see Thomas drawing closer. He could feel the terror within Carrie as the two men reached their destination beneath a large tree on the edge of the field to carry out their heinous act. Matthew sensed a shift within Carrie as she suddenly felt the need to fight back. The man who had taken her upon his horse dismounted and pulled Carrie down onto the ground where she violently landed on her side. As he approached her, Carrie quickly stood and grabbed his face with both hands using her nails to rip into his flesh. The man screamed in pain as she scratched him so deeply that streams of blood quickly appeared.

"Why, you little bitch!" he screamed. "You gonna pay for that!"

Carrie turned to run the other direction only to be met by the second man who grabbed her and threw her to the ground where she landed on her back. He jumped on top of her while the other man quickly knelt down by her head in order to hold down Carrie's arms. Matthew sensed Carrie's helplessness of the inevitable overcome her. Then out of the corner of his eye, Matthew saw Thomas reach them.

Upon seeing his wife in this position, Thomas' emotional state instantly shifted. Fear and panic gave way to something far more powerful. Rage.

Matthew could feel it in Thomas as he reached the two men holding his wife captive. Thomas lunged at the man holding down Carrie's arms, sending him violently to the ground. Thomas did not hesitate to use this opportunity of brief disorientation to begin striking the man who lay slightly stunned. It was at this moment that Matthew fully appreciated Thomas's intimidating size and sheer strength. He towered over them and his huge arms were fully flexed ready for battle.

Thomas held the man by the shirt collar with his left hand and with a clenched, right fist, he quickly landed at least five or six solid punches to the man's head and face, each blow growing in force. It was as though Thomas had crossed a threshold from which there would be no return and with that realization, came a force completely unleashed.

As he was about to strike the man again, Thomas saw the other man lift himself off the ground, releasing Carrie from her entrapment. She lay motionless, however, too afraid to move or know what to do next. Thomas released the man in his grasp, who was on the verge of unconsciousness. He collapsed onto the ground like a lifeless rag doll, his face swollen and bloodied.

The other man ran to his horse standing next to the tree in order to grab his whip, but Thomas was too quick as he anticipated the move and bull-rushed the man, sending him flying into the tree. The man let out a scream of pain as his back hit the trunk. Thomas used this next window of opportunity to continue his assault on his wife's attacker. This time, Thomas struck the man in the stomach and sides several times as he alternated between his left and right fists.

Matthew could not only sense Thomas's rage but now his thoughts.

How dare these men threaten his wife. How dare they think of her as a piece of property.

How dare they think of her anything less than the amazing woman that she truly is.

A person. A human being. The one he loved more than anything.

With each blow, a fury grew within Thomas. He was not only defending his wife's honor and safety but now striking a blow to the lifelong oppression that his family had endured for generations.

The man began coughing up blood as Matthew heard the cracking of bones, a sure indication of broken ribs. Thomas then grabbed the man by the collar with his right hand and held up his left fist to land a strike upon the man's face when he faintly heard Carrie's voice behind him.

"Thomas," she said softly. "Please."

Her soft words reached his heart, and he realized that he was losing himself to his own rage. Carrie knew this as well, which compelled her to speak in order to reach her life partner before it was too late.

Thomas released his grip on the man who lifelessly fell to the ground. He ran over to Carrie still resting motionless on her back. Thomas knelt down beside his wife and gently placed his left palm against her cheek. His knuckles were raw and bloodied. He didn't notice the condition of his hands until they were in direct contrast to her beautiful flawless face. Thomas could not hold back the tears as she looked deep within her hazel eyes.

"Takes me home, my love," she quietly whispered with tears in her eyes.

Thomas slid his huge arms beneath his wife and gently lifted her off the ground as he stood.

Matthew felt the relief within them that the ordeal and immediate threat had passed. Carrie rested her head on Thomas' massive chest as he carried her across the field. Matthew sensed Carrie's feeling of security, an assurance that she and Benny would always be safe with Thomas around. His commitment and love for them was not only unwavering but also enveloped them in a protective shield. He would never let anything happen to them. He would sacrifice anything for them.

Then Matthew sensed something else begin to surface within them both—dread of what was to come.

Thomas walked over three miles in one-hundred-degree-plus heat carrying his wife back to their little shack of a home. Thomas gave no notice to the sweat that dripped from his brow or the screaming pain from his back and muscles.

The extreme intensity of the experience left Matthew physically and emotionally depleted. He realized, however, that it was not yet over as the scene changed again. It appeared to be the next day, and three white men armed with guns and whips came to their home early in the morning. They came to collect Thomas who would be severely punished for what he had done. As they stood outside waiting for him to walk out, Thomas turned to face his beloved wife.

"Don't you lets our little boy sees this," Thomas said with a resolve within his voice that he hoped would strengthen Carrie for what was to come next.

Tears streamed down Carrie's face as she gave an affirmative nod, unable to utter a single word. They embraced, and Thomas walked outside.

The men took Thomas to a gathering place in the center of the plantation and tied him to a post just like the one his father had been bound to many years before. They ripped the shirt off his back to expose his bare skin. The entire plantation gathered around to witness the punishment, a requirement of all slaves to deter further retaliation.

Carrie stood ten feet away facing Thomas in hopes that her close proximity would somehow provide him comfort. Thomas knew they would not kill him or permanently damage him physically since he was the strongest and hardest worker on the plantation. He was too valuable to them. They would surely levy a significant whipping, however, with the intent of breaking his fighting spirit.

Carrie knew better; that's why she had to be there for him. She could not bear to see him tortured and in pain, but she had to be strong for him now. She hoped her presence would serve as a reminder of who he is: an amazing man, husband and father whose love and strength could power the sun.

Matthew gained an incredible insight: The belief in another human being only further propels them forward and strengthens their own belief in themselves.

Benny stood in front of his mother looking at his father, not sure why his father was being punished. He could not have been more than seven years of age at that time. Thomas looked into his son's eyes and saw the fear in his precious little boy and wished he could send Benny away from all of this. Far, far away.

Carrie then spoke. "Look at me!" she said with great strength in her voice. "I's right here."

Thomas looked up in response to his wife's command, and they looked directly into each other's eyes. As the white man raised his right arm holding the whip, she grabbed Benny's head, and at the last moment, buried his face within her brown dress to shield his eyes while simultaneously covering his ears to muffle the sound.

The whip came down and struck Thomas with such force that it sliced through his flesh like a surgeon's scalpel, sending needles of pain coursing through his entire body. Thomas did not let out a sound as he suppressed the urge to let out a scream of agony. He merely let out a grunt while keeping his jaws clenched to prevent his mouth from opening. With each lash, Matthew felt the searing physical and emotional pain emitting from Thomas and Carrie. She saw each gruesome strike but never looked away; nor did he. Tears freely flowed from each of them as their gaze remained fixed on one another. Each one trying to remain strong for the other, for they knew this would not define them. This would not take away their hope for a better life. This would not break their spirit nor rid their true desire: To be free.

Mercifully, the scene changed again, and Matthew found they were back at the river where the family embraced for the final time. The most powerful emotion erupted into Matthew's consciousness. Love. Pure love.

Matthew's breath was taken away. Now he understood more fully what had transpired and led this family to the pivotal moment standing at the river. Now he could fully comprehend the depth of the couple's sorrow in parting and Thomas' extreme desire to free his family of this life. Matthew could sense within Thomas the pain of separating from his boy and wife as his heart began to shatter into a thousand pieces. It felt as though someone had plunged both hands into Thomas' body and ripped open his chest cavity. He felt every bone crack and muscle tear as some faceless invader grabbed his heart and ripped it out. It was a pain that invaded Thomas' entire physical, mental and emotional being. It felt like someone had thrust a steel-bladed sword straight through Thomas's spirit and a darkness descended upon him.

The unbearable pain completely overwhelmed Matthew. His mind began to race as countless thoughts and questions emerged.

How could this be possible? How could Thomas summon the strength to carry out his action to sacrifice himself and either live without his wife and child or to even die in the process? To ultimately say goodbye forever?

But then Matthew immediately knew. He could feel the truth. It all boiled down to the love they shared. Thomas sacrificed himself for the ones he cherished in this life in order to provide them with a gift, loving them more than his own life. Loving them so much, he was willing to let them go to set them free and keep them safe. Loving them so much that it gave him the strength to face his own pain. It was a love much deeper than any kind of romantic notion a person could fathom. A love whose power could only be understood through the experience of one's divine spirit

It was *true* love.

Thomas was able to draw on the power of that love and rise above his own pain in order to save them. He loved them that much, and Carrie and Benny knew that.

Matthew then sensed Carrie's thoughts and feelings. Her mind and heart suddenly became consumed with the reality of caring for Benny without her husband's love and strength by her side. Panic began to consume her as she thought, *I can't do's this alone withouts him.*

Matthew could actually feel the tears flowing down her face. The notion of them never seeing one another again nor sharing this life together was suffocating. She would miss the countless times they awoke in the morning when she felt the warmth and comfort of Thomas's large strong arm draped over her in protection. Then she thought of his eyes. Oh, how she would miss his big, beautiful brown eyes and see within them the love and peaceful confidence that made him such a stabilizing force within their lives. But she realized that Thomas was right. This was the only path; she, too, had to summon the strength for their boy. She could not allow Thomas' precious gift of sacrifice to be in vain. She must allow him to be the man that had always protected and provided for them and for him to follow this inner calling of love. Carrie must now carry the torch in the next journey of this life.

For their boy.

To be free.

A simple and fundamental truth of existence.

The power of the emotions was now so overwhelming that it literally knocked Matthew off his feet, thereby breaking the physical connection with Carrie and Thomas as he fell backwards into the water. His eyes quickly regained focus but his body thrashed about in convulsive spasms preventing him from being able to control his physical movements and also temporarily hindering his ability to speak.

Samuel walked over to Matthew and grabbed his right arm. He pulled Matthew to his feet and held him around his shoulders in an attempt to steady the young lad.

"This will pass in a few more seconds, Matthew," Samuel assured him.

Matthew was completely and emotionally spent. He was numb. He looked at Samuel directly in the eyes.

"Wha . . . what happened?" Matthew mumbled.

"You entered their chakra energy field," Samuel explained.

After a minute or two, Matthew found he had regained control over his bodily movements and could more easily talk.

But then, as the numbness subsided, a wave of emotion overcame him. He fell to his knees and began to cry uncontrollably.

Samuel knelt beside him and placed his arm around Matthew in an effort to comfort his pupil.

"Oh my God," Matthew began struggling to speak. "That was the most intense experience of my life."

"I know," Samuel replied. "But you handled it remarkably well."

Matthew paused a few more moments to collect himself but now a new emotion burst forth, and it was directed toward Samuel.

Anger.

"Why, God damn it?!" he lashed out toward his guide.

Not surprised, Samuel calmly replied, "Why what, Matthew?"

Matthew had no one to justifiably direct his anger to except the only other person present; Samuel had to be the recipient. After all, he was the one who brought him to this place and exposed him to this extreme experience. He grabbed Samuel by the shirt and began to shake him.

"Why did this have to happen?!" Matthew raged. "Why did this good family and these good people have to go through this? They didn't deserve it! They shouldn't have to suffer!"

His anger quickly subsided, and he released his guide. It was as though he had to let it out so he could let it go. Matthew stared down into the water and saw the reflection of the family standing next to him sharing their last embrace. Sadness settled within him and he spoke softly.

"Why did they have to break apart?" he asked desperately.

Samuel got down at eye level with Matthew who was still on his knees in the water.

"Matthew, there are a great many things to learn, and one of them is the fact that we all have a journey," Samuel began to explain. "Each one offers a rare opportunity."

Matthew looked up at Samuel and gazed directly into his eyes. "And what would that be, Samuel?" Matthew asked.

Samuel paused a moment before responding. "To grow and evolve, Matthew," Samuel replied. "The circumstances or situations that come into our life or that we are born into can be extremely difficult at times, but they enable our growth, especially when we have the strength and courage to face them and move through it." Samuel paused and looked back at the embracing family again before continuing with his explanation.

"The greater the challenges, the greater the triumph," Samuel continued very purposefully. "And the greater the triumph, the greater our growth and evolution as spiritual beings."

Matthew pondered his guide's words for a moment.

"I doubt I would have the strength and resolve to do what they did," Matthew surmised as he continued to process everything he had just experienced. "To survive as they did and make those sacrifices while having to put up with such intense pain."

Samuel placed both his hands beneath Matthew's arms to hoist him to his feet while still directly facing the young man. "Yes, you do Matthew," Samuel retorted.

Matthew saw the confidence in Samuel's eyes and the expression he wore. "And what makes you say that, Samuel?" Matthew asked.

"Because you are special, my friend," Samuel replied. "You willingly chose to take this journey, accept the challenge contained within, and you are here with me right now doing so."

Matthew looked down into the water, seeing his own reflection and then turned his gaze back to the slave family still frozen in the moment.

"They truly are remarkable people," Matthew began. "I feel like I know them so well now. I feel so connected to them, especially to Carrie and Thomas."

Then Matthew remembered something Samuel had told him about the experience and how this was possible. "You said something about a chakra field," Matthew began. "What is that?"

"A chakra is an entry point into the spirit, Matthew," Samuel explained. "Almost like a mini-gateway that allows us to experience the true essence of who we are and what we've experienced in our lives."

"What happened to me?" Matthew inquired with great curiosity as he thought back to his physical reaction after the connection was broken. "Why did I react so violently and lose control of myself?"

"That usually happens the first time you experience it, but yours was especially bad because you absorbed the energy signatures of both people at the same time," Samuel replied encouragingly.

Matthew looked back at his teacher. He wanted to tell Samuel that he had no interest in ever doing that ever again. Just as he began to open his mouth, however, the words would not come. Somehow Matthew knew that this was part of the journey. As mentally, emotionally and physically exhausting as this had been, he knew that the lessons contained in the experience could not have been merely verbalized by his guide. Somehow Matthew realized that he had to not only witness these events but also *feel* them. He had to become immersed within them to gain full understanding and insight.

Realizing that Matthew was now "back" and able to more easily think and process more clearly, Samuel resumed the lesson at hand. "So tell me, young one, what did you learn from this chakra experience about this family? What did you sense at the core of their very being?" he asked, returning to his original question.

Matthew now knew what exactly his guide was expecting to hear. In spite of the unpleasant nature of his chakra reaction, an intellectual rationalization would never have so strongly conveyed the true answer to Samuel's question.

"The most intense and powerful feeling, Samuel, that I sensed was love," Matthew replied as he glanced back to the slave family again. "That seemed to be the root of what drove everything, including the sacrifice that Thomas made."

Samuel smiled and gave an affirmative nod as he listened to Matthew's words.

"A force so powerful that Thomas sacrificed everything he knew, valued and loved in order to give his wife and son a chance at a free life," Samuel added. Seemingly able to read Matthew's thoughts, Samuel then provided another perspective to Matthew's experience and observations thus far.

"Matthew, this was tragic, but it's also an unbelievable example of and testimony to humanity's POTENTIAL!" Samuel said emphatically. "Humanity, in its purest form, is spiritual, loving and a powerful force to be reckoned with. It also demonstrates the capacity of the human heart to endure the most intense pain because of its infinite capacity for one thing."

Matthew looked at Samuel, because the answer suddenly burst forth into his mind. Love.

Despite the pain from his chakra experience, Matthew felt the enormity of the love the slave family shared among them.

Samuel smiled as he knew the connection Matthew just made.

"The ability to love so wholly, Matthew, is also the source of strength that allows us to survive periods of great pain and experience true healing after we face such trying times," Samuel explained.

"Before making the link with Carrie and Thomas, I don't think I could have fully understood that statement, but I think I do now," Matthew noted. "At least I am beginning to, anyway."

"In the end, their spirits triumphed over all else," Samuel concluded.

Struck by Samuel's words, Matthew looked away from his guide toward the slave family as he reflected on that concept for a few moments. Thinking back to when Thomas was tied to the whipping post, Matthew contemplated how the couple stayed the course in spite of such great suffering.

"In the end, Matthew, they won," exclaimed Samuel. "What they knew at the core of their being was to be free."

"But they were separated," Matthew lamented. "It wasn't fair! They should have gone to freedom together."

"I know, Matthew," responded Samuel with compassion. "It's painful to even conceive of how they coped with the separation, but yet again, this provides another example of how the spirit triumphed. Carrie and Benny did not let Thomas sacrifice in vain. They honored Thomas's love and sacrifice by ultimately healing from the pain and then going on to live a life to the fullest as he had desired so deeply for them."

Samuel paused a moment to allow the words to come to Matthew that would further connect his new insights to the journey he was now on.

"You see, Matthew, your first dream sequence provided you a glimpse into unlocking the mystery of The Oval," Samuel stated. "I will help you unlock your potential so that you will find the answers you seek. In order to do so, I must teach you about the human spirit."

Matthew had become so consumed by this lesson that he had almost forgotten the purpose of it all: unlocking the secret of The Oval, which Matthew was beginning to realize may carry a life-altering consequence with its unveiling. He turned back to gaze upon the African American family again. Unlike his first encounter with them, he deeply connected with their struggle and triumph, whereas before, he mostly could only imagine. He would never have seen, or more importantly, felt the apparent good which came from this one story of sacrifice and triumph.

"Samuel," Matthew began with heightened interest. "Tell me more." Matthew then realized there it was again—his own desire for "more" he had been craving all his life.

Samuel smiled and realized that something more had been awakened within his pupil, and he was now ready and willing to receive more truth. Samuel's purpose, which had yet to be fully revealed to his pupil, was now gaining a strong foothold.

Samuel paused momentarily as he looked at Matthew, trying to assess how much to reveal at that precise moment. He realized that Matthew's ability to enter the chakra's of two souls, absorb them, and recover so quickly while retaining his own sense of self was truly remarkable and rare. Yet again, this is what he expected of Matthew, who had more than proven himself thus far.

"It's something called 'The Five Levels of the Spirit,'" replied Samuel. "I won't divulge them all at once but one at a time as they build upon each other, like a pyramid."

Eager to demonstrate his learning thus far, Matthew quickly offered his own insight into these levels.

"Level One is Love, isn't it?" Matthew asked eagerly.

"Not exactly," Samuel answered. "Love is the foundation of all things, and you certainly experienced that here. I am talking about Levels of the Spirit that build off a force of love that infuses us with passion and purpose."

Matthew's interest grew greatly as he hung on his guide's every word. "So what is Level One, Samuel?" he asked anxiously.

"Level One is freedom," Samuel answered, looking directly into Matthew's eyes.

After Samuel's statement, Matthew felt a bit foolish as to why he didn't ascertain the obvious on his own especially after his slave dream sequence.

"Matthew, I can tell you are disappointed in yourself for not beating me to the punch, but don't lose heart," Samuel said encouragingly. "You are doing amazingly well!"

"The Spirit seeks freedom?" Matthew reiterated as he brushed Samuel's compliment aside, suddenly feeling the need to prove himself worthy.

"Yes, Matthew," Samuel continued. "But it's not always as obvious as this case, which led you to experience Level One in the most literal sense. It means freedom in all of its various forms. The human spirit has a natural tendency to react to any limitation or confinement placed before it."

"Such as?" Matthew prompted.

"Such as freedom from a great many things that goes beyond the bondage of slavery," Samuel answered with great purpose. "Freedom from things, like emotional scars from one's childhood that forever skew your perceptions of life; freedom from depression, disease, addictions, or irrational fears. Freedom means so many things on so many levels."

Matthew felt his understanding begin to take shape, but there was something still missing. "How does Level One apply to The Oval?" Matthew asked.

"What is it that you seek?" asked Samuel, answering Matthew's question with yet another question.

"I want to know its secret," noted Matthew. "I want to know what it is, where it came from and what its purpose is." Matthew then got right to the heart of the matter. "I want you to help me unlock my potential," he said.

Samuel smiled as he noticed Matthew's eager expression for the "more" he so desired.

"Freedom is the first step, Matthew, because you are seeking knowledge," Samuel explained. "In other words, you wish to be free of ignorance as it relates to this mysterious object that catapulted into your life and understand its meaning. You wish to free yourself from your old ways of limited thinking that will help you in your journey for that 'more' you desire."

Samuel struck a strong chord within Matthew with his last comment. How could Samuel sense that?

"This inherent drive to be free, Matthew, fuels levels of thought and feelings that, in turn, leads you to understand your deepest desires as a spiritual being," Samuel further explained. "It can also thrust us into confronting our worst fears as well."

"Then what do these thoughts do for us?" Matthew asked, not fully understanding.

"These thoughts and desires can provide the catalyst to start some amazing explorations of mind, body and soul, as well as achieve miraculous accomplishments," Samuel replied.

"So, this spark to be free that exists within us is what you call Level One?" confirmed Matthew.

"That's right," Samuel responded. "This free spirit exists within all of us and cannot be extinguished. The key is to allow it to grow, as all too often, many try to ignore it or even suppress it. When you let it out, it can lead you down a path of incredible growth and accomplishment never before considered possible. The spark of thoughts and ideas are often times preceded by two simple words."

Matthew's head tilted to the side and raised one eyebrow in silent question.

"What if," Samuel said.

Matthew was soaking in all of Samuel's words instantaneously as they rolled off his tongue. His mind was now racing, and he couldn't stop himself from the rush of adrenaline fueled by the excitement he now felt from the possibilities presented before him. After pausing a few moments, Matthew glanced back one last time to the African American family who risked everything by listening to their free spirits and unleashing their own potential. Grateful for their actions and the miracle of this most amazing chakra experience, Matthew then turned his attention back to his guide with a higher sense of purpose and determination.

"Samuel," Matthew began. "I want to go onto Level Two."

Samuel responded with a huge smile.

"Come then, my young friend," Samuel replied as he gently placed his right hand behind Matthew's back and nudged him toward the transport. "It's time to leave this place and move forward."

They both walked side by side toward the hover disc. Samuel stepped onto the platform first. Just as Matthew was about to do the same, Samuel called an important observation to Matthew's attention.

"Matthew, don't step onto the transport just yet," Samuel noted.

"Why not?" asked Matthew surprised.

"Look down," Samuel commanded.

The young man immediately looked down. He was both shocked and simultaneously elated by what he saw. A clear indication that something big was beginning to shift within him and the expanded awareness of his own potential.

Matthew was standing next to the hover craft ON the surface of the water.

CHAPTER 8

COURAGEOUS CHOICES

Matthew stepped onto the glowing transport disc and took his place next to Samuel. His guide placed his right hand upon the smooth, blue marble of the navigation ball, and they began to lift off. They slowly floated upward as Samuel next engaged thrusters to propel them forward. Matthew looked down as they passed over the African American family he had come to know so deeply. After taking one last look behind him as if to say goodbye, Matthew turned his attention back to Samuel.

"I have one other question, Samuel," noted Matthew as they were traveling above the river bed. "How is it possible that I discovered the picture of Carrie and Benny? Was I really there?"

"I was wondering when you were going to ask that question," replied Samuel. "You were really there, Matthew, but not in the way you are thinking."

"What do you mean?" responded Matthew.

"You were there, but you were witnessing it as if you were watching a show or movie," answered Samuel attempting to frame the concept in a manner that would aid his pupil's understanding. "You noticed you weren't able to interact with anyone, right?"

"Yeah," replied Matthew. "It seemed so real, though, like I was actually there. You were there, Samuel, because I saw you look directly at me. What's up with that?"

Samuel paused a moment in order to choose his words carefully. He knew now was not the time to fully disclose everything to Matthew, especially if his suspicions were correct on who Matthew really is. The young man could, in fact, be the one for whom Samuel had been searching.

"First off, Matthew, your experience was very real. It was through the power of your mind and spirit that you were able to enter into this ripple of space-time," Samuel began. "Secondly, I was there watching you to see how you would react and to monitor your thoughts and emotions along the way. We needed to assess your capacity and desire to challenge yourself in ways you've never before experienced."

"That's why you called yourself a dream monitor?" confirmed Matthew.

"That's right," Samuel replied.

Matthew was suddenly annoyed at Samuel for intruding into his mind and life the way he had, especially with so little explanation. "Why are you monitoring dreams anyway?" Matthew inquired. "And who is the 'we' you just mentioned?"

Ignoring Matthew's impertinence, Samuel responded kindly, "In due time Matthew. You are not quite ready yet. We must forge ahead in your journey, my friend."

Matthew was quickly learning that Samuel was not only unflappable, but infinitely patient.

"Ah, here we are now," announced Samuel.

Their transport began to slow as Matthew's attention turned from Samuel back to their immediate surroundings. They were still apparently in the deep south, along the same river. Matthew glanced backward in an attempt to gauge the distance traveled using the position of the slave family from whom they just departed as a reference point. They were nowhere in sight. Matthew surmised they have been traveling at a far greater speed than he would have guessed, or maybe they made some turns to mirror the contour of the river. Samuel brought the transport to a full stop, and they were now hovering a good twenty feet above the water.

"I don't understand," said Matthew. "Why did we stop?"

"We must exit here in order to move onto your next step," replied Samuel. "Don't you remember the portal connection along the energy ripple we followed that brought us here?"

"Yes, of course," responded Matthew as he looked all around their current position to find the gateway. "How could I forget it? But I don't see one anywhere."

"Look down, Matthew," instructed Samuel with a small smirk.

Matthew crept to the edge of the hover disc and peered below into the river. Sure enough, he saw the now familiar circular gateway and contained within it, the white, glistening liquid energy fluctuations. At first glance, the gateway was difficult to detect as it almost blended perfectly with the river itself. Only upon closer examination would someone be able to find it. The hover disc then began to float downward.

"I'm not going to get wet again, am I?" Matthew asked nervously.

"Do you want to?" Samuel answered with another question.

"NO!" Matthew quipped.

"Then Matthew, I would suggest that you shouldn't focus on what you *don't* want but focus on what you *do* want," advised Samuel.

"How exactly do I do that?" asked Matthew with a sense of urgency as their transport was now only a few feet from the portal and the water's surface.

"You must train your mind, Matthew, to re-direct your thoughts away from the idea that when you enter the portal, water will pour over you," Samuel instructed. "Your mind is used to creating its own reality based on the paradigm of thinking you were taught. The notion of 'seeing is believing' is ridiculously limiting. Remember Matthew, I'm here to help you open yourself up to a new way of thinking. If you believe you will get wet, then surely that will be the reality you create for yourself. But if you believe you won't get wet and you envision that you will enter the portal successfully as you are engulfed by its energy, then you will not."

"Oh well, why didn't I think of that?" Matthew said sarcastically.

Samuel laughed out loud and continued their descent. Matthew closed his eyes and took a deep breath to clear his mind and think only the thoughts Samuel had suggested. Within a few seconds, they began to enter the gateway as the transport platform fully submerged within the energy of the portal. Matthew knew they had made contact, because he could feel a tingling sensation within his feet, which gradually moved up his ankles, legs and torso. Matthew's heart rate escalated, and he tried to calm himself by breathing deeply with his eyes closed. As more of his body submerged within the gateway, a sensation of weightlessness overcame him. Parts of his body now engulfed within the portal felt as light as a feather, and those parts outside the portal felt too heavy to even lift. They had now entered the gateway up to Matthew's neck at which point he decided to open his eyes and take one last look around. As he opened his eyes, his line of vision was just a few inches above the water's surface. His brain processed this "reality" as a sense of panic swept over him. At that moment, Matthew's head became engulfed by the wave of energy within the gateway, and the blinding white light impaired his vision momentarily as it had done the previous two times.

They emerged on the other side of the connector exiting the slavery scene. Matthew collapsed onto the deck of their transport as he readjusted to feeling the weight of his body. It was as if someone had suddenly re-activated the gravity that kept them aboard their transport. Unexpectedly, a small amount of water then showered his head and shoulders. Matthew looked up only to see the back of Samuel's legs as he stood operating their hovercraft. Matthew strained to pull himself off the floor and within a few moments found himself standing shoulder to shoulder with his guide.

"Sorry, Matthew," Samuel apologized. "It does take some getting used to entering a portal feet-first. Got a little wet there, huh? You let the seed of doubt creep into your mind when you opened your eyes, didn't you?"

"Yes," answered Matthew as he lifted his T-shirt up to his face and forehead in an effort to dry them. As soon as Matthew's eyes fully adjusted, he realized they had re-entered the same labyrinth of energy ribbons appearing as a golden web of fibers. Matthew still gazed in wonder at the endless web of gateways. Although they appeared to be moving forward, the energy ribbon upon which they now glided had numerous curves and turns making it difficult for Matthew to gauge their speed or distance. Their hovercraft slowed, and they came to a connection where five different ribbons intersected into a single gateway. Matthew immediately noticed the phenomenon and was compelled to ask the obvious question.

"Why are there five different 'threads' converging into this single portal?" he asked.

"I'll explain that in a bit, Matthew, but first things first," responded Samuel who was ready to get down to business. "We need to enter this gateway for your next lesson of the Spirit."

Samuel guided the craft into the portal, except this time, he elected to enter it backwards. Matthew was now experiencing the entry and re-entry of a space-time gateway for the third time. As soon as the blinding, white light dissipated, a breathtaking scene of natural outdoor beauty greeted him. He could feel the warm rays of the mid-day sun upon his face. The sky was a brilliant, bright blue without a cloud in sight, and he closed his eyes while taking a deep breath, filling his lungs with clean, crisp air. As Matthew looked slightly to his left and right, he quickly assessed they had entered into a chain of mountains and were apparently hovering above one of its peaks. He could see the sharp drop on all sides but felt a sense of peace and communion with nature. A hawk flew directly overhead letting out a screech as it peered from the heavens down the mountainside in search of its next meal.

The serenity of this most pleasant scene was suddenly disrupted as Samuel rotated the hovercraft one hundred eighty degrees clockwise so they faced the opposite direction from their entry point of the portal. As they rotated, Matthew caught a glimpse from the corner of his right eye the apparent reason for entering this particular gateway. Standing at the edge of the cliff directly in front of them was a young woman. Samuel guided the transport slowly forward as they approached her from behind. Matthew suddenly felt compelled to jump down onto the ground and run over to her. Giving into this urge, he impulsively leapt, falling about three feet and landed on the ground. He quickly jogged the remaining ten or so feet to the summit's edge where she stood. He walked over to her left so he could see her profile. She stood five feet, three inches in height. Her long, blonde hair was pulled back into a ponytail as the sun highlighted the beauty of her natural color and her beautiful, blue eyes. She was a very attractive girl with a fit figure as Matthew surmised that she must be close to his own age. She was wearing a red T-shirt and light blue shorts. It wasn't until he began to examine her face more closely that he noticed her unsettled expression. By this point, Samuel had approached them on the hovercraft as he swung around in order to face Matthew. Samuel navigated their transport beyond the edge of the cliff where he now suspended in mid-air directly facing the two young teenagers.

"She looks upset," Matthew commented as he continued to study her facial expression. Matthew then had a horrible thought. "She's not here to throw herself off, is she?!" he asked in a sudden panic.

"Matthew, look down on the ground on either side of her," Samuel instructed.

Complying with Samuel's request, Matthew noticed that flanked on both sides of the young woman were suitcases resting on the ground.

"I don't understand," Matthew lamented. "This doesn't make sense. Why would someone who is possibly suicidal climb a mountain and bring along two suitcases?"

"We've come to our next teaching moment, Matthew," Samuel noted. "Her name is Kate, and if you were thinking that she is roughly your age, you are correct. She was born and raised in a small farming town in Southern Indiana with a population of approximately twelve hundred people. She has never really traveled beyond her small self-contained world except to occasionally visit relatives in Illinois and Ohio."

Matthew quickly wondered how Samuel could possibly know this information about Kate or why it mattered, but that wasn't the burning question on his mind at the moment.

"What is she doing here?" Matthew asked again as his eyes never left the girl.

"She's reached a pivotal decision point in her life, Matthew," Samuel stated as his tone grew more excited. "We are here, because Kate epitomizes the Second Level of the Spirit!"

Samuel paused a moment before telling his student what must come next. "Matthew, you know what you need to do, don't you?" Samuel asked.

Knowing full well what Samuel was referring to, Matthew nodded his head but he instantly became filled with dread. "Can't you just tell me?" he asked Samuel. "That last one was God-awful."

Samuel gave Matthew another one of his reassuring looks. "Matthew, remember that every experience is critical to your growth, that to merely say the words would not allow you the opportunity to embrace the full lesson," Samuel replied. "It wouldn't allow you the opportunity to *feel* the truth."

Matthew knew full well that would be Samuel's response, but he indulged his feelings of avoidance nonetheless by raising the question. He turned his attention back to Kate and slowly raised his right hand and placed it gently on her petite left shoulder. Matthew then saw the glowing circular light between Kate's eyes begin to shine brighter and brighter until, once again, he was fully engulfed by its energy.

The experience was similar to the prior chakra entry as Matthew began to feel Kate's spirit. Just like his slave family sequence, many of the young girl's key life events flashed across his mind. Although the visual experience followed the same structure, the feelings were quite different. Something incredibly powerful was present within Kate that he could strongly relate to. It was a dream of some kind, and she, too, was longing for something more that went far beyond her traditional small-town upbringing. Somehow, she was destined to do something completely different with her life.

The events continued to pass through Matthew's view. The traditions of their family unit and the love they shared were very strong, quite similar to Matthew's own family. He sensed the safety Kate felt while with her parents and siblings. Then a scene slowed to a Christmas of a few years ago with Kate opening a present. Matthew felt her excitement as she ripped open the wrapping paper. It was a telescope. Matthew felt her elation, and he could only respond with a huge smile and a small laugh.

The Christmas scene quickly disappeared as more events passed until Matthew realized that the telescope changed everything for Kate. That was the key for her. That was the trigger which helped her focus on what she truly wanted and where she felt her calling would be. Matthew saw countless hours being spent on the small roof top outside her bedroom window, staring up into the heavens with her new treasure. She was filled with awe and wonder. Matthew knew that feeling all too well.

Then, the maddening pace of what passed through her chakra slowed and stopped as another pivotal event in her young life came into focus. The prevailing emotion Matthew sensed from Kate in that moment was fear, a very strong sense of fear and doubt. Suddenly, Matthew saw the scene play out within Kate's chakra.

"Kate, how many times do I have to tell you!" said a man within the new scene. "The world is a very scary and dangerous place."

Matthew could see Kate as a young adolescent as the scene came into full view. Kate was probably thirteen or so years of age. She was standing in what appeared to be the kitchen of her childhood home. Matthew surmised the man who was sitting at their kitchen table was her father, and Kate stood next to him holding a book. It was a book with stars on the cover.

"You need to get these crazy thoughts out of your head right now, Katie bug," he said discouragingly. "If you plan on venturing too far from home one day, your mom and I can't keep an eye on you. God only knows what will happen to you then. You are better off staying here in Indiana with us, honey. Besides, we don't have that kind of money to afford to send you off to some school in Chicago. It's a huge city. People are mean. They don't care for each other like we do here in our small town. It's got all kinds of crime!"

Matthew then saw Kate turn and run out of the room, up a set of stairs and into her bedroom. Flinging herself onto her bed, she burst into tears. He could *feel* her discouragement. He could *feel* her sadness. He could *feel* what could only be described as some kind of betrayal. Matthew could sense how much she truly loved her dad, but that made his reaction all the more hurtful. She felt that his reaction was a contradiction to the love they shared, because she didn't feel supported. More than anything, she wanted his approval and blessing to pursue her dreams. He knew how much this meant to her. Then the doubt crept into her mind as Matthew tapped into her thoughts: *Maybe Daddy is right.*

Her feelings became Matthew's. His heart ached from the experience, but then suddenly, a fundamental shift occurred within his host. Kate pulled herself out of her bed and walked to the window. She opened it up and began to crawl outside onto the roof. Surprised by this sudden emotional shift and physical movement, Matthew walked over to the window and peered outside.

Kate sat perched upon the roof holding her telescope in her hands. It was night time, and the stars were clearly visible in a black tapestry from which their brilliance could shine with divine brightness. Peering through the eye piece, Matthew felt a surge of awe. He felt her emotions and tapped into her thoughts as the young girl dreamt of life on other planets, how someday mankind would travel to other systems. To discover life on other worlds! Kate's excitement could barely be contained as she thought of such possibilities.

I'm not going to stay in this little town, she thought to herself. *I will find a way. I will go somewhere to study the stars.*

Suddenly the scene changed again, and Matthew saw Kate standing on the edge of the cliff right where they first found her. In that very moment, more emotions flooded Matthew, so incredibly intense that he became overwhelmed and practically shut down. Without warning, the white light of Kate's chakra began to fade, and Matthew found himself flat on his back. His body was shaking but not as violently as the first chakra encounter with Thomas and Carrie.

"I feel sick," Matthew said as he slowly turned on his side.

Fortunately, that simple act seemed to help his nausea, and within a few seconds it had dissipated. This one was much shorter than the last and certainly less intense, for which he was very thankful, but he also felt a bit disappointed. He wasn't ready to leave. He remembered the connection he felt with Kate and how much he could relate to her desires. Matthew stood to see young adult Kate still standing before him on the cliff and Samuel hovering in front of them on the transport.

"Well, what did you experience?" Samuel asked.

Matthew turned to look at Samuel.

"Before I answer, Samuel, why was that one so short?" Matthew asked.

"I deliberately wanted this one to be short, Matthew, because you are still adjusting to the entire chakra experience," Samuel explained. "The last one was incredibly intense, and I knew that you should only have a short session with Kate to allow your mental, emotional and physical being to continue adapting. Now, getting back to my question, what did you see and feel within our new friend?"

Matthew then turned his head to look at Kate again before he responded to his guide's question.

"I saw a moment in her life involving her dad," Matthew replied. "There were a lot of emotions. She felt fear, doubt, betrayal, love but there was something else there too."

"What was that?" Samuel replied curiously.

Matthew paused for a moment, and the word he was searching for came to him almost instantly.

"Hope," Matthew stated.

"Interesting," Samuel encouraged. "Tell me more."

"It's pretty clear from what I saw and felt, that Kate has spent her whole life in this small farming town," Matthew continued. "Her dad was lecturing about the world being a dangerous place and that she shouldn't consider leaving the safety of their little world. I'm guessing that her parents were probably born and raised in this town, too. I could feel the love between the two of them, but his lack of support was crushing her. His words infused so much doubt into her that she ran away."

"Ran away?" Samuel repeated.

"At first, she ran to her bedroom to cry alone," Matthew replied. "I felt her need to let it out but not in front of her dad. But that's when I felt something stir within her. She almost instantly stopped sobbing and went to a safe place." Matthew paused a moment in an attempt to find the proper words to convey what he felt within Kate and how to describe this safe place to Samuel.

"She went to a place inside herself," Matthew clarified. "A place where she found comfort. Somewhere where she could allow herself to dream. A place where no one could intrude or take anything away. She went onto the roof outside her bedroom window and peered up into the night sky with a telescope. I could feel her excitement and the wonder of what could be possible come into her mind. Then I felt her excitement grow as she thought of all the possibilities. This safe place is where she could let out her deepest desires and be free."

Matthew could hardly believe how he was able to so clearly understand and articulate all of this. His only explanation is that somehow, this chakra business provides insights that go far beyond any simple observations.

"It's amazing, isn't it, Matthew?" Samuel began. "How much of our beliefs and perceptions of the world are shaped at such a young age by our environment and upbringing. How beliefs can be passed from generation to generation regardless if they are accurate or not."

"But I didn't sense that her dad was being mean," Matthew quickly countered.

"So, what do you think it was then, Matthew?" Samuel asked, hopeful that his pupil would probe deeper.

"I think it was simply that he was afraid," Matthew replied. "Afraid to consider the possibility that she may leave. Afraid for her safety and well-being. I think his intentions were good, because he was worried about her and wanted to protect her."

Looking away from Kate, Matthew glanced back toward Samuel. "So why are we here, Samuel, seeing Kate standing on the edge of this cliff?" Matthew now asked.

"Matthew, what was the first Level of the Spirit?" asked Samuel.

"Freedom," replied Matthew.

Samuel gave his pupil a reaffirming smile.

"It's obvious that Kate has this special spark within her that is propelling her toward a different life, despite the beliefs she has learned from her parents," Samuel added.

Matthew immediately knew what beliefs those were, including the one that emphasized to young Kate that the world outside the familiar confines of her little farming life is a big and scary place. But Matthew knew that her parents weren't being malicious or manipulative as they only wanted her safety and well-being as a top priority. It wasn't completely their fault as their own frame of reference was based upon the only the life they knew. Matthew felt a very strong kinship with the young woman. He had an understanding of what Kate dreamed of while looking up at the countless stars shining down from the blackness of space and marveled at the expansive universe. He wanted to unravel the mysteries of different galaxies including the pursuit of discovering life elsewhere.

"She dreamt of something more," he suddenly commented to Samuel.

Samuel nodded back in response to Matthew's comment.

"This still doesn't explain why she is standing at the edge of this cliff," Matthew noted.

"Matthew, Kate's passion, combined with how smart she is, has led her to this critical point in her life," answered Samuel. "She's about to spread her wings and fly to new heights and witness new wonders."

"She's not about to jump, for God's sake, is she?!" Matthew asked with alarm, looking back at Kate and feeling an instinctive need to grab her.

"Just watch," Samuel replied calmly.

Samuel then swung the hovercraft around to Kate's left so as to position himself directly next to Matthew standing on the ground. Matthew glanced over to Samuel as his mentor glided over to his present position. At that moment, he detected a loud rumbling noise within his right ear. It was so startling that Matthew's head jerked in that direction as he felt his heart skip a beat. The loud noise was emitting from a large bus that swiftly pulled up in front of young Kate. A bus, which appeared to be levitating in mid-air.

"What's going on?" Matthew demanded. "What is this?"

"Matthew, just watch," Samuel replied trying to encourage patience within the young lad.

Kate bent down at her knees and picked up both suitcases resting on either side of her. She then walked up the steps of the bus, pausing a moment and looked back out from the door. A small tear streamed down her face as she took one final glance with a sad look in her eyes. She wiped away the tear and then smiled, turned and resumed boarding the floating bus. Matthew turned his head to look directly behind them in an attempt to appreciate the view that appeared to invoke within Kate such a sense of sadness.

Yet again, another unexpected twist occurred. What he saw behind them was not the mountain view with all its splendor of natural beauty as when they first exited the gateway, but a different kind of beauty. Matthew saw what he presumed to be Kate's family standing at the curb of a bus station smiling and waving goodbye as her mother was clearly holding back her own tears. Kate was the oldest of four children with two younger brothers and a sister. Matthew realized the bus station was part of her little farming town.

It was beginning to make sense.

Matthew turned back around to see the bus no longer levitating but stood firmly upon the paved road as the mountain scene completely disappeared. The bus closed its doors, and Kate settled into a window seat. She looked out of the window and blew her family a kiss as the bus drove off, bound for some destination unknown to Matthew.

"You see," Samuel began to explain. "After graduating high school, Kate applied at several colleges, one of which is located in Chicago. This school actually offered Kate a full scholarship. Do you know why this was so huge for her, Matthew?"

Matthew pondered a moment before answering as he reflected on the emotions he felt within Kate's chakra: the excitement of an amazing future filled with potential but also the terror of going beyond the familiar.

"She just took a very brave step," Matthew responded.

"She most certainly did," Samuel confirmed. "To take that brave step, Matthew, she had to move forward, but to do that, she had to get beyond a barrier that existed within herself. Would you like to venture a guess as to what that barrier was?" Samuel studied Matthew's facial expression as he sensed the intense reflection transpiring within his pupil.

Matthew looked at the bus in the distance and then back at his guide. Again, a single word floated into his consciousness that would directly answer Samuel's question.

"Fear," Matthew simply stated. "She had to move beyond her fear."

"That's exactly right, Matthew!" Samuel excitedly replied looking very pleased with the progress the young man was making. "She had to move beyond all her fears that had been instilled in her at a young age, and this choice allowed her to fulfill the freedom her spirit desired," Samuel continued. "She was waiting for the bus that would drive her seven hours away from home and all that she had ever known in order to attend her first year of college."

"What is she going to study?" Matthew asked.

"You probably already know, Matthew," Samuel commented. "She plans to study astrophysics."

Matthew looked back at his guide with an expression of wonder. Kate had done it—realizing her dream to learn about the stars. Speechless, Matthew glanced downward at the ground as he tried to fully comprehend the experience.

Samuel realized the time was at hand for another critical revelation in Matthew's journey. "In order for the spirit to triumph and move beyond the First Level of Freedom and embrace its true desires, it must have something else to take the next step," Samuel stated. "A step that is critical in not allowing a dream or desire to wither away and die." Samuel paused a moment as Matthew looked back at him with immense focus and desire to know the answer. "Do you have any idea from the insights you gained by knowing Kate much more deeply, what that might be?" Samuel asked intently.

Matthew took pause as he realized that the residual effects of Kate's chakra experience left an imprint of other feelings and thoughts on Matthew that he just accessed within his own soul. It was a myriad of emotions that she felt just before stepping onto the bus that flooded Matthew's consciousness just before the chakra connection was broken. She felt exhilaration, excitement, gratitude, sadness, joy and fear all at once. But the latter emotion did not stop her. That's when Matthew realized the answer to Samuel's question and how Kate demonstrated Level Two of the Spirit.

"You are talking about the Second Level of the Spirit!" Matthew stated excitedly. Then he realized what the second level truly is. "It's courage," Matthew stated confidently. "Courage is the Second Level of the Spirit."

Samuel rendered a huge, approving smile as he nodded.

Then Matthew had to ask the most obvious question that next came to mind.

"So, why all of this?" Matthew inquired as he raised his right arm and motioned in a one hundred eighty degree area. "What was the whole mountain scene all about?"

Samuel looked his young friend square in the eye as though he couldn't wait for Matthew to ask that question. "Ah yes," he began. "Excellent question, my young student. What we witnessed was the mental display of Kate's thoughts and emotions that we tapped into."

"Come again?" Matthew asked.

Samuel let out a chuckle at Matthew's response. "Simply put, Matthew, Kate felt she was standing before a cliff ready to step into the terrifying, yet exciting, unknown," Samuel explained.

Matthew then realized that her choice to get on that bus was no different than his own as he took hold of Samuel's hand and stepped into the darkness to embark upon his own journey. Samuel placed his left hand on Matthew's right shoulder and gave the young man a reassuring nod as he sensed the connection Matthew just made.

"Well, let me put it to you this way," Samuel continued. "All of Kate's thoughts and emotions resulting in her actually stepping onto that bus was like scaling a mountain and then standing at the summit miles above the ground. She was grateful and exhilarated at the potential future before her, but as you said, she was also scared out of her mind. In the end, she conquered her fear and made a courageous, conscious choice by taking the first step into a much larger world."

Then Samuel had a thought of how to solidify Matthew's understanding of Level Two by linking it to someone whom Matthew would surely know. "You are familiar with the name Winston Churchill, right?" Samuel asked.

"Of course," Matthew responded, a bit offended.

"Mr. Churchill was once quoted as saying, 'Courage is rightly esteemed the first of human qualities because it is the quality which guarantees all others.'"

Independent choice. Personal courage. Matthew felt an unexpected sense of embarrassment. He once again felt this whole lesson had been dreamt up just for him. He himself was only attending college less than an hour from his home and now found himself thinking of what other options he may have. He stood there wondering why he had never considered going somewhere far away, more adventurous or somewhere his father had never gone.

Samuel extended his right hand to Matthew inviting him back on the transport disc. Matthew grabbed a hold of Samuel's hand hoisting him aboard. He detected the inner conflict growing within his young pupil and felt compelled to say something.

"There are many callings we may have that require us to be courageous, Matthew," Samuel began. "Yours and Kate's are not the same. I don't see her on this transport, do you?"

Matthew felt his pride returning just a bit. *That's right*, he thought. *Chicago is nothing compared to this freak show I am now starring in.*

Samuel laughed.

"Freak show? What does that make me?" Samuel inquired greatly amused.

There it is again, Matthew thought. *How can he do that?!*

Even though Samuel had earned Matthew's trust, he had to express just how unsettling it made him feel that his guide has this most unnatural ability to intrude on his thoughts.

"It kind of pisses me off that you can read my mind," Matthew complained.

Samuel began to realize that he couldn't keep the truth from Matthew much longer, but he also sensed that the timing still wasn't right to reveal his true purpose. "I don't know why you would feel that way," Samuel offered while smiling innocently, in hopes of making light of the present situation and to ease Matthew's discomfort.

Then Samuel changed the subject by pulling them both back to the lesson at hand.

"Matthew, can you appreciate both the differences and similarities of Level Two between Kate's choice and that of Carrie, Benny and Thomas'?" asked Samuel.

It was obvious to Matthew that Samuel had no intention of addressing his concern, at least not at the moment. Rather than push the issue, he elected to resurrect the topic again another time when it felt right. He then tried to focus on the topic at hand and the question Samuel had just asked.

"Well," Matthew thought aloud. "Benny, Carrie and Thomas all had to be extremely courageous in order to be free. They risked not only bodily harm but also the reality of their family being broken apart."

"Go on," Samuel encouraged.

Matthew attempted to formulate the explanation in his mind but he could barely utter the words because the emotions of the slave's chakra were still very fresh in his own spirit. Rather than thinking of the answer, he suddenly felt it. "Having been there during those final minutes, I could feel the intense sadness more powerfully, the courage to say goodbye and move on in love," Matthew said with a soft tone.

Samuel was amazed by the depth of Matthew's abilities he continued to demonstrate.

"Matthew, I am truly stunned at how well you are doing and make such a profound connection," Samuel said proudly.

Matthew had no idea how he was doing it either. He had no logical explanation, but perhaps that has been his problem all along. Maybe more answers would come to him from deep within rather than by him trying to think everything to death.

"Level Two," Samuel continued. "Means not only having the courage to move beyond our darkest fears but also beyond the deepest pains we may encounter in life's journey as well."

Matthew thought again what an inspiration Benny, Carrie and Thomas were to him. What deep and profound lessons he had learned because they had the courage to embark on their quest for freedom amidst life-threatening dangers but also the courage to say goodbye for a greater cause. Thomas possessed a courage Matthew could barely fathom. Carrie and Benny had the courage to continue living to the fullest even amidst the greatest pain they had ever known in losing the most important man in their lives.

Then Matthew pondered how the source of such strength in the human spirit could help a person move forward on their journey in spite of horrific pain. To courageously heal from intense heartbreak. The answer suddenly burst forth within him.

Love. Love is that source of incredible strength.

"We have one more stop, Matthew, before moving onto our next gateway," Samuel hinted as he broke Matthew's train of thought.

"Alright," Matthew replied, feeling ready for a change. "Where to, next?"

"You made a most interesting observation as we approached this particular portal that I wanted to come back to," answered Samuel.

"I did?" Matthew asked most curiously, unable to recall saying anything particularly interesting.

"You'll remember once I take you back," noted Samuel.

Samuel guided the disc over the edge of a mountain that suddenly appeared. They descended at least one hundred feet down the side of the cliff. Within a few moments, he slowed the hovercraft to a complete stop. Still suspended in mid-air, Samuel turned the hovercraft to face the side of the mountain, at which point Matthew realized he had guided them to their portal exit. Samuel maneuvered them into the gateway as they emerged onto the other side, returning them to the expansive web of energy ribbons in the space-time continuum. Instead of moving along an energy ribbon in search of another portal, Samuel stopped their transport shortly after they emerged where they had just witnessed Kate's personal journey into courageous self-discovery. Samuel then rotated the craft in order to face Kate's portal ring one last time.

Matthew quickly recalled the question he had asked Samuel when they approached and entered the gateway the first time.

"That's right," Matthew began with a sense of certainty after seeing the gateway again. "I noticed that this portal had five golden ribbons connected to it."

Matthew then took a moment to study it more closely in a way not possible while they were in forward motion the first time they approached it. He picked one thread and attempted to follow its beam through the web as it curved and moved in and out of other similar ribbons contained within the labyrinth. Finally, Matthew could faintly see the end point of this single thread emitting from Kate's gateway intersecting with another portal seemingly miles away.

"Now watch closely, Matthew," instructed Samuel with a hint of wonder in his own voice.

At that moment, the outer rim began to glow with increasing intensity as it emitted the familiar blinding, white light. Prepared this time, Matthew shielded his eyes until the light faded. He then noticed that a sixth golden ripple of energy had shot out of the portal and made its way through the web. Matthew tried to follow it with his eyes which proved to be more difficult given the speed at which it moved and the constant weaving in and around other similar threads along the expansive web. Finally, however, Matthew saw it "connect" to another portal in the distance marked by a grand flash of light.

"What was that?" Matthew asked excitedly.

"Wait, Matthew, it's not over," Samuel replied.

Suddenly, a golden ribbon came flying into Matthew's left peripheral vision. Just as he turned his head, a seventh thread was joined to Kate's portal, again emitting an explosion of white light.

"Wow! What's going on? Why does that happen?" Matthew said with astonishment.

"What did you see?" asked Samuel.

"What I thought I saw," began Matthew, attempting to answer his guide's question. "Was a new ribbon coming from *within* Kate's gateway that joined with another portal in this huge grid. Then a new, seventh ribbon coming *elsewhere* from a different portal seemed to shoot out and made a connection to Kate's."

Matthew stared in wonder at Kate's gateway where he witnessed this most spectacular sight.

"That's exactly right," commented Samuel. "I suppose you want me to explain?"

Matthew glanced quickly at Samuel. "Well, you *are* my guide," Matthew smiled.

"Matthew, do you remember how I first described this place?" Samuel asked.

"I remember you saying something about it being some kind of space-time continuum," responded Matthew. "I just assumed that since we used the transport disc to ride these energy threads within the web to different gateways, they must be some kind of way for us to enter points in time?"

"Very good," Samuel encouraged. "But to fully answer your original question as to why there were so many threads connected to Kate's gateway, I needed you to see firsthand these new connections being formed."

"What are these connections?" Matthew immediately inquired.

"Well, it's really quite simple, Matthew," answered Samuel. "Kate's courageous choice to move forward coupled with her thoughts and emotions are the cause of these new connections."

Matthew looked at Samuel with a look of pure befuddlement. "I don't quite follow."

"You see, Kate's choice, spawned from her deep desires, has now set off a sequence of events within the space-time continuum which will lead her to new experiences," Samuel explained. "She will not only experience new things but also *draw to her* the events and people that she needs to fulfill her desires. Think of it as a radio signal that she emits, with a unique frequency that will guide Kate along her journey as the path unfolds, so she can fulfill her inner calling. It's almost like a magnet, where she made a choice and it creates a ripple effect that not only impacts herself but other people as well. The people she meets along the way have a very important purpose in connecting with Kate. They may not only help her in her own progress, but she in turn may help them on *their* journey in pursuit of *their* dreams."

As Samuel spoke, Matthew made an important connection in relation to his guide's last remarks. "Is that why one ribbon seemed to originate from within her gateway and another seemed to originate elsewhere from within the web?" inquired Matthew as he felt a little pride from his observations.

"Yes, Matthew, that's exactly right!" Samuel replied excitedly. "That's why I wanted to introduce you to this concept. This is important as we move into the next Level of the Spirit. Matthew, you have no idea how expansive the Universe is and how the individual and collective spiritual energies of people interact within it."

Matthew was taken back somewhat by Samuel's last statement. He felt like he was beginning to understand, but it was also overwhelming at the same time. The young man wanted more clarity, and his mind began to flood with questions. Samuel then interrupted his thought process as though he knew that perhaps Matthew should slow down a bit.

"I'm sorry, Matthew," Samuel said abruptly. "I'm getting ahead of myself. Just like Kate, Thomas, Carrie and Benny, your path will continue to unfold on your own journey as you continue to make courageous choices. You will understand so much more when the right time comes and you are ready."

Matthew then felt a twinge of frustration that Samuel would drop teasers like that without furthering his explanation. *But I do feel ready now*, Matthew thought.

"Are you ready to continue to the next step?" Samuel quickly asked, sensing his pupil's eagerness.

Matthew spoke not a word as he gave an affirmative nod. He was now incredibly anxious to see what other wonders awaited him.

"Onward we go," responded Samuel.

Matthew now knew Samuel was holding back something huge. He could *feel* it—a revelation of epic proportions. Realizing

Samuel would not divulge it just yet, Matthew tried to quiet his mind, trust his guide and not jump ahead.

Samuel engaged the transport yet again as it shot straight up in search of the next energy ribbon that would lead Matthew to Level Three.

CHAPTER 9

BELIEF

Samuel guided the transport along the web as he weaved through the path of a new golden stream of energy. Unlike his previous experiences, Matthew felt they were traveling in a vertical position moving up a new ribbon. Also unlike previous times, Matthew witnessed the continuous expansion of the web as new threads were being created and connected to various portals just as he observed with Kate's, from which they had exited moments ago. Golden, glowing ribbons flew all about them as they traveled through the labyrinth with each new connection exploding in flashes of brilliant, white light. Matthew became fixed in awe as his eyes tried to absorb the spectacular beauty of the scene. The infinite flashing of lights were reflected in his eyes as Matthew quickly realized his breath had literally been taken away. Within what felt like a minute or two, Samuel slowed their hover disc as Matthew forced himself to look away from the beauty of the continuum. He instinctively looked directly above them, seeing how they had arrived at the next portal.

"You don't really get much of a chance to pause and admire, do you?" Matthew commented.

Samuel realized that he had been pushing his pupil quite hard, given Matthew's readiness and ability to take on so much. "Are you feeling a need for a break?" asked Samuel with concern.

Being a typical eighteen-year-old, Matthew could have extreme peaks and valleys where he could stay up all night at times or sleep until noon. Here, however, he felt an amazing sense of energy. His mind was alert, and his body felt incredibly alive. "Are you kidding?" Matthew excitedly responded. "I've never felt so good."

"Pure spiritual intelligence," Samuel commented coolly, as though it were the most natural response in the world.

"What does that mean?" Matthew inquired.

"It means mind, body and spirit come into harmony toward a single focal point, Matthew," Samuel replied.

Oddly, Matthew knew exactly what Samuel was talking about without really knowing how. Somehow he understood it perfectly, which was yet another example of the impact this mystical journey was having upon him.

"Wow," Matthew uttered, for it was the only word he could conjure up at that moment to express his feelings. He had no idea why it all seemed to make such sense but relished in the fact that it did. Thus far, Samuel had guided them into and out of portals in a variety of fashion. They entered facing forward, backward and from the top while approaching feet-first. It was quite apparent that Samuel planned to enter head first from the bottom of the next gateway this time around.

"I believe I know what you are thinking, Matthew," Samuel interjected before Matthew had a chance to even ask his next question. "Why are we entering the portals from different positions?"

There it was again. Samuel demonstrating his skill in reading into what Matthew was thinking or feeling in the moment.

"I have started to notice," commented Matthew passing up the opportunity to call his guide out again on his unnatural ability.

"We'll come back to that later," Samuel replied.

"Then why did you bring it up?" Matthew asked, frustrated at being baited.

"In due time, Matthew," answered Samuel. "I need you to merely make a mental note of it."

They entered the portal and emerged on the other side. Matthew realized that he had grown more accustomed to the experience as his vision returned to normal more quickly than before. The images his eyes transmitted to his brain took a few moments to fully register, but within seconds Matthew recognized the surroundings. The transport disc was now hovering within the bridge of the spacecraft Matthew had taken for a joy ride in one of his previous dreams. He found himself again among the crew of the shuttle, Centurion. Similar to their arrival within the slave gateway, everyone was suspended in a motionless state.

"Do you recognize where we are?" Samuel asked.

"Yes," replied Matthew. "We're in my second dream. I remember that there was a crew of five people on board this spaceship named Centurion. The captain's name was Logan, and they were in trouble. He was sending a message to their base that they were caught in some kind of gravitational pull coming from this planet. I think he called it planet 317."

"And the date?" inquired Samuel looking directly at the young man.

Matthew paused for a moment to reflect back when the feeling of disbelief crept into his consciousness after he recalled hearing Logan utter the month and year. "May something, in 2311," Matthew responded. "But how is that possible?"

"Very good memory, Matthew, and hold your question a second," noted Samuel. "What point in your dream sequence are we at right now?"

Matthew immediately looked out the observation window before them and noticed they were still orbiting the planet.

"It looks like we've entered the time just before Captain Logan gave the order to crash land," Matthew replied. "How does this represent Level Three?"

"I don't want to launch into that just quite yet, no pun intended of course," Samuel commented as he gave a little grin at his clever play on words to which Matthew rolled his eyes in typical teenage fashion. "How do you suppose this is an example of the first two levels?"

Matthew paused a moment to reflect before he responded. "Well, humans have always wanted to explore space and achieve what seemed like the impossible," exclaimed Matthew, mildly surprised by how quickly he was beginning to solidify his understanding.

"How does that illustrate freedom?" prompted Samuel.

"To grow our understanding of the universe and find life on other planets," Matthew replied. "To know that we aren't alone. To see if we have a connection to something bigger out there."

Samuel listened intently and wanted to expand upon Matthew's remarks. "The collective human mind craves something at a very profound level," continued Samuel. "You already said it actually."

Matthew thought back a few moments ago to retrace his steps. "I said humanity wants to understand the universe more and our place in it?" Matthew stated with a hint of uncertainty.

"Exactly!" responded Samuel enthusiastically. "Trust your instincts, Matthew. You know more than you realize. The answers often reveal themselves when you trust yourself, and they can surprisingly bubble up to your consciousness from deep within."

Matthew gave Samuel a brief nod as he was beginning to realize how true a statement that was based on all of his new experiences—to not only know the truth but to feel it.

"It can be summed up in one word, Matthew," Samuel continued. "Knowledge. This deep desire to pursue knowledge, to better themselves, is fundamentally hard-wired into the mind of humanity and is a perfect example of Level One. Collectively, mankind wants freedom from ignorance. Freedom from the lack of understanding. Freedom to solve the infinite mysteries of the Universe and your place within it."

Samuel could tell his words were making an impression as Matthew's face appeared most thoughtful. Matthew could completely relate as his mind gravitated to The Oval that catapulted him into this entire sequence of events and somehow drew Samuel to him. He sensed there was something very big at play here and that his destiny was tied to this quest. *But what could that be?* Matthew thought to himself. Pondering his own question only further intensified his desire as morsels of understanding continued to present themselves. His thoughts were interrupted as Samuel levied yet another question for Matthew to answer.

"How does this dream sequence show us Level Two of the Spirit?" Samuel asked.

Matthew almost felt insulted by the question because it seemed so obvious. "Space travel must take immense courage and commitment," Matthew responded.

Samuel realized he needed to help his pupil dig a bit deeper beyond the obvious. "Of course," Samuel began. "The people aboard this ship certainly must have had the bravery and discipline to leave their home planet to be a part of such a journey. But it goes well beyond that. Do you think they were alone and got to this point by themselves?"

Matthew gave Samuel a quizzical look. "What do you mean?" Matthew asked.

Samuel motioned all around the bridge with his right arm as he repeated the question in a different manner. "Don't you think there was a complete support system that led these brave explorers to this point?" Samuel inquired as he reframed the question.

Now Matthew began to grasp what Samuel was leading to. "Oh, I understand what you are getting at," he commented, beginning to understand. "I'm sure they had an entire team of people involved."

"Yes, Matthew," Samuel continued. "But there is one thing that I want you to realize, though."

"What's that?" Matthew asked. He began to appreciate that rarely is the answer Samuel is searching for so obvious.

"Those who made this possible goes far beyond the crew aboard this ship and it even goes beyond the team of people on Earth who are also a part of this mission," Samuel stated with heightened emphasis.

Still not clearly comprehending Samuel's point, Matthew had to continue to seek clarity.

"What do you mean?" Matthew asked with heightened interest. "Are you talking about their families or something?"

Samuel was quite pleased with Matthew's insatiable desire to probe deeper. "This mission spans hundreds of years and thousands of people, Matthew," replied Samuel. "The multitude making this exploration possible crosses many generations of scientists, astronauts and engineers who all shared this dream. They shared the same passionate vision to make interstellar travel a reality."

Matthew realized that he truly wasn't thinking in the context of just one team working toward this end goal.

"They were no less courageous than those who actually stepped onto the ship and left their home of planet Earth," Samuel further explained. "They displayed the courage and perseverance in overcoming incredible odds and a steady mainstream mentality that constantly discouraged them. The naysayers continuously told them that interstellar travel was impossible. They tried to convince those brave pioneers that their scientific theorems were faulty; the materials to construct a durable spacecraft did not exist on Earth; the technology required existed only within science fiction or it would be too costly. Every imaginable road block was erected only for those who would not be denied to overcome them. Therein also lay one of the fundamental conditions of humanity. Where there is a mountain, people will be challenged to climb it and not stop until they succeed." Samuel paused a moment as he noticed Matthew look around the bridge absorbing the critical lesson at hand.

"I never would have even thought about that," Matthew openly admitted. "How the hard work of others helped the crew to achieve their dream to be here."

"The crew's predecessors had the courage, Matthew, to not only overcome external challenges but also moved beyond those moments of doubt they sometimes found within themselves," continued Samuel. "Even though it took a few generations to accomplish this vision, which started with a single thought, there was always a man or woman who would pick up where the last generation left off until the progression of science and technology brought this end goal into reality. They clung to their vision. This is yet another example of true desire and true courage."

Samuel could tell that Matthew's mind was abuzz with activity as his pupil began to grasp the vastness of interconnectedness involved in this one example. A connection to people, events and places that goes well beyond the scene that appeared before them.

"The advancement of scientific or social theories isn't based upon the safety of old thinking but breaching the insanity of new ideas that push beyond common beliefs," Samuel stated with authority. "There are countless examples throughout history, Matthew, of heretical ideas that exploded into the consciousness of mankind all because one or a few individuals had a moment of genius sparked by a thought. A thought they consciously and courageously pursued."

Samuel realized that the foundation has now been set for Matthew to continue his own growth through a very important and profound connection to this specific dream sequence. A realization of how one courageous act by one individual can set into motion events that can impact one life or many. Such acts can possibly even impact thousands spanning decades and centuries. Samuel then turned to face Matthew and placed both his hands on Matthew's shoulders, for he had another huge connection to divulge to his student.

Matthew, realizing his guide had an important point to make, made himself look away from the crew on the shuttle bridge and directly at Samuel to give him his full attention.

"Now Matthew, what I am about to tell you next might blow your circuits, but it's important for you to understand, nonetheless, as you continue your journey," Samuel stated emphatically.

"Alright," Matthew replied, unsure what it was that Samuel was about to share but sensed it must be critical given his level of intensity.

"One of those pioneers whose ideas and scientific theories which formulated a critical foundation making this possible was our very own Kate!" Samuel said with excitement and wonder.

Matthew's facial expression quickly changed as he looked away from Samuel for a moment to gaze upon the shuttle scene yet again. He attempted to fathom the true depth and incredible connection that Samuel had just revealed. His mouth dropped open slightly and his mind began to ponder how Kate was connected to all of this—a connection that spanned hundreds of years.

Samuel smiled as he clearly saw Matthew's slight bewilderment over the depth of what he just revealed.

"We can exit this gateway, Matthew, re-enter the space-time continuum and trace one of the ribbons back through a series of portals to the one within which we witnessed Kate make her historic decision to get on that bus and pursue her dreams," Samuel further explained. "That's why portals are continuously making new connections as life unfolds and choices are made which connect people and key events."

Matthew's mind immediately catapulted him to Kate's dream sequence as he recalled the feelings of fear and doubt which she had to overcome in making her brave choice.

"What if Kate had never gotten on that bus, Matthew?" Samuel asked. "What if those specific ribbons never became connected to the portals within the continuum?"

Matthew tried to fathom the alternate realties within his mind, and it became very apparent to him the staggering effect Kate's courageous choice could have had on the future of so many people if she hadn't followed through with her own dream, if she hadn't pursued her inner calling. "Then it's possible that none of this may have happened," Matthew stated as he looked directly into Samuel's eyes, clearly demonstrating his new level of profound understanding.

"Exactly, my young friend!" Samuel confirmed. "And so it goes in any choice a human being makes each day. To summon the courage that leads them to that next step. It doesn't matter if it is on a large scale such as this, which has led human beings to interstellar travel. It could even be on an individual basis such as a single parent choosing to work two jobs while pursuing a college degree in order to provide their child with a better life. But even then, that one child, if given the right opportunity in life, could spawn something huge. It's about facing life's challenges, recognizing what they desire in order to live that free life and to summon the courage each day in each choice they make, even when obstacles arise. People do this especially when they feel there is a greater good at play. It sets forth an unfathomable sequence of events that you are now just beginning to realize. These examples show the true depth and power in shaping our lives and even the lives of others as we make those courageous choices!"

Matthew was blown away, and his mind was operating at an unprecedented pace. His understanding was now exponentially growing, but it went far beyond an intellectual level that he could sense and even felt the truth flowing deep within himself. It was almost as though something had been unlocked and a spark of fire ignited.

Samuel sensed Matthew's recognition and grasping of these latest truths and that he was indeed, ready for more.

"So let's get back to the topic at hand, which is Level Three of the Spirit," Samuel continued. "We just took a big-picture perspective here, Matthew, of what has led this particular crew of five brave souls to this precise moment in time. What about the first two levels of spirit as it relates to the Centurion crew predicament?"

Still pondering the incredible connection to Kate, Matthew tried to pull himself back into the present, so he could adequately reflect before responding to his guide. He then replied thoughtfully. "Freedom to them must have meant filling their own desire to experience space travel and all of its unknown mysteries firsthand," Matthew began. "As you called Kate a star gazer, I think you can call these guys the ultimate sky gazers, but I can't even imagine how much courage they must have had to actually leave Earth and our own solar system to get here."

"Yes indeed, Matthew, and that now leads us to Level Three of the Spirit," noted Samuel.

Samuel motioned to Matthew in the direction of Captain Logan sitting motionless in his captain's chair. Matthew knew what Samuel wanted him to do. As with the others, he needed to physically touch Logan in order to enter his chakra. Matthew stepped off the transport and took a few steps toward the captain. He took note of Logan's focused facial expression as Matthew lifted his left hand to place it on Logan's right shoulder.

The second his fingers touched Logan, Matthew immediately began to see the circular white light emerge in between the captain's eyes. Within seconds, he became engulfed by the light and was immersed in Logan's thoughts and emotions. This time, it was at the very moment of the crisis aboard the shuttle as the crew worked furiously carrying out the captain's orders in hopes of averting a disastrous crash landing. Logan was barking out orders, lights were flashing, the alarm siren screamed out of control, and violent thrusts jerked the crew in all directions within the cockpit. Matthew immediately reacted to the extreme intensity of Logan's mind and soul as his own body tensed with a rush of adrenaline sweeping through his entire being. Matthew sensed the fear one would fully expect under such duress. But oddly, it was in the far background of Logan's mind and spirit. It was not the predominant force that could easily consume a person when faced with their potential doom.

Matthew tried to "reach" out to feel more and to let his own guard down in order to fully experience Logan's mental and emotional state at that very moment. It was harder than he expected, because Matthew was afraid of what he might experience. His fear not only stemmed from the notion of taking on such intense feelings from another person but also the possibility of discovering his own feelings in the process. His caution was especially extreme after his first chakra experience and the terrifying possibility of becoming in touch with his own deepest and darkest fears.

Matthew tried nonetheless. He realized that he had to move beyond his fear in order to gain the full appreciation of this next lesson. He had to make his own courageous choice and get through the first two levels himself at this very moment, just like Samuel was saying a few minutes ago. Each day and each moment is presented with a series of choices that enable us to move forward and grow.

Suddenly, Logan's thoughts became his. The captain's emotions came through to Matthew with increasing clarity and focus. Matthew realized that Logan was not allowing the fear to consume him.

How? How could he possibly hold this fear back and not totally lose it? Matthew wondered. Matthew again sensed the fear present within the captain. He started to feel its power grow, and it was frightening. It was a fear that could morph into sheer terror in an instant—a terror that could immobilize a human being. Then he heard Logan talking to himself.

God damn it, Tom! Think! If we don't act quickly, the ship is going to be torn apart. All these lives. My God! My crew!

Matthew suddenly felt a convulsion through his body from the intensity of the emotion. His back arched, and Matthew began to feel as though he was being pulled into the vortex of a tornado, the center of which led to a terrifying darkness. Logan's thoughts continued to pierce Matthew's mind.

Focus Tom! You can do this. They can do it. Delta sequence! That's it!

As quickly as this terror welled within his host, Matthew felt it begin to dissipate. Logan's stream of consciousness began to focus on that next choice—because he did not panic. Fear faded away into the background and in its place, Matthew then began to sense something else—a growing confidence. A confidence in the decision that the captain made to avert certain destruction. *But where was this confidence coming from?* Matthew thought as he continued to search for the answer within Logan's chakra.

Then he felt it. He realized what Logan was doing. Logan was invoking a disciplined mind to hold his destructive thoughts and fearful emotions in check. Matthew could not believe how strong Logan was. It was incredible how the captain was able to do this with so much at stake and the pressure of making a split decision where each second could mean the difference between life or death.

Then more came through that Matthew could sense. He felt an overwhelming surge of warmth within his body. His tension gave way to clarity. Matthew felt a growing faith. He sensed Logan's trust, and finally, he could tell that the captain believed in what he was doing.

Where was this faith and trust coming from that's giving him such strong conviction? Matthew thought to himself. The more Matthew opened up, the more he felt Logan's mental and emotional state growing stronger and more confident. Then Matthew understood. He sensed it. Logan had faith in himself. This morphed into belief in his choice.

Matthew next felt a transference of this faith go out from Tom. Yet another twist that he could never have possibly understood except when experiencing the intensity of it all through the captain's chakra. It was faith in a greater power. Somehow, Logan knew this was not the end. This transference began to come through more powerfully to Matthew. It was in a higher power. A faith in God perhaps, but Matthew couldn't tell for certain. Being a spiritual person, himself, Matthew didn't need to mentally rationalize this feeling because he just understood. Somehow, Matthew understood what Tom was feeling, and it helped erase the doubt. But then, Matthew felt yet another surge. This time a faith that was directed toward something specific—the crew.

Yes! Matthew thought.

Logan had faith in his crew and entrusted his own life to the men and women of the ship. Logan *knew* that they would get through this, in large part because he trusted that the crew would carry out his orders to the letter. That they were prepared for this from countless hours of training and working as one unit, preparing for any conceivable circumstance they could encounter in deep space. They were a family now and loved each other.

As quickly as the chakra experience overcame Matthew like a tsunami of thoughts and emotions, it began to fade. At first,

Matthew did not want to leave it. Unlike the painful experience of the slave's chakra, if felt absolutely thrilling to be in a place where you felt such trust and faith. Even more amazingly, to be in such a place during an intense situation where one could be lost forever.

Lost to fear and panic. Lost in darkness.

Matthew felt a hand on his own shoulder as it gently pulled him backward. As with the previous chakra experiences, his body succumbed to a limp state. Matthew stumbled to the floor and landed flat on his back. He was dizzy and disoriented but there was something else this time. He felt an emptiness. He missed those feelings that he had tapped into through Logan's experience. Matthew felt the need to get back there.

"Are you alright, Matthew?" Samuel asked concerned.

Matthew slowly began to sit up but didn't want to attempt to stand just yet until he felt his legs return. Samuel knelt down beside his pupil and put his hand on Matthew's back to help steady the young man.

Samuel was then taken a bit off guard when Matthew asked, "Why?" Samuel raised his eyebrow in question.

"Why did you pull me away?" Matthew inquired more specifically. "It felt so wonderful."

Samuel gently patted Matthew on the back in an attempt to comfort him. "I know, Matthew," Samuel began. "As real as it all felt, you were merely tapping in, and not experiencing it on your own. I was concerned that to leave you exposed much longer might lead you to become overly dependent and hamper your own growth."

Matthew took some deep breaths to regain his wits and allow the post-traumatic stress to pass through his body.

"So tell me, Matthew, this experience from Logan's chakra, what did it teach you about Level Three?" Samuel asked, getting back to the topic at hand.

Matthew was still feeling a sense of loss but realized that he had to invoke some mental discipline of his own now to come back to the moment and address his guide's question. "It's hard to put it into words Samuel," Matthew began. "I sensed different things but one thing I felt for sure was trust."

"Good, Matthew, but you mentioned something more. What else did you *feel* within Tom?" Samuel asked.

Matthew paused a moment before responding and looked at the captain sitting motionless in his chair. "I felt Tom's faith," Matthew replied succinctly.

Samuel shot Matthew a smile. "Describe it for me," Samuel encouraged wanting Matthew to express his full experience.

"He started to allow some of the fear to well up inside him from their situation, especially when he thought about his crew," Matthew described. "But I could definitely sense his mental strength keeping that in check and preventing it from overpowering him. A discipline of sorts, I guess you could say. Then, as he tried to keep this overwhelming fear from gripping him, an idea came to mind as to what command he should give next to save the ship and crew. Once he knew what to do, I felt a surge of confidence begin to grow."

"Yes, Matthew!" Samuel shouted out. "Then what did you sense?"

"That's where I realized that he began to trust," Matthew continued. "To trust himself. Then I felt a growing sense of faith. A faith in himself, but something also happened, Samuel. It was so powerful that words hardly describe it." Matthew then looked at Samuel to make direct eye contact with his guide.

"Try," Samuel said with a tone of slight amazement.

"His faith began to take on more than one . . ." Matthew's words faded briefly as he struggled for a moment to find the right thing to say. "Dimension. I could sense his faith in a greater power beyond himself. I don't know how religious of a man Tom is, but I could sense without question that God, or whatever he would call it, would help him get through this crisis."

Samuel nodded as he listened intently to his pupil's explanation.

"Yes, Matthew, but I can tell you have more to describe," Samuel commented.

Matthew's strength returned and he stood. His gaze moved away from Samuel and began to look around the cockpit of the ship at the various crew members still in a motionless state. "He had faith in his crew and trusted them," Matthew stated. "All of this trust and faith led him to somehow know that they would pull through it."

"Matthew, I have never seen someone with such a natural ability to 'tune into' the chakra's of other beings as yourself," Samuel complimented. "This is one example, my friend, of Level Three of the Spirit," Samuel revealed.

Matthew looked back at his guide in great anticipation over what Samuel would divulge next.

"Level Three is Faith, Belief and Knowing," Samuel clearly stated. Samuel paused a few seconds as Matthew's gaze returned to meet his mentor's eyes.

"Once a person embraces their desire to be free, embrace a dream or inner calling, and then have the courage to pursue it, they inevitably are faced with the next Level of the Spirit in order to continue their progress," Samuel explained.

"That's how he knew!" Matthew suddenly blurted out as he interrupted Samuel in mid-sentence.

"How he knew what?" Samuel asked with great curiosity as to what Matthew would next say.

"That they would make it," Matthew commented. "He let faith overcome his fear which then gave him the clarity he needed to know what to do next. Then he just knew they would get through it."

Samuel smiled and gave a most deliberately reassuring nod. "Once you know what you want, embrace it and have the courage to move forward, a person must then summon trust and faith in order to achieve any goal or vision," Samuel further explained. "This faith has multiple connotations, or as you put it, my young friend, multiple dimensions."

Matthew gave Samuel a quizzical look to prompt his guide to further his explanation.

"It often requires faith in something larger than yourself," Samuel stated trying to provide more clarity. "Many times, we are faced with a decision, Matthew, that sometimes cannot be logically or rationally thought through within the mind. There is an element of intuition or gut feeling that sometimes accompanies decisions or actions that are necessary to reach your dreams. Listening to this intuitive feeling inherently means that you are placing an element of faith which goes beyond yourself. Having that faith in God or in whatever way people may refer to it."

Samuel placed his right hand on Matthew's left shoulder as he divulged another key point. "Where I come from Matthew, we have an expression for it," Samuel commented.

"What's that?" Matthew asked with great curiosity.

"We refer to it as the *intelligence of the whole being*," Samuel stated. "Intelligence goes well beyond just mere mental intellect, Matthew."

Then Matthew felt compelled to launch several questions toward his guide. He wanted him to elaborate more on this concept, and he finally wanted to know exactly where Samuel was from.

Why hasn't he told me yet? Matthew thought in frustration.

But as soon as Matthew was about to open his mouth, Samuel interjected with more information. It almost seemed like his mentor didn't want him to go there. At least not yet.

"The other dynamic of faith also means you have to trust and have faith in yourself," Samuel explained. "Those who embark on any mission or goal in life must not only summon the courage but also a faith in oneself to encourage that first step. It also means you must trust along the way as the two conditions are so interwoven. Initially, that faith may only be a tiny seed but can eventually blossom and grow along the way as we progress."

"Yes, but you can't ignore what your mind is telling you," argued Matthew. "I might want to take a hot bath but if a thermometer is telling me the water temperature is two hundred degrees, I'm not going to jump in and get burned. Don't you also need some common sense along the way?"

"Absolutely, Matthew," replied Samuel, respectful of Matthew's simplistic argument. "The mind, body and soul must work in tandem. Just as I mentioned, it's the intelligence of the whole being. What I am referring to is that the road to growth and achieving an inner calling may not be nicely or neatly laid out before you when you summon the courage to embark on it. Even though you may have the end point firmly embedded in your mind, an element of faith is required that the road will continue to be revealed, the pathway will unfold along the journey and you will receive the necessary guidance along the way."

Samuel paused again to allow Matthew to continue to digest his words.

"This is especially true when you actively ask for help and guidance," Samuel commented as he planted yet another seed within Matthew's mind and soul. "We will come back to that point later though."

Why does he keep doing that!? Matthew thought to himself with growing frustration in response to his guide continuing to bait him with new information. His wanted to know everything right then and there.

"You studied Dr. Martin Luther King in school, didn't you?" Samuel asked breaking Matthew's current stream of thought.

"Yes," replied Matthew immediately wondering why he would randomly bring that up.

"Dr. King once likened faith to a stair case," continued Samuel. "You need not see the entire stair case but merely take the first step!"

Samuel's words made a sudden impact as Matthew could immediately relate the analogy to his own choice when he stepped into the darkness with his guide. He had no idea what to expect or what would come next but he took that first step nonetheless. Then a question popped into Matthew's mind that he wanted Samuel to address.

"You mentioned that Level Three is faith as well as belief," Matthew commented. "What's the difference between the two?"

"Ah, yes," responded Samuel. "Once you place your faith in something or in a direction, Matthew, what tends to happen?"

Matthew thought for a moment before answering.

"If all goes well, I supposed your faith can grow," Matthew answered very simply.

"Exactly," replied Samuel. "That small seed of faith I mentioned earlier can grow and balloon if properly nursed. Level Three of the Spirit *starts* with faith, Matthew, and as it grows, that faith then becomes belief. You begin to really *believe* in what you are doing. You believe that you are on the right track. You believe in yourself, others and God. Then, Matthew, something really transformational happens, which ultimately leads a person to yet another state. It's almost the final 'stage' of Level Three."

"What's that?" Matthew asked with heightened intensity.

"*Knowing* then happens deep within yourself," Samuel said with a calm confidence as he placed his hand over Matthew's heart. "A person who steps forward in courage not only has faith in the notion of accomplishing their goal and where they need to go, they then begin to believe it and ultimately that belief morphs into a knowingness," Samuel explained. "They begin to know which helps them erase any doubt. As successes are experienced along the way, the growth in faith is gradually accompanied by enhanced belief."

"And eventually that belief grows into a sense of knowing," Matthew stated as he made the connection glancing back in the direction of Captain Logan.

"Exactly," Samuel replied.

Noting Matthew's glance at Logan, Samuel wanted to make sure his pupil fully understood how this dream sequence relates to Level Three. "The situation in the shuttle, Centurion, is a great example of Level Three," Samuel continued. "Why would this crew withstand months and even years of intense training in order to accept the challenges and unknown obstacles before them when they left Earth?"

"Because they had faith and believed in the cause," replied Matthew without hesitation looking back at his guide.

"They not only had faith and belief in the cause, Matthew, but also faith in themselves and their fellow crew members," Samuel stated. "They had faith in the ideas which propelled them. They had faith and believed in all those before them who blazed the trail which led them to accept their mission and make it possible. This included Kate, even though they didn't know her since she pre-dated them by hundreds of years!"

Samuel turned and looked directly at Logan who was still sitting motionless in his captain's chair, his arm reached out in mid-air at the control panel before him. "The crew also had faith and believed in their captain and each other," Samuel continued. "They managed to invoke the necessary courage and faith, knowing that their captain would successfully navigate this life-or-death situation. They had faith that each member would perform their duty and function to the best of their ability to avert a disaster. To be successful, they moved beyond themselves in faith under extreme duress. Faith, Matthew, encapsulates not only in something much larger outside yourself, but also belief in oneself and others as well."

Matthew looked around the cockpit of the shuttle, Centurion, and more closely studied the facial expressions each crewmember wore during this crisis. He more fully appreciated the extreme focus visibly evident within their eyes. It must have taken nerves of steel to maintain that level of focus and mental discipline under such terrifying conditions.

"Even though I realized that I was not really part of this situation in this dream sequence, I was still terrified during the part where I didn't know if we would safely crash land on the planet," commented Matthew. "But when I entered Logan's chakra, I fully understood how that anxiety can turn into terror during such an intense moment."

"Absolutely, Matthew!" Samuel responded as he too glanced around the cockpit at the crew. "Fear is one of the most basic emotions of humanity. The key is how we choose to react to fear. Summoning the courage is the critical component of Level Two, as we already talked about. Level Three is the next step, as faith then becomes one of the tools by which we follow through with that courageous choice in any given situation. I'm certain these brave explorers were very scared, but it was their faith that enabled them to overcome that fear in maintaining their composure and to discipline their minds not to let destructive thoughts overpower them."

Matthew looked around again at the crew and appreciated the mental and emotional discipline they displayed to survive this horribly stressful ordeal.

"Every fearful situation we encounter, whether great or small, entails a choice of how we are going to react," Samuel commented. "Fear can immobilize a person from achieving their dreams and prevent us from truly growing."

Matthew looked away from the crew as his attention turned toward Samuel with yet another inquisitive look. "What happened to them, Samuel?" Matthew asked with concern.

"They were rescued within seven days," Samuel answered. "Although they weren't able to repair the damage to their ship, their ingenuity saved them as they found a way to repair the communications satellite and radio their base."

There was something else Matthew had begun to wonder about and decided now was as good a time as any to bring it up. "I have another question for you, Samuel," Matthew began. "Where does God fit into this equation of faith?"

"Ahhhh, yes," Samuel said with a slight nod. "I was wondering when you were going to ask me that, Matthew."

"Well?" Matthew prompted.

"We sometimes refer to God as the Creator or The One," noted Samuel.

"We?" Matthew said curiously. "Who is the 'we' again?"

"I'm sorry, Matthew, but please hold that second question," Samuel requested. "I'll tell you more very soon, but first let me answer your question by showing you something that may help you understand better."

Samuel stepped onto the platform of their hover disc and Matthew immediately followed. Samuel then engaged the navigational ball and rotated ninety degrees to their right. Matthew noticed the portal seemingly appeared out of nowhere.

"When did that pop up?" asked Matthew just now noticing the gateway.

"It's always been there, Matthew. You just didn't notice it when we first arrived," Samuel replied. "It's almost a metaphor for so many living on Earth right now."

"What?" Matthew asked.

"So many people walk in a state of confusion," Samuel began. "Lost in their own lives, because they are lost within themselves. Some never develop the self-awareness to Level One, or they get stuck in Level Two, or they dabble in Level Three but retreat in fear or doubt. If they could get to the third level, they would see the paths all around them to which they were so blind to before."

"So, you're saying I am stuck in Level Two?" Matthew asked with concern.

"You just noticed the portal, didn't you?" Samuel asked.

Matthew suddenly realized the depth of Samuel's comments and how his guide answered his question with yet another question. He, himself, was beginning to broach Level Three, because if that weren't the case, he would never have noticed the existence of this new portal. The path was truly beginning to unfold before him.

As Samuel engaged the hover disc, he continued to be amazed by his pupil's progress. Samuel searched within himself and then reached outward for guidance as to what should come next and at what pace he should continue to introduce Matthew to these critical lessons. In spite of his tremendous progress, Samuel realized that Matthew still had no idea who or what he is and how immensely important he has become. This only further propelled Samuel to continue the journey with Matthew and his own commitment to revealing the divine truth. Samuel now knew, without question, he had finally found the one for whom he had been searching.

CHAPTER 10

POWER OF FAITH

They entered the gateway and re-emerged into the space-time continuum on the other side as Matthew experienced the usual blinding white light, distorted vision and brief feeling of weightlessness. The young man turned back to view the Centurion portal they had just exited and saw many interconnecting golden ribbons extending outward in all directions. The connections to this gateway were so numerous that it was almost impossible to count. Samuel deliberately selected one of the threads protruding from the bottom of the gateway. As soon as their vehicle made contact with the selected ribbon, they were instantly swept away within its current. Their transport was catapulted across the expanse of space-time, weaving their way through the ever complex web of gateways. Within a minute or two, Matthew could see the end of the energy ribbon they were riding on and their presumed end destination. This time, however, Samuel did not reduce their speed as they approached, and Matthew grew concerned.

"Shouldn't we be slowing down?" Matthew asked nervously.

"No," Samuel said rather flippantly. "Your mind is growing, expanding and making more connections, Matthew, so I can start to speed up."

Matthew suddenly felt the need to brace himself for impact since he had no idea what to expect. They had previously entered all other portals in a much slower and cautious manner. He grabbed Samuel's arm just before they slammed into the energy field of the gateway. Given their rate of speed upon impact, Matthew theorized that the visual and physical effects would pass within an instant. He did not expect what actually happened next.

Instead of accelerating the process of adjusting to the effects of entering the energy field, time seemed to slow down. Matthew's vision was not blinded by the brightness of a pure, white light. Instead, he could see very clearly. He could see Samuel standing there at the navigation control of their hover craft but appearing very differently. It was as though he saw Samuel's physical form being outlined by some kind of energy signature. It was a glowing aura of light emanating numerous fluctuating colors all around him—white, gold, blue and even purple. Matthew found it difficult to fully distinguish all of them as they constantly shifted and flowed from the edge of Samuel's body. Something then compelled Matthew to look downward as he caught a glimpse of himself. He held up his left hand and saw a similar colorful array of energy outlining his hand. Like Samuel, it extended to his entire being. It was breathtakingly beautiful. Amazed and also slightly frightened, Matthew was rendered speechless.

Their transport finally emerged on the other side of the gateway. Motion and vision returned to normal as Matthew looked up from his hand and saw Samuel standing at the control panel. His guide turned to look at his young passenger standing directly behind him, still showing signs of confusion and disbelief.

"I told you, Matthew. Your mind is expanding and capable of handling far more now and at a greater pace," Samuel injected quickly.

"But you looked so different just a few seconds ago!" exclaimed Matthew. "It was as though I could see the energy surrounding our bodies."

"You did indeed," Samuel replied. "You are now starting to truly 'see' for the first time. But first things first, Matthew. We've arrived at our next destination and your next lesson."

Matthew had to briefly search his memory banks for the question he had asked Samuel which led them to this stage. "Oh, right," noted Matthew. "Where does God fit into Level Three of the Spirit."

"Look ahead of us," Samuel instructed as he stepped to the side to reveal the view directly in front of their current position.

They still appeared to be in space, but instead of the view of the Centurion and the planet in the Orion system, Matthew saw a beautiful, glowing planet with spectacular, blue oceans and brown-green colored land masses resting within the blackness of space. Overwhelmed, Matthew realized he was looking at his very own planet Earth. His transcendent moment was short lived, however, as he was startled by the rush of a rumbling engine that came within one hundred feet above their heads. He felt his stomach practically jump into his throat as his heart pounded intensely.

"What the hell was that?" demanded Matthew.

"That's your next lesson of Level Three, my friend," Samuel said with a smile. He immediately engaged the thrusters on their transport and began to accelerate. It was clear that he was in pursuit of this unidentified flying object that just passed overhead traveling in the direction of Earth. Within a matter of seconds, they were flying side by side with the spacecraft, and Samuel kicked the transport disc into high gear. They quickly passed the spacecraft as Matthew realized they were now speeding toward Mother Earth. Just as quickly as Samuel accelerated past the spacecraft, they slowed to a complete stop. Samuel then rotated their transport ninety degrees to the right. From this new vantage point, they could see the Earth on their left and the approaching spacecraft to their right. Looking straight ahead, Matthew could see both objects within his peripheral vision. The ship quickly approached them from the right side as its clear objective was to reach the bright, blue planet.

"Any guesses, Matthew?" Samuel asked as he glanced in the direction of the spacecraft.

Matthew looked at the approaching spaceship and back again at Samuel as he couldn't render any kind of guess. "I have no idea," Matthew replied, shaking his head. "Am I supposed to know what that is?"

"Are you familiar with the Apollo space missions from the sixties and seventies?" Samuel inquired.

"Yeah," Matthew replied as he looked at his guide curiously. Then something triggered his memory. "Actually, I think that was the name of the space program then, right?" Matthew stated uncertainly.

"Correct," Samuel replied. "In fact, there were several Apollo missions. What we are seeing now is Apollo 13."

Matthew glanced back at the approaching craft as his mind quickly recalled a tidbit of information. "Isn't that the mission where some kind of tank exploded on their ship?" Matthew questioned as he realized that perhaps his information was coming from a movie he had once seen with his family.

"That's right, Matthew," Samuel confirmed. "That's the mission where the famous expression 'Houston, we have a problem' first came about."

Matthew turned his head to more closely study the approaching spacecraft. He then noticed severe damage to the ship's hull on one side which further confirmed his theory.

"They never landed on the moon and had to return home immediately," Samuel stated as he continued to set the story line for the young man. "One of the main problems they had to deal with was not only damage to their ship but also to some of the equipment they needed to stay alive for the journey home. Do you know what happens to a person if they are confined to a space with no ventilation?"

"They would run out of oxygen," Matthew replied as he felt the answer was a bit obvious.

"Yes, that's true, but the crew had ample oxygen supplies," Samuel countered. "Even with oxygen, they would still die if it weren't for one critical piece of equipment."

Matthew looked back at the ship again trying to conjure up the answer his guide was obviously in search of, but it was to no avail. "I'm sorry, but I'm not making the connection," Matthew conceded.

Samuel looked back at the ship and then to his pupil. "Well, when a person breathes, they release carbon dioxide, right?" Samuel asked.

"Yeah, so?" Matthew quipped still not understanding what any of this has to do with Level Three.

"They not only needed oxygen, Matthew, but also a way to get rid of the carbon dioxide they exhaled," Samuel continued. "The equipment that performed this simple yet crucial task was damaged. Without these carbon dioxide 'scrubbers' as they were called, the crew would die before they reached Earth. They would literally suffocate."

Matthew looked at his guide with a growing sense of impatience. "Samuel, why are you going into such detail about this one thing?" Matthew asked with frustration creeping into his tone. "What does that have to do with God and Level Three? What does this space mission have to do with any of it?"

Samuel turned to directly face his pupil, clearly sensing Matthew's growing impatience.

"It is another example of all three levels, Matthew, and I need you to understand what these brave men were faced with!" Samuel stated with a sense of urgency. "It's also going to help you make the connections you want to know about Level Three."

Matthew took a deep breath to calm his mind and temper his impatience. Samuel hadn't steered him wrong yet, and he needed to remind himself of that fact. "I'm sorry, Samuel," Matthew stated apologetically. "I just want to know the answers and find the truth."

Samuel smiled at the young lad and placed his right hand on Matthew's left shoulder.

"I know, Matthew, and you are doing amazingly well," Samuel encouraged. "You have learned so much, and I sense in you that desire for more. The more I expose you to, the greater your passion to pursue the truth becomes. That, my friend, is a true indication of why we are here and why it has unfolded so fast for you on this journey. You have no idea the ridiculously fast pace we are moving at."

Matthew felt his impatience wane and a brief moment of appreciation blossom over what he had learned thus far. A small sense of pride also crept in with Samuel's compliment.

"Thank you, Samuel," Matthew replied.

Matthew looked back at the Apollo spacecraft to focus again on the task at hand. "So what's next?" he asked.

"You know what the crew had to do in order to deal with this life threatening situation?" Samuel inquired.

Matthew paused a moment to ponder the possible answer before responding. "I assume they had to figure out how to dispose of their carbon dioxide," Matthew replied.

"Yes," Samuel began. "But they first had to wait, Matthew. Wait for the team of engineers back on Earth to figure out how to modify and adapt any kind of material they had on board that could do the job of those broken scrubbers and keep them alive."

Matthew reflected a moment on what it must have been like to be completely reliant on others to solve a problem to which the end result would be your own life or death. Each passing moment must have felt like an eternity. Matthew realized that he would have likely gone mad in the process when his own life depended on an answer to a problem. Not to mention the notion that the solution was merely an "if" and not a given. He truly couldn't fathom that possibility as he tried to place himself in their situation and imagined what it must have been like.

"Wow," Matthew whispered under his breath as he continued to watch the approaching spacecraft. "Talk about having faith and patience in others."

"Exactly," Samuel responded in hearing his student's comment. "Pretty strong testimony to Level Three in and of itself, wouldn't you say? In the end, Mission Control engineers managed to find a way using only materials available to the astronauts on the ship to make a simple device that would work and keep them alive."

Samuel quickly glanced at the approaching ship and then back to his student, thinking of what Matthew needed to hear next. He definitely felt the struggle within the young man. "Like I said, Matthew, Level Three starts with faith, and from faith, comes revelations that strengthen ones belief," Samuel began with great emphasis. "From this faith, a way will be revealed, which can include inspired thought or clarity of action that will enable you to achieve your goals or solve a problem. It's from this level that we open ourselves up to magical things happening. Once you do and they are revealed, then you move into a heightened state of awareness where you know you are on the right path."

Matthew wanted to fully grasp this, and he tried to imagine what it must have been like at the NASA building when they were trying to solve this problem back on Earth. He wished they could go there now so he could truly experience it.

"Samuel, how exactly did it work?" Matthew probed. "How did they even go about trying to generate ideas? Where did they even start?"

Samuel's excitement grew as Matthew demonstrated his continuous desire to open himself up to more truths. "I'm sure they took inventory of what materials the astronauts had on the ship as a starting point," Samuel noted. "The team of engineers on Earth had no idea at first how they would do this, but they had faith and perseverance to solve this problem. To them, failure was never an option because of what was at stake. The answer was shrouded in a fog of uncertainty, but all it takes is one inspired thought which can then lead to numerous ideas, ultimately leading them to a solution."

Samuel paused a moment as he saw the familiar contemplative expression adorning Matthew's face. "Do you suppose their troubles were over then?" asked Samuel, wanting to help Matthew realize the severity of the astronauts' plight.

"I'm guessing, no," Matthew replied as he learned a long time ago that Samuel's lessons often contained multiple levels.

"Not by a long shot," noted Samuel. "They had to conserve energy with only one liquid oxygen tank left, so they shut down almost all of the electronics, including the systems which provided heat to the ship."

Matthew thought about that for a second and realized how cold space must really be. "It must have been freezing in there," Matthew commented.

"It was so cold, Matthew, they could see their breath," Samuel responded. "Not only that, once they did turn the power back on, they ran the risk of short circuiting the electronic equipment, which was yet another risk of certain death."

"In the end, though, everything worked out fine," Matthew stated with a hint of uncertain hope in his voice as he reached within his memory again to recall the outcome.

"They faced so many obstacles, so many challenges mentally and physically whereby the slightest mishap or miscalculation could lead to certain tragedy," Samuel exclaimed. "In the end though, Matthew, their resolve prevailed. Their faith in themselves, each other, in the team of engineers and their faith in the unseen enabled their safe return to Earth."

Matthew let out a small breath of relief as he just became aware of the tension within his body as he thought of the hair-raising situations the astronauts were faced with.

"Going back to your question, Matthew, the reason we are here is for you to witness the miracle of the unseen," Samuel continued. "The crew and NASA team were not alone in their quest to save these men."

Matthew's head tilted slightly as he gave Samuel his full attention. "What do you mean?" he asked.

"Take a look," Samuel instructed as he raised his left hand and motioned toward the Earth.

Matthew saw a beam of white light suddenly appear from the direction of Earth. He turned his head to adjust his line of vision directly toward the bright blue planet. The pure, white beam shot skyward beyond the planet's atmosphere. It was very similar to that of a beacon but with a greater intensity and purity. Then Matthew saw yet another beam of light shoot into space. Both beams originated from the North American region of the globe. Although it was difficult to tell from their current vantage point, the land mass from which the beams were emitting their glow seemed to be coming from the United States. Much to Matthew's surprise, more beacons suddenly appeared as they projected and converged into a single point above the Earth. Within seconds, there seemed to be thousands of these lights filling the sky and illuminating the darkness of space surrounding the planet. Matthew was blown away by the beauty before them.

"What is that?" Matthew asked with awe.

"Those, Matthew, are the prayers of millions of people across the world," replied Samuel.

"Prayers?" Matthew repeated in disbelief as his eyes remained affixed to the scene before them. "How are those beams of light, prayers?"

"I really can't explain it right now. You need to experience it firsthand," answered his guide.

He engaged the transport without warning, and they sped toward Earth. Within seconds they were situated right next to the concentrated focal point of the white beams of light which now took on the form of a perfectly shaped sphere whose brilliance emitted a warmth unmatched by anything Matthew has ever experienced. Now that they were much closer, Matthew could see what appeared to be millions of golden light particles floating within the sphere of white light.

"Okay, Matthew," Samuel began. "I want you to reach out and touch the orb of light."

Samuel's statement caught Matthew off guard. He forced himself to look away from the sphere in order to shoot his guide a look that conveyed his trepidation. Yet, Matthew also felt an intense desire to comply with Samuel's instruction. Their eyes locked onto one another, and Samuel gave him a reassuring nod. Matthew was just getting used to entering people's chakras, but this seemed to be an entirely different proposition all together.

He then turned to face the orb again. It had grown even larger and brighter as it was now being fed by even more light beacons that continued to grow and expand before his eyes. Matthew then slowly stepped to the edge of the transport, lifted his right arm and reached out until his hand became fully engulfed in the sphere.

The sensation was unreal. The beauty of the light paled visually to the feelings and images that flooded his mind's eye and penetrated his soul. He felt incredible warmth enter his body.

The images that came to him were of people, thousands upon thousands of people who all had a singular focus in their minds and hearts. He saw them in churches of all faiths. He saw them in synagogues, mosques, candle light vigils outdoors, and even individuals praying within their homes. Some were clutching Bibles in prayer. Some were holding rosaries. Some focused on statues of religious figures Matthew didn't even recognize. Some were crying while pleading in desperation. Some felt a confident peace as they asked God for help.

The pace of these images increased as he not only took in who and where they were but also the feelings conveyed during these prayerful moments. Moments united on a global scale for the sake of a single purpose: bringing these men of Apollo 13 home. *Bring them home safely. Please, God, bring them home.*

Matthew sensed empathy, concern and anxiety among the millions engaged in these prayers. Then he felt a strong sense of projection. A projection of feelings and emotions sent to others outside themselves. Every single person was sending strength, courage and hope to the astronauts of Apollo 13 and to their loved ones, asking God to aid the efforts of all those involved in returning these men home safely.

It was unreal. Matthew's own emotional state became utterly over whelmed. *My God!* Matthew thought to himself. *Millions of people praying for these men whom they don't even know.* Then Matthew felt something else come through. It was a sense of connection. A connection through a unity of brotherhood and humanity. No matter the race, religion or nationality, they were praying for their fellow human beings. They were all so desperately hoping these men would be okay.

Matthew fell to his knees sobbing, and in doing so, his hand pulled away from the orb of light. His tears, however, were not out of sadness but out of the sheer beauty of this miraculous event. He felt the overwhelming sense of love. Love was at the heart of it all and was the driving force behind the purity of the lights which streamed across the Earth's atmosphere into this single focal point.

But why? Matthew suddenly thought amidst the overpowering emotions he now felt. *Why was it focused on a single orb hovering above the Earth?* The power of the experience would forever change him. It was as though he had just touched something that was truly divine. It was though he reached up and touched the face of God.

Samuel walked over to Matthew, knelt down to his left, and placed his right hand gently on Matthew's back. "It's amazing, Matthew," Samuel spoke softly, aware that Matthew was overwhelmed and immobilized.

Matthew regained his composure and looked up at Samuel with tear-filled eyes.

"It's amazing how humanity is capable of such incredible beauty," Samuel began. "How crises such as this can unite your kind in pursuit of an ultimate good. A good that calls for the miraculous through focused prayer and faith which can change the outcome of events or circumstances seemingly outside of their control."

Matthew then glanced back at the Earth, the beacons of light, and the ever-growing sphere. He stared at the scene before him as his guide continued to explain.

"As the word spread across the United States and then across the world, people began to pray," Samuel explained. "They prayed for God to return them safely home. They prayed for the astronauts to be brave and courageous. They prayed that these men and their loved ones not lose faith. They prayed for all those working around the clock at Mission Control to do everything in their power to bring them back safe and sound."

Matthew looked back at the orb of light and again at Samuel in order to ask his guide the next question that came to mind. "How is it that we can actually 'see' these prayers?" Matthew inquired softly in his overwhelmed emotional state.

Samuel glanced at the sphere himself as he thought of the best approach to explain the phenomenon to his pupil. "This realm that we have entered and traveled in has expanded your awareness," Samuel replied. "You have opened your mind and spirit, thereby taking some brave steps to open yourself to experience and see infinite possibilities. This heightened perception actually includes seeing things beyond what you might not physically perceive. These prayers powered by sincere and loving hearts possess a real energy and as you continue to tap into your true potential, you can begin to see things that you felt impossible."

Matthew gave Samuel a blank stare of disbelief as he pondered his teacher's response.

Determined to keep Matthew engaged and pull himself back to the present, Samuel helped him to his feet and levied yet another question to the young man.

"What did you notice this time as we entered the portal that brought us here?" asked Samuel to address Matthew's earlier observations.

Trying to bring his mental state into focus, Matthew paused a few moments to recollect his prior experiences. "I noticed that we entered each portal from different positions and at different speeds," Matthew replied as he wiped away his tears with his right shoulder.

"Yes, Matthew," Samuel encouraged. "What about this *last* experience?"

Matthew thought back again to that specific moment when they entered the last portal, and the images came flooding back.

"When we went through the last gateway so fast, the opposite of what I expected happened," Matthew commented. "Time and motion seemed to slow down. My eye sight wasn't blurred or blinded like all the times before but instead, I could still see you standing there on the transport. The thing is, though, I didn't see you as I normally do."

Samuel turned to his right to directly face Matthew. "Go on, Matthew," Samuel prompted. "What did you see that wasn't 'normal?'"

"I could see your physical body outlined by some kind of glowing light," Matthew replied. "A light of different colors. It was almost like I saw your energy signature, or spirit or something."

Samuel gave Matthew yet another affirming smile. "There is a reason why I took us into the gateways at different positions and speeds," Samuel explained. "It's to help you understand that to grow and expand our knowledge of life and the Universe, we must consider all angles or viewpoints. It can help open you up to new possibilities. Perceiving different situations gives us new information and experiences all the time. When we entered the last portal, you caught a glimpse of the real me and the real you. We are so much more than our physical bodies. As people enter Level Three of the Spirit of faith, and eventually knowledge, they begin to reach beyond themselves and tap into something much bigger."

Samuel turned and motioned with his left arm toward Earth.

"Those beacons of light, Matthew, represent the pure energy emitted from the prayers and meditation of all those spirits concerned for the astronauts," Samuel continued. "Their focused thoughts and strong emotions are generating a powerful energy signal that you can now see with your new abilities. Their sincerity and genuine heartfelt concern is why the white beams of light appear so pure."

Matthew looked back at the beams and the sphere again as he continued to appreciate its sheer beauty and perfection. The question that started this whole new experience came to mind again, and he then looked back at Samuel for the answer.

"So, how does God fit into this equation?" Matthew asked.

"It's simple," Samuel replied. "God gave humanity this ability. He gave you this power, the potential to discover it and ultimately use it, once you know you have it!"

Samuel placed both hands on Matthew's shoulders as he looked directly into his eyes to emphasize the next critical point. "God is love, and when we return to that state of love, miraculous things happen. Now Matthew, watch what happens next," Samuel instructed as he moved towards the back of the hover disc positioning himself directly behind Matthew. It was clear Samuel intended to give him an unobstructed view of the upcoming event.

Matthew turned his attention again toward mother Earth, which shined more beautifully by the spectacular light show that now engulfed it. Then, Matthew quickly realized the purpose of Samuel's action. More beams of light appeared all over the globe and began to move and bend in unison, converging into the central sphere of light that Matthew had touched just moments ago. The additional lights enlarged the sphere even further, which expanded at a rapid rate. Within seconds, the orb exploded into a blinding flash, forcing Matthew to shield his eyes. Astonishingly, the explosion created two large beams of pure, white light that extended out of the sphere. One of the beams shot past their hover transport and directly engulfed the Apollo 13 spacecraft. Matthew could feel its warming energy causing him to enter an incredible state of bliss. He could feel the hope, resolve, perseverance, joy, faith and love all over again. The other large beam of white light was sent back toward Earth in the direction of the United States.

Matthew looked on both in disbelief and wonder as his spirit was never before lifted to such a heightened level of perception. Samuel then stepped forward to the navigational control, realizing that it was time to conclude this lesson.

"You see Matthew, all those involved in this crisis were not alone; they were aided by the thoughts and feelings of millions back on Earth," Samuel explained. "One beam engulfed the Apollo spaceship to aid the astronauts. The other beam was sent to the team of scientists and engineers on Earth to help them overcome the challenges before them that would save these brave men's lives. What seemed like an impossible task, hope, faith and love revealed a way. God enabled this through his creation of humanity and your connection to one another. The One gave you all such amazing abilities and power, especially once you learn to tap into it."

Finding himself unable to pull his gaze away from the miraculous beauty before him, Matthew cleared the emotional lump within his throat before speaking. "I'm seeing a miracle in action, aren't I?" Matthew asked as the tears of joy welled up in his eyes.

Samuel smiled. "Yes, you are, Matthew," he responded in a heartfelt voice. "Because all those on Earth praying, were focused on a single, noble endpoint. An endpoint founded in goodness and love, my young friend. Such amazing, unseen miracles are possible."

Samuel placed his hand on the navigation ball, but just before he engaged the hover disc, he turned his head slightly in Matthew's direction to convey one more point to his pupil. "But it's so much more than that, Matthew," Samuel continued with a hint of excitement in his voice. "You have no idea what amazing things still await you if you choose to continue down this path and uncover your destiny."

Samuel turned his head further in order to see Matthew in full view. "And not only that, the amazing secrets that will be revealed to you next," Samuel encouraged.

In a flash, all beams of white light dissipated. Matthew wasn't thinking of any destiny for himself at that moment but merely savoring the beauty of this amazing experience that had penetrated his spirit.

"Kinda makes you wonder," Matthew began.

"Wonder what?" Samuel asked curiously.

"What other problems we could solve if we did this all the time," Matthew stated as his thoughts drifted toward war, famine, disease, poverty and numerous other challenges that has plagued mankind's existence on Earth.

He's getting so close! Samuel thought to himself. There was no mistaking what must come next. "Are you ready to move on to Level Four?" Samuel inquired.

Matthew took a deep breath, looked at his guide and nodded.

Samuel rotated their craft and headed back toward the portal from which they had originally entered the miracle that was Apollo 13.

CHAPTER 11

AWARENESS

The hovercraft exited the Apollo gateway and emerged yet again within the web of ribbons in space-time. Matthew was still carrying the residual feelings of joy, happiness and disbelief from the lessons learned from his Level Three experiences. He was lost in a meditative peace and was oblivious to the next ribbon Samuel had chosen. The web continued its expansion as ribbons made new connections to portals throughout the infinite expanse of the continuum. There were new threads flying all around them. Matthew was distracted at the moment as he pondered the lessons Samuel had exposed to him thus far.

His mentor had found a way, however, to penetrate Matthew's introspection as he guided their transport into the portal. They emerged on the other side to a most puzzling sight. They were apparently within an enclosed arena at the center of which was a boxing ring. Even more peculiar was the fact that the building was empty with the exception of two men sparring within the ring. Having emerged from the gateway towards the upper most deck of the arena, Samuel began to move the transport slowly down the sloping design of the seating in order to view this private boxing match. As they descended, Matthew carefully watched the two men jab, counter jab, and dance around the ring looking for just the right opportunity to land a crucial blow. Their movements were fluid and almost synchronized as though the event had been entirely choreographed. The hovercraft had reached the edge of the ring and Samuel elevated the transport to improve their view.

From a closer vantage point, Matthew observed they were both white males of similar height and even physical stature. They weren't overly muscular as one would expect of a professional boxer but in decent shape. One of the men had red hair and both had fair skin. In fact, the two men seemed to be perfectly matched as though they were a mirror image of one another except for one obvious peculiarity. One of the boxers was wearing a ski mask pulled down over his head with the customary holes only for the eyes and nose.

"What is this?" Matthew asked, greatly confused. "Why are we here watching this boxing match, and why the heck is one of them wearing a ski mask?"

"I'm sorry?" replied Samuel, apparently enjoying the match so much that he was unable to draw his gaze away from the boxers to look in Matthew's direction.

"Don't you see it?" Matthew inquired.

"See what?" responded Samuel.

"Why is one of them wearing a ski mask?" Matthew asked again. "Also, where is the crowd?"

"Don't worry, Matthew. You'll get your answers soon," Samuel replied as he was still quite focused on the match itself.

"Who are they?" Matthew asked now, wanting to skip over his prior questions in hopes Samuel might answer that one directly.

"His name is Ronald," Samuel noted. "He is the man boxing in the center of the ring."

"Which one is Ronald?" Matthew asked, frustrated as he glanced back at Samuel. "The one with the mask, or without?"

"Yes," Samuel answered. "Now watch closely."

Samuel motioned toward the ring re-directing Matthew's attention to the boxers before them. Suddenly, the unmasked fighter landed a mighty right hook to the chin of his opponent. The blow stunned the masked boxer with such force that he was catapulted backwards landing flat on his back. He appeared to be knocked out cold, as he lay motionless on the floor mat.

Matthew took a step forward to the edge of the hover disc, eager to observe the next sequence of events, curious to see if the downed boxer was harmed. Interestingly, however, the victorious fighter then walked to his opponent and knelt down beside him. Matthew's intense focus heightened at the unexpected twist. The victor then pulled off his red boxing gloves and placed them on the floor of the ring. He reached down with his left hand, grabbed the top of the ski mask and with a quick motion, pulled off the mask.

Matthew was stunned by what he now saw. The newly unmasked boxer looked identical to the man who knelt beside him. The two men didn't just look similar but appeared to be identical twins. Still closely studying the faces of both men, Matthew asked the next obvious question.

"Are they twin brothers or something?" Matthew inquired.

"No, Matthew," Samuel replied. "I already told you that this is Ronald."

"You mean, they both are named Ronald, right?" Matthew asked, attempting to make logical sense of it all. Matthew wondered why he would even attempt to be rational when so many things he had witnessed thus far transcended logical observation at first glance.

"Matthew, you must stop trying to lead with the limited view of what you perceive as logical or possible from your old paradigms but continue to open your mind to infinite possibilities," Samuel exclaimed. "What you are seeing is a mirror image of the same person."

Suddenly, the environment began to change. Noticing some strange fluctuations in the lighting of the arena, Matthew quickly took in a three-hundred-sixty degree view of their current surroundings. The empty seats began to fade away, and the downward sloping structure of the arena flattened as though someone were pushing the floor up to create an even walking surface. Finally, the walls themselves began to collapse inward as the once-large sports facility closed in on them.

Matthew then turned his view once again to the two boxers in the ring, but much to his surprise, the boxing ring was gone. In its place stood a square wooden kitchen table. Sitting at this table on a matching spindle chair was Ronald, who was now alone. The physical environment had transformed, and they now found themselves hovering in an ordinary kitchen.

"What just happened?" Matthew asked slowly and deliberately.

"Well, similar to our experience with Kate, we are seeing a glimpse into the mind of our new friend, Ronald, who has just ever so effectively demonstrated Level Four of the Spirit," Samuel succinctly stated. "The ribbon, upon which we followed into this gateway to this very moment, was a key decision point in Ronald's life. He has been engaged in an intense battle from which he has emerged victorious."

"A battle?" Matthew repeated with utter confusion. "A battle with whom and over what?"

"Matthew, I think you know what must come next," Samuel said as he motioned in Ronald's direction.

Matthew looked back at Samuel. His guide certainly has shown consistency in how he has enabled Matthew to "absorb" these new teachings. He stepped off the transport and onto the yellow-tiled kitchen floor to the right of the table. He walked over to Ronald, who was of average height from what Matthew could tell, had receding red hair, fair skin, green eyes and most likely in his early to mid-thirties. Matthew then placed his left hand on Ronald's right shoulder. Immediately, Matthew saw the chakra begin to glow and open between Ronald's eyes. As its brightness expanded, the intensity of the first emotion and thought was quite clear. Ronald was incredibly conflicted.

Within Ronald's chakra, Matthew absorbed his host's thoughts and feelings as they entered his awareness at a maddening pace. The young man realized how quickly his abilities had increased, because he found it much easier to follow and process them, despite the speed with which they flooded his consciousness.

Suddenly, one scene within Ronald's mind came into focus. Matthew could see Ronald sitting at a cubicle which he could only assume was his work place. Then his thoughts focused further, and his host was actually talking to himself.

"Come on, Ron! What are you waiting for?! Everything will be fine. You've got everything ready to go. I can't do this anymore. I'm dying a little bit every damn day!"

Matthew then felt a surge of emotion from Ron at that moment. Ron felt trapped, but he was trying to suppress those feelings to summon enough confidence to do something. Clearly, he was trying to give himself a pep talk.

The scene changed again, and Matthew quickly surmised he was retracing some past event that set the stage for why his host felt so much conflict. Within this new scene, Ron was sitting in his parked car in a vacant lot in front of a building with a "For Sale" sign posted. It was obviously some kind of business. Matthew paused for a moment, because there was something oddly familiar about the building. Yet another surge of emotion from Ron at that moment pulled Matthew's attention from the vague familiarity of the location. Matthew felt his host's excitement. Ron was feeling excited about a future filled with possibilities.

Possibilities of what? Matthew thought to himself as he tried to dig deeper into Ron's memories to discover the source.

Then the scene changed again as more events passed quickly within Ron's chakra. Matthew continued to observe as well as feel the corresponding mental and emotional states of his host along the way, a process Matthew quickly thought was both a curse and a blessing. A curse, because the intense nature of the feelings his hosts unknowingly shared were sometimes devastatingly painful. A blessing, because it helped him understand them in a way that would otherwise take years if he had known them personally.

The next scene slowed, and Ron was now sitting at his kitchen table again. He was busily filling out some paper work. Matthew couldn't exactly tell, but they appeared to be official forms of some kind. The young man focused more closely and realized it was a bank loan application. Matthew began to connect the dots.

Then the current scene was swept away by more thoughts, emotions, conversations with loved ones and images of pivotal events. The scenes continued to quickly change, but one in particular slowed down, allowing him to see Ron many years earlier when he was merely a child of eight or nine. It definitely was a significant moment within Ron's chakra that invoked a very strong emotion. Matthew saw him sitting in a booth in a restaurant. On the table sat a pizza and around the table with Ron was who Matthew presumed to be his family. His mother, father, two brothers and two sisters were all there with him. Ron was obviously the youngest of five children. They were all very happy as they laughed and talked with each other.

Matthew could feel why this memory was so significant to Ron because of the emotions associated with it. He could feel the warmth and joy within his host. He could feel the peace and safety of all being together. He felt the incredible connection with each other and the familial love they shared.

Once again, Matthew was swept away within Ron's chakra as the images and events fast forwarded through his life at a maddening pace. Suddenly they stopped yet again. Ron couldn't have been more than eleven or twelve years of age. The scene was an outdoor basketball court. Ron was playing a game of one-on-one with a much larger boy with some of his peers watching the game. Matthew guessed that the larger boy must have been at least a three or four years older and as such, Ron was being dominated on the court. The older boy was having his way until there was a play where he ploughed Ron over causing him to fall flat on his back. The older boy taunted his younger opponent.

"You suck! You play like a pathetic little girl."

The other kids watching let out a laugh, causing Ron to feel sickening embarrassment. Matthew sensed Ron's pride shriveling with each cackle from the onlookers. The older and much larger kid had challenged him again. Ron just wanted to run away but tried to suppress the urge and summon the courage to resume their game.

Then Matthew saw another boy come into his peripheral vision. Matthew realized that something significant must have transpired in this particular memory of Ron's for it to linger like this.

"*Hey, Ralph!*" the newcomer said. "*Why don't you take me and my little brother on in a game of two-on-two. Choose anyone you want here to be your teammate.*"

Matthew turned his attention to the boy that just appeared, and it was unmistakable they were clearly brothers. He looked just like Ron with red hair and a round-shaped, freckled face. The boy had a similar build but taller.

Then Matthew felt it. There was a shift within Ron mentally and emotionally. Just seconds ago, he was flat on his back, feeling completely beaten down and dejected. Then the sudden appearance of his older brother changed everything. Matthew felt confidence return within his host as though he had been thrown a life vest and the odds had turned in his favor. It felt like a strong wind inflated Ron's sails. Matthew sensed the incredible connection on the court between the two brothers as they shared a glance and Ron's brother cracked a brief smile.

The next few moments of the scene played out in a manner that Matthew found most inspiring. The two brothers were unstoppable. They managed to anticipate each other's moves and those of their opponents with absolute ease. Matthew could tell the pair spent countless hours playing basketball together, and it definitely showed. The two brothers gave their opponents a good old-fashioned beat down. When the game ended, Ron's brother approached him and ruffled his hair.

"*That was pretty brave, little brother, taking on that asshole one-on-one. But you need to believe in yourself. Do you know why?*"

Ron shook his head in response.

"*Because I believe in you. You could have taken him on and beaten him without me, Ronnie. Just remember that. Believe in yourself, little brother.*"

Matthew could feel the swell of pride within Ron as well as the appreciation and respect toward his brother, how he always had Ron's back without fail.

The scene was swept away as quickly as it appeared, replaced by another significant moment in Ron's life. He was standing in front of a casket. Ron couldn't have been more than thirteen or fourteen years old. It was the eldest brother, who moments ago Matthew saw alive and vibrant playing basketball with his younger brother. Ron stood there with tears streaming down his face.

Matthew's heart sank. The depth of pain was unbearable. Then Ron's memories came flooding into his mind while standing there looking at his brother's lifeless body. He could not have been more than sixteen or seventeen years old at the time of death. Memories of when they were younger played back: Boys playing football in the backyard with their neighbors; the countless hours playing basketball with the hoop affixed to a backyard tree; the excitement they collectively shared as a family of five children waking up on Christmas morning.

Those memories and many more flashed across the landscape of Ron's mind. With each one, it was like a thousand daggers plunging into his heart which only deepened the sense of loss that came with such relentless fervor. The grief was overpowering, inescapable. Matthew's knees buckled as he looked for a way out of absorbing it all.

He didn't want to be there anymore. He just couldn't bear it. He likened it to the pain he felt with the breakup of the slave family. An unimaginable sorrow, such an incredible sense of loss. Ron was totally despondent as he could not fathom life without one of his older siblings. His oldest brother, who was so important in his young life, was now gone. An empty chair stood at the kitchen table where he once sat. How fragile life truly is and how those whom we love so deeply could be here one day and gone the next.

Matthew pinpointed the cause of death within Ron's chakra and memories. A drunk driver killed his brother in a car accident. Matthew was beside himself in anger and sadness. He was not only drowning in the pain of his host but in anger at the utter waste of an incredible life. Ron's brother had been taken from their family in an instant that would forever change their lives. At that moment, Matthew felt that if the person who caused this were standing there before him, he would plunge his fist into their chest and rip out their heart. Because that's how Ron felt, that his heart had been ripped out with the loss of his older brother.

As quickly as the scene appeared, it was whisked away as more flashes of his host's life events bombarded Matthew. He saw and felt images of Ron's remaining adolescent years, college life and young adulthood. Matthew was so thankful to be able to move beyond the tragic event of Ron's brother's death, but the feelings of loss haunted him nonetheless. To lose a sibling, especially at such a young age, was unfathomable to Matthew as he continued to feel Ron's immense pain plaguing him for years. He felt a void for which there was no simple remedy but only time could heal. Matthew wanted to escape this horrible feeling but resisted the temptation to break the connection with his host, because he knew there was still more to learn.

Matthew decided to dig deeper, trying to break through the pain. He sensed something incredibly powerful and beautiful, deep within Ronald. Matthew found it as more images and emotions came to the forefront. It held an undertone of strength, courage and faith whose foundation was that of pure love.

It was the memories and feelings within Ron toward his family. His devoted parents were the foundation that Ron always relied upon and of course his three older surviving siblings. They were there for each other, and their brother's death only deepened the connection and appreciation for one another. Matthew sensed there were countless hours of tears shed in one another's arms to help them all move beyond the tragedy. They banned together throughout the years as they drew even closer and shared in their major life events. They all eventually married, and some started families of their own. Matthew felt the sense of loss all over again when their father passed away from cancer and again when their mother succumbed to the debilitating disease of

Alzheimer's. Matthew not only knew Ron at this deep level but also the members of his family through Ron's eyes.

The images and feelings continued to flood Matthew's awareness as he felt all the major joys and tragedies of life through his host's experience. But through it all, Matthew felt within Ron this net of interconnectedness with his family as their names and faces appeared before him. The matriarch and patriarch of the family were Theresa and Ed. He then saw the faces and names of Ron's siblings, their spouses and their children. There was Di, Edward Henry, Jonathan, Jessica and Francesca. He saw Karen, Michael, Jon, Diane, Nick, Eddie Joe and Gina. Then another came into focus. It was Ron's cousin Jane whom he admired so much for her strength and was so instrumental in helping him through his extremely difficult divorce. There were the powerful loving prayers of his aunt Jane as well numerous other friends and extended family providing him strength throughout all of life's difficulties. It served as a constant reminder to Ron, never to lose hope and to maintain his faith. Matthew witnessed the countless hours around the dinner table as this family shared home cooked meals, stories, life experiences and lots of laughter. It was a safety net where Ron always felt loved and supported because they were always there for each other.

Matthew could relate, for that was his own experience with his family whom he loved and now appreciated more than ever. Then he became aware how much he missed them.

The swirling imagery within Ron's chakra slowed a final time as Matthew then saw him sitting at his kitchen table alone. He then understood very clearly Ron's inner conflict that Matthew initially sensed upon entering his chakra.

My God! Am I crazy?! Ron thought to himself. *I'm about to quit my job and leave my company. Ten years. Can I walk away? Can I really walk in tomorrow and quit?*

Matthew felt the powerful feeling of doubt gain a foothold within Ronald's mind.

Jesus, I can't do this! How can I quit this stable job and start my own business? I should just keep the fifty thousand dollars I've saved and invest it or something. I could lose it all, not to mention the loan. My God, two hundred thousand dollars of debt! A pizza parlor? Seriously, Ron?

Matthew felt a knot form within his stomach, because that's how Ron was feeling at that very moment. His host was being consumed by stress, uncertainty and fear.

But then Matthew sensed a shift within Ron.

Ron then stood up, went to the corner of his kitchen where a black leather briefcase stood on the tile floor. He bent down and pulled out a yellow folder. Ron returned to the kitchen table and sat back down as he opened it. He pulled out some pictures of the building that Matthew had just seen in a previous vision. He also looked at his application for the bank loan that was accompanied by a letter of approval. Matthew noticed something else. It was another photo within the file that Ron immediately picked up.

It was a picture of his entire family a long time ago when they were mere children sitting around a semi-circular booth at a restaurant. The same scene Matthew had witnessed moments ago now captured in a photo that his host clearly treasured. They were all there in the picture adorning huge smiles. All the children were leaning into one another, crammed into a tiny space amidst the spacious booth. Matthew felt a brief reprieve from the stress over Ronald's contemplative string of thoughts as it was replaced by this incredible warm feeling invoked by this simple photo from the past.

Matthew now better understood the source of Ron's dream of owning his own pizza business. Why he wanted to risk everything. It was so clear.

Ron's passion was about family and togetherness. Seeing other families share what he experienced as a child and having a fun place in the community to gather. For others to form the kind of memories that would forever shape people's lives in a positive way and never forget the beauty of such moments. Especially when tragedies happen in life and everything can change in an instant, just like what happened to him at an all-too-young age.

To never take anything or anyone for granted because of that very fact.

It was about love.

It was also about leading a life that he chose and to follow his passion while earning a living at something that he wanted to do.

Matthew then felt another shift within his host.

Dream Ronnie. Dream! Why not? Why not me? Why can't I do this? What if! I NEED to do this. I'm letting my thoughts get carried away.

Ron looked down at the picture of his family again, and Matthew sensed a surge of confidence within his host. Matthew now understood how the tight connection with his family would now be his source of strength to take that leap of faith. Thoughts of another person came into Ron's mind. It was an incredibly dear friend and influential person from his work place. Her name was Karen, and she had been with him through thick and thin. She had been so encouraging and inspiring throughout this whole process, especially given the tragedies of her own life she had to overcome. Ron then realized how ridiculously blessed he truly was, because he was surrounded by so much unconditional love and support. A powerful thought then emerged that would push Ron onward toward the summit of his dream. All of these amazing and beautiful people in his life believed in him, and it was time he believed in himself. Ron put the picture down and looked out the window where he saw the sun peering through.

"*I can't let fear and negativity control me anymore,*" Ron whispered to himself. "*I won't die a slow death at a job I hate. God damn it, Ron, you can do this now. STOP doubting and start DOING!*"

Ron then looked upward. "*Help me brother! I need your strength.*"

Then it was as though his brother answered him from beyond as a word came into Ron's stream of consciousness.

Live. Live, brother. Just live.

Matthew felt the swell of confidence continue to grow within his host. All those doubtful and negative feelings quickly dissipated. Matthew could sense that Ron's connection to his deceased brother was somehow still present. That he had been resurrected in some way and made his presence felt. Like a confident loving hand upon Ron's shoulder.

At that moment, Ronald delivered the "knock out" punch to his negative line of thinking. A blow to obliterate his fear and to believe in himself again just as his brother had reminded him so many years before.

Matthew felt a rush of adrenaline within himself in reaction to Ronald's personal victory. The excitement of taking a risk and the leap of faith to do so. To summon the courage to take that step in pursuit of a dream. To be free.

Matthew now understood what happened. He now understood what he witnessed upon entering the portal and who Ronald was "boxing." He was engaged in a battle with himself. The boxing ring was merely a manifestation of his thoughts and emotions at this poignant time where Ron was faced with a decision that would forever change the direction of his life.

Matthew then felt the familiar pull upon his shoulder as Samuel called him back from within Ronald's chakra. It was time to leave.

As usual, Matthew opened his eyes while on the ground. He was laying on his side, not recalling how he ended up there, but at least the disorientation wasn't nearly as strong this time.

"So, Matthew, tell me what insights have you gained from our new friend," Samuel inquired as he knelt down to help Matthew sit up.

Matthew took a deep breath to clear his mind, closed his eyes, and slowly moved his head around in a circular motion to stretch his neck.

"I now understand why we saw Ron boxing when we entered the gateway," Matthew began.

"Why is that?" Samuel inquired.

"Ron was in a struggle," Matthew replied.

Samuel nodded affirmatively. "A struggle with what?"

"A struggle within himself," Matthew replied. "He was in a battle with his own mind. Ron was trying to overcome his negative thoughts, and that was the masked version of himself in the ring."

"And what was the one key, undercurrent driving those thoughts?" Samuel asked intensely.

Matthew knew immediately. Not on an intellectual level, but an emotional one due to his experiences within Ronald's chakra.

"Fear," Matthew simply replied. "It began to overwhelm him and cause him to doubt. It was shaking his confidence. It was almost like the fearful part of his mind was trying to gain control."

"Yes, Matthew!" Samuel said excitedly. "But what happened?"

Matthew paused for a moment and looked directly at Ron sitting motionless at the kitchen table.

"He caught himself, Samuel," Matthew noted. "He began to recognize that his line of thinking was taking his mind into a dark place of fear and doubt. But then, he found the inner strength and mental discipline to suppress those dark thoughts and focus on his goal. To focus on his passion and ultimately, his dream. To believe in himself."

Samuel gave his pupil a huge approving smile. "Excellent, Matthew," Samuel continued. "What you witnessed within Ron was an example of Level Four of the Spirit."

Matthew thought about how one could quickly synopsize his experience in relation to the fourth level. Before he could conjure up what he thought Level Four pertained to, however, his guide let him in on the secret.

"Level Four of the Spirit is Self-Awareness," Samuel exclaimed. "Overcoming negative thoughts, emotions and of course, the associated fear which potentially holds us back in pursuit of our dreams, requires the spirit to be self-aware."

"Like what you said about monitoring our thoughts?" Matthew.

"Yes, exactly," Samuel replied. "As a being moves into Level Four of the Spirit, they begin to train and discipline themselves to monitor their thoughts. It is as though they guard themselves from wrong thinking, which can prevent them from realizing their full potential. The power of negative thinking or emotions like fear, jealousy, resentment or anger can actually stop you from accomplishing anything *before* you even start! It can stop you from growing and evolving." Samuel paused a moment as he noticed Matthew look away from him and back at Ronald, continuing to process the lesson at hand.

"Those who set out to achieve their dreams, Matthew, must go through the first three Levels of the Spirit, but it's Level Four which guides them through potentially rough waters along their journey," Samuel continued. "Anyone who sets out to achieve something specific in life or to push themselves to new levels of growth, may encounter significant obstacles, but those within Level Four don't let their minds run away in negativity. They don't give up. They persevere and can only do so when they possess the right mindset."

Matthew looked back at Samuel as his last statement struck a chord within the young man.

"You should know the power of letting the mind 'run away' with a thought pattern which may spiral out of control," commented Samuel.

Matthew knew immediately what his guide was referring to as thoughts of his jungle scene in search of the chest and key came to mind. Samuel could tell by the expression on Matthew's face the connection his pupil just successfully made.

"When I gave you a challenge, you immediately associated the word 'challenge' to a difficult task," Samuel explained. "Since we were within the power of your own mind to create your reality at that moment, your mind chose what you believed to be one of the most difficult terrains to search for the chest and key in. Then what happened?"

"It got worse as it went on," Matthew replied. "I started having more problems and even bigger challenges."

"Exactly, Matthew," Samuel confirmed. "Your mind and the scene it created began to run away from you. I helped you center yourself, channel your thinking, and brought back some order and discipline to your thoughts."

"You have heard of the great spiritual teacher, Buddha, haven't you?" asked Samuel.

"Yes," replied Matthew.

"Buddha was once quoted as saying, 'All that we are is a result of what we have thought,'" Samuel commented. "The human mind, Matthew, is an incredibly powerful thing, a power that humanity is only now beginning to scratch the surface in understanding."

Matthew looked away from his guide back toward Ron who was still sitting at the kitchen table. He noticed the expression upon Ron's face changing from worrisome and anguished to one of peace. In fact, Matthew saw the formation of a slight smile. He realized the moment when Ron took control of his thoughts, appearing as a knock out to the masked opponent in his mind, directly corresponded to the reassuring peace and positive emotions that Ron now felt.

"Matthew, I think you are beginning to realize that the expression 'attitude is everything' has a very deep and profound truth within the realities of the human mind," Samuel exclaimed. "Those who possess defeated thoughts before they embark on any task, great or small, will surely create a self-fulfilling prophesy of failure."

Matthew realized how right Samuel was about that often-used expression, as thoughts of his own life experiences skirted across his mind.

"Those, on the other hand, who have progressed through the first three Levels of the Spirit and enter Level Four, will have faith and knowledge as weapons to combat any negative thinking. They do not allow their mind to control them but rather they control it!"

The notion of letting his mind control him terrified Matthew as the dark memory of a time in his life suddenly emerged before he could suppress it.

Samuel noticed the quick shift in Matthew, for he knew what the young man was suppressing, but the guide also knew that now wasn't the time to address it, so he continued the lesson.

"Everyone has dreams, Matthew," continued Samuel. "No matter how grandiose or small they may seem, whether it be interstellar travel or starting your own business. It comes from the same source."

Matthew looked directly at Samuel as his words continued to penetrate deep into his own understanding. He began to experience the holistic intelligence that Samuel referenced to earlier. This went well beyond the intellectual mind, as it encompasses something so much bigger.

"The human spirit," Matthew spoke softly.

Samuel placed his right hand upon Matthew's left shoulder and gave his pupil a reassuring squeeze. "Yes, Matthew," Samuel affirmed. "The human spirit is what propels us to move beyond ourselves or external influences, to move beyond our fears, many of which are deep-seated issues we may have carried since childhood. But the self-aware spirit recognizes the desire to be free, to summon the courage to move forward and to have that faith to navigate difficult times. Of course, this can also mean we must confront our personal demons. It is embedded in every decision of every moment in every step that takes us forward in a positive direction of growth, Matthew, no matter how seemingly large or small. Each step forward is in and of itself a triumph as we move toward our desired destiny."

Matthew's understanding of Samuel's words seemed to be much easier than he would have ever anticipated. He felt that he was grasping the messages contained within these lessons at a much deeper level. Once again, his only explanation came from his experiences contained within the chakra's of his hosts as the only plausible explanation to truly absorb the whole truth of the lessons.

To understand something intellectually is one thing. To understand something through emotion is even more powerful.

"Samuel?" Matthew began. "There was something very familiar to me about the building I saw within Ron's chakra that he planned to buy for his business."

Samuel smiled.

"It should, Matthew, since you have been there several times," Samuel replied.

Matthew shot his guide a look of confusion.

"Does the name 'Eddie's Family Parlor' ring a bell?" Samuel asked.

It took a few seconds for Matthew's brain to register what Samuel had just stated, and then it hit him like a bolt of lightning. He had been there many times over the years with his own family. In fact, for many years it became a family ritual on Friday nights when Matthew and his siblings were younger. It was their favorite place to go. It was so much fun with video games, air hockey, pool tables, and the pizza was so delicious. Then the astounding truth of this connection burst forth into Matthew's consciousness. How amazingly wise Samuel was to choose a lesson to which he had such a strong emotional connection to himself.

"You, your family, friends and their families are the perfect examples of the types of people Ronald dreamt of attracting to his business," Samuel stated. "He held true to the vision, Matthew, and it became reality for our new friend as well as for you and many others over the years."

Matthew looked back one last time at Ron sitting there at his kitchen table, pondering those two little words, "what if," in the context of what may have never been.

What if Ron had never summoned the courage to pursue his dream?

What if Ron had let fear overcome him during that pivotal moment at his kitchen table?

What if Eddie's Family Parlor had never existed?

How many lives have been positively touched by Ron's dream?

How many new connections were formed within the space-time continuum because of what Ron accomplished?

It was almost mind-numbing, especially when he thought back to his own positive experiences and memories at Ron's parlor, because he had made it to the Fourth Level of the Spirit. Then Matthew's mind drifted to yet another question: How many other things never happened in this world because someone let their fear and negative thinking stop them from doing what they dreamt of?

"It's truly amazing isn't it, Matthew?" Samuel asked interrupting his student's stream of thoughts.

Matthew gave Samuel a raised brow.

"How the choice of one human being had such a positive, profound impact on so many others spanning so many years," Samuel commented. "Not only that, but all of these unsuspecting people didn't even realize the obstacles Ron overcame and how he truly allowed his spirit to triumph over his pain to navigate the challenges of life."

Matthew realized then how much gratitude he now has for Ron's personal triumph, and he actually felt a strong connection to him. Matthew realized that he actually felt incredibly proud of Ron.

"Okay, Matthew, it's now time to go," noted Samuel realizing it was now time to conclude this part of the lesson. Samuel then turned toward the transport still hovering within Ron's kitchen and was ready to step onto the platform when Matthew suddenly interrupted his forward motion.

"Wait, Samuel," Matthew blurted. He glanced one last time at Ron still sitting motionless at his kitchen table.

"What is it, my dear lad?" Samuel asked as he paused in response.

"There was something else I felt within Ron's chakra," Matthew stated.

"What's that?" Samuel inquired with great curiosity.

"Ron's connection to his brother was still very real and very present even *after* his death," Matthew said with great wonder as he continued to gaze upon Ron.

Samuel wasn't completely taken aback by his pupil's observation but still a little bit surprised that Matthew would bring this concept up so soon. He looked at Matthew with a sense of his own wonder that actually took Matthew by surprise.

"What?" Matthew asked. "Did I say something wrong?"

"Oh, Matthew, on the contrary," Samuel replied. "I am so incredibly proud of you and so excited about what lies ahead for us both."

Matthew's head tilted inquisitively at Samuel's response.

"We will come back to your question later, eager student," Samuel encouraged. "Trust me on this, okay?"

Matthew gave an affirmative nod. Of course he would trust Samuel, for he had earned it implicitly. There was one other question, however, on his mind about Ron's achievement that he hoped Samuel could address.

"Then can you answer this question?" Matthew inquired.

"I'll try," Samuel commented, not certain what would come out of his pupil's mouth.

"Why did Ron name his business, 'Eddie's Family Parlor,' and not after himself?" Matthew asked most curiously.

Just before stepping onto the transport, Samuel turned toward Matthew in order to address his student's question. "You already know the answer to that, Matthew," Samuel replied.

Matthew turned his attention away from Ron and looked back at his guide because he was right. Matthew did already know the answer.

Eddie was the name of Ron's brother whose life tragically ended too soon.

CHAPTER 12

POINT OF NO RETURN

Samuel engaged the navigation control, and their transport began to ascend vertically. Looking around them, Matthew was unable to see an exit portal. "Um, where are we exiting?" Matthew asked, slightly alarmed. He anticipated hitting the ceiling of Ron's kitchen.

"Look up," Samuel quipped.

Sure enough, as soon as Matthew looked toward the ceiling, he saw the now familiar view of the flowing energy field contained within the circular structure of each gateway. Samuel slowly guided the hovercraft into the portal, and they emerged on the other side. Matthew glanced behind them as they sped away from Ron's portal. He was now able to fully fathom the significance of Eddie's Family Parlor. Matthew could see hundreds of individual energy ribbons connecting to the gateway they had just exited, an indication of special moments and events that had taken place at this restaurant over the years. It was the only establishment of its kind in their small Indiana town and had become so much more than a place to meet and share a meal.

Matthew turned back around with a smile on his face again, thinking of all the fun times that he and his family had over the years. His thoughts then drifted to the Friday night get-togethers with his classmates after football or basketball games which forged enough incredibly fond memories to last a lifetime.

Did Ron know how many lives he touched because he moved through the first Four Levels of the Spirit? Matthew pondered if Ron truly could appreciate the significance of his personal triumph.

Ron had the courage to pursue his dream and took a leap of faith, which blossomed into courageous belief to stay the course despite any negativity he may have encountered. His accomplishment was especially impressive as he had won the inner battle against his own negativity.

"Are we moving on to Level Five now?" Matthew asked as his thoughts moved ahead.

"Not quite," replied Samuel. "We still have more to learn about Level Four."

Matthew felt a small twinge of impatience. He believed he was ready and had learned so much thus far. Why didn't Samuel feel he was ready?

"Where are we headed then?" inquired Matthew.

"Right here," replied Samuel as he slowed the transport to the next gateway.

Then another question occurred to Matthew. "How do you know which ribbon to follow, Samuel, and which gateway to enter?" he asked.

"I was wondering when you were going to ask me that," Samuel replied. "You will better understand once we get into Level Five, so hold that thought for now."

A small seed of frustration sprouted in Matthew's thoughts, but knowing more about self-awareness, he did his best to acknowledge it, take a deep breath, and continue to trust his guide.

The transport penetrated the flowing energy field of their next gateway as they exited the web-like continuum of space-time. Emerging on the other side, Matthew was taken aback by the severe environmental conditions. They were in the midst of a blinding snow storm. Not only that, but they apparently had landed on what appeared to be a mountain. The wind was incredibly intense, and the snow came at such a furious pace that Matthew could barely see anything. His face was being pelted by the rapidly-falling snow. The wind not only made it bitter cold but added a stinging sensation from the snow as it struck his cheeks. Folding his arms across his chest in an attempt preserve body heat, Matthew looked down at the floor of the hover disc and noticed that snow began to accumulate on their transport. The high winds also made talking a challenge.

"What is this?!" Matthew was mildly annoyed and yelled to be heard over the wind. "I can't see anything! Where are we now?"

"Why are you yelling?" Samuel asked.

"Because of all this!" Matthew responded as he motioned around with his right arm. Looking directly at Samuel, Matthew noticed that his guide didn't appear to be the least bit cold or bothered by the winter storm in any way. In fact, Matthew realized that there was absolutely no snow accumulating on Samuel's side of the hover disc.

"Hey!" Matthew protested. "Why am I the only one freezing and getting snowed on?!"

"Matthew, it's just like the slave dream we visited where you took a swim in the river," Samuel began. "As is always the case, your mind is creating your reality, my friend. Just like in all the other portals we have visited, we are merely observers. Your mind is convincing you that it must be cold, and you are simply going along without any conscious choice in the matter. You must discipline your mind and embrace what you know and not what you think is real."

"Oh, that's just great," Matthew responded as his teeth began to chatter. "Is this why we are here—for you to test me again?" He knew if that were the case, he had just failed yet again. Matthew didn't want to hang around the scene any longer. He longed to jump to the Fifth Level right now.

"That's not why we are here, Matthew, but it was a nice side lesson, don't you think?" Samuel said with a smirk. "The real reason is about half way down this snowy mountain."

Samuel engaged the transport yet again and guided it off the mountain top. They began to descend the side of the mountain blanketed by several feet of snow. Their vertical descent began to slow and surprisingly, the snowfall began to ease a bit. With the improved visibility, Matthew caught sight of a mountain climber. Samuel brought the hover craft to a full stop once they were approximately ten feet above the poor soul huddled on a ledge attempting to stay alive.

"What is she doing?" Matthew asked with a slight panic in his voice. "Why would she be so foolish as to start climbing a mountain in a snow storm? Does she have a death wish or something?"

Samuel glanced down the side of the mountain toward the climber.

"The person is a young woman, Matthew, and her name is Donna," Samuel replied. "No, she does not have a death wish. Once again, we are caught within her own mind as she moves along her personal journey of self-discovery."

"We have to help her!" Matthew demanded with great concern. "Lower the transport, and I will reach down and grab her."

"No, Matthew!" Samuel yelled. "This is her path. She must choose the way. People in her life have helped all they can, and it's time for her to stand up and make a choice. Besides, you know this isn't how it works."

Amidst all of the climbing and winter gear Donna was wearing, Matthew noticed that her back pack was attached to some ropes which hung down so far that he couldn't see where they led to. It was as though she was being weighted down on the mountain that she was struggling to climb.

"Choose what?" Matthew asked. "And what are those ropes hanging down from her back pack?"

"Matthew, self-awareness not only means monitoring your thoughts but also your emotions as well," Samuel continued. "They go hand in hand. It also means that you must sometimes let go of those things which hold us back."

Matthew was confused by Samuel's last statement, but his attention turned from his guide's comments as Donna suddenly lost her footing and slipped off the ledge she was attempting to climb. She landed about eight feet below with a force that caused her to cry out in excruciating pain.

"Samuel, we have to help her, damn it!" Matthew exclaimed even though his rational mind knew better of what these dream sequences truly represent. He wished he could at least free her from the tethered back pack to lighten her burden.

Matthew looked at Samuel and then back at Donna who was visibly writhing about on the snow-covered ledge in pain. Compelled to compensate for his own helplessness, Matthew stepped to the edge of the transport. Looking down to gauge her position, Matthew jumped as he aimed to land on the ledge where Donna lay.

"No, Matthew! Not yet! I need to prepare you first," yelled Samuel as he watched Matthew free-fall toward the mountain side.

Matthew landed about two feet from Donna to her right, but the force of the impact briefly knocked the wind out of him. Fortunately, the snow was deep enough to help cushion his fall, but Matthew instantly felt the sting of cold run through his body and the ensuing shock through his system. Trying to remain focused on the task at hand, Matthew scrambled to his feet and leaped to the aid of this stranded soul.

"Hey, lady! Are you alright?" Matthew asked, knowing full well there would likely be no response, but he still felt compelled to try.

He knelt down beside her and saw her face twisted in pain as tears ran down her cheeks. Snow continued to fall now at a maddening pace, and the wind blew with such force that the flakes periodically flew sideways. With no other course of action to take, Matthew thought that maybe he could try to at least help her to her feet. He reached down to grab her underneath her right arm, and then it happened. The familiar white light appeared from his host's forehead as Matthew quickly became engulfed within her chakra.

The first thing that struck Matthew was the intensity of her emotions as they flooded his consciousness. Most were of a painful nature as he tried to distinguish their source within her life. Matthew detected fear, of course, but there was more.

He sensed feelings of rejection, disappointment, unworthiness, a lack of self-confidence and then a very strong one came through.

Self-loathing.

Matthew buckled over in physical pain from the intensity of the exposure as the white light still shined brightly. Then the images of her life became slightly visible as the light started to fade. As with the others, Matthew began to see the life events that shaped Donna from early childhood and beyond. He saw her playing at parks, being read to by a woman who radiated a loving peacefulness. Matthew knew immediately that the woman was her mother. Donna, who was probably four or five years of age at the time, was sitting on her mother's lap listening to her mother read to her. Matthew felt the warmth of love and peace in that very moment contained within his host's chakra. It was a wonderful reprieve from the intense negative feelings he felt moments earlier.

But as quickly as it came, the scene faded and more images flashed across his vision. Then another image slowed down, coming into focus, and like a radio picking up signals from the airwaves, Matthew honed in on the emotions contained within this particular life experience.

It was intense sadness and an incredible feeling of loss. Matthew knew this feeling as he was still raw from his visit with Ron. Donna, who may have been no more than ten years old, was standing beside a casket and sobbing uncontrollably.

Her mother had died.

Then a man whom Matthew could sense was her father walked up and picked Donna up but she resisted. Kicking and screaming, Donna yelled, *"No, no, no! I won't leave her. Mommy! Mom! I need you!"* Donna screamed as her dad carried her away.

Matthew had to turn his eyes away from the scene, because the pain was too great to witness any further. His heart sunk, and his own eyes began to well up with tears. To lose a parent at such a young age struck a chord within himself which was something he never wanted to face. Matthew felt the desperation in young Donna. The need to cling. The need to find her mother. The need to have her peaceful presence and love back. The bleak emptiness now left within her little heart was overwhelming.

As quickly as the scene appeared, however, it dissipated. More images flew by once again from left to right as key events from Donna's life flashed into view. The emotions within these scenes penetrated his soul. They slowed again, and this time Donna appeared to be in her thirties.

Matthew found it odd that they had leapt so far ahead in her life. She was sitting in a coffee shop. A man was with her as they sat at a small table. He had salt and pepper hair worn just above the ear, and he was wearing black, rectangular, wire-rimmed glasses. The gentleman appeared to be an intelligent fellow, at least judging from his appearance. He wore a pair of tan dress slacks and a blue blazer. Two cups of coffee rested on the table, steam rising from each. Reaching into Donna's memories, Matthew drew out the man's name—Steven.

It was then that Matthew noticed Donna's shiny black hair, a trait he didn't perceive while on top of the mountain where he first found her, given she was wearing a ski mask. Matthew also noticed her amazingly beautiful blue eyes, a rarity considering her dark complexion. He stared into them for a moment as he began to appreciate the full extent of Donna's physical beauty.

"*Donna, please,*" Steven pleaded, desperation clearly in his voice. "*Please come with me.*"

"*But what if they don't like me?*" Donna replied.

"*My family will love you,*" Steve countered. "*It's time you met them. Please. I promise it will be okay.*"

Matthew walked over to the table to observe them more closely. He immediately noticed Donna's body language. Her arms were folded, her face down and she was slumping into her chair. Steve reached over to touch her arm. Matthew then felt the tension rising in her body as he did so.

"*What if they don't think I am good enough for you?*" she asked.

Matthew felt the insecurity within Donna. He felt her discomfort from Steve's touch. He felt her distrust and disbelief in herself. A strong feeling of unworthiness was present and a most powerful sense of self-loathing.

Then Matthew picked up something else. It was a wall, a wall of self-protection. He couldn't understand why it was present, but it was there nonetheless.

"Donna, trust me," Steven stated. *"They will see what I see."*

"Oh, really?" Donna said in disbelief. *"What's that?"*

"A beautiful, kind and loving woman," he stated gently. *"An incredibly amazing and special person. A person whom I love."*

As he spoke, Steven placed his index finger beneath her chin and gently lifted upward to engage Donna's eyes. Matthew felt her guardedness lessen a bit as their eyes locked. He could feel the warmth and sincerity coming from her suitor who clearly cared very deeply for her. Matthew could immediately sense that Steven was a special soul himself, a gentle and kind man.

Just as she was about to say yes, Matthew felt a resurgence of panic within Donna. She was beginning to pull away and erect the wall once again. She was beginning to let her thoughts and feelings get the better of her. Matthew then pinpointed the source. Donna had an intense fear of male intimacy.

"No!" Matthew said instinctively. "No, let him in damn it! Don't retreat!" Matthew pleaded as he stared at his host in a feeble and desperate attempt to communicate with her, in hopes he might alter her past.

Donna pulled her head back to disengage Steve's touch, swung her legs out from under the table, and began to stand up from her chair. Matthew could feel her fear continue to rise as she clearly began to retreat from the situation causing her discomfort.

What just happened? Matthew thought to himself.

The scene was whisked away, and more events flashed across Matthew's view, except there was something notably different this time. The scenes flashed by in the opposite direction, going from right to left. It was as though they were going back in time through Donna's life. Matthew sensed he knew the answer to what just happened with the man at the coffee shop. Why she retreated so quickly after flirting with the idea of accompanying Steven to meet his family.

A new scene slowed into view. It was teenage Donna this time. She was in a room, her bedroom, Matthew quickly surmised. She was crying into her pillow. Then a male figure appeared at her doorway, and Matthew sensed within his host that it was her father. He merely stood there wearing an angry expression. Matthew noticed he was holding a bottle in his right hand. Donna's father was a very large man. Just as tall as Matthew, well over six feet but with substantially more body mass. Matthew squinted as he attempted to make out what her father was holding. As the light in the scene fluctuated, he realized it was a bottle of whisky. Then the man spoke.

"Get up!" her father yelled. *"Get down here and make my dinner, you worthless piece of shit! You haven't amounted to anything, and you won't amount to anything ever!"*

He raised the bottle to his lips and took a swig.

Matthew felt the damage to Donna's emotional state as each word out of his mouth inflicted a sting of pain. The infusion of doubt and destruction to her spirit was over-powering. It was like a dagger thrust into her heart with each word. She wanted to curl up and die.

Matthew sensed that this systematic abuse must have been the prevailing presence in Donna's life for years since her mother died. The source of her strong sense of self-loathing became much clearer, why she had such distrust of Steven in the coffee shop and her fear of real intimacy.

Donna was still crying into her pillow when her father stepped into her room and walked over to her bed.

"Get up!" he yelled again.

He then grabbed her under her right arm and violently lifted her up out of the bed. As he forced her to her feet, he then pushed her to the ground where she landed on her side while striking her head against the wall adjacent to the door. Matthew then noticed her head was bleeding profusely. Matthew grabbed his own temple feeling the throbbing pain as if he had been thrown against the wall as well.

Her father then walked over to her and continued his verbal assault.

"You worthless piece of shit!" he continued. *"Get up and go to the kitchen and make my God-damn dinner!"*

Matthew then felt an emotional shift within Donna as she momentarily stopped crying and looked up at her father. Rage.

"I hate you," she said in the coldest tone she could muster.

She was clearly attempting to strike an emotional blow to the man who was supposed to be her protector. The man who was supposed to take on the role of two parents in her loving mother's absence. The person that was to help form her sense of self-worth, not to break it down. He was supposed to be there to support her and love her unconditionally. Matthew sensed a strong sense of betrayal from the frail, young girl. When your own parent, your own flesh and blood turns on you, it becomes the ultimate betrayal.

Matthew then sensed her longing, the longing for her father's love and approval. In spite of his horrific treatment, Donna couldn't still help but feel that need. She could feel that void in her life, and sadly, she hated herself for it.

Donna's father walked over to her. Their eyes locked as Donna forced herself up from the floor with her head bleeding, as neither was willing to back down. Then he began striking her repeatedly with his right hand. He struck her on both cheeks as his hand swung back and forth.

Matthew felt the physical pain and couldn't take it anymore. He lashed out.

"God damn you!" Matthew yelled. He ran to Donna's defense. Allowing the rage to overcome him, Matthew began to form a fist and started swinging in the direction of her attacker as he positioned himself in between them in an attempt to shield her from further harm.

Never before had he felt so much anger.

Never before had he felt so much rage.

Never before had he allowed himself to lose control in a way where he physically assaulted another human being with such ferocity. Matthew obviously had aggression from playing football, but this was very different. It was personal, and he became consumed. He wanted to teach her father a lesson and beat him into submission much like he had done to his daughter all her life. He wanted to come to Donna's aid and save her.

Matthew swung as hard as he could with both fists, each swing alternating between his left and right. Each punch landed on either side of the man's face or torso. Of course, nothing affected the situation. There was no noticeable change in her father as he continued to strike his own child. It was as though Matthew were striking an inanimate object with no feeling while her father was able to swing through Matthew's presence into Donna's face.

"Stop it!" Matthew screamed in desperation while striking the drunken man to no avail. "You're supposed to love her and protect her, God damn it! Leave her alone, you son of a bitch!"

Matthew sensed he was beginning to lose himself as he felt the rage, the pain, the hurt, the betrayal, the beaten-down physical and psychological effects of the abuse that Donna had endured for years.

Then Matthew felt a pressure on both his shoulders. It was Samuel. His mentor was trying to pull him back. In a matter of a second or two, Matthew quickly realized he was on his back looking up and no longer contained within Donna's chakra. His breathing was rapid and labored. Samuel then knelt next to Matthew as he looked over his pupil.

"Matthew, it's okay," Samuel said trying to comfort his young friend. "You're back."

Samuel lightly tapped Matthew's face in hopes of retrieving him from the intense chakra experience.

As Matthew looked up, Samuel's face was blurring distortedly. He could barely make out his features and the motion caused him to feel nauseous. He then closed his eyes for a few moments in hopes to relieve the sickness building within his stomach.

"Here," Samuel said as he grabbed Matthew by the right arm and tried to coax the young man to sit up.

Matthew responded by rolling onto his right side and pulling himself off the floor of the transport. He could get no further than his knees.

"Keep breathing," Samuel encouraged as he placed a reassuring hand on Matthew's back.

"I began to lose myself," Matthew said while still out of breath.

"I know," Samuel replied. "What you did was brave but very rash. I needed to talk to you first before you leapt into the situation."

"Why?" Matthew asked.

"I think it's obvious now, don't you?" Samuel responded. "I needed to warn you and prepare you for what lay ahead—how to guard yourself from the possibility of losing yourself. I needed to prepare you for the intensity of what you were going to witness and feel."

Matthew still knelt on the deck of the transport with both hands resting on his thighs. His nausea improved and his breathing became more controlled, but he was still reeling emotionally from the experience. He still felt the pain, hurt, anger, betrayal and rage present within him.

"I don't understand," Matthew said in protest. "She fell down the mountain. I just wanted to help her! Why doesn't she take off her back pack and make it easier for herself? Why does her back pack have these tethered lines running down the mountain?"

Samuel gave an affirmative nod. "Because, Matthew, she is clinging to the past," responded Samuel. "That's what those lines fixed to her back pack represent. As you saw, she has had an incredibly difficult life. She grew up without her mother and with an alcoholic father who made her question every beautiful thing about herself and destroyed any sense of positive self-esteem."

"That still doesn't explain what those lines are," Matthew stated, clearly frustrated.

"The back pack she is wearing with the cords dangling down the mountain side is the emotional pain and negative way of thinking in her past that she has been unable to let go of," Samuel continued. "One of the things Donna desired most was to meet a kind and loving man, fall in love, and ultimately get married. She was looking for the type of man who was the opposite of her father. Two years ago, Matthew, she met such a gentleman, as you saw, and Steven has helped Donna begin to recognize the real beauty within herself that she has denied for over thirty years. He has set Donna on the path of self-discovery that would help her heal the wounds she has carried all of her life. He has been trying to get her to believe in herself."

Matthew looked back at Donna again still lying on her back on the side of the mountain. She was writhing in pain. He realized that she wasn't truly climbing a mountain with some of the worst possible conditions, but rather, it represented her struggles, the scars and pain within herself that she had been trying to overcome her entire life. It represented her journey.

Matthew glanced up and down the mountain, noting how far she had progressed. She was over halfway up the summit but still had so much ahead of her.

Samuel could tell Matthew was beginning to make the connections to the scene at hand to Donna's chakra and felt compelled to help him fill in the gaps. "Donna's healing process and spiritual growth has been linked *within her own mind* to that of climbing a mountain," Samuel began. "She has made tremendous progress. The tether lines you see strapped to her back pack are the demons of negative thoughts and emotions associated with her past that she must choose to confront and eventually shed, or she will not reach the top of her own mountain. The same can be said of the high winds, bitter cold and blinding snow storm. Those represent the mental and emotional state of her spirit. Steven has entered her life to set her on the right path. He is someone who believes in her, a person who truly sees her for the amazing spirit that she is. She is beginning to confront her demons, Matthew, so that she can finally move beyond them, but it can be a very painful process."

Matthew looked all around him as he once again noticed the steep ledges, jagged rocks, heavy falling snow, and the strong winds swirling about. He then began to appreciate the desire to be free of such burdens and the courage to confront them.

Because he understood. He understood it all too well.

Samuel paused a moment to look back at Donna.

"It's not the literal mountains we conquer, Matthew, but ourselves," Samuel stated solemnly.

Matthew began to shake his head, because this whole thing struck a chord within him. He suddenly lashed out. "How would she be able do that?!" Matthew pleaded. "How does a person let go of such deep pain carried for so long?"

Samuel paused a moment before he replied, capturing Matthew's gaze.

"Donna must finally confront the pain and recognize that all of these horrible events and conditions of her past life were not her fault," Samuel replied. "To acknowledge it, let it out, and finally let it go. She is now at a point in her journey where she must consciously make a life-changing decision, Matthew."

"What's that, Samuel?" Matthew inquired as he looked back at Donna.

"That her past will no longer determine her present or her future," replied Samuel. "Donna has immense potential, but she must finally address the things within herself she has avoided all her life. The next key step in her journey of self-discovery is to see the wonderful being she truly is and to embrace it. Donna has begun to realize that she possesses the beautiful light of a divine spirit, but clinging to the pain of the past is limiting her future growth."

Samuel, still kneeling next to Matthew, placed his left arm around his pupil's shoulders as they both looked toward Donna, immobilized on the side of the mountain.

"Matthew, it's time for Donna to finally love herself," Samuel stated with finality.

Matthew looked away from the young woman to look directly at his guide. He felt something stir deep within himself.

"Once a person truly can love themselves, they will unlock something so huge that miraculous things can start to happen," Samuel stated as he sensed Matthew's own struggles. "It will enable them to have the unbounded capacity to love and give to others. Then, my young friend, more miracles can happen as that love returns to you in ways you can't even fathom."

Matthew looked away from Samuel to check on Donna. He felt the connection so strongly to her struggles in more ways than one. Matthew realized that Samuel knew this as well.

"The future is determined by our present thoughts and choices," Samuel emphasized. "In each moment, Matthew, we have a choice for a better life, and it is entirely dependent upon what we choose to think and believe right now, the future you envision for yourself."

Samuel knew this lesson was intended to help Matthew open something within himself. He knew the deep-seated secret Matthew had been carrying for years now, and it was time he finally confronted it. It was also why he could sense the edge of panic swelling up in his young prodigy.

Matthew's breathing and heart rate quickened, and he began shaking his head, because he did not want to go there.

"Matthew, as terrifying as it can be, confronting our past pains and limiting beliefs allows us to diffuse the power they have always held over us, so that we recognize them for what they are and let them go," Samuel encouraged. "To finally be liberated, Matthew, by realizing that what you now know is more important and powerful than any negative line of thinking or feeling from your past."

Matthew looked down toward the deck of the transport and Samuel bent over in an attempt to make eye contact again.

"To finally be free," Samuel said. "The past can no longer hurt and limit us. It takes the self-aware spirit to address those things that hold us back and to not allow them to control us any longer. To recognize that when the mind begins to wander into a dark place, a person can catch these negative thoughts before they balloon into negative feelings."

Matthew struggled to reconcile Samuel's words with his own inner conflict.

"That's what growth is all about, Matthew," Samuel continued. "We begin to see our true beauty, learn more about ourselves by processing those things in our lives that created limiting assumptions and feelings, so that we may finally let them go."

Because if you don't do this, you can become lost and fall into a black hole, Matthew thought as his own fear began to well up within him.

Samuel could sense he was beginning to get through to Matthew but that the struggle was still crippling the young lad.

"As soon as Donna can do this, Matthew, she can focus on what's in front of her and not what's behind her," Samuel concluded. "She not only will take off her back pack but her spirit will then effortlessly fly up the rest of the mountain!"

Matthew glanced down at Donna again who had picked herself up. He could hear her faint screams as she reached deep down within herself to resume her climb. Matthew then looked up at his guide. "Then what, Samuel? What happens then?" he asked.

"Once the self-aware spirit can do this, Matthew, their minds can fill with the good in their lives and thoughts of the future they wish to create," Samuel replied. "Then she will completely shift her line of thinking and feel the joy of a hope-filled future of happiness, gratitude, and most of all love, replacing the darkness that once consumed her."

Matthew closed his eyes and took a deep breath. The powerful emotions of Donna's chakra still lingered inside of him. This whole experience awakened something that was deeply buried. Matthew had never wanted it to emerge again as he had tried to safely keep it locked away deep within his own spirit.

"Amazing, isn't it?" Samuel asked as he sensed his pupil needing to focus his energy in a positive direction.

"What's that?" Matthew replied as he opened his eyes to see the snow and wind intensify, which ironically coincided with Donna's brave choice to resume her climb.

"How interwoven our mental state is with our emotional state and how the self-aware spirit learns to understand that connection," Samuel stated.

Suddenly a gust of wind blew down the mountain, and Matthew's face felt the stinging cold once again. He glanced over at Donna who continued climbing, with each step accompanied by a scream of agony. She was courageously moving through all the pain she had endured in her life. She was working to move forward and confront her demons.

"Matthew, we both now know why you were brought here," said Samuel calmly.

Immediately, Matthew felt a surge of helplessness. *No,* he thought. *I can't do this.* This was too much. He didn't sign up for this, suddenly longing for his simple life. He had forgotten why he was even there. What was the purpose of this experience? What was the purpose for all this pain? Then he remembered. The mystery of The Oval.

Samuel had grown quiet, sensing that his pupil was now caught up in his own deep, internal struggle.

Then an idea struck Matthew like a bolt of lightning; it didn't need to be this God-damn difficult. There is no reason that the path must be this hard. He quickly remembered where they were: the space-time continuum.

Matthew slowly looked up at his guide kneeling on his right. The wind blew Matthew's black hair about, and the snow continued to fall at a rapid pace, but Matthew didn't care nor did he really notice. He became hyper-focused, putting on a determined look, and Samuel grew concerned as he saw the shift in his student's demeanor.

"I know what to do," Matthew said softly.

"What do you mean?" Samuel asked

"I am ready to figure out the mystery of The Oval," Matthew replied. "I know how to do that right now."

Samuel grimaced. "No, Matthew, you are not fully prepared," Samuel warned. "Haven't you noticed that your chakra experiences within each host have become more intense and personal?"

"Yes, of course!" Matthew snapped. "It's become too intense, and I don't want to do this anymore! I'm done, Samuel. It's time to jump to the end."

Samuel shook his head in response.

"Matthew, you must trust me that I know how to lead you to that point," Samuel countered patiently. "That's why I needed to prepare you in advance before entering Donna's chakra, but you rushed in far too quickly."

"There is an easier path, Samuel," Matthew said with even more determination and stillness in his voice.

"What are you talking about?" Samuel asked, growing more concerned.

"We are in the space-time continuum," Matthew exclaimed. "All I need to do is find the ribbon that will lead me to that moment where I discover the secret of The Oval and figure out how to open it!"

This time Samuel lost his patience. "No, Matthew, you can't!" Samuel pleaded. "It doesn't work that way. You must stay the course!"

Samuel's words felt like a sharp lash against his soul. *No. Not this time,* Matthew thought to himself. Samuel can't make him continue this way.

He is of a free mind and spirit.

He has a free will.

He can choose his own path.

Matthew shook his head from side to side as he slowly looked up at his mentor to make eye contact. "No, Samuel," Matthew said in a cold voice. "Not this time. I know what to do."

"No, you don't Matthew," Samuel warned.

Matthew realized that Samuel was not going to support him in this line of thinking. He assumed his guide would try to stop him. Matthew decided that now was the time to act as he quickly jumped to his feet.

In response to Matthew's sudden action, Samuel began to lift himself up, but his pupil already anticipated his reaction. While Samuel was still trying to raise himself up, Matthew placed both hands on Samuel's shoulders and pushed as hard as he could. Samuel lost his balance and fell onto his back.

Matthew then leapt to the navigational control at the front and instinctively grabbed it as he had seen Samuel do many times during their travels. The transport lunged forward. Matthew nearly lost his balance, and he quickly glanced behind his shoulder to check on Samuel who again lost his balance and fell on his side.

Matthew quickly looked around for the gateway and saw it at about eleven o'clock from their current position along the side of the mountain. Navigating the transport was far easier than he had anticipated, his intuition guiding the disc through the movements of the navigational ball. Matthew accelerated and tried to navigate the transport amidst the high winds and heavy snowfall. Within a few seconds, he successfully reached the portal. The white flash of light engulfed them briefly as they passed through to the other end of the energy field. Matthew then saw the expanse of the space-time continuum, but one small problem suddenly occurred to him that he hadn't fully considered.

Which ribbon would lead him to *his future?*

Matthew then brought the hover disc to a complete stop. Surprisingly, Samuel then fell forward from the sudden lack of motion just as he had managed to stand up and regain his balance. Matthew realized he may not have long before Samuel tried to stop him. He feverishly looked throughout the massive web. It must be here somewhere. Given that the continuum was ever expanding and changing, it made trying to locate the correct thread all the more difficult.

Where do I even begin? Matthew thought to himself.

The answer then appeared out of thin air. A new ribbon suddenly emerged from under the transport and shot out in front of them. It was as though he had created the path with his own will. Without hesitation, Matthew engaged the transport and began to ride along the ribbon. He sped up, in fear that he might lose it and managed to stay with the thread through all of its twists and turns. A few hundred yards ahead of them, the ribbon suddenly stopped at a gateway which strangely had no other connections. Within a few seconds, they reached the portal where Matthew disengaged the transport and came to a full stop just before entering. Only then, did he realize how frantic his breathing had become.

"What's wrong, Matthew?" Samuel asked.

"Aren't you going to stop me?" Matthew questioned as he turned his head to look back at his guide standing just behind his left shoulder.

"No," Samuel answered. "It's now clear that this is what you must do right at this moment. But prepare yourself, Matthew. It's not what you are expecting."

Matthew turned forward to face the gateway to his destiny.

Of course this is what I am expecting, he thought to himself. *To fast forward through time to the moment where I finally unlock the secret of The Oval. Where I will finally understand what it is and how to open it. I will finally know what its purpose is and why it has entered my life.* All of the painful experiences and lessons learned thus far had culminated to this defining moment.

Matthew did not delay any further and quickly engaged the transport shooting them forward.

Samuel knew that this moment for Matthew would be like nothing he expected but was necessary for his pupil to continue on his critical journey. Matthew had no idea of what was on the other side of the gateway. Samuel realized this next step could determine if, indeed, he had truly found the one for whom he had been searching virtually his entire life.

CHAPTER 13

GREAT PARADOX

The familiar stretch of white light lasted only a few seconds as they passed through the portal. Then without warning, the transport jolted to a complete stop. Unprepared, Matthew was thrown off the disc, flipping over head-first but didn't immediately fall to the ground. He became suspended in mid-air as time momentarily stood still. He turned his head slightly to find some kind of bearing in hopes of seeing something familiar. He hoped, perhaps, to see his bedroom and himself holding The Oval just before opening it. But all Matthew could see was darkness.

Within a few moments, his weightless suspension quickly dissipated as gravity returned without warning. His flip from the transport was completed by a violent landing on his back, but fortunately, he landed on something soft. In fact, he brushed his hands along the ground and recognized the familiar texture immediately—sand.

Matthew moved his legs very slowly to check if he had injured himself in any way. He then lifted his right arm followed by his left. He felt fine despite the sudden jolt to his body and mental state. Matthew raised his head up as he caught a glimpse of light off in the distance directly in front of him.

The view was not what Matthew expected. The glimpse of light he saw was tinted yellow like that of the sun and came peaking over a sand dune immediately in front of him about fifty yards away. But this was no ordinary sand dune. Matthew quickly scrambled to his feet and spun around in a three-hundred-and-sixty degree turn. He now found himself apparently in the middle of a desert, a desert whose sand was pure black.

Matthew knelt down on his right knee and scooped up a handful of the blackened grains with his left hand. He stared in disbelief as he opened his fingers to let it sift through and fall back to the ground. He turned to look behind him where the transport hovered above the ground. Samuel stood there looking at his young friend.

"What is this?" Matthew asked.

"You are seeking answers, yes?" Samuel replied with a question.

"Yeah, but this is not what I expected," Matthew said as he stared at the landscape. The terrain contained numerous rolling mounds of sand, dunes of various heights and ripples within the sand whose patterns appeared almost perfect as though made by some intelligent design.

Samuel stepped off the transport and joined Matthew on the ground. He approached the lad from his right. Matthew was still trying to make sense of it all when he felt Samuel touch his right shoulder.

"Go to the top of the dune and find the light," Samuel instructed.

Matthew looked at his guide whose eyes conveyed his usual calm. He then stepped forward and began to scale the dune. His heart rate increased with each step until finally he could no longer contain himself and began to run up the steep hill. Matthew reached the top where the brightness of the light caused him to shield his eyes. As he held up his right hand, Matthew tried to look through his fingers to find its source. Strangely, the yellow light began to morph into a bright white, the kind of white light he had been experiencing while entering the chakras of his various hosts along this journey. The brightness began to fade enough for Matthew to lower his hand and catch a glimpse of something in the distance. He saw the outline of two figures standing next to each other with one visibly shorter than the other. The light continued to fade, and the figures came into focus. He then realized what he was looking upon. Immediately he felt a sense of dread spawn from his soul. A swell of panic ensued, ready to burst forth and overwhelm him like a volcanic eruption. It was ready to consume him as it once had a long time ago.

"Oh no, you don't!" Matthew screamed back at Samuel who was now scaling the dune and almost to the top where Matthew stood. "God damn you!" Matthew yelled as he turned to face his guide. Get out of here you son of a bitch! Stop this right now!"

"Matthew, it's time you faced this," Samuel said calmly.

As soon as Samuel reached the top of the dune, Matthew lashed out by striking him with his right fist across the jaw. Samuel's head quickly jerked from the force of impact, but his forward motion was unaffected.

"Get the hell out of my chakra, Samuel!" Matthew protested. "I'm not going there! I'm not going to do this!" Matthew then grabbed the front of Samuel's black shirt with both hands.

"No!!" Matthew yelled in sheer desperation as he shook his guide as hard as he could. Terror and pain continued to grow uncontrolled within him.

Samuel raised his left arm and placed it upon Matthew's right shoulder as they faced each other. Samuel spoke not a word but looked directly within Matthew's eyes attempting to reach his young prodigy. Samuel looked at Matthew, trying to convey to the young man that this was what must be done now if he were to continue on this journey and that he would be there with him through it.

Matthew realized he had no choice. The only way out of this was to face it and move through it. Realizing that, Matthew had an incredible sinking feeling that it was time to face his past, to face the pain he had attempted to bury and conceal, not only from everyone in the world, but also from himself.

He loosened his grip on Samuel's shirt and momentarily rested his forehead on Samuel's shoulder, wishing there was another way. His mentor responded by placing his hand on the back of Matthew's head. Matthew then slowly turned. Suddenly a strong wind emerged. The scene became clouded by the black sand now swirling around them.

There before him was a little boy, no more than eight or nine years of age. He had sandy brown, straight hair and wore a red and blue striped shirt with a white collar. He clutched in his right arm a stuffed animal. It was a small, gray elephant.

Tears flowed down the little boy's face. He was trying to be brave. He was trying to hold back the tears, but he couldn't hold it all in. It just wasn't possible.

Wearing a brown flower-patterned dress standing behind the little boy was an elderly woman bearing an expression of deep sorrow and worry. They were looking out the living room window facing the front of a house. She clutched the little boy's shoulder from behind while her right hand gently stroked his hair. It was the little boy's grandmother—Matthew's grandmother.

Matthew immediately fell to his knees as all the emotional pain came flooding back into his awareness. It was all there, the moment when his mother was taken away in the ambulance. The panic, pain, sorrow, fear, helplessness and abandonment. Then the blame crept in. It was somehow his fault. If only he had been better. If only he hadn't been so needy. Overwhelmed, Matthew looked down at the black sand and began to weep. He couldn't do this. It was too much.

Samuel knelt down beside Matthew and placed a reassuring hand on the young man's back.

"Matthew, it wasn't your fault," Samuel explained. "Your mother's mental breakdown was not of your doing. She needed help, and it had nothing to do with you, your dad or your sisters. She was very sick."

Matthew took a deep breath, looked up at the scene again before him, and then locked eyes with his guide. "I know that now," Matthew said as the tears continued to stream down his face. "But I didn't then. She attempted suicide, for Christ's sake!"

Then all the same questions that plagued Matthew for years re-emerged. "I kept wondering, why?" the young man lamented.

"Why wasn't I enough to live for, for God's sake?! Why wasn't our family enough?"

The memory of walking into his parents' bathroom that day still haunted him. He heard a loud thud from within, only to discover his mother had collapsed on the floor. When he walked in to investigate, he saw the blood streaming from her wrists.

By now, Matthew was sobbing uncontrollably as the well of emotions overcame his sense of control. He had struggled his entire life to maintain that control, because he knew and feared more than anything what losing control could mean. Samuel tried to help his pupil wrap his mind and spirit around that pivotal moment in his life.

"Matthew, you now know within your rational mind that your mother's mental sickness was never meant to hurt any of you deliberately," Samuel began. "She lost control, but she has progressed on her own journey to wellness and would never do something like that again. What your mind cannot take away is how you were hurt by it and how profoundly it affected you in ways that no one knew until later."

Samuel paused a moment as he gently reached down to lift Matthew's chin up in order to make eye contact. "So, it's time Matthew, right here and now, to finally deal with this cross you have carried," Samuel said encouragingly.

As he looked at Samuel again, Matthew noticed out of the corner of his eye that the scene had changed amidst the back drop of the blackened sand storm. This time, he saw himself in the most darkened state of his life. Fourteen-year-old Matthew was sitting on a floor next to a bed that had leather straps dangling down its side. He wore a flimsy, light-blue cotton gown like those issued in a hospital. His hands were on either side of his head as his elbows rested upon his bent knees with his feet planted on the floor. He noticed the hospital band wrapped around his younger self's left wrist. He was rocking rapidly back and forth as he sat on the floor. Matthew remembered how completely immobilized and trapped he had felt.

Fourteen-year-old Matthew was imprisoned within his own mind.

He was admitted into a mental institution as psychiatrists and medical staff tried to understand how to help this tormented young teen. The emotional trauma came flooding back into older Matthew's consciousness. Try as he might to extinguish this experience from his mind and soul, Matthew reconnected with the hopelessness and depression, the feeling that he was a pure freak. His mind had betrayed and decimated him with uncontrollable thoughts. It reduced him to a state of dysfunction from which he felt there was no return. He had fallen into a black hole with no way out. He felt totally isolated and alone where no one could understand him or seemingly help him. No one could reach him. He was on the brink of suicide as he was no longer in control of his own mind. He was gripped with fear all the time.

Still kneeling on the black sand, Matthew sat back and stared at his younger self. He wished he hadn't been brought to this moment that he so desperately desired to forget or change as he felt all of those overwhelming emotions yet again. This was why he had to keep it locked away.

Samuel got down on both knees to turn Matthew's gaze upon himself. He knew he had to help his young friend out of the darkness and finally release the control it had over him all these years.

"Matthew, look at me!" Samuel commanded as he reached down toward Matthew's face and physically moved his head up to his own line of vision again. The wind began to grow stronger as the black sand storm intensified and swirled around them.

"We both know why you were brought here," Samuel continued. "You are on your own journey of self-awareness."

"This is not what I wanted, damn it!" Matthew yelled in desperation. "It's too hard!"

Samuel ignored his pupil's rejection.

"Matthew, you must fully accept what happened to you. Process it and understand it, so you can be free," Samuel stated encouragingly for Matthew to finally open up and face his demons.

"There's nothing to understand," Matthew retorted. "It's over!"

Samuel would not be deterred.

"My God, there is so much you need to understand!" Samuel said with compassion. "So much of our negative or destructive behaviors, thoughts, and emotions come from scars inflicted upon us at a young age when we can't process them in a healthy way. Especially when one doesn't get the help needed to be able to cope."

"But it still hurt and terrified us all," Matthew responded as his voice cracked under the emotional distress. "She was just gone after the ambulance drove her away. She was gone for months. We barely got to see her. My dad was overwhelmed. It took her years to recover. To become the person and mother she used to be."

Samuel sensed the depth of Matthew's pain and suffering that had tortured him throughout his life and hoped he could help Matthew finally deal with it once and for all. "Of course it was horrific, Matthew. You didn't get the help you needed, especially at such a young age," Samuel continued. "Your mother needed help and your father found a way, but he didn't know what to do for you and your sisters. So left to your own devices, you conjured up your own explanations and theories of what happened that sadly led you down a dark path mentally and emotionally."

Matthew tried to focus again on his guide as the tears poured from his eyes, but it was becoming more difficult with the black sand whirling around them. He looked back on the scene of his hospitalization.

"I kept asking myself, 'why?'" Matthew stated again. "Why? What did I do wrong? Why wasn't I good enough? I kept thinking I was the cause of her breakdown somehow. Why wasn't I enough to live for?"

Matthew began to sob uncontrollably again.

Samuel felt the battle within his pupil's soul. "Matthew, this incredibly traumatic event of your young life led to your own mental and emotional illness a few years later, didn't it?" Samuel asked.

Matthew remembered the anxieties and fear he constantly felt from that point forward. How his mind conjured up every imaginable tragedy that could befall him or anyone in his family. How he felt that all he could do was pray and beg God for help. Asking Him to prevent any of his fearful thoughts from coming true. Then, it grew to an obsession which in turn resulted in more and more ritualistic behaviors that eventually left Matthew completely helpless. It began to take over his life. The dominating thought was either his parents, sisters or he himself would die.

As his condition worsened, he became more withdrawn until he could no longer function in normal society. This resulted in a serious depression that completely engulfed him. He felt he would never be released from this tortuous state and feel normal again. It was like he had been imprisoned by his own mind but didn't know how to break free. Thoughts of taking his own life as the only means of escape, began to form. Matthew then reconnected with the self-loathing he had within himself. His parents recognized how ill their son had become and hospitalized him. Matthew recalled that eventful day when his parents walked into the kitchen and saw him lying on his side upon the floor whispering something that no one else could hear or understand. He was clutching a knife in his left hand.

"Once the mind starts to wander into a dark place, Matthew, more bad thoughts fueled by dark emotions are sure to follow," Samuel stated. "Negative thoughts attract more negative thinking, leading a person into a downward spiral, and that's what happened to you, isn't it?"

Samuel realized it was time to shift Matthew's perspective. "Matthew, I want you to look at that young teenage boy," Samuel instructed.

Matthew, still kneeling in the black sand, turned his gaze away from Samuel and onto the scene at hand.

"You must recognize that you found the will to pull yourself out of that terrible state, and you did so with no medical intervention or real psychiatric assistance, because they didn't know what to do for you at the time," Samuel began to explain. "Since then, you have gone on to achieve remarkable things. You must give yourself credit and celebrate that, Matthew. You displayed tremendous resiliency. You went through the first three Levels of the Spirit in trying to cope with your illness. You desired to be free from it, found the inner strength to be courageous, and had the faith that you would get better. A belief that God would help you. You summoned an inner discipline that was well beyond your years."

Samuel paused a moment, sensing that he was reaching the young lad. "But these scars which you never addressed took their toll on you, didn't they?" Samuel asked, knowing full well the answer from his knowledge of Matthew's young life.

Matthew looked back at Samuel and then again at his younger hospitalized self, sitting on the floor.

"You decided that you had become weak by letting those terrible thoughts bring you to that immobilized state," Samuel stated.

Matthew fully remembered that feeling of being out of control mentally and emotionally.

He remembered what it felt like at night when the resident nurses came into his room, put him into bed, and fastened the leather straps to his wrist. He was completely restrained like some kind of animal. They kept him confined, fearful of Matthew's instability and the concern that he could harm himself. But then Matthew remembered the moment when he reached deep down within himself where he vowed never to return to that state. Where he would rise above the insanity and re-enter the world. Where he would beat this. He would win. He would be strong and no longer allow his mind or his emotions to take over and reduce him to such a condition. Matthew finally nodded his head in response to Samuel's question.

"As you reached deep within yourself, you had to find a new focal point beyond the obsessive thinking," Samuel continued. "You found something beyond the dark emotions of fear, depression, hopelessness and self-hatred. You needed to latch onto a light, a light that would guide you. To help you crawl, fight and pull yourself out of that dark hole and give you a sense of hope for a new beginning."

Matthew knew exactly what Samuel was getting at and where he was headed. He again gave his guide an affirmative nod as he continued to stare at the present scene.

Samuel knew what must come next as he continued kneeling before Matthew. "You created this image of yourself as the All-American kid," Samuel began. "Great student. Great athlete. Good religious boy who never did wrong. Trying to be the perfect son. To be the perfect person, in hopes you would never go back to that state or perhaps somehow prevent your mother's instability again."

Matthew looked at Samuel, realizing how amazingly true those statements were.

"You became a truly remarkable testimony of the strength of the human spirit as you accomplished everything you set out to achieve, especially after you had fallen so deep," Samuel stated with wonder. "You could have turned to drugs or alcohol or lashed out in destructive ways, but you knew, even at such a young age, that it would only lead to more pain. You showed such wisdom and strength!"

Matthew reflected on his accomplishments, giving him a brief reprieve from the overwhelming negative feelings associated with the past that could have easily led to his demise.

"But over time, something else began to happen, though," Samuel continued. "You decided to become everything to everyone, which eventually created your identity."

The lump in Matthew's throat from all this past pain rendered him speechless. He returned Samuel's gaze, not even questioning at this point how his guide knew all of this intensely personal history.

"You eventually began to live, not for yourself, Matthew, but to please others," Samuel succinctly stated. "And during this incredible journey, something even more tragic came into play."

Matthew was suddenly perplexed. What more could have taken place that he already didn't know?

"You determined at a young age that you could not have emotional needs," Samuel explained clearly, hoping to draw a final connection for his pupil. "And that, somehow, having emotional needs would make you weak or drive people away. Even worse, Matthew, you were terrified that in doing so, you might return to that time and place when you couldn't function. You saw that as a precursor to your mother's breakdown and to your own. You were afraid to fall back down into that deep, dark hole, so you buried a part of the real you."

The wind began to pick up even more. The black sandstorm whirled around at such a rapid pace that Samuel, who was still kneeling directly in front of him, was barely visible. Matthew could not deny anything Samuel had just said. He could utter only one response.

"Yes, it's true," Matthew whispered, barely able to speak.

"Why?" Samuel questioned. "When you are such an amazing and beautiful spirit?" Samuel already knew the answer, but he needed Matthew to say it out loud.

Matthew gasped for air against the sandstorm. "Because," Matthew began as he struggled with the words. "I felt that if anyone knew the real me, they wouldn't like me. If they knew what truly happened, I would be labeled as a freak. I would be rejected. I would be abandoned." Then Matthew paused, knowing what needed to be said next but didn't want to say it aloud. "I felt I couldn't possibly be loved for who I truly am," Matthew said with great strain in his voice.

"So, it was safer to be the all-American," Samuel commented. "To bury all of the pain and emotion from your illness deep within yourself, but in doing so, you cut a part of yourself off and then grew to hate it. You blamed your problems all on that, didn't you?"

Matthew nodded.

"But Matthew, you have known the truth all along that something so huge within ourselves cannot be locked away forever," Samuel continued. "It must come out one day and be addressed. You have always known this, but you were terrified to go there. There are two beings in this universe whom we can never lie to.

Matthew strained to see and hear Samuel as the wind continued to intensify.

"You can never lie to God or yourself," Samuel yelled over the noise of the storm. "You were terribly insecure, Matthew, and felt such inadequacy, that you were compelled to over-compensate," Samuel further explained. "You worried about what people would think of you. Do you know where all insecurity stems from?"

The lump in Matthew's throat grew so painful from his despondent state that he once again found it impossible to speak. All he could do was shake his head.

"Fear," Samuel replied. "Insecurity stems from fear when we let it grip us or find a foothold within our consciousness. It was fear that drove your mind to the brink of uncontrollable thinking, to the brink of insanity. Your childhood and adolescent trauma left you fearful of being abandoned and unlovable. From that fearful place, Matthew, we may think or do irrational things that can be destructive. Fear can deny our true selves, because it can eventually consume and even imprison us. It can cut us off from a part of our true being."

Matthew swallowed hard in an attempt to regain control again. He didn't want to deal with all of this baggage. He had gone on to lead a normal life again filled with success and accomplishments that he was proud of. He never wanted to return here to this place within himself, ever. Then Matthew felt a shift from within and his voice suddenly returned.

"All I wanted, Samuel, was to come here and see *my* future-self unlock the secret of The Oval," Matthew said through gritted teeth. "I wanted to see how I would do it, what was contained inside, its purpose, or if I would even do it. Not to reopen these God-damn wounds and hold me back!"

"Matthew, it doesn't work that way," Samuel explained urgently. "You are intended to deal with this in order to move forward in your journey. To not do so, would be inevitably what holds you back!"

Then Samuel realized that he had to convey something crucially important to his young friend.

"Not only that, Matthew, desiring to see into the future is one of the greatest paradoxes of the universe," Samuel stated intently.

"What?" Matthew replied. "What are you talking about?" Matthew's voice grew louder to speak above the noise of the wind. The vortex of sand swirling about grew so intense that Samuel was no longer visible. A feeling of abandonment began to grow within the teenager, but fortunately, he could still hear his guide's voice and resisted the urge to further panic.

"Matthew, you wanted to jump to the end," Samuel yelled. "You wanted to take control and skip to the end result."

"So?!" Matthew responded indignantly. "That's what I want, damn it!"

"I know, Matthew, but if you were allowed to see that, it could change everything!" Samuel replied. "If you were granted the vision of knowing how you solved this problem right now or even if you solve it at all, that could change the end result you desire!"

"That doesn't make any sense, Samuel!" Matthew complained as his voice cracked in frustration.

Samuel took a deep breath, knowing that Matthew still resisted what he must confront. Somehow, he had to get through to him. "To know the future would ultimately put that future at risk!" Samuel clarified.

"Why?!" Matthew retorted defiantly.

"Because you would be given a vision into something that could alter your current stream of thoughts and emotions, thereby changing your decisions along the way," Samuel replied. "And changing your decisions, reactions, thoughts and emotions along the way in solving a problem or working through a difficult time in your life could ultimately lead you down a different path that you might not have intended. You could lose your motivation, because you think you already know the end result, but the end only comes with each step in the present journey. Thinking you already know the outcome could *change* the resulting future. Your mind and spirit would lose that compelling drive in the present, and your journey of learning and self-discovery could be jeopardized."

The wind blew even harder, and Matthew felt the sting upon his exposed skin as the sand struck him with incredible force. He was now straining to hear his guide.

"Each step contains lessons for further insight and growth, and you don't want to put that at risk!" Samuel pleaded. "Those opportunities for growth lie in every choice of every moment. To know the end would influence the journey and thereby jeopardize that very end you seek!"

Matthew truly didn't want to hear it, but he sensed the truth deep within his spirit.

"That's why it's called The Great Paradox, Matthew," Samuel concluded. "To alter your steps now would alter your future. You have been given a tremendous gift."

"What's that?" Matthew questioned as he held up his right hand to shield his eyes from the storm.

"To be given the chance to confront your deeply buried pain, recognize it for what it truly is, and then be free once and for all," Samuel shouted.

Matthew placed his hands on his thighs and leaned forward. He didn't know if he truly understood, but Samuel had earned his complete trust. He realized that his faith must come into focus and that his guide would not lead him astray, even though he didn't fully comprehend its meaning just yet. God had sent Samuel to him for a reason, to be that focal point of light in this dark place and help him navigate through it.

Samuel was right. Matthew realized that his approach to close himself off to his past, made things so much worse in the long run. The mere fact that he had no desire to ever open up this black void deeply buried within himself was proof of how terrified of it he really was and how much control he had given it. It had limited him, causing him to live in fear in so many ways. He had been denying a part of his true self.

All of a sudden, Matthew noticed Samuel had completely disappeared. The panic he suppressed just moments ago resurfaced.

"Samuel!" Matthew shouted in desperation.

No response, which only heightened his fear.

Am I truly all alone now? Matthew immediately thought. *Here, lost in this black desert of pain and misery?*

He had to find Samuel. He had to find him somehow. He couldn't do this alone. Now reduced to a terrified state, Matthew attempted to stand and frantically search for his guide but the wind knocked him down on his left side. He screamed out again, "Samuel! Where are you? I need you!"

At that point, visibility was so poor, Matthew couldn't even see his arms or legs. Was he falling back into the black hole again? Was he losing himself again? Matthew struggled to simply get back on his knees. Then he felt a sudden urge to look up into the blackened sky and yell out.

"Take me, God!" he screamed. "Please take me! I am so much more than this. Make it stop. Please make it stop!"

Matthew then let out a blood-curdling scream of pain. The ground shook violently as the decibels rose from his agonizing cry. Suddenly, Matthew felt a warmth grow from within himself. He felt it at the center of his chest. He immediately looked down, and that's when he saw it.

A glimmer of white light.

The light grew brighter, and with it, the intensity of the warm feeling. He felt his chest about to explode as it got brighter and hotter. Matthew thrust his chest outward in response, and he let out another scream as though to release the light and allow it to burst forth. Just as soon as the heat became unbearable, there was an explosion of white light that pierced the darkness of the black sandstorm.

Matthew screamed again, expelling all the air in his lungs. He was unable to take another breath. Physically taxed and lacking oxygen, his body collapsed onto its left side. He passed out for a few seconds and then began to breathe again almost immediately. His head now rested on the sand, and he slowly opened his eyes.

The wind had inexplicably calmed. The sandstorm had passed, and he saw Samuel standing over him out of the corner of his right eye. Matthew slowly turned his head to face his mentor, relieved in knowing his guide was with him again.

Samuel looked down and smiled at the young man.

"What just happened?" Matthew asked weakly.

Samuel knelt beside his pupil.

"You've done a most remarkable thing, Matthew," Samuel began. "You faced your worst fears and confronted your demons. In doing so, you opened yourself to the complete you, to the whole you. How do you feel?"

Matthew pushed himself up with his left arm and sat up. He still felt weak and could only make it back to his knees. He looked at Samuel and then took in a three hundred sixty degree view of the landscape. He noticed a calm breeze blowing, and something else caught his attention. The sun was shining brightly amidst a beautiful blue sky.

"I feel . . ." Matthew paused to find the right word. "Lighter."

Samuel gave Matthew a huge smile and placed both hands on his shoulders.

"It's because you faced the pain that you buried, understood it, diffused it and let it go." Samuel stated proudly. "That piercing white light was the fullness of your incredibly divine spirit being released."

Samuel paused a moment to view the beautiful blue sky and feel the warmth of the sun shining down upon them. He then looked back at his young friend.

"Matthew," Samuel began. "You are now free. This past pain can no longer hurt you or hold you back."

Matthew looked to Samuel again and knew his guide was right. He realized that he finally had access to his complete self. He had never felt so free. He never felt such hope. A tremendous burden that he had been carrying for years had been lifted. The entrapment of all that darkness and pain had suppressed a part of himself, but now it was all out. The fear he once felt about his past was now gone.

"I am incredibly proud of you, Matthew," Samuel said as he gave the young man a squeeze on the arm.

Matthew gave a quick smile to his guide in response to the validation.

How could any of this be possible? Matthew thought. *Who is this man? How does he understand me so well? How could I have been so blessed to have Samuel come into my life?*

"Matthew, it's time for you to accept the truth," Samuel said.

Matthew responded with a quizzical look.

"You are an amazing soul," Samuel warmly continued. "You are very loveable. You are incredibly strong and courageous. You have a tremendous fire and passion that has always burned within you."

Samuel then realized that he needed Matthew to know more of what was in store for him.

"You have a power that is beyond your wildest imagination, and it is time for you to fully unleash it," Samuel stated excitedly. "To become that vessel of divine goodness and purpose. To unleash your full potential upon the world."

Still kneeling, Matthew stared down into the black sand, attempting to not only understand Samuel's words but to *feel* them as truth.

"What must I do?" he asked.

The excitement grew within Samuel. He was now certain of who and what Matthew truly is. These last sequence of events proved it beyond a doubt. He had found him. He had truly found The One for whom he had been seeking.

"You must finally accept who and what you truly are," Samuel answered. "That's why I am here."

Confused, Matthew asked, "What am I, Samuel?"

"You are an amazing spirit whose purpose is beyond comprehension," Samuel replied. "You are THE KEY!"

The weight of Samuel's words took Matthew off guard. He briefly studied Samuel's expression and could instantly sense the significance and excitement radiating from his guide.

"What does that mean?" Matthew inquired.

"I will absolutely show you, Matthew, but in order to continue down your path, it's time you leave this pain, suffering, and fear behind," Samuel responded. "It's time that you let go of all preconceived notions of who you are. It's time you begin to understand your true potential and accept your whole self."

The intensity of his emotions had left Matthew drained and literally brought him to his knees, but in doing so, he realized that this was needed. It was needed, because he was finally opened and whole. Nothing brings us to our knees faster than facing our pain and darkest nightmares. In doing so, we also finally address them and grow. We get to be free.

"So what do I do to realize this potential?" Matthew asked.

"By taking the next step in your journey and focusing on the light," Samuel answered. "You are pure light, Matthew."

"How do I focus on the light?" Matthew inquired, ready and very eager now to continue moving toward his future.

"It's so simple, Matthew," Samuel began. "So incredibly simple."

Matthew searched within his mind and soul, but the answer that was so obvious to Samuel eluded him.

"You LOVE YOURSELF," Samuel replied intensely. "We combat our dark fears by focusing on the divine spirit within us. The divine spirit within us is pure light and love. Moving toward the light, Matthew, will open doors, new insights, and attract more light into our lives. Then, something else miraculously happens."

"What's that?" Matthew asked eagerly, hanging on Samuel's every word.

"Our divine purpose in life comes further into focus," Samuel answered.

Matthew pondered his mentor's words. We need to recognize the pain for what it truly is and choose to turn away from it after acknowledging its power over us. Then he could release the hold it had upon him, realizing that he is not the embodiment of those negative thoughts and emotions. Matthew's mind turned toward Samuel's last comments.

What does he mean by divine purpose? Matthew thought.

Samuel nodded affirmatively as though he could read Matthew's mind and the connections he was trying to make.

"You have released your pain and scars to the divine light, Matthew, and are now free of it," Samuel continued. "You retain the lessons but have let go of the pain and the fear along with it. We embrace all of our experiences for the growth they represent. We accept all that we have been through and know those experiences are part of our whole selves but we don't stay in darkness. It is a huge part of becoming a whole, healthy person."

Samuel realized it was time to conclude this part of Matthew's journey and the profound lessons embodied in the experience. It was time for Matthew to keep moving forward.

"The greater the pain we move through, the greater the growth we experience, making the triumph of our spirit that much more immense," Samuel stated. "And the greater the growth, Matthew, the greater potential we possess in achieving our destiny!"

Matthew continued to process his teacher's words. The past can no longer hurt him if he chooses not to allow it. To recognize it now for what it truly is and release it; it was finally time to embrace his whole self and recognize his remarkable spirit, whose purpose is beyond what he previously believed possible. His desire for "the more" couldn't be realized because of his intense fears and limiting beliefs. The fear led to him rejecting a part of his true being, but having Samuel help him shine a light upon it, it was now dissipated. Things were going to be very different now, and he felt an amazing positive energy flow through him.

Then a simple truth resonated within his spirit: darkness cannot coexist with light. Choosing to embrace the light within himself ultimately means choosing a life of love and it all starts with loving himself. It was finally time to let his true being shine for all the world to see, because Matthew loves Matthew. He no longer had to be afraid to pursue what he was called to do, even though he didn't know what exactly it was just yet.

The Key, Matthew thought to himself. *What did Samuel mean by that?*

Matthew finally realized there were tears of joy streaming down his face.

He leaned forward to pick himself up off the ground. As he did so, a single tear dangled from the tip of his nose and slowly dropped to the sand below. Then a most amazing thing happened. The tear immediately disappeared within the black sand, and a sparkle of light began to flash just beneath the surface. He paused a moment, remaining on his right knee and stared in wonder. The flashes of light continued a few more seconds before the black sand began to move. Matthew was too mesmerized to be afraid.

A portion of the sand began to rise as if a seed had been planted, and a new growth began to emerge from the ground, taking on a familiar shape. The black sand sparkled as the shape moved up toward Matthew, slowly twisting and turning. After several seconds, Matthew realized what had just emerged.

It was a single rose.

The sparkling, black rose began to intensify in color. What appeared to be hundreds of sparkling lights began to randomly flash before Matthew's eyes. As they did, he could actually hear the small points of lights as they gently rang like angelic bells from heaven. The sparkling then focused into a single bright flash from which Matthew briefly shielded his eyes.

When the light began to fade, Matthew lowered his hand to see a few flashes of light slowly drop to the ground like the embers of an open fire floating in mid-air. He then noticed the black sand flower had changed yet again. It now possessed the color of a real flower. The stem was a perfect hue of green, and the petals were a brilliant red. He reached down with his left hand to touch it and felt pure velvet. Matthew gently caressed the rose with all of his fingers and felt a lightness stir within his soul. Out of the corner of his right eye, Matthew saw Samuel approach but couldn't bring himself to pull away from the flower's beauty.

"Wonderful isn't it, Matthew?" Samuel asked.

"Incredible," Matthew replied slowly. "What is it? What just happened?"

"Another miracle," Samuel answered.

"What?" Matthew said still staring at the rose in disbelief.

"From this intense pain, something magnificent was born," Samuel continued.

"And what was that?" Matthew asked as his gaze remained fixed on the flower.

"The recognition of your real beauty," Samuel replied. "Your true essence of divine light and love."

Samuel felt a stirring within himself now. He was so ridiculously proud of his young prodigy for the new insight Matthew had gained by addressing that part of himself he had closed off for years.

"The darkest caves we fear entering most, Matthew, most often contain the greatest treasures," Samuel said with a gentle confident tone. "And the greatest treasure you just found was yourself."

Matthew smiled and let out a small gasp of air as the truth of Samuel's words powerfully resonated within him.

"Come now, it's time to go," Samuel commented as he knelt down and placed his hand upon Matthew's shoulder.

Matthew resisted a moment, not wanting to leave. He did not want to feel the absence of the beauty, peace and light of the rose.

"It's okay to leave now, Matthew," Samuel reassured him. "You aren't leaving anything behind. It's coming with you."

"How?" Matthew asked.

"Because it's always been inside you, Matthew, and you have finally let it out," Samuel responded. "You will now carry it with you wherever you go, and everyone will see the real you."

Matthew finally looked up at his mentor who gave him the warmest smile. Samuel stood first and motioned with his right hand for his pupil to join him. Just before Matthew stood, he slid his left hand down from the pedals to the base of the stem. He gently pulled the flower toward him and detached it from the black sand, whose expanse only accentuated the deep hues of the rose.

Matthew gently held the stem with his left hand while cupping the flower with his right as though it was as fragile as glass. He held the flower to his chest, directly over his heart. They walked their way back to the transport and stepped onto the platform. Samuel stepped forward to engage the navigational ball.

"That's not necessary, Matthew," Samuel commented as he glanced at Matthew holding the flower.

"You said I could take it with me," Matthew replied.

"I said it would always be with you wherever you go, because it's always been inside you," Samuel answered.

Matthew then felt a growing warmth coming from the flower, and rather than clutch it tighter for comfort, he instinctively let it go. The rose floated in the air right before his eyes and began to slowly rotate. It again emitted a brilliant white light until it was void of all color yet retaining it's perfect shape. It slowly floated toward Matthew until it was within inches of his body. With a blink of an eye, it plunged itself into Matthew's chest. His heart felt a surge of warmth and his breath was momentarily taken away.

He felt peace, and love.

Matthew fell to his knees again at experiencing pure joy. His chest was heaving from his rapid breathing, and he could see a few sparkles of light radiating from his body.

Samuel smiled as he turned around and engaged the transport. It lifted off and their vehicle returned to the gateway from which they entered.

Matthew didn't look back at the black desert they left behind. He felt no need to for he was finally free. He only looked forward to what lay ahead with gratitude, peace, hope, and wonder. His guide believed in him, and now he was beginning to genuinely believe in himself. Samuel said that he was The Key, and Matthew pondered what that truly meant, but he now knew that the truth would be revealed.

His destiny would unfold, and he was never more ready to embrace it.

CHAPTER 14

FINAL LEVEL

Samuel guided the transport to the portal directly ahead of them. Never before had Matthew thought about the power of the human mind and the opposing forces at play. He never pondered how learning about oneself can provide such insight. It can unlock why we think or behave the way we do, but more importantly, discover who we truly are and how life's journey aids in our quest to grow. However, only if we are open to new possibilities, new ways of thinking, and start to pay attention can it all be possible.

Samuel slowed the transport and entered the gateway. As they emerged into the web, he brought their craft to a complete stop.

"Are you ready to enter into Level Five?" Samuel asked.

Determined and confident, Matthew replied, "Absolutely."

Samuel merely smiled back at his prodigy reassuringly. He engaged the transport one final time, and off they went. Samuel must have thought Matthew was truly ready to embark on this final leg of the journey as they flew across the web at an incredible speed. The various ribbons upon which Samuel guided their craft caused them to move in all directions. The curves, sharp turns, and continuous up and down movements would certainly have made the most avid roller coaster enthusiast ill.

Matthew didn't flinch a muscle or bat an eye at the turbulence. This, without question, was a clear indication that he had truly begun to open his mind to the limitless possibilities available to him.

After a few minutes, Samuel came to an energy ribbon like no other they had encountered thus far. Matthew immediately took notice of its uniqueness. The diameter of the golden ribbon of energy was at least three times that of the ones they had been riding along. It was much wider than that of a skyscraper, extending vertically from their current position.

Matthew looked around in a complete circle and was shocked by the vastness of the web, the endless threads and gateways to which they were connected. He could see it all unfolding, as the web was in constant motion. Matthew was amazed at the sheer quantity and speed of ribbons flying about the endless continuum as they formed new connections far beyond his view.

"Where are we now?" Matthew asked, looking back at his guide. "Why have we stopped?"

"I just wanted to show you something, Matthew, before we enter the final gateway of your journey," Samuel responded.

Matthew assumed his guide was referring to the large ribbon before them.

"You noticed this thread is different," Samuel prodded.

Matthew looked at the large ribbon again.

"Yes. It's much larger and runs up and down," he answered. "Why is that?"

"It's because we have entered the center of the space-time continuum, Matthew, and the energy ribbon you now see before us is the heart of it," Samuel replied. "This marks the beginning of the web itself created by The One from which all things were born."

Matthew paused for a moment, trying to comprehend Samuel's words. He looked up the supposed "trunk" of the space-time continuum and saw a gateway in the far distance. The sheer beauty compelled him to take pause and admire the incredible sight. The threads extending outward from the gateway were so numerous, they emitted a solid glow, which rained down upon the web in a mushroom shaped fashion. Matthew soaked in this incredible phenomenon. He could actually feel the intensity and purity of the golden light upon his body. It was a feeling of pure joy, love and hope that lifted his spirit. He became filled with an unexplained bliss as all past cares, worries, fears and limitations were wiped away. Matthew tried to savor this amazing moment in his young life. He could not take his eyes off this extraordinary sight but had to ask the burning question in his mind.

"Is this heaven?" Matthew asked excitedly. It did not even occur to him until now that maybe he might have passed on to the other side and not even realized it.

"Not exactly, Matthew," Samuel replied. "And no, you're not dead, my young friend. Rather than try to explain it to you, let me just show you."

Samuel then engaged the transport and they began to rise up the energy ribbon. They reached what Matthew assumed was the master portal at the very top and his heart began racing.

From this one gateway spawned thousands and maybe even millions of golden threads which created the web all around them.

Matthew's excitement intensified at the thought of what lay ahead of them on the other side. In usual fashion, the white flow of energy engulfed them as they disappeared within the portal. Matthew's vision blurred as all light and colors stretched just before the bright light briefly blinded him. Within a few moments, they emerged on the other side. It took a few seconds for his eyesight to return to normal at which point his brain finally processed the image before him.

They had entered an open space with no visible walls, ceiling or floor. There were no objects or scenery of any kind. Samuel slowed their transport to a complete stop and disengaged their engine as they "landed" on an invisible floor. Matthew's immediate thought was, *Where have we landed, and how could we have landed without a visible platform*? But despite the disbelief, Matthew had felt the craft jolt slightly as it physically landed within this void.

Samuel nonchalantly stepped down from the deck of the hovercraft. Turning his head to look at his guide fully, Matthew was shocked by Samuel's action, as he expected him to immediately fall due to the apparent lack of a floor. Surprisingly, however, Samuel's left foot with which he led his descent, struck a solid surface followed then by his right. He was clearly standing unattached from their transport, seemingly levitating in mid-air. Matthew then took a step forward toward the edge of the hover disc platform only to see that Samuel stepped onto what was now a visible path. It was a path apparently made of red brick. Sizing up the rough dimensions, Matthew estimated it was approximately four or five feet wide.

"Come on, Matthew, step down with me, and let's take a walk," encouraged Samuel.

"Take a walk to where?" Matthew replied as he looked all around at the vastness of nothing which surrounded them. "I don't see anything!"

"We've entered into The Room of Infinite Possibilities," Samuel replied. "You and I are going to walk along this path that will lead you to the next leg of your journey. This is where I can best show you Level Five of the Spirit."

Samuel realized he should provide more details to his pupil to emphasize the importance of this place. "This is the place from which all possibilities are created and realized," Samuel continued, "It represents the capacity of the human mind and spirit and your true potential."

"Oh, is that all?" Matthew said as he looked about nervously. "Why didn't you say so in the first place?"

Samuel let out a small laugh, but he motioned to his pupil to step off the hover disc and join him on the path.

Looking down at Samuel, Matthew could see the calm, confident and reassuring look in his eyes. Then he looked at Samuel's feet which clearly were standing on this visible brick path. He lifted his gaze in an attempt to follow the direction of the path, but much to his surprise and discomfort, the path ended about ten feet from where Samuel stood. It didn't just end; it completely disappeared into thin air, which of course, did nothing to bolster Matthew's confidence.

Sensing Matthew's hesitancy, Samuel reminded, "Matthew, don't forget the lessons you have learned so far. What is Level One?"

Matthew rolled his eyes in response to Samuel's question. "Really, Samuel?" Matthew began impatiently. "Do we need to have a review? I get it. I remember."

"Then why, Matthew, are you doubting this moment if you 'get it?'" Samuel countered, knowing Matthew needed a refresher to overcome his doubt.

Matthew opened his mouth, ready to counter his guide's argument, but then he realized that he had nothing. Samuel had just helped him, yet again, make a quick connection of self-awareness which was needed.

"Level One is Freedom," replied Matthew, tempering his tone.

"That's right, Matthew," Samuel replied. "I know you chose this journey, because you had that fire and burning desire. Now, what is Level Two?"

"Courage," Matthew responded without hesitation.

"Which you have definitely summoned and displayed thus far," Samuel confirmed.

Matthew began to actually think and recall all he had been through, including facing his darkest demons. Looking back to appreciate the progress made does not happen often enough on life's journeys.

"And Level Three?" Samuel quizzed.

"Level Three is having faith that can strengthen our beliefs," Matthew succinctly answered.

"Okay," Samuel continued. "Now it's time, right here, right now, to invoke the courage I know you have. Trust me and yourself to have the faith to continue on to the next step of this journey. I know you cannot see beyond the path immediately before us, but it goes back to believing in the choices you have made thus far, believing in the vision you now have for yourself. You cannot deny or abandon that, Matthew. Every being's desire to lead a life by their own design lies in the freedom of choice, and each choice is in the present."

Samuel paused a moment to allow Matthew to absorb his words. "You have chosen exceptionally well thus far, Matthew," Samuel encouraged.

Matthew looked back up at Samuel, feeling more at ease and confident again. Then he remembered what Samuel had said. He was The Key, and hopefully that would soon be revealed, which stirred a bit of anxiety but excitement as well.

"Also, Matthew, don't forget about Level Four," Samuel reminded. "You mustn't let your mind trick you and hold you back. Don't let it impose limitations through negative thinking or fear of things that we may not yet fully understand. Sometimes our fears seize control of us. In the greatest moments of growth in our lives, we actually have to let go and allow the path to unfold before us. We have to have faith that we will be guided along the way and be tuned into the clues we need to move forward."

"Self-Awareness," Matthew said aloud.

Samuel gave an affirming nod as he watched Matthew process these truths with his usual contemplative look. Matthew closed his eyes and took a deep breath. For a moment or two, he began to repeat the meditation mantra, "Om," that Samuel had taught him during his jungle sequence in order to calm and clear his mind. He was not about to come this far only to allow fear or negative thoughts hold him back. Feeling much calmer, Matthew opened his eyes and stepped off the transport wearing a huge smile.

"Well done, Matthew," Samuel praised. "You've taken your first step into Level Five."

"I have to ask," Matthew commented. "Why is the path only a few feet long and then disappears into thin air?"

"This is one of your first lessons of Level Five, Matthew," Samuel answered. "There are times in life when a person has no idea how they will accomplish their dreams or resolve a current problem. They may have no clue where assistance will come from, but they know one thing, especially once they enter the Fifth Level of the Spirit."

"What's that?" Matthew asked curiously as he studied the red brick path more closely.

"They know they will accomplish what they set out to do," Samuel stated intensely. "The mere fact that they have this clear vision of the end point in mind enables them to achieve it, because they know that their path will be revealed and that they will get the guidance they need. They stay true to their vision and have faith that the path will unfold as it should."

Matthew paused to further reflect on his teacher's words. He had summoned the resolve thus far and was not going to allow himself to fall short of his vision: Unlocking the mystery of The Oval. Revealing his destiny. Learning how he was The Key and discovering the reason for the burning desires he felt since he was a young boy.

"I assume we're supposed to walk along this path then?" Matthew inquired as he took a few steps forward to find himself shoulder to shoulder with his guide. Matthew could see the edge of the path just a few feet away, and he suddenly had a light-hearted moment of humor.

"It's going to be a short walk," Matthew commented with a short laugh.

"Let's get started and see what happens," Samuel said wearing a bit of a smirk himself.

Samuel looked away from his student and took a huge, deliberate first step along the short brick pathway. Matthew immediately followed suit, and as they quickly approached the edge of the pathway, an astonishing thing occurred: An extension of the walkway suddenly appeared out of nowhere. Another twenty feet of brick "roadway" simply materialized. To make things even more interesting, the newly laid path had some twists and turns along the way.

Matthew smiled in wonder at the sudden development. Then again, he realized that this journey of his has been nothing short of incredible, so why should he be surprised by anything at this point? Now he realized anything was possible, and there was no doubt about it: This path and journey thus far had been designed specifically for him.

"So what is Level Five of the Spirit, Samuel?" Matthew asked.

"Let's start here, Matthew," Samuel replied as he then suddenly stopped in his tracks.

Matthew looked around, above and below them, only to see more of the same as when they first arrived on the transport—nothing.

"What are we looking for?" Matthew asked looking back at his guide.

"This," Samuel replied. He raised his left arm in an upward sweeping motion.

Matthew gasped as his eyes grew wide.

Samuel's arm motion had somehow transformed the endless sea of nothingness into a most extraordinary scene of beauty. They seemed to have been transported to a valley with snow-capped mountains and towering pine trees. At the base of this valley was a crystal-clear lake whose water sparkled in the light of the sun. Matthew was so taken back by the beauty of this serene place that he did not notice they were standing in the middle of the lake itself. After a moment or two, he finally glanced down only to see that their red brick path was still visible as it hovered just above the surface of the water. The path was leading them to the distant shoreline.

Samuel smiled in response to Matthew's expression of awe. "Striking, isn't it?" Samuel asked.

"Beautiful doesn't even do it justice," Matthew muttered as he slowly spun around. "It just seems so pure."

"Would you believe me if I told you we are in prehistoric Europe, in an area known today as France?" Samuel asked.

That definitely caught the young man's attention as he shifted to make eye contact with his guide. "A few days ago, Samuel, the answer would have been no," Matthew responded.

"And now?" Samuel inquired knowing full well the response he would get from his pupil.

"Now, I absolutely believe you," Matthew stated. "I guess that's part of my getting through Level Three and Four. How prehistoric are we talking here?"

"It's roughly twenty-five thousand years ago by Earth's measure of time," Samuel answered.

"So, why are we here?" Matthew asked. "I would have thought we would be looking to the future for examples of Level Five. As pretty as this is, what does prehistoric France have anything to do with it?"

"Don't let your mind try to bulldoze along too quickly or make snap judgments," Samuel warned. "We are here for a very good reason."

"Which is?" Matthew prompted.

"To lay the foundation, Matthew, as we enter Level Five," Samuel responded as something caught his attention in his peripheral vision. "Ah, here we are. Just in time to see an old friend."

Samuel shifted his gaze away from his student toward the shoreline directly in front of them. Matthew followed Samuel's gaze to catch some movement along the bank of the lake.

"Shall we?" Samuel asked as he signaled with his left arm for Matthew to commence walking toward the shore.

Matthew complied and began stepping forward. As they gradually drew closer, Matthew could see what caught Samuel's eye. It was a man, from what Matthew could tell. When they came within ten or fifteen feet from the bank, the mysterious figure was fully discernible. The Caucasian man was roughly five and a half feet in height with long brown hair. He was holding a wooden spear with the tip pointing downward toward the lake. He stood motionless about knee deep in the water with his spear at the ready and his eyes intently focused on something. He was wearing a chest plate made of light-colored wooden material, and his face was decorated in ornate colors and patterns. He was also wearing light brown, leather-skinned pants. Matthew's thoughts quickly drifted to his jungle scene where he had the most unpleasant meeting with the native, hoping this would not have the same outcome.

Matthew's attention was brought back to the moment when the man suddenly plunged his spear into the lake directly beneath his feet. He then bent over reaching down into the water to retrieve the spear. When the man's arm emerged from the water triumphantly holding his recovered weapon, Matthew could see a fish wiggling on the end of the spear. The man smiled, clearly pleased with himself at securing his next meal.

"This, Matthew, is an ancient European man whom your people officially named Cro-Magnon," Samuel explained. "Ever hear of him?"

Matthew continued to study the man's behavior and physical appearance.

"Yeah, I remember the name, but I don't know anything about them," Matthew replied, briefly glancing in Samuel's direction. "So what does this have to do with Level Five?"

"Matthew, before we go there, I want you to take a very long look at this fellow from thousands of years ago," Samuel instructed. "What do you notice?"

Matthew looked back at the man and further studied Cro-Magnon.

"He's wearing the type of clothing I would expect of such an ancient person," Matthew began. "I suppose the first order of business would always be about survival, like what he is doing now."

"That's true, but is there anything you notice about his physical features other than his face paintings or clothing?" Samuel prompted.

Matthew was unable to come up with the specific answer his mentor obviously wanted. Ready to admit defeat in failing to make the correct observation, Matthew responded, "No, I don't see anything unusual about him, except he seems shorter than average."

"Exactly!" Samuel replied excitedly.

"What?" Matthew said, surprised. "How can that be the right answer?"

"Well," Samuel continued. "Here we have the case of an ancient human being who roamed the Earth between ten to forty thousand years ago, and yet his physical appearance is for the most part very much like your own. Look at his head, Matthew. Is there anything unusual about its size?"

Once again, Matthew studied the man intently with a narrowed focus. Try as he might, Matthew was unable to find any significant variations to the man's features.

"I don't see anything that different," Matthew replied.

"Right again," Samuel encouraged. "His head and brain are slightly smaller but certainly not to the casual onlooker."

Matthew thought for a moment about Samuel's choice of words. In particular, how "casual" is it to be seeing a live image of an ancient human being? Maybe for his guide, this was normal, which in turn, brought Matthew to recall some of the subtleties in Samuel's comments throughout their journey. He remembered Samuel using words or phrases such as, "by Earth time," or "your people." Then the big one was Samuel referring to him as The Key. Matthew made yet another mental note to address this at a more suitable time, but now clearly wasn't it.

"I'm sorry, but I still don't see how this has any connection to why we are here or to any Levels of the Spirit," Matthew commented.

"Matthew, this ancient human being is all about untapped potential awaiting boundless possibilities!" Samuel stated with intense excitement. "At this stage, Cro-Magnon had started to create sculptures, paintings, body ornaments, engravings, and even music."

"Untapped potential?" Matthew responded with an inquisitive look.

Pointing to the Cro-Magnon man standing before them, Samuel posed a series of questions.

"How do you suppose that humanity went from this, to you?" Samuel asked. "How did humans go from spearing a fish at the end of a wooden stick, to creating submersible machines that explore the oceans miles deep? How did humanity go from a strictly land-bound species, to navigating the seas, or creating airplanes to fly and ultimately leave the confines of the planet to walk on the moon?!"

Matthew felt he had the perfect answer to all of Samuels's questions. "We figured it out, I guess," Matthew stated.

"How?" Samuel asked, encouraging Matthew to further expound on his short response.

"Humanity became smarter in using more of our mental power?" Matthew elaborated uncertainly.

"Yes!" Samuel affirmed. "Unlike any other species on Earth, the brain development throughout ancient history has driven humanity's progress. How much do you know about the human brain?"

Matthew became confused and a bit frustrated yet again as to why they were now having a biology lesson when he is supposed to be learning about Level Five. He thought for a moment. He truly didn't know that much about the brain.

"I thought I once heard that it weighs around six pounds on average and made of a very dense tissue," Matthew replied. He became increasingly confused about where Samuel was headed.

"Okay, Matthew, let's get a bit of education on the brain for a minute," Samuel began. "Your modern day scientists have estimated that the brain contains approximately one hundred billion brain cells. As the brain is stimulated and new learning occurs, these brain cells, or neurons, are connected by something called dendrites. The creation of dendrites drives more interconnection of neurons which, in turn, has driven humanity's advancement."

"Meaning we get smarter," Matthew muttered, amused.

"Yes, meaning you get smarter," Samuel affirmed with a smile. "Let me try to put some perspective on the vastness of the possible intellectual power of humanity. Right now, most computers have the computing capacity, in mathematical terms, ten to the power of twelve. Do you know what scientists estimate the computing capacity of the human brain is?"

Matthew thought for a moment, realizing that he had no idea what the answer was, but he did know one thing. Computers today can do amazing things that go well beyond his level of understanding.

"Not a clue," Matthew responded.

"Try ten to the power of eight thousand!" Samuel answered knowing he would elicit disbelief in his pupil.

"That's incredible," Matthew commented. Matthew silently chuckled at the thought that he truly was not able to "compute" this comparison.

"Do you know, Matthew, how much of the human brain that present-day scientists believe you currently use?" asked Samuel.

"I'm not sure, maybe twenty percent?" replied Matthew.

"Five to ten percent," Samuel stated. "Think about that for a minute. Right now, you and your present-day people use only a fraction of your current brainpower. Not Cro-Magnon, but you!"

"How much of his brain capacity do you think this fellow used?" Matthew suddenly asked, curious at what the starting point might be.

"Probably less than two percent, Matthew," Samuel surmised.

Matthew paused to reflect on his teacher's comments. It was indeed a staggering concept that in twenty-five thousand years, humanity advanced from Cro-Magnon to the beings that traveled in the Apollo space craft and yet only increased their brain productivity by a few percentage points.

"So, is Level Five of the Spirit about the growth of the human mind?" Matthew inquired.

"Oh Matthew, it's much bigger than that, my friend," Samuel said intensely. "That is certainly one element of Level Five, but we are here to understand HOW humanity has and will continue to unlock their own boundless potential. The mind is a very powerful tool."

Samuel paused for a moment to reflect on what must come next to further Matthew's understanding. The answer came to him. "But there is something else, Matthew, that you must understand," Samuel continued.

"What's that?" Matthew asked.

"You need to experience it firsthand," Samuel replied.

He then raised his left hand and incredibly managed to "rewind" the scene to a few minutes in the past when Cro-Magnon stood motionless in the water just before spearing his meal.

Matthew quickly realized what Samuel was referencing. His guide wanted him to enter the ancient man's chakra. "Are you serious?" Matthew questioned in disbelief. "How?"

"Just like you have done numerous times now," Samuel replied.

Matthew couldn't wrap his mind around this proposal. "But he's 25,000 years old!" Matthew blurted in protest. "I don't even speak his language. I don't even know what the hell his language is!"

Samuel turned and looked Matthew square in the eye. "You don't need to, Matthew," Samuel said. "Trust me."

Matthew realized, once again, he must comply. His guide continually shows him the way, and he must continue to trust if he is to progress further through his journey. Turning away from Samuel, he walked over to the edge of the walkway which ended right next to his prehistoric friend standing in the water. Uncertain of what to expect, Matthew nervously reached out and touched the man's left shoulder with his right hand. The white light engulfed him and then quickly faded.

Something was very different. There were no images of the past and no stress or worries of the future. No significant events that shaped the emotional complexities of this man's current life came through at all. In fact, Matthew could not sense or feel any kind of strong emotion emanating from his host. Something far more unique than his past chakra experiences was at play. Matthew suddenly felt his senses come alive as though they were magnified one hundredfold.

He took a deep breath and filled his lungs with the fresh mountain air, the scent of pine trees lingering. He suddenly heard a bird chirping and noticed out of the corner of his eye that it was perched in a tree more than twenty feet away. He felt the coldness of the water on his legs as though he were truly standing in the lake with his host. He felt the wooden handle of the spear but with such detail that every grain of the wood within his grip could be felt. Matthew then managed to see the fish beneath the water with incredible detail. He was focused on the fish yet aware of everything around him.

Matthew found himself completely immersed in the environment in which he stood as though he were the Cro-Magnon trying to catch the fish. It all came to life at once. Like nothing he had previously experienced. No need for interpretation. No need to decipher the meaning. No language barrier to overcome.

He was one with all that surrounded him.

Matthew found it incredibly invigorating to be in this heightened state of his senses. There were no words to clearly articulate it. The only thing that came to mind was a feeling of existing in tune with the energy of life all around him. Somehow, he was totally immersed within the environment where he not only felt its energy but was an active participant in it. The intensity was profoundly invigorating and also filled him with a deep sense of peace.

He didn't want to let go but soon felt the familiar pull on his shoulder as Samuel called him back. It seemed only seconds ago he had entered Cro-Magnon's chakra, but as Matthew had grown accustomed, "time" slips away very quickly. It was likely far longer than he would have guessed. The white light flashed as his hand pulled away from his host.

Matthew took a moment to take in a few deep breaths and allow his vision to return to normal. He immediately noticed the dulled nature of his senses. Matthew looked all around him in an attempt to appreciate the beauty yet again. It wasn't the same, and he felt his senses were almost crippled.

Samuel knew what his pupil was experiencing. Without prompting, Matthew spoke.

"Wow," Matthew began. "That was intense. I've never felt such incredible sensations before." Confused, Matthew questioned his guide, "So how does *that* relate to Level Five?"

"One word, Matthew," Samuel replied. *"Presence."*

Although Matthew knew the general meaning of the word, he now had a true experience of it through this last chakra. He had a much better understanding of what it means to be fully present.

"You know what's amazing?" Samuel asked. "How humanity in your time has become insidiously distracted!" Samuel said with frustration.

Matthew paused for a moment to think about that notion.

"As 'advanced' as your people have become, they have also lost the ability to truly live in the moments of life," Samuel continued. "You are in the electronic age of cell phones, computers, television and internet with access anytime, anywhere. This has driven the insatiable need to be connected on an *external* level all the time in the name of political or social agendas, careers, busy schedules, and any other reason people conjure up."

Matthew looked at Samuel as he thought of how all those things that seemed such a normal part of everyday life can have such a negative effect on our abilities.

"What our prehistoric friend clearly showed you, Matthew, was truly being in the present moment of existence," Samuel explained further. "A trait that so few of your people now have an ability to appreciate and even practice."

Matthew nodded affirmatively in recognition of a level of understanding that exceeded logic.

"So, this state of presence is Level Five?" Matthew inquired with great curiosity, trying to seek a deeper understanding.

"Not quite, Matthew, but it is a critical key to Level Five, because without presence, you will miss the signs and the ability to 'plug into' something far greater and more powerful than you could possibly imagine," Samuel replied looking directly into his prodigy's eyes for emphasis.

Matthew's attention shot up tenfold at these words.

"It's time now to leave our friend, Matthew, and continue the journey," Samuel stated.

Suddenly, his guide raised his left hand, and in a vast sweeping motion, wiped away the scenery of ancient France with Cro-Magnon man. Matthew now found themselves back within the same vast room of nothingness but only for a few seconds. Samuel repeated the sweeping motion transporting them into an entirely different scene.

Matthew looked up to see a bright blue sky lit by the mid-day sun. His attention then turned to immediately behind them as his ears detected the sound of crashing water. As he turned, Matthew could see the source of the sound far beneath them as the waves from an ocean crashed and sprayed a fine mist against the side of a steep cliff, a cliff that Matthew quickly realized they weren't standing on but levitating in front of. Even though their feet were clearly planted on the red brick "suspension bridge," it was a bit unnerving as Matthew looked on both sides to see what appeared to be a one hundred-foot drop to a rocky shoreline. Matthew kept his calm, however, and casually walked along the pathway until it led them to the edge of the cliff where it continued on the ground from there.

"Where are we now?" Matthew inquired.

"Ancient Greece," replied Samuel. "About 300 B.C."

Matthew's mind raced with excitement as to what could possibly be awaiting him in ancient Greece. The last experience with Cro-Magnon man was incredible.

They walked along as the pathway gradually revealed itself every twenty feet or so until they reached the summit of a hill. A white, stone structure appeared before them. The circular structure possessed towering white pillars. Matthew immediately recalled the photos of coliseums in a history book of Greek architecture. Matthew gained a further appreciation up close of its impressive size. As soon as they entered the roofless building, Matthew realized they weren't there to admire the architecture.

They were staring at a man wearing a long, white tunic and standing in front of a podium. He appeared to be of average height and weight, had a black, receding hairline but a very full beard. His current facial expression gave the indication he was deep in thought. Matthew then noticed he was holding a feather. Very peculiar, thought Matthew, until he soon realized it was a quill as the man dipped it into a small container of ink and began to write.

"Do you know who this person is, Matthew?" Samuel inquired.

"He looks a little bit like my Uncle Joe," Matthew responded with a bit of humor.

Samuel chuckled a response.

"Good guess, but it's the ancient Greek philosopher, Aristotle," Samuel responded. "He wrote about such subjects as politics, ethics, physics, metaphysics, poetry, biology and zoology just to name a few. He was a student of Plato and a teacher of Alexander the Great."

Matthew was mesmerized as he tried to fully grasp being in the presence of a person who shaped so much of human history.

"To increase your understanding of Level Five, I want to mention one tidbit of information regarding one of Aristotle's theories," Samuel commented. "But first, I would like to ask you what you see him doing?"

Matthew looked more closely at Aristotle.

"He's clearly writing something down," responded Matthew. "I guess he is taking notes."

"Notes on what?" Samuel asked.

"How am I supposed to know?" Matthew responded irritably.

"I don't mean exactly the specific topic but in general, what is generating these notes?" Samuel asked again.

Matthew looked again at Aristotle who seemed quite excited about what he was feverishly recording on his scroll. "I guess he might be writing down his thoughts on whatever subject he is thinking about," Matthew replied.

"Ah, yes indeed," Samuel confirmed. "Our ancient philosopher and scientist is writing down his thoughts. He had incredible passion to expand his own knowledge of the Universe, especially when he felt it was for the betterment of his fellow man."

Matthew continued to marvel at the scene now before him. *Aristotle,* he thought to himself. It didn't seem possible.

"One of my favorite quotes of Aristotle, Matthew, is, '*All human beings, by nature, desire to know,*'" Samuel commented.

Matthew thought for a moment. That quote certainly resonated with him in relation to The Oval and the Levels of the Spirit his guide has shown him.

"What tools or instruments do you see?" Samuel asked, compelled to keep Matthew's focus on the task at hand.

"Nothing but a quill," Matthew replied.

"Is that all?" Samuel prompted.

Matthew knew that look of Samuel's just before dropping a new lesson onto his lap.

"What is this theory of his you wanted to mention?" Matthew inquired ignoring his guide's last question.

"Come on, Matthew," Samuel responded a bit indignantly. "You know by now that I'm not going to let you off that easily."

Matthew looked at his guide.

"He only has the quill," Matthew re-stated.

"Well," Samuel began. "You know the best way to find the answer to the question I asked."

Matthew obviously knew what Samuel wanted him to do. He walked over to the ancient philosopher and stood immediately to his right. Matthew's heart rate began to escalate. The excitement of what he was about to do was mind blowing.

Aristotle! he thought to himself.

Matthew slowly lifted his left hand to touch the man's right shoulder but paused with his hand in mid-air, just inches away from his host. Matthew looked at Samuel with a huge smile which Samuel reciprocated while motioning to his pupil to proceed. Matthew entered the philosopher's chakra as his hand made contact. The white light engulfed Matthew and quickly faded with a light haze remaining, which again differed slightly from his past experiences.

Matthew immediately felt Aristotle's presence and all that was associated with it. He felt a rush of adrenaline followed by an intense focus. There was no infusion of past or future events within Aristotle's life that streamed into Matthew's consciousness. It was similar to Cro-Magnon, in that Aristotle was fully present in the moment while being aware of all that surrounded him. The huge difference, however, is what his host was focusing on. His mind, body and soul all seemed to be converging on a single thought. A problem that needed to be solved. But it was much more than a problem.

Matthew's excitement grew as he stood there watching and experiencing the emotional rush of this man who seemed to be on the verge of an enormous breakthrough. It was about truth. A truth about humanity's existence and the place we have called home as a species for thousands of years. It was something about the Earth itself.

Matthew then began to tap into Aristotle's mind. He became one with his thoughts, and suddenly, concepts and theories raced across his consciousness. Again, Matthew realized that there was no language barrier. He was able to comprehend everything that Aristotle was thinking and contemplating that very moment.

His host was quickly writing with each surge of excited thought and concept that flooded his mind. Matthew glanced down at the scroll recording his thoughts and saw a sketch of the stars with numerous arrows coupled with a landscape drawing underneath it, a landscape that Matthew quickly realized was Aristotle's rendition of the Earth.

Matthew then heard voices. All spoke in Greek, but he understood them nonetheless.

Aristotle was recalling, with great accuracy, past conversations with others, but what Matthew quickly surmised is that his host was asking them questions. He was trying to tease out information from these people.

But who? Matthew thought. *Who were these people?* Then Matthew saw Aristotle sketching a ship on the ocean. He now understood that the people whom his host had interviewed were sailors.

Suddenly, a burst of white light within Aristotle's chakra temporarily blinded Matthew. A moment of truth exploded into Aristotle's mind, sweeping his soul and body into a state of pure bliss. Aristotle dropped the quill and stumbled backwards to the white brick steps upon which he had been standing, clumsily falling onto his back side.

Yes, of course! Aristotle thought. *Pythagoras was right!*

Being so attuned to his host, Matthew also fell to the ground with the overwhelming emotions. Matthew realized he had just witnessed a miraculous discovery born within the mind of one of the greatest philosophers and teachers ever known. A discovery of a simple truth now universally accepted as fact.

The Earth is round.

Aristotle remained in his euphoria where he had perfect clarity. Matthew could feel the profound sense of knowing that this great thinker now became immersed within. Time stood still for a few seconds and then, without warning, Matthew felt a surge of energy welling within himself, a surge of energy coming from within his host.

Aristotle suddenly leapt to his feet, thrust both arms into the air and let out a tremendous bellow that echoed across the land. His heart was filled with pure elation, propelling him to dance about uncontrollably. Matthew could not contain a huge burst of laughter from coming out and joined Aristotle in his dance.

But then Samuel called him back.

As suspected, Matthew did not want to leave, as his spirit fed off the elation projecting from his host. He reluctantly broke the link, and the flash of white light faded. Matthew then realized he was on his knees. His breathing was heavy and a feeling of emptiness poured into him.

"Oh my God!" Matthew shouted. "He had this incredible breakthrough. I not only understood it, Samuel, but I felt it!"

Facing Matthew directly, Samuel knelt down, grabbed Matthew from beneath his left arm and helped his pupil to his feet.

Matthew didn't realize how dizzy and weak he had become from being in the chakra.

"You witnessed a birth, Matthew," Samuel commented.

Matthew looked at Samuel. Although it was a most peculiar way to explain this experience, Matthew understood perfectly what Samuel was trying to convey.

"A birth of truth," Samuel further explained. "A move from mystery to revelation. It was a most profound discovery from this single individual, Matthew, who devoted his entire life to seeking knowledge."

Matthew looked away from Samuel and back at Aristotle who was still dancing about, allowing himself a few more moments of celebration.

"Do you have any idea how significant discovery was, Matthew?" Samuel asked.

Matthew felt he understood the significance from the perspective of his host but didn't fully comprehend much beyond that. Matthew shook his head back and forth as he stared in wonder at the great philosopher still immersed in celebration.

Samuel paused a moment to contemplate how best to articulate the magnitude of Aristotle's discovery.

"Matthew, do you realize the notion of a round Earth did not begin to gain broad acceptance until about a thousand years *after* Aristotle's discovery?" Samuel noted. "Not only that, but it would be several centuries later when travelers would even attempt to sail around the world to finally dispel the notion that the Earth is flat."

Matthew looked back at his guide as the importance of the last comments began to take a foothold. Then a question formed within his mind that he wanted to ask his guide.

"Who was Pythagorus?" Matthew asked. "Aristotle said he was right."

"Pythagorus was another philosopher and ancient scientist in 570 B.C. who first theorized that the earth was round," Samuel replied. "It was Aristotle who confirmed it based on his own theories providing what he felt was irrefutable evidence. Aristotle obviously didn't have the benefit of satellite photos or telescopes in deriving his hypothesis. He didn't have his own ship to sail around the world."

Samuel looked away from his apprentice and fixed his gaze upon the great philosopher. At that moment, Aristotle stopped his celebratory dancing and resumed passionately writing his ideas.

"Then how, my young friend, could this man from so early on, have possibly deduced that the Earth is round?" Samuel asked.

Matthew was beginning to truly fathom the significance of the point that Samuel was making. How could Aristotle have conjured up this theory? He had no instruments available to him, but Matthew did have a very important frame of reference to give him some insight.

"It was clear from his chakra that he began to piece together clues," Matthew replied. "He must have been working on this for a long time, since he had written a lot of notes. He observed, asked questions of sailors, and came up with more theories until he managed to make some conclusions."

Samuel gave Matthew a huge smile as he began to clearly understand what happened.

"He used his mind, the power of thought and reflection, as his only tool in coming up with his theory," Samuel further elaborated. "Through his observations of the horizon and the mere fact that ships sailing south would see the southern constellations change their position in the sky and appear higher gave him the clues he needed in confirming the theory of a round Earth must be true."

Matthew understood yet wanted more clarity.

"How did he develop this awareness?" Matthew asked as his desire to learn more propelled him to dig deeper.

"Ah yes!" Samuel said excitedly. "You've just made a connection of your own, Matthew. His life was consumed by thought. He could piece clues and observations together, make connections and ponder them, thereby, raising his own awareness."

To further Matthew's understanding, Samuel proposed another challenge.

"What happens when a person exercises a muscle?" Samuel asked.

Having been an avid weight lifter, Matthew immediately knew the answer.

"It gets stronger," Matthew replied.

"So it is with the human mind," Samuel continued. "The more you use it and challenge yourself with new ideas and concepts, the more you initiate the building of dendrite connections within the brain itself. The possible connections are virtually limitless!"

Samuel then turned and began to walk along the red brick path. "Come, let's take a look at another example," Samuel instructed while motioning to his prodigy to join him.

Matthew followed his teacher as they walked shoulder to shoulder along the path. He turned his head back toward the ancient philosopher to take one last look. Matthew felt overwhelming gratitude for this experience. He was grateful for Aristotle and his contributions to human development. There is no way to fully comprehend the significance of this experience by reading it in a text book. The fact that he got to feel it and know it from the perspective of the human spirit was incredible and surreal.

Within a few seconds, Aristotle faded away along with the ancient Greek structure and ocean-side scenery. Matthew then faced forward and a completely new scene instantly appeared. Before soaking in his new surroundings, however, Matthew had a spark of potential insight of his own just then. It was as though the experiences, observations and lessons learned thus far had begun to form even more connections within himself. A possible theory of his own burst forth.

The human mind . . . the space-time continuum.

Dendrites form connections to synaptic nerves within the brain, infinitely expanding the potential for growth and knowledge. The web is always expanding with new ribbons connecting to new or existing gateways. Are these facts a coincidental parallel or is it something much bigger? Is it another truth of The Universe waiting to be discovered?

They continued to walk along the brick path as Matthew's sense of anticipation grew.

CHAPTER 15

REVELATIONS

Their red brick path had now led them along a cobble stone street in a city unknown to Matthew. He immediately realized they had not yet emerged within the twenty-first century as they walked by some horse-drawn carriages. Several two- and three-story homes lined the street appearing almost as a single structure due to their close proximity.

The red path turned off the cobble stone road only to lead them up the stairs to the doorway of one of the homes. The two men followed the pathway up the steps to the dark wooden front door. Samuel gripped the knob and the door swung open as he simultaneously motioned to Matthew to step inside. As soon as he did so, the young man detected faint music emanating from somewhere within the house. Judging from the type of sound, it was unmistakably a piano. Samuel then followed his pupil through the doorway heading toward their next lesson. Matthew glanced down and noticed how unnatural their red brick path appeared in contrast to the dark wooden planks of this obviously historic home.

"Where are we now?" Matthew inquired as they continued walking.

"Germany, around 1778," Samuel replied.

Matthew was absolutely loving this, because the knowledge now coming to him in these most recent chakras had been so uplifting. He thought back to the intense experiences from his earlier hosts and the painful lessons contained therein. Lessons and understanding that he now realized was an absolute necessity, especially when confronting his own deeply buried demons.

Matthew began to appreciate, now more than ever, how moving through intensely difficult and painful situations and dealing with them along the way not only helps us grow, but makes us stronger and more resilient in the process. He was also feeling incredibly blessed from the insights gained from his latest hosts, because the chakras were not only so positive but seemed to have accelerated the rate of his learning and comprehension.

They followed the path straight ahead, making their way through the foyer and dining room. Turning a corner, they approached an adjoining room with solid dark wooden French doors that were presently closed. Samuel grasped the tainted metal knobs with each hand and slowly opened them inward to reveal a study.

The previously muffled sounds now filled the air with clarity and fullness. Matthew was better able to appreciate and admire the beauty of the performance as he began to marvel at the skill of the pianist who sat on the other side of the instrument out of view. Matthew noticed a gentlemen standing at the side of the piano looking down at his pupil presumably engaged in a lesson. Both Samuel and Matthew slowly walked around the somewhat stern-looking instructor to bring the performer into view. Matthew's gaze immediately fell upon the pianist responsible for creating such a skillful melody. Much to his surprise, the person sitting upon the piano bench was a young boy.

Anticipating his confusion, Samuel then turned to his own prodigy to pose a question.

"Any idea who that is?" Samuel asked.

"No, but he's amazingly talented!" Matthew replied enthusiastically. "Who is he?"

"I assume you have heard the name, Ludwig van Beethoven?" Samuel inquired.

Matthew looked at the boy in astonishment. He had always enjoyed all styles of music, but by far his favorite genre was classical in spite of his young age. He always found it to be so inspiring, because something about it moved him deeply.

"No way!" Matthew said as his excitement magnified one hundredfold at the prospect of entering the composer's chakra. "He is one of the most famous composers in history. I never really thought of him as a performer though. How old is he?"

"He's about eight years old here," answered Samuel. "His father discovered his musical ability very early in life, and he was only ten when one of his compositions was first published."

Matthew was amazed as the young lad effortlessly moved his hands and fingers along the keyboard. "Who's the grumpy-looking fellow looking down on him?" Matthew asked as he glanced in the direction of the adult male standing next to the boy.

"That's his father," Samuel responded. "He was his teacher until about eight or nine. Matthew, did you know that starting in his twenties, Beethoven began losing his hearing?"

"No, I didn't," Matthew replied in shock as he looked back at his guide. "So, was that the end of his composing days?"

"Not by a long shot," answered Samuel. "In fact, Beethoven eventually went completely deaf but continued to compose amazing works."

As much as Matthew had been thriving in his latest experiences, he still could not make the connection to this elusive Fifth Level of the Spirit. "I don't understand how this relates to Cro-Magnon, Aristotle and Level Five," Matthew stated, hoping Samuel would finally reveal it to him.

"You're ready to get to the point, aren't you?" Samuel said with a smile. "I'm going to have to answer your question with another question. How do you suppose child prodigies are created?'

Fighting the frustration of Samuel not giving him a direct answer, Matthew paused to reflect on the question.

"I've never really thought about it before, to be honest," Matthew replied while studying the young Beethoven and his flawless, fluid movements upon the piano. "I would guess that maybe it's a combination of the fact that they might have been born advanced somehow, and their parents recognized it."

"But Matthew, how do you suppose they are born that way?" Samuel asked. "How is it that their development can be accelerated beyond what would be considered 'normal'?"

Once again, Matthew was at a loss for an explanation that made sense to him. It was at that moment he realized how mesmerizing the music had become.

Samuel then motioned Matthew to walk over to the young boy.

"Well, my seeker of truth and knowledge, why don't you walk over there and take another step on your quest," Samuel encouraged.

Matthew began to walk toward the piano directly in front of them. He stepped off the red brick path and onto the wooden plank floor. Matthew immediately noticed a creaking noise as he placed his full weight upon it. It all seemed so real.

Matthew walked around the left side of the piano, passing Beethoven's father. He stopped directly behind the boy and raised his left hand. He placed it upon the musician's left shoulder, who continued to play uninterrupted. Matthew entered the chakra and became fully engulfed in music. His hands and fingers suddenly came to life as they instinctively began to mimic the movements of the young boy.

It was completely effortless.

Then Matthew realized there was no sheet music from which the young lad was playing. An astonishing discovery given how the music flowed from the movements of his hands and fingers. Then the white light customary within the chakra began to grow in intensity, and although it caused Matthew to instinctively squint in reaction, his vision detected an explosion of stars within the room itself. There were numerous points of light which then began to swirl about the room as they danced in synchronicity to the music flowing from its creator.

Sheer beauty.

Sheer perfection.

Matthew began to lose himself further as he found himself rhythmically swaying to the music. There was nothing logical about the experience. There was no rational thought of any kind. In fact, Beethoven was not even thinking at all. The music merely flowed through his soul, and Matthew could feel its presence. Somehow, it just came to the young composer. It felt he was harnessing something outside himself, and he was acting as a conduit. Matthew could feel the surge of musical energy and Beethoven's piano channeled this force. It was as if this music was meant to be revealed by the young prodigy. He somehow could access it from some unseen place.

Matthew closed his eyes and tried to fully immerse himself. His own spirit began to feel the spectrum of notes swirling about the room as they pulsated through him as though he too became a conduit through which this musical genius burst forth. He felt wonderful and alive. Just as he became deeply engrossed, Samuel called him back.

Matthew broke the connection, and the room returned to normal. He took a deep breath before speaking. As he looked up at Samuel, Matthew realized that his hands and fingers were still twitching in response to Beethoven's movements. Rather than be alarmed, Matthew's breath was taken away as he stared down at his hands in disbelief.

"Don't be frightened, Matthew," Samuel assured

Matthew looked up at Samuel in response. "I'm not scared," Matthew responded. "I'm shocked."

"I know it seems shocking, Matthew, but it's an expected outcome," Samuel commented.

"Expected outcome?" Matthew repeated inquisitively.

"Yes, from entering into a plane of existence that is much bigger than you can fathom right now," Samuel continued. "Your mind and spirit has been exposed to an endless sea."

Matthew's mind was attempting to still wrap itself around the experience and make some sense of it.

"Let me explain it in a different way," Samuel began. "There are numerous cases across history, some famous and others not, of people becoming advanced in all areas of human development. Think about Einstein and his scientific advancements, Da Vinci and his art, or Beethoven in the creation of his music. Think about inventors such as Thomas Edison or Henry Ford."

Matthew looked away from the boy and gave his guide a quizzical look. "Yeah," Matthew replied. "What about them?"

"Okay, Matthew," Samuel began. "These cases point to fundamental evidence where within every generation, humanity can experience quantum leaps of development. Such things are possible when the mind and spirit manages to breach Level Five of the Spirit."

Matthew's excitement grew as he realized that his mentor was about to reveal the final level.

"Level Five of the Spirit is Universal Awareness," Samuel succinctly stated.

Matthew paused a moment, trying to comprehend this next truth. Then a question immediately formed within his own mind. *What's the difference between Self Awareness and Universal Awareness?* He thought.

"Universal Awareness?" repeated Matthew. "What exactly do you mean?"

Samuel took a step closer to emphasize the importance of his words.

"Do you believe that the only plane of existence, Matthew, lies in the physical world?" Samuel asked.

"No, of course not," Matthew replied. "I believe we are spiritual beings, and certainly the lessons I've had only strengthens my belief. I believe that when we die, we leave our bodies and move into heaven or some other place that people may name differently."

Samuel nodded his head in response. "Universal Awareness, Matthew, is when a being realizes that they are part of a much bigger plane of existence!" Samuel explained excitedly. "They not only become aware of it but also try to 'tap' into this other plane to advance their own knowledge and growth."

Samuel paused a moment to find the words to further explain this concept. "To seek the Truth of Being," Samuel emphasized.

Matthew spoke not a word but merely shot his guide a look of confusion.

"Think back to what you noticed upon entering one of the gateways during your journey within the space-time continuum," Samuel prompted. "You saw me and even yourself very differently. Do you remember that?"

Matthew thought back for a moment to the various portals they entered and exited and quickly recalled the one to which Samuel was referring. "I could see your silhouette not as your physical person but as though you had some kind of energy surrounding you," Matthew replied.

"Yes!" Samuel responded. "We are so much more than our physical bodies, Matthew, and the energy signature, if you will, of our spiritual selves are active participants in this invisible plane."

Matthew glanced down at the floor for a moment attempting to absorb it all. He realized that if Samuel had revealed this to him a few gateways back, there was no way he could have possibly fathomed this concept. He looked at Beethoven displaying his artistic genius, and Matthew could now understand what Samuel was referring to. He felt it during this last chakra.

Samuel could tell that Matthew was now opening himself up even further and he grew more excited. Based on what he was now sensing from his pupil, he could reveal even more information. "Where I come from, we have given it a specific name," Samuel continued.

Matthew's gaze moved away from Beethoven to Samuel. He tilted his head with narrowed eyes, curious to what Samuel was about to reveal.

"We call it the Unified Life Force or The Fourth Dimension," Samuel explained. "It's a field of energy which binds all living things together. This connection is so strong, that life as we know it on the physical plane would not exist without the Fourth Dimension. Most people go through their entire lives thinking they live within a purely self-contained physical realm with no connection to other people or living things."

Suddenly an epiphany came upon Matthew with Samuel's last words. His mind raced through all that he had been exposed to within his various hosts' chakras. The key word that created a link for Matthew to this Level Five concept was "connection." How connected we all are and the interwoven fabric of our lives is not by random chance. Matthew was beginning to realize how vast this connectivity truly is, and another revelation came to him as he continued to dwell on this. Connections can span multiple lifetimes within this plane. So many believe that death severs the connection, but Matthew now knows the truth and recognizes the illusionary nature of this old paradigm. If all this is true, then, does time really even exist? Is it yet another illusion created by man during a time when our development had not yet progressed past limited knowledge and where our beliefs compelled us to only think linearly? Our perception of reality was limited to only what we could physically see.

Matthew's deeper understanding of the world suddenly opened the flood gates to endless possibilities. He began allowing himself to explore the vastness of his own spirit and his place in the Universe. He had always felt an inexplicable connection to some unseen force, and now Samuel had given him an incredible insight for understanding it through the existence of this Fourth Dimension. Matthew excitedly locked eyes with his teacher's, at a loss for words in trying to convey his thoughts and emotions. He was too overwhelmed to speak.

But that didn't matter, because Samuel knew what Matthew was thinking and feeling. He returned Matthew's gaze with his own excitement and nodded in understanding. Matthew was not only able to comprehend the truth more fully, he was feeling it saturate his spirit, the place where divine truth resides. The key is to recognize it, unlock it, and tap into it. Samuel's purpose had been to help Matthew unlock his true potential and realize the incredibly important destiny that awaited him.

Matthew excitedly grabbed hold of Samuel's shoulders, bursting from the elation of his deeper understanding. "Samuel!" Matthew shouted, unable to say anything else.

Samuel returned the gesture by placing his left hand on Matthew's right shoulder as the two directly faced one another. "I know, Matthew," Samuel began as he smiled at the young man. "You've taken another huge step into a much bigger plane of existence and understanding."

Matthew returned the smile and even let out a short burst of laughter. After a few moments, he let go of his guide and his breathing slowed.

Samuel waited a few more moments to let Matthew calm down enough to continue the lesson.

"Do you know what is contained within the ULF, Matthew, besides these infinite connections?" Samuel asked.

For some inexplicable reason, a single word flashed into Matthew's consciousness as he stared back at his guide. "Knowledge," Matthew said softly, still trying to catch his breath.

"Yes," Samuel said confidently. "It embeds knowledge and wisdom. You see, Matthew, in building more connections to advance the mind, we can build receptors to all of the information which exists within the ULF. Our individual minds and spirits can touch this expansive Fourth Dimension, which aids us in advancing our own development. All past and future discoveries exist there. Remember, it's our spirits that drive us, and the mind only acts as a powerful tool to enable our growth and understanding."

Samuel paused again to allow Matthew a moment to process his words.

"Level Five of the Spirit is when we become aware of this Fourth Dimension and consciously begin to interact with it," Samuel explained. "That's why this level is called Universal Awareness because of the recognition that we are part of something so huge."

Matthew looked back at Beethoven again as another question came to mind.

"So, people like Aristotle and Beethoven were aware of this Fourth Dimension, which is why they became so advanced?"

Matthew asked. "How did they know about this unseen field of energy and knowledge?"

Samuel appreciated Matthew's line of thinking, because he knew how deeply his pupil desired to know even more by making these personal and universal connections.

"That's the fascinating part of this whole thing, Matthew," Samuel said excitedly. "Human kind's awareness of the Fourth Dimension has been growing and evolving over thousands of years as people throughout history engaged in deep reflective thought about human existence and their place in the Universe. Beethoven and Aristotle probably were not fully aware of the ULF at the time, but yet they were somehow able to access it and extract from it the intelligence that enabled them to excel in math, science and music. Their spirits were drawn to it, and the individual receptors in their minds grew at an advanced rate for people of their time as they unknowingly tapped into the ULF. They didn't entirely know what is was or explain it, but *they could feel it and were drawn to it!*"

Samuel paused a moment as yet another example came to mind that might help his prodigy continue to grasp this latest truth.

"Isaac Newton!" Samuel suddenly blurted out.

"What about him?" Matthew asked somewhat startled. "He discovered gravity or something."

"Mathew, it was so much more than that," Samuel continued. "He not only discovered gravitational force but also the Universal Laws of Motion. His advancements in math and physics were astounding especially given he lived in the 1600's. His spirit drove his insatiable curiosity about life and the Universe itself. His mind and soul tirelessly strove to unlock the knowledge within the Fourth Dimension which lead to critical discoveries in math and physics that furthered humanity's understanding of the Universe. He gave future scientists the tools of how to enter space!"

Samuel's last statement sent a shockwave of connection through Matthew. He instantly thought of all the threads connecting the portals of the Shuttle Centurion crew, Mission Apollo and even Kate. All of them could easily have a ribbon within the space-time continuum connecting to a portal within which Isaac Newton made these profound discoveries.

Samuel could tell these latest truths were sinking in within the young lad at a deeper, more profound level.

"Even though Newton didn't know what this force was or even had a name for it, he was still drawn to it, began tapping into it and in a way, used his own words to describe it," Samuel continued.

"What do you mean?" Matthew asked.

"Newton likened the Fourth Dimension to an expansive sea, Samuel began. "*I do not know what I may appear to the world; but to myself I seem to have been only like a boy playing on the seashore, and diverting myself now and then in finding a smoother pebble or prettier shell than ordinary, while the great ocean of truth lay all undiscovered before me.*'"

Matthew continued to wrap his mind and spirit around Samuel's explanations. In doing so, another idea came into focus. "So, Level Five isn't necessarily the fact that human kind has advanced over the years because we've used more of our mental power, but more about letting our spirits motivate us and being drawn to this unseen field. Eventually even becoming aware of it." Matthew stated, seeking more clarity.

"Exactly!" Samuel responded. "Humanity has and will continue to advance due to their ability to form connections in their own brain development, but the conscious awareness and connection to the Fourth Dimension is what will increase the speed of your growth and the magnitude of possibilities to become limitless."

Matthew nodded as he thought of how much more humanity can grow and accomplish if we progress like this on a global scale. It was mind-numbing.

"The real power here, Matthew, is first opening up one's mind to the existence of this plane and then knowing how to tap into it," Samuel said passionately. "Once a person does this, they will be astounded by how much they can grow and accomplish. It's the power of the spirit which propels us forward. The mind's intended purpose is to be a powerful tool aiding our development and accomplishing our evolutionary goals."

Samuel looked around one last time at the scene at hand of Beethoven and spontaneously decided that another example was in order to help his young pupil further expand his knowledge. "Let's look at another example which should help you understand the potential of this life force and not only our connection to it but also the powerful connection between mind, body and soul," Samuel stated as he raised his right arm to change the scene. Samuel swept away 18th-century Germany along with young Beethoven. In its place were beautiful rolling fields of golden wheat that swayed to and fro moved by a gentle breeze. The familiarity of this country farm setting to his own Indiana hometown brought unexpected warmth to Matthew. He immediately noticed the paved country road which ran along their now familiar brick pathway. He then caught a glimpse in his peripheral vision of a distant figure approaching. Matthew turned his head to look closely. It appeared to be a white woman quickly running alongside the edge of the paved road. Within a few short moments, she had quickly passed by them. Matthew felt a sudden jolt as their pathway unexpectedly began to move.

"I didn't know this thing could move," Matthew quickly proclaimed. "Well, I guess I shouldn't be surprised since we are in the room of infinite possibilities, right?"

Samuel chuckled an affirmative response. Their moving sidewalk quickly caught up to the unidentified female jogger. Matthew was now able to see more details. The woman was of average height, roughly five feet, five inches tall. Her long, straight, black hair was pulled back into a pony tail which danced about to the movement of her running. Judging from her youthful and attractive appearance, Matthew estimated this woman to be in her late twenties or early thirties. He took careful note of her face. Her eyes were a large, beautiful brown color and her facial features looked very Mediterranean. He would have guessed Italian or Greek.

"Who is she?" Matthew asked.

"Her name is Wendy," Samuel replied.

"Why are we watching her exercise?" Matthew asked the obvious question.

"We're witnessing an example of the huge, potential connection between the human mind, body and spirit, especially when they can work in tandem," Samuel answered. "Not only that but how the energy of the Unified Life Force is a part of us that enhances that connectivity within ourselves."

Matthew still didn't quite understand what his teacher was referring to, as Wendy seemed to be doing something very ordinary. "You mean when we push our bodies to get stronger and into better shape?" Matthew inquired.

"Not exactly, Matthew," Samuel replied. "You see, Wendy is a very spiritual person, and she has just entered the early stage of Level Five of the Spirit. A belief began forming years earlier that there had to be something bigger at play in life. A force that was very strong and existed both beyond herself and within herself. She felt it but couldn't quite understand or name it."

"What does that have to do with our watching her jog along this country road?" Matthew asked, confused.

"You know what I am going to suggest to you next, right?" Samuel asked in reply.

Matthew's mind raced as he continued to digest all of these new concepts his mentor has been introducing. Each chakra experience was incredibly unique and immensely enlightening. He no longer approached each one with trepidation but rather with an excited anticipation of what would be revealed next. It allowed him to grasp this new knowledge much more firmly and profoundly. They were to Wendy's right as the moving sidewalk matched her pace perfectly. Matthew reached out with his left hand and touched her right shoulder.

The white flash brought Matthew to another place within his female host's chakra. They were no longer jogging along a country road but rather, appeared to be in the examining room of a doctor's office.

Matthew immediately sensed Wendy's unease. She was feeling very afraid. There was great anxiety milling about her consciousness. He noticed her glance at the clock. Each tick of the second hand took an eternity to advance. She looked around the room searching for anything to occupy her mind. Wearing a gown, Wendy stood and began to study a medical chart of the human muscular system. He sensed her reading the words but her mind could not concentrate as it merely went through unfocused motion. She was searching for anything to distract her.

Matthew could tell there was something very wrong. Wendy was fearful of receiving some potential bad news. Their attention was drawn away from the chart by the opening of the exam room door. A tall, gray-haired man with black-rimmed glasses and blue lab coat walked in. Matthew and Wendy's reactions were both the same as they saw the facial expression which adorned the man's face. They both suddenly felt a real sense of dread.

"Wendy, we have the results from your biopsies," the doctor began. *"We have confirmed that the lump in your left breast is cancerous. We need to check your lymph nodes to see if it may have spread."*

"Oh shit!" Matthew said as the well of emotions began to flood him.

Wendy stumbled backwards into the exam room table and almost fainted upon hearing the news.

Matthew suddenly felt immense compassion, sadness and deeply-rooted concern for this soul with whom he had just become acquainted. He wished he could take it all away. He wished he could take away her pain and fear. He wished he could take away this horrible realization of the potentially life-threatening condition. Somehow Matthew knew Wendy and what a good person she is who would never hurt anyone. A kind-hearted soul filled with love.

Wendy began to tear up. Matthew sensed thoughts of her worst fears coming to fruition. A deep sense of darkness and hopelessness flashed through her mind. Matthew felt it all. The darkness was beginning to overwhelm and consume her, an experience Matthew knew all too well as he tried to contain his own panic-stricken reaction.

"Wendy, no!" Matthew yelled out. "Fight it. Please!"

Matthew knew that there was no way to interact with her or influence the outcome, but he couldn't help himself. Within a few moments, however, Matthew felt a fundamental shift in her mental and emotional state, and he sighed in relief. Wendy was not going to let this beat her down. She spoke to the doctor who just delivered the devastating news.

"Okay, doctor," she began. *"Tell me what we do next. What do I need to do to beat this?"*

A sense of resolve began to take hold in her mind and soul. Matthew's connection with Wendy deepened as he quickly learned more about the type of person she is and her sense of beliefs. He sensed her bravery and positivity. Wendy was summoning the courage to deal with her reality.

It was then that Matthew saw a light begin to shine. This time the light shone from within Wendy herself and pierced through her chest. It started to displace the dark thoughts of her assumed demise as she began to place her focus on one particular kind of light.

The light of hope.

She was not going to become just another cancer patient.

She was not going to become another statistic.

She was going to be herself and not be denied what she knew as truth.

She is a strong, wonderful, loving, immortal spirit who can overcome obstacles and would not allow herself to wallow in worry, fear or self-pity. She would fight and grow in the process. Wendy would stay focused not knowing the outcome but have faith. She would pray and ask for help, strength, courage and guidance. This would put to the test what she always had believed about the unseen. What she always felt was true. She would have love, support of family and friends as well as her beliefs at her side as weapons in her fight.

Matthew walked over to Wendy, astounded by her sudden strength. He looked deeply into her huge, beautiful brown eyes and became almost completely lost in them. He admired her long, black hair and began to appreciate her physical beauty. Far more importantly, he felt the beauty of her spirit which radiated a spectacular light, a light fueled by love, including a love for herself.

He walked closer and stood directly in front of Wendy, knowing she couldn't see him or feel his presence. He did so nonetheless and embraced her with a warmth and compassion that he never before felt toward a person he had never before met. He knew her now, though. He could see her. He felt her at the core of her being, and she inspired him. He wanted to help her, but all he knew how to do in that very moment was to wrap Wendy in an energetic embrace.

"Take my energy, Wendy," Matthew said lovingly as he whispered into her ear. "I believe in you. You can do this. You are so strong."

Matthew opened his eyes to a white flash as he exited Wendy's chakra. Samuel had a hold of Matthew's left arm this time. He had to exert some extra force to pull Matthew out of Wendy's chakra.

Matthew was dizzy but Samuel steadied him. When his vision returned to normal, Matthew noticed they were moving alongside Wendy as she was jogging. Matthew felt a sense of relief. Wendy had made it. She overcame her sickness and was a healthy strong person with more vibrant life ahead of her.

"Matthew, we aren't done here with Wendy yet," Samuel commented sensing Matthew's relief.

Matthew looked Samuel in the eye, wary of the implication of Samuel's words. "What do you mean?" Matthew asked, slightly panicked. "She's fine, right?"

"We are actually intruding on her thoughts and feelings at the moment, Matthew," Samuel replied. He then moved his arm in a sweeping motion and the scene changed again.

While still focusing on his guide, Matthew then noticed the absence of the country scenery out of the corner of his eye, the paved road and Wendy. Matthew then turned his attention to a woman who was now lying in a bed. In fact, as Matthew glanced around the new surroundings, it was painfully obvious that it was Wendy lying in the bed of a hospital room.

"What happened?!" Matthew demanded. "How did she go from a strong body that was exercising just a second ago to being bed-ridden in a hospital?"

"What we just previously witnessed was Wendy's mental visualization," Samuel replied. "Because Wendy has started entering Level Five, she not only believes but knows that her spirit is a part of something bigger than the limited confines of her physical body. Yet she also knows that her spirit controls her mind and body and how they are all interconnected."

"I'm sorry, but I don't quite follow," Matthew said while staring at the very ill woman lying motionless in bed. It was then he noticed the sparse clumps of hair as most of it had fallen out from what he could only assume was some kind of chemo therapy treatment.

"Wendy knows that if she channels her thinking properly and only pictures herself as a healthy, physically strong person void of any disease or limitations, she will get better," Samuel began to explain. "In addition to taking on the treatments of modern medicine, Wendy believes that her mind and spirit can help heal the disease presently growing within her. She learned how to meditate to help her relax and focus on her own divine light. By holding onto the thought of wellness and strength, she is tapping into the power of the Fourth Dimension and channeling the energy at a subatomic level to actually change the cells of her physical body."

Matthew looked back at Samuel to directly ask the next question. "She is actually healing herself?"

"Yes," Samuel answered. "She absolutely believes that she will recover faster and help heal herself in tandem with the treatment given by her doctors. Matthew, I want you to think of Wendy's present condition in relation to the Five Levels of Spirit."

Matthew paused a moment as he related all that he has learned to his current chakra experience with this amazing soul he has now encountered. "She obviously progressed through Level One, as she desires to be free of her illness," Matthew began in response to Samuel's question. "She has reached Level Two by being courageous enough to battle this disease. Wendy took the next step to Level Three as I felt her faith, belief and sense of knowing in something bigger. I also felt within her chakra a moment of self-assurance and control of her thoughts after the devastating news, so she is definitely self-aware and went to Level Four."

Matthew paused because he had a flash of self-awareness within himself at that moment. He was amazed how easily he could articulate the answers to Samuel's question and retain all the previous lessons so effortlessly. Samuel was quite pleased how quickly Matthew has progressed and the ease with which he continues to make such connections.

"She has reached a point in her own development, Matthew, that Wendy knows beyond a shadow of a doubt the existence of the interconnectedness between mind, body and spirit," Samuel continued. "Wendy knows that she will aid the efforts of modern medicine by channeling her thoughts, energy, and emotions toward the wellness she desires for herself. She knows she must not only think positively while she visualizes her healing but must also try to feel positive as much as possible. She can feel the strength of her spirit and the powerful draw to some unknown field which you and I now know as the ULF." Samuel looked away from his pupil to fix his gaze upon the young woman lying in the hospital bed.

"Let me ask you a fundamental question, Matthew," Samuel continued. "Do you think that Wendy could channel the energy of her spirit and mind if she were to remain in a state of sadness or hopelessness?"

Even though there was only one logical response, Matthew felt the need to answer the question, because he knew the answer at a spiritual level based on what he experienced within her chakra.

"Of course not," Matthew replied. "It goes back to what you taught me in Level Four about self-awareness. Our thoughts and feelings go hand in hand." Matthew was thrilled by his ability to recall exactly what Samuel had said and instantly connect it to something else. There was something about this mystical journey which endowed Matthew with more mental clarity than he had ever known.

"Precisely!" Samuel said excitedly. "Tell me again, my young friend, what is the most powerful feeling or emotion that humanity possesses?"

Matthew knew immediately, without question now.

"It's love," Matthew stated confidently. "The greatest force in life is love. But Samuel, it's also unrealistic for people to not have the full spectrum of emotions. How could someone in Wendy's condition sometimes not get sad, depressed or scared? She's human, for God's sake. We all are!"

"Of course, Matthew," Samuel responded. "That's very true. We must feel what we need to feel as spiritual beings with powerful emotions. It's okay to sometimes get sad or afraid. But the key is to not dwell in the space of darkness and negativity for too long and to courageously pick ourselves up or actively seek out support of others to help pull us out of a hole. That's where our self-awareness comes into play, because our minds can then find a way to take over and spiral out of control. It can create this illusion of being cut off from the divine within us and our connection to The One, other people and the Fourth Dimension. The darkness can consume us if we let it, as you know all too well, my young friend."

I most certainly do, Matthew thought to himself.

But now things will be different, because Matthew has defeated his demons and he is well-armed with strength, courage and the awareness to navigate life so much more than he ever thought possible. On top of that, these incredible insights his guide continues to help him gain propelled him into an incredible anticipation of what is yet to come.

Looking very pleased, Samuel turned away from Wendy to face his young student who continued to grasp these powerful truths at a profound level. Samuel placed his right hand upon Matthew's shoulder.

"People in a state of love, Matthew, have the ability to create and manifest incredible things in their lives as it puts the spirit in a state of peace that strengthens their connection to themselves and the Unified Life Force," Samuel further explained. "Wendy has started down this path, because she loves herself. That's the first step of Level Five."

Matthew looked back at Wendy with immeasurable gratitude for the gift of deeper understanding through experiencing her immense personal challenge.

"Wendy has learned that the peaceful tranquility between mind, body and spirit is critical to lead a happy and healthy life," Samuel went on. "Even though she may not think of it as the Fourth Dimension or some kind of Unified Life Force at this moment, she still knows and feels its existence and the potential of tapping into its energy *and the power that is within herself* to heal her body. Can you imagine the potential once one knows of our own divine power and our connection to this massive unseen plane?"

Matthew moved toward Wendy and stood to the left of her hospital bed. He reached down with his left hand to touch hers, and a perplexing thought entered his mind.

"How is it that she became sick then?" Matthew inquired.

"Because for a period, Matthew, Wendy forgot and became entrapped by the tyranny of her day-to-day life," Samuel replied.

"What do you mean?" Matthew asked looking back at his guide.

"For a while in her life, Wendy became consumed with her job and career," Samuel responded. "She began to get wrapped up in advancing her 'outside' self as her friends and co-workers encouraged her to continue to get promoted. She let the thinking of the masses override her own sense of being and began to identify herself with only her job. She let every problem and stressful situation at work become a life or death situation. Over an extended period of time, Matthew, do you know what happened?"

"Her body gave out on her?" Matthew quickly replied assuming that was the answer.

"Why?" Samuel asked probing his pupil to explore his response more fully.

"Because of the connection between the mind, body and spirit that you just mentioned," Matthew responded as though the answer was obvious.

Samuel nodded in response to Matthew's answer.

"Our emotional and mental state, Matthew, have an immense impact on the healthy functioning of our physical bodies," Samuel stated. "Wendy let her thoughts create emotional stress which then caused a state of disharmony in her body. She became out of balance and lost focus on maintaining her mental, emotional, spiritual and physical health."

Matthew felt a surge of desire well up within him that has happened now countless times throughout his journey. Learning these new truths of existence only fueled his desire for more.

"But how does a person knowingly reach Level Five?" Matthew asked earnestly. "You mentioned how much power and knowledge exists there. How we can interact with it and even ask for help?"

"Ah yes," Samuel replied, beaming from ear to ear. "That's what we are going to explore next. There is still so much more, Matthew, and your extreme drive and eagerness to explore it is well founded. Do you know why?"

"No?" Matthew replied with a quizzical expression.

"Because you are being powerfully drawn to it, and you are able to feel it at that spiritual and energetic level," Samuel replied excitedly. "You almost feel a magnetic pull don't you? A pull to something massive."

How does Samuel know all of this? Matthew thought. He nodded affirmatively to his guide. Matthew then glanced back down at Wendy.

"Will she be okay?" Matthew asked, concerned. "Will she make it?"

"What do you think, Matthew?" Samuel said in reply. "Actually, what is your insightful *feeling?*"

Matthew calmed his mind and then closed his eyes. He again reached down and placed his right hand upon her own resting calmly upon the bed. He took a deep breath and slowly exhaled as one word came into his stream of consciousness—*Yes.*

Samuel placed his left arm across Matthew's shoulders to indicate that it was time to go.

Matthew opened his eyes and turned to walk away as Wendy and the hospital room disappeared. He still had no idea what was to come next in the revealing of his significance. The young man and his mentor resumed their walk along the red brick path moving ever so closer to Matthew's true power.

His true purpose.

CHAPTER 16

PURPOSE

"There are actually four stages of Universal Awareness, Matthew," Samuel began to explain as they walked along the path. "The first is recognizing that we are spiritual beings and are part of a much larger, unseen plane of existence."

"You mean they begin to consciously feel the Unified Life Force?" Matthew asked.

"Exactly," Samuel replied. "They begin to, not only recognize there are unexplainable mysteries beyond the physical body, but start to feel the energy of the Fourth Dimension and its presence in their lives. A person enters stage two when they feel this truth and also begin to understand the interconnection between mind, body and spirit. They start to realize the immense potential when all three co-exist in a state of harmony."

Matthew wasn't surprised by the first two stages, given what he has learned thus far through Samuel's guidance. His anticipation intensified, however, upon hearing there were more stages beyond the first two.

"So, what's stage three?" he asked.

"Stage three, Matthew, is one of the most amazing revelations of all," Samuel stated excitedly. "The one that can change everything! It's when a person recognizes that they are not passive participants in the Fourth Dimension. They begin to realize that as intelligent, spiritual beings, they have the ability to fully tap into this powerful field."

Matthew immediately recalled the information Samuel had told him before, where all knowledge and truth exist within the ULF. "So the third stage is when someone realizes they have the

287

ability to use this universal field to help themselves evolve and learn?" Matthew questioned.

"That's right," Samuel answered.

"How exactly, Samuel, can a person tap into the Fourth Dimension?" he asked earnestly.

Samuel paused a moment to form the right words in order to help set the context for his young prodigy. "This happens once the spirit and mind becomes aware of their own infinite possibilities and the power they possess," Samuel explained. "They begin to realize that this other plane, not only exists, but that they can become active participants within it. This realization allows a person to tap into the Fourth Dimension to bring forth new discoveries and help them realize their dreams or solve problems. Like I said before, Aristotle may not have consciously been aware of the Fourth Dimension but through the powerful focus of his mind and spirit in those moments of quiet self-reflection, fundamental truths were revealed to prove Pythagoras' theory. He drew forth the answers and truth he was seeking by connecting to this field of energy and knowledge. You can almost think of the knowledge and intelligence contained within the Fourth Dimension as a Universal Mind, if you will."

"So in a way, his intentions were somehow released into this plane, and he was able to eventually get the answers he wanted," Matthew reiterated.

"Exactly, Matthew," Samuel confirmed. "The key difference in stage three is when a person not only feels the presence of this divine universal field where unfathomable intelligence and knowledge exists but they realize they can actively tap into it."

Matthew then felt a burning desire to know how to consciously do this. How does a person, once they know of the Fourth Dimension, tap into this immense field?

"Samuel, I'm still not clear on *how* to do this," Matthew urged, hoping Samuel would address that next.

"Matthew, it's easier than you think," Samuel responded. "You need only take time out of every day to quiet your mind, to center yourself. You can do this by prayer, meditation or even sitting quietly to calm the mind and body where you can release your intentions or ask for help in solving a problem. You can open yourself up to receive the inspired thought you need, the intuition of what to do next, or even ask for people to enter your life. Not only that, Matthew, this infinite, dynamically expanding field works both ways."

"Both ways?" Matthew questioned. "What do you mean?"

"You will become connected to others not just based on what you need or desire but what others may call forth from this field as well, to aid them in their own journey of growth," Samuel answered. "Connections form all the time in life, because either they are intended to help you, or you are intended to help them. There are also situations when paths cross for mutual benefit between people. A person in stage three not only understands this but they become in tune to the synchronicities of life. They understand that there can be meaning with every encounter with another person."

Matthew pondered deeply on Samuel's words. He tried to let them absorb into his own consciousness and penetrate any self-imposed barriers that may still be lingering. The space-time continuum was certainly strong testimony in relation to this third stage. He thought of all the portals with multiple connections contained therein and how Samuel's words rang true from all that he has seen on his journey.

Samuel noticed his pupil's contemplative expression and grew excited as more words came to him that would help deepen Matthew's understanding. "Let me give you a simple example of the power within the Fourth Dimension and how we interact with it," Samuel began. "Have you ever noticed that when a person you have not seen or heard from in a long time suddenly pops into your head and then you may see them or hear from them shortly thereafter, seemingly out of the blue?"

Matthew thought for a moment, and there was no question that he had experienced that phenomenon in his life but always dismissed it as chance. He gave Samuel an affirmative nod.

"Your mind and spirit sent an energy signal that led them to you in a moment of reconnection," Samuel explained.

"Or they thought of me and then came into my mind," Matthew said with excitement realizing the potential of this vast field.

"Exactly!" Samuel said. "Let me give you another example. Think of inventors who at first might struggle resolving whatever problem they are attempting to solve. They may struggle with a solution, but when they finally take a break and get their minds off their trouble, what tends to happen?"

Matthew stared at the brick path they were walking on, mulling over the answer to his guide's question. After a few seconds, he realized what Samuel was alluding to, at which point he looked up smiling.

"You are beginning to understand, Matthew," Samuel said sounding very pleased. "The genuine desires of their spirit attract solutions from the Fourth Dimension, and they suddenly get an inspired thought or idea. Imagine what humanity can accomplish by consciously leveraging the Unified Life Force."

"Do you mean to tell me that no one in the history of humanity has ever discovered this truth?" Matthew asked in disbelief.

"Not at all, my young lad!" Samuel replied. "We have seen great examples of this throughout the history of human existence. The difference, Matthew, is simply more people must progress on a collective, global scale of consciousness."

Matthew shot Samuel his usual quizzical look when something didn't quite make sense.

"Let me explain it in another way," Samuel continued. "Human kind has been heading down a track of potential greatness. Any advancement has been due to those quantum leaps we talked about before. Some people either advanced their intellectual and spiritual development that allowed receptivity to the ULF or were born with inexplicable gifts through a powerful connection to this field with little or no knowledge of it."

"Like when Beethoven became a musical prodigy at a ridiculously young age," Matthew affirmed.

"Precisely," Samuel replied. "Some beings are born with their minds already 'pre-wired' to tap into the ULF for certain areas of human development. Examples span across thousands of years in all areas of human existence. Science, technology, literature, music, morality and spirituality have been created or advanced when an individual spirit receives inspirations or flashes of greatness from the Fourth Dimension."

Matthew immediately thought of his chakra experience with Aristotle and the enormity of his connections that came from such inspired thought in proving that the Earth is round.

"Like I mentioned before, all universal truths and knowledge exist in this field," Samuel continued. "You can almost think of it as the Universal Mind. The Universe is intelligent and has been created out of divine thought. Think back to what you saw with the oak leaf. You were able to see that leaf in a way you had never before experienced. You could see that leaf at a subatomic and energetic level. Was the creation of that leaf or tree a chance event of nature?"

"I'm guessing it wasn't," Matthew replied.

"No, it wasn't," Samuel stated. "The intelligence of the divine Universal Mind spawned the creation of a tree and how it would exist on the physical plane. There is a growing theory among scientists on Earth that is so incredibly simple yet captures the essence of existence and our divine truth of being."

"What's that?" Matthew asked anxiously.

"The Universe and everything within has arisen from thought!" Samuel stated dramatically.

Matthew continued to reflect, now knowing that the power of the mind, as a tool, can aid the spirit in breaching Level Five, how some are born almost pre-wired to tap into certain areas of the ULF based on their strong mind-spirit connection to this plane, such as in Beethoven's case, without even knowing it. But once a person does know, the possibilities grow exponentially. Then another insight stopped Matthew in his tracks. An example from one of his past experiences within the web had displayed the incredible purity of how love and prayerful thoughts from millions of people on Earth aided the astronauts of Apollo 13. Those thoughts and prayers took on an energy form that he could actually see and touch.

"So, thoughts and feelings from our mind and spirit possess energy of their own," Matthew stated as his own connection began to take hold. "And that's how we interact with the Fourth Dimension. That's how we shape things and the world around us. How it impacts our lives!"

Samuel noticed how Matthew had stopped and turned back to see his pupil staring at the red brick path. He knew that Matthew had yet another breakthrough and sensed his racing thoughts making profound connections that continued to expand his awareness. "The combined force of mind and spirit is a most powerful one to be reckoned with," Samuel exclaimed. "It possesses the power to actually create your reality."

Matthew hung on every Samuel's every word. Since leaving Wendy's hospital bed, they were still in the room of infinite possibilities, and Matthew stared into the view of nothingness as his mind exploded in thought. He was not only comprehending these incredible new connections intellectually, but somehow another dimension deepened his understanding. He felt the truth within himself now, how God had given everyone such tremendous potential, especially as our knowledge and awareness of it comes into focus, how knowing the truth in our spirits affirms the thoughts in our minds, how the two work in tandem. He began to realize the immense possibilities of how releasing thoughts and prayers into this unseen plane can help us attract solutions, gain knowledge, and shape our lives. With his experiences from the space-time continuum, he now knows this power forms the connections to other people. The resulting events in our lives not only aid in achieving our desires but furthers our own growth as spiritual human beings. Matthew realized that what he had been drawn to his entire life was the desire to unlock these truths, discover the true divinity within himself, and understand the powerful connection to this divine field. It could almost be likened to that of a beacon. This journey had expanded his understanding of the enormity of connections to others through this field, but it was far greater than he could have ever imagined. He never thought that such connections extended beyond to others that may have come before your own birth and even after your death.

Pausing for only a moment or two, Samuel was set to reveal another critical secret. "Here is yet another universal truth of stage three," Samuel continued. "The power contained within the mind-spirit connection can control and manipulate the physical world. You not only have the ability to access the knowledge and wisdom of the collective divine mind within the Fourth Dimension, but you also have the potential to do incredible things in the physical plane as your connection evolves."

Matthew shot his guide a look of astonishment. Samuel immediately thought of an example to help cement this concept for Matthew in a most personal and profound way.

"What happened when you woke up after your space shuttle dream and you looked at yourself in the mirror?" Samuel asked. "What did you see?"

Matthew didn't need to think for very long. "I saw that I had bruised my forehead," Matthew replied. "It was bruised in the exact place where I hit my head when I was thrown to the floor during my dream sequence."

"But how would that be possible under the old paradigm of thinking?" Samuel asked, shrugging his shoulders. "You were lying in your bed and yet when you awoke, your mind actually triggered a response within your body because of how real it all seemed."

"I thought I might have fallen out of bed and hit my head on my desk but just didn't realize it until I woke up," Matthew responded, thinking back to the logical explanation he conjured up when it happened.

"Well, Matthew, you and I both know the truth," Samuel encouraged. "The mind and spirit's power over the body is immense. What if these perceived limitations did not exist and the connection between mind, body and spirit was fully recognized? Tibetan monks have learned to do incredible things with their bodies just through the channeling of their mental and spiritual energies. They have been witnessed to do such things as raise their body temperatures to such a degree that you can place a wet towel on their backs, and their body heat would dry the towel."

Matthew was astounded, because the evidence was now irrefutable.

"What one perceives as real, my young pupil, is driven by what is held within your mind and the beliefs you've been exposed to in the past," Samuel continued. "If we aren't careful, our mind can allow self-imposed limitations to dominate. We both know that so much of what someone believes to be impossible is merely an illusion. There is yet another key!"

"What's that?" Matthew asked.

"We cannot allow the mind to control us, as you know all too well," Samuel concluded. "Spirit rules the domain of the mind, not the other way around. The mind is a part of us and a most potent tool, but it must not control us."

Matthew immediately thought of Level Four and the self-awareness of not allowing the mind to get carried away on a road of negative thoughts or limiting beliefs. He remembered how the pioneers of interstellar space travel in his Centurion shuttle experience didn't allow the old paradigms to deny them what was previously thought impossible. Matthew could sense there was more to this part of the lesson that Samuel wanted to reveal.

"Samuel, you just said that we have the ability to do incredible things in the physical world," Matthew commented as he began to formulate another question. "Is it just related to controlling our bodies?"

"No, Matthew, it isn't," Samuel replied eagerly. "It can go far beyond that."

Matthew's intrigue intensified as even more questions began to form. Could Samuel mean that we can do something else within our physical plane of existence? Something previously thought to be impossible? Then his mind thought of an example to test Samuel's statement on the potential of our physical abilities.

"You don't mean something crazy like being able to levitate an object using only our mind and spirit, right?" Matthew asked, wanting clarity.

"Matthew, don't forget that you have been exposed to an incredible amount of knowledge and truth," Samuel reminded. "You need to remain open to all these incredible possibilities of your potential."

"I mean, Samuel, come on!" Matthew protested. "There are certain laws of physics that can't be ignored."

Samuel realized that Matthew had a moment of retreating to the familiar, but he knew how to turn his pupil around. "You are absolutely right," Samuel replied.

Matthew felt a twinge of disappointment, because he realized how badly he wanted the potential of manipulating the physical world to truly be limitless.

"Do you know why you are right in that example, Matthew?" Samuel inquired.

"Because it truly isn't possible," Matthew answered. "Like I said, there are laws of physics at play, like gravity."

"Let me tell you something, Matthew," Samuel began. "In general, we don't one day wake up and begin to do incredible things like moving objects with the power of our mind, because it's a journey. It's an evolutionary process where we begin to realize our potential and explore it. We unlock it, have breakthroughs of discovery, and that doesn't usually happen overnight. In your example, a person may harbor a belief they can levitate anything they focus upon, but they must invest in the process of seeking the truth and growing in their knowledge of what they desire. Belief is a powerful thing, but it must propel us to continue to seek answers within the Fourth Dimension and allow us to grow in truth. It's also not an excuse to foolishly put oneself or others in harm's way either. A being entering Universal Awareness may want to understand the possibilities of levitation but certainly wouldn't do something that could hurt themselves or others, because they hadn't yet figured it out."

"So, you *are* saying it's possible to move objects solely using our mental and spiritual energies?" Matthew asked again, trying to distill Samuel's somewhat long-winded response.

"Let me give you another example of your potential," Samuel tried again. "Do you recognize this?" Samuel then raised his right hand, moved his arm in a sweeping motion and immediately summoned another scene. Their path was now suspended above another large body of water. In a short distance away, Matthew caught sight of a fishing boat. The fishermen were dressed in simple, brown robes as they busily cast their nets to the side of their vessel. Further in the distance, an image appeared of a similarly dressed man approaching the boat along the surface of the water. The approaching man didn't have the benefit of a boat to propel him along the lake nor was he swimming. The man making his way toward the fishing boat was walking *on the water*.

Matthew immediately recognized the scene at hand and fell to his knees. His body became completely limp as he was witnessing yet another miracle. He was witnessing one of Jesus' miracles. It was all so overwhelming. The tears welled up once more from the sheer awe of the scene now before him. Another lump in his throat rendered his ability to speak useless.

"I can see that you know who this is," Samuel commented as he looked away from Matthew and watched Jesus approach the vessel. "Jesus realized the true potential of humanity in his teachings and in his actions. He could manipulate the physical plane to heal the sick, walk on water, and turn water into wine. How could he perform such miracles?"

Matthew attempted to gather himself in an effort to respond to Samuel's question. He stared intently at Jesus, unable to pull away his gaze. *How is this all possible?* Matthew thought to himself yet again. *Who is Samuel?* Matthew took a deep breath and tried to answer.

"Because God granted him great power to show us the way," Matthew replied as his voice cracked under the emotional strain.

"Matthew, Jesus possessed the spiritual advancement which gave him full control over the physical plane," Samuel continued. "He could, on command, use the power which exists in the divine field created by The One to manipulate his physical world. In addition to his most important teaching of living in divine love, what was one of Jesus' other key messages during his time on Earth that you now find written in the Bible?"

His gaze still fixed on Jesus, Matthew shook his head, unable to derive the specific answer Samuel wanted.

Seeing that Matthew was incapacitated with emotion, Samuel continued his lesson. He knelt down in front of his pupil and cast his line of vision directly into Matthew's tear-filled brown eyes. "He said that even the least of God's people possesses this same power," Samuel clearly stated. "And Matthew, that power starts with love. It is fueled by love that allows us to connect to our true divine spiritual nature which in turn enhances our ability to connect to the Fourth Dimension! "

Still kneeling, Samuel turned his torso slightly to the left, raised his left arm, and the scene of Jesus walking on water quickly disappeared. An awe-inspiring view of the Universe now appeared with thousands of stars shining brightly amidst the blackness of space. There were galaxies filled with planets swirling about Matthew as if he was immersed within a three-dimensional planetarium encompassing all that now existed in the Universe.

Matthew's breath was momentarily taken away by this magnificent view. He stood and slowly turned in a complete circle to fully absorb everything surrounding him. It was yet another incredible experience that moved his spirit in ways he never thought possible.

"So, Matthew, after gaining more knowledge from the lessons throughout the course of your journey and being taught one of the most ancient secrets of existence, I have a question for you," Samuel said, shifting Matthew's attention back to him even as he appreciated the purity of his prodigy's emotional state. "What really limits us?" Samuel inquired.

Due to his awe inspired state, Matthew just noticed that his breathing was suspended this whole time and took a deep breath. He then focused on his response to the question. Still gazing at the vastness and beauty of the scene at hand, he replied hesitantly, "Ourselves?"

"Good, Matthew," Samuel encouraged. "Ourselves, negative thinking, and limiting old beliefs. Even those who may have been exposed to this knowledge or even witnessed miracles, still manage to find a way to dismiss and disbelieve. They limit themselves."

"But why?" Matthew asked, looking at the beauty all around him. "Why disbelieve?"

"There are many possible reasons, Matthew," Samuel replied. "Fear is a big one."

"Fear of what?" Matthew inquired.

"There are many forms," Samuel began to explain. "Fear of having such hope perhaps. Fear of letting go of comfortable, old beliefs. Fear of believing they are worthy due to past experiences that have hurt them which led to dysfunctional ways of thinking. The ego tries to be the one in control; much of the self is driven by the ego. Anything that threatens its existence causes a response of fear, dismissal or disbelief. It's from this place of ego and insecurity that negative thoughts can begin to form. It's from this place that our mind can begin to run away and take control." Samuel paused as another question came to mind.

"How can we dispel negative thought?" Samuel asked.

Matthew immediately knew the answer.

"By recognizing it, and seeing it for what it is," Matthew replied. "Having self-awareness."

"Exactly!" Samuel affirmed. "And the understanding of interconnectedness between our mental and emotional states. By consciously focusing on one, it influences the other. Our true nature, Matthew, is to exist in a state of joy and love. When we follow our joy in a state of love, doors will open where there were previously walls and the path will unfold. Virtually anything is possible within this divine field of the Fourth Dimension."

Samuel paused again to allow time for his young student to continue processing the lesson.

"Humanity possesses an insatiable appetite to advance itself," Samuel continued. "Why does this happen, Matthew? Why does human kind as spiritual and intelligent beings want to continue to advance and solve the mysteries of the Universe?"

Matthew wrestled with his teacher's question, but a profound answer eluded him at the moment.

"Because that's just how we are," Matthew responded.

"That's right," Samuel said excitedly. "That's how The One has programmed humanity. It is your birthright to bring forth all that which is possible. There is an internal drive to advance both as individuals and also as a race. Matthew, there are many examples of people in Earth's history who understood the magnitude of your immense potential as human beings."

"Like who?" Matthew asked.

Samuel thought a moment and began to quote several people:

> *Whether you think you can or cannot do something, either way you are right.*
> —Henry Ford.

> *We make our universe as we go along.*
> —Winston Churchill.

> *All that we are is a result of what we have thought.*
> —Buddha.

> *It is our duty as men and women to proceed as though limits to our abilities do not exist. We are collaborators in creation.*
> —Pierre De Chardon.

"One of humanity's most significant documents talks about God, your divine nature as spiritual beings, and your immense potential," Samuel stated with a sense of awe. "A potential that includes the ability to interact within the divine field of creation!"

Matthew looked away from the spectacular scene of the Universe for just a moment to make eye contact with his guide. "You mean the Bible?" Matthew questioned.

"Absolutely!" Samuel replied. "In the book of Matthew, chapter 21, verse 22, it states: '*Whatsoever ye shall ask in prayer believing, ye shall receive.*'"

Samuel's words strongly resonated within Matthew as he, once again, not only believed with his intellect but felt the truth within his soul. He looked away from his guide to further admire the scene and reflected on how such infinite power and beauty within the cosmos was not a chance event. There was without a doubt, a divine intelligence at play. Matthew grew even more excited as he thought of how humanity's advancement, spanning tens of thousands of years, has led them to this point as a race. Our knowledge and understanding of these truths as intellectual and spiritual beings has expanded exponentially. He thought of how we are potentially standing on the verge of yet another massive breakthrough as a species. Humanity truly could be on the cusp of a whole new renaissance of intellectual, emotional and spiritual development.

Samuel knew exactly what Matthew was internalizing and where his line of thought was leading him. He then had another inspired thought to help Matthew continue his progress.

"A new kind of science has emerged on your planet that you may have heard of, called quantum physics," Samuel commented.

Matthew was so lost in thought that Samuel's voice slightly jolted him back into the moment.

"Yes, I have heard of it, but I don't know much about it," Matthew softly replied as he continued marveling at the scene and all the possibilities it represented.

"What your scientists theorize to be quantum physics is actually the study of the Fourth Dimension!" Samuel explained.

"Our desires, beliefs, and intentions are released into it and ultimately create the reality of our lives. These thoughts and emotions can be very powerful in enabling our interaction with this divine field. We are interacting with it at a spiritual and kinetic level."

Samuel paused a moment before saying the words necessary to emphasize the next key point for Matthew to understand. "But here is another key, Matthew," Samuel continued earnestly. "People interact with the Fourth Dimension whether they realize it or not."

Matthew was taken off guard by this last statement. "What?" Matthew asked. "What do you mean? Like the example with Beethoven or Aristotle?"

"Yes, but it's even broader than that," Samuel began to explain. "You saw the immense potential through their experiences, but it's not limited to just prodigies. Think of it this way: If you conceptually accept that the thoughts and feelings spawning from our minds and spirits are energetically charged, then whether you know of the ULF or not is of no consequence, because they are still released into the unseen."

Then Matthew had a flash of connection to Samuel's explanation from his own experiences. How during his own little test to find the chest and key created a flow of unfortunate events because his mind and emotions ran out of control. "That's why Level Four is so critical, isn't it?" Matthew asked drawing on his newly formed comprehension. "We don't want to limit ourselves and the possibilities to actually achieve our dreams and discover how to do it, because negativity creates a wall but self-awareness can help us prevent it."

"That's right, Matthew!" Samuel confirmed. "It creates a disconnection within yourself and hinders the link to the divine field of the Fourth Dimension. But the energy from negative thoughts and feelings still can be released into the ULF and unfortunately, can potentially attract more negative things into our lives."

"And then it can become a vicious cycle," Matthew stated as he looked at his guide, thinking again of his own experiences.

"Yes," Samuel said. "When you asked me how to consciously tap into the Fourth Dimension, I told you that a person can start by centering themselves through calm, focused feelings and thoughts, like when you pray or meditate. This is one key reason why our focus must be on creating good, positive things for ourselves and others. Those who continually focus on the negative, will ultimately only get back what they put out, which is more negative things in their lives. The self-aware soul can break that cycle!" Samuel looked out into the vastness of the Universe as he paused a moment to reflect and appreciate its awesome power. "So, Matthew, that's why you need to understand this key point. Your 'signal,' if you will, and interaction with the divine field can be magnified even more when you try to stay in a state of peace, joy and love."

Matthew immediately thought of how the same theme keeps repeating itself in his lessons: The foundation of all that is possible revolved around that one most basic and powerful force—love. He began to realize how centering oneself not only helps connect to the divine field but also connect to the divine within oneself. It's love that drives the connection within ourselves and to others. But does this mean we enter a state of joy as a result?

"Samuel," Matthew began. "You just said that our connection to the Fourth Dimension can be enhanced by trying to be in a state of peace, joy and love. So, does that mean joy is a natural outcome of feeling peace and love?"

Samuel was quite pleased with Matthew's continual desire to grow in knowledge and understanding. "It certainly does, Matthew," Samuel answered. "But there is something else that can help you enter a joyful state."

Matthew looked at Samuel and tilted his head questioningly.

"When one sets out to achieve something, and he or she is successful, what typically happens?" Samuel asked.

Pausing for a moment, Matthew replied, "It gives you a sense of accomplishment."

"Yes, Matthew, that's true, but what is the underlying feeling?" Samuel probed further.

Instantly, the obvious answer came to him. "Joy," Matthew responded.

"We can also bring forth joy by following our passions and callings from within," Samuel simply stated. "So, Matthew, why don't more people follow their joy? Why don't they follow their passion!?"

"Maybe some don't know it's even an option, or they think of excuses why they can't," Matthew replied.

"Either they don't know it's an option, or they allow the negative mind to take control and conjure up excuses or reasons not to follow a dream," Samuel emphasized. "They may be able to move as far as Level Three but falter in Level Four as they allow their thinking to slip into a negative state. In the absence of self-awareness, they may become fearful by suddenly conjuring up all the reasons in the world why they can't follow their passion."

"And we can't be in a state of peace, joy and love within ourselves if we are focused on the negative all the time," Matthew stated as he looked at Samuel for confirmation.

"Exactly, Matthew!" Samuel said encouragingly. "We need alignment and connection within ourselves to continue to evolve and grow. This then will enable an even greater connection to the Fourth Dimension, and as you now know, stage three of Universal Awareness is to know about this connection and begin to leverage it." Samuel paused again to reflect how better to find the right words and examples to further help his student grasp these truths. "Like I said before, there are numerous past teachers and leaders of Earth who gained insight into the potential of human kind," Samuel continued.

Matthew was amazed by how Samuel knew so much about past and present people from history to keep using as examples. He again wondered who Samuel truly is and how he could possibly know so much. Before Matthew could say another word to ask his guide to explain this inexplicable knowledge, Samuel went on with this explanation.

"They realized the importance of thoughts, beliefs and human emotions that shape a person's life," Samuel continued. "They began to understand that the natural state of the human condition is that of a spiritual being capable of great things and finding ways to overcome obstacles to realize their dreams and discover new truths."

Matthew looked at Samuel as his mind continued to build the connections to all that he has learned. "Who are you talking about, and what did they say that you would know that?" Matthew asked.

Samuel began to rattle off quotes from people, some of whom Matthew recognized and others not.

> *Men are not prisoners of fate, but only prisoners of their own minds.*
> —Franklin D. Roosevelt.

> *The treacherous, unexplored areas of the world are not in continents or the seas; they are in the hearts of men.*
> —Allen Claxton.

> *With the realization of one's own potential and self-confidence in one's ability, one can build a better world.*
> —Dalai Lama.

> *Never underestimate the power of dreams and the influence of the human spirit. We are all the same in this notion: The potential for greatness lives within each of us.*
> —Wilma Rudolph.

> *You must do the things you think you cannot do. The future belongs to those who believe in the beauty of their dreams.*
> —Eleanor Roosevelt.

No pessimist ever discovered the secret of the stars, or sailed to an uncharted land, or opened a new doorway for the human spirit.
—Helen Keller.

Believe it can be done. When you believe something can be done, really believe, your mind will find the ways to do it. Believing a solution paves the way to solution.
—David J. Schwartz.

"If a person can fully comprehend the power within them in reaching Universal Awareness by knowing how to tap into the Unified Life Force, they would have tremendous power to shape their lives and destiny to what they desire most," Samuel stated with great intensity.

Matthew was again overwhelmed but also excited at the same time. Samuel was helping him unlock his own potential. He was about to move forward into his new young life with renewed optimism in achieving his inner calling and the desire of doing something so much bigger than he imagined. So much more than he or his family envisioned for himself. Matthew could now sense that he was getting very close to unlocking that truth. He was close to unlocking his true calling.

"The will of the human spirit, Matthew, has such power when we choose to believe in it and embrace it," Samuel stated while looking all around him at the great expanse of the Universe. "It is the will of our spirits that has enabled people across the ages to achieve great things, large or small. It has propelled countless people to rise above tumultuous or painful events in their own quest to better themselves and improve their circumstances or those of others. How else could people endure such intense pain, physical or emotional, to find ways to keep going and pursue their dreams or purpose?"

Another word suddenly formed within Matthew's mind. *Perseverance.* He realized that it truly is the will of the spirit that drives us through adversity. It is what keeps us going, especially when life may knock us down. It's the power from which we draw upon to pick ourselves up, but we must make that conscious choice. Struggles take on many forms across all walks of life in a human being's existence. It is human to have defeatist thoughts and feelings of depression when we encounter difficult, painful times. The key is not to surrender to them but to keep turning to the light of our spirit which possesses an incredible power to moves us forward. It transcends rational thought. It defies logic. Matthew's mind flooded with thoughts of some of the souls he touched in his journey thus far who endured incredible suffering or the doubt of those around them only to rise above it—Thomas, Carrie, Benny, Kate, Captain Logan, Donna, Ron and Wendy. When we embrace the power of our spirit, it not only propels us beyond unimaginable pain but can inspire us to achieve the "impossible." So many beings fundamentally want to reach for the stars, dream for a better life, or relentlessly pursue solutions to problems such as finding a cure to diseases that has plagued mankind such as cancer. Matthew then fully appreciated at that moment how our spirit is fueled by the powerful force of love. We keep fighting the good fight, moving forward, evolving and growing because we do so for the people in our lives we love for whom we have to remain strong or our belief in a cause that would benefit many. We also receive motivation to keep going because we love ourselves as well. We may not even realize it at the time but we feel that inner drive which propels us. The strength of our spirit and our connection to others through the power of this divine field of the ULF which exists all around us comes from the same source—love. We tap into this field by tapping into our own divine powerful spirit, thereby unlocking our incredible potential and enabling miraculous things to transpire.

Samuel sensed these latest teachings further ignited the flame within his prodigy to pursue his true destiny, and it was now burning like the fires of a newly formed star. "The Triumph of the Spirit, Matthew, happens at each of the Five Levels," Samuel continued. "Our journey is to build up to that final, climactic moment when we reach a state of peace, joy and love in connection with this divine field of the Fourth Dimension. This enables the real power that each human spirit possesses within themselves. You now know that the highest and purest power in the Universe, Matthew, is love. Putting oneself in this state of love inevitably leads us to new levels of the spirit as we grow and evolve to even higher levels of existence." Samuel paused yet again as another question for Matthew came to mind. "Do you know why, Matthew, love forms a more powerful connection to the Fourth Dimension?"

Matthew felt the need to take a deep breath and close his eyes to allow the answer to come. To practice what he had been taught on how to tap into the ULF and into his own divine intelligence. This wasn't something that could be intellectualized and studied like some academic test. This was now something so much bigger and deeper. This whole experience had somehow awakened him. He need not struggle but let it flow. After a few moments of reflection and quieting his mind, he responded. "God," Matthew murmured with his eyes still closed. "It brings us closer to God." Matthew opened his eyes to be met by Samuel's warm smile.

"And getting closer to God, Divine Being, The One or whatever term someone may use, ultimately brings us in connection to our true divinity as spiritual beings with immense potential," Samuel added.

With their red brick path still suspended in space, Matthew marveled again at the incredible beauty before him of infinite galaxies swirling around their life-giving suns, the sparkling glow emitted from the tail of comets hurtling across the Universe, and the hues of multi-colored rings surrounding various planets. Matthew was speechless as his mind and spirit continued to absorb this most wondrous sight and all that he had learned thus far.

"The vastness and beauty of the Universe is absolutely limitless," Samuel stated. "A part of reaching Universal Awareness, Matthew, is when a being realizes that the same universal beauty, energy, power, and love, which exists out here, really exists within themselves as well. Just look and you'll see it."

Samuel stepped aside to reveal what appeared to be a mirror image of Matthew standing directly before him. Within seconds, however, the image changed, and Matthew saw his spiritual energy signature as a golden light. It suddenly grew brighter until an eruption of blinding, white light filled the entire expanse of the Universe. It was as though the energy and brightness of a star had just exploded, its light released across the vastness of space.

Matthew felt an amazing rush of warmth overcome him as the light engulfed his very being, and a gust of wind blew through him, lifting his spirit. He felt love powering the light which beamed from it source—himself. It was though he had just witnessed the birth of a star, a star whose creation actually came from within himself and has now been released for all to see. It was beautiful.

Samuel studied Matthew's face as it reflected the awe and joy his prodigy was clearly experiencing. He realized that it was almost time to reveal the final truth. "You see, Matthew, the potential of humanity as intelligent and powerful beings is truly immense as long as they don't limit themselves," Samuel reminded.

With the backdrop of space and a view of the Universe still surrounding them, Matthew felt compelled to finally ask the question which had been burning in his mind throughout the entire journey. He turned his gaze back to Samuel. "Why are you here, Samuel?" Matthew asked. "Who are you? I've noticed some of the things you've said during our time together like you've been 'monitoring' me and the people on Earth. It is like you aren't from Earth."

Samuel stepped to Matthew's left, directly in front of him, and placed his hand upon the young man's right shoulder. "It's time now, Matthew," Samuel responded, knowing Matthew was ready to take the final step. "The answer to that is in the fourth stage of Universal Awareness."

With these recent inspiring truths that touched the core of his soul, Matthew nearly forgot that Samuel had told him there were four stages within the final level. How could there possibly be more?

"Alright, Matthew," Samuel began. "This last piece is so incredibly important, because it pertains to you, me, The Oval, and what this is all about. It's time you know why we are both here and how we are connected. It's time you know who and what we both are."

Matthew's heart began to pound in anticipation of what Samuel would next reveal. He would finally know what that burning desire for more he felt his entire life truly is and why it has propelled him so powerfully.

CHAPTER 17

THE LAST STEP

The two men were still standing on the red brick pathway suspended amidst the infinite beauty of space looking directly at one another.

"As a person moves into and through Level Five, they begin to feel a fundamental shift within their own state of consciousness as a cosmic spiritual being," Samuel began to explain. "Divine love begins to consume them, and they may start to feel some kind of inner calling. A spark within them begins to burn, driving them toward some purpose until it eventually ignites into flames of passionate pursuit to those who embrace and nurture it!"

Matthew couldn't believe it; he knew exactly to what Samuel was referring. Somehow, he knew. It was that sense of knowing there was so much more to this life beyond what was traditionally taught. It was that insatiable desire to find the truth and unearth what was deeply buried within himself. Matthew had always felt compelled to allow his true nature to burst forth into existence once he knew how to unlock it. He was no longer afraid to do so. He had always felt some kind of inner calling, and Samuel was helping him understand it. He was guiding him to it. Matthew now could fully appreciate why he felt this inner pull and what a powerful force it truly is. A calling which if ignored or denied by the ego, would leave a person wandering the Earth in a state of constant searching. They would be driven to fulfill a calling and ultimately discover divine fulfillment of their purpose. It grows and evolves into an alignment of one's true nature with God's loving intent for us. Matthew now knew he was in stage four of Universal Awareness.

"Yes, Matthew!" Samuel encouraged, knowing exactly what his pupil was thinking and feeling. "It's time you answer your calling. The fourth stage of Level Five is when you *surrender to your divine calling* once you discover it. Then you can ask for God's help and leverage the power within the Fourth Dimension to aid you in your divine quest."

"A divine quest," Matthew softly repeated while still looking directly at his mentor.

"Yes," Samuel confirmed. "What I am talking about is the final stage of Universal Awareness where we awaken to and accept our divine purpose in life. Following our passion where we use our God-given talents in fulfilling that purpose."

Matthew looked away from Samuel for just a moment and gazed once more at the incredible beauty of the Universe. Although Samuel's words resonated as ultimate truth, he still didn't know exactly what his purpose is, in spite of all that he has learned. Matthew looked back at Samuel to ask him to finally reveal what his calling is, but his guide still had more to convey to his young prodigy.

"This divine calling, Matthew, inevitably leads us to help others in small ways, large ways, or anywhere in between," Samuel continued. "We connect to the love within us and of others through God's divine presence. That's why the knowledge and energy within the ULF can only be used for good purposes and never to harm others. Once we answer our divine calling, we can ask for help, pray for guidance, await answers, and the serendipitous events orchestrated by The One through the Fourth Dimension will get us where we are ultimately supposed to go. In a way, Matthew, we die to our ego self and begin to embrace the eternal being within us, whose foundation is love and whose actions are driven by following the Divine Code."

The Divine Code.

Those last words struck a powerful cord within Matthew but that would have to wait a moment. A more pressing question burned in his mind and soul that he had to address with his guide before anything else. "What, Samuel?" Matthew began. "What is my true calling?"

Then suddenly it happened before his guide uttered another word. It was as though God whispered directly into his ear. The Key. Samuel had revealed it a few lessons ago. Somehow, Matthew knew that was the answer.

"You referred to me as The Key," Matthew rushed on. "I am The Key."

"Yes, Matthew. You are The Key!" Samuel replied excitedly. "You are The Key, and I am The Seeker."

"The Seeker?" Matthew questioned. "What is The Seeker?"

"We both have an incredible connected purpose," Samuel proclaimed. "My purpose was to find and guide you. Your purpose is to carry out a critical event in Earth's short existence, which is why you are The Key. You emitted a signal intended to be found by me. Hence, I am The Seeker whose purpose was to not only find you but unlock your potential. You are The Key that will trigger a sequence of events forever changing the future of your kind."

"What am I to do?!" Matthew asked with great anticipation.

"You asked to do this, Matthew," Samuel proclaimed before addressing Matthew's question. "Part of my growth was to work through this process to find and teach you. My purpose is to help you remember the fundamental truths that exist within your divine realm of being."

"I don't understand," Matthew replied.

"Don't try to wrap your mind around it, Matthew," Samuel instructed. "Merely try to access this knowing from within your spiritual self where all truth lies as it helps you draw upon the divine intelligence within the Fourth Dimension. Don't forget that the mind is merely a tool, albeit an exceptionally powerful one, where the ego resides and can hold us captive to old, destructive beliefs if we are not careful. It can manipulate us into thinking how separate we are from God, others and even from our own divine spirit."

Samuel's latest words helped Matthew remember a connection. "Because we all come from the same source," Matthew began. "We all come from the divine field of love." Matthew immediately thought of how the mind can create such doubt and fear within ourselves.

Samuel gave his prodigy another affirming smile. "You are a very old soul, Matthew," Samuel stated. "Souls range in their levels of existence and development just like people on Earth. You are part of a special group of beings commissioned by the Angelic Realm to take on missions of unique purpose in helping others."

Matthew's mind was racing. He was resisting the urge to disbelieve. It began to form, but he took a deep breath in an attempt to center himself and gain access to his spirit in order to diffuse what his logical mind found nearly impossible to grasp. He was trying to access the spiritual intelligence that existed within that his mentor spoke of. "So what is my mission, Samuel?" Matthew asked. "How am I The Key? The Key to what?"

Without warning, a strong wind began to blow.

"You are a connector, Matthew," Samuel answered emphatically. "You are a bridge. A bridge that connects beings to one another!"

A bridge? Matthew thought. *What could that possibly mean?*

"I have fulfilled my purpose as The Seeker by finding you and helping you remember who you are," Samuel continued to explain. "My purpose was to help you unlock your true potential and help you realize the purpose that you already knew deep within yourself. As The Seeker, I had to find you amidst the billions of souls on Earth. I tapped into the divine power within the Fourth Dimension as the brightness of your spirit and vibrating energy signature led me directly to you."

"How do I bridge people?" Matthew asked. "What does that even mean?"

Samuel placed his hand on Matthew's shoulder. There was a heightened intensity in their connection, knowing his mentor was about to deliver another huge revelation.

"You are to bridge worlds, Matthew," Samuel stated very clearly.

Matthew took in a quick breath in response to his guide's astonishing statement.

"You not only are to bridge entire worlds," Samuel began. "But also help bridge people to the divinity that exists within themselves."

Although momentarily stunned, Matthew knew deep down this was "the more" he felt his entire young life. It was both overwhelming and incredibly humbling at the same time. Nonetheless, this was his true divine purpose.

"We are here to help the people of Earth break free from these self-imposed limiting perceptions and connect to the source of their divinity of God's love," Samuel further explained. "It's time for humanity to experience another quantum leap but this time on a global scale."

The same question pertaining to his guide's origins still plagued Matthew. Samuel sensed it and decided it was time to finally reveal this truth. "I don't come from Earth, Matthew," Samuel said before his prodigy could ask. "I am from another planet within the Universe."

The expression upon Matthew's face shifted to one of complete disbelief.

Samuel then raised his left arm and pointed his index finger. The power that Samuel apparently possessed caused the scenery of the Universe to change again. Stars, galaxies and entire planets suddenly zoomed past them as Samuel somehow pulled his own galaxy and planet into view. Matthew now found themselves hovering above a planet whose beauty and majesty could only be rivaled by that of Earth. There were oceans and land masses just as one would expect, but the brilliance of the colors was a sight to behold. Matthew saw multiple shades of blue and purple within the waters of Samuel's planet. The landmasses ran the entire spectrum of landscapes and colors. There were snow-capped mountain ranges, lush green forests, open plains and areas of land that appeared to be emanating a very bright light. It was a light that one would only presume could exist within large industrial cities.

Matthew's heart pounded within his chest as his level of excitement could only be matched by his level of disbelief. He had always dreamed of other galaxies and planets with intelligent life and how such a discovery would rock the world. He had always fantasized of such an event happening during his lifetime, and he now found himself standing before visible proof.

It was amazing, beautiful, exciting and mind-numbingly incredible all at once. Yet, Matthew realized that such things were possible now that he opened up to his true self and allowed his spirit to be his guide on this journey through Samuel's tutelage.

"What's the name of your planet, Samuel?" Matthew quietly asked as his gaze remained fixed upon the planet before them.

"We refer to my home world as Epoh," Samuel answered.

"It's beautiful," Matthew said with wonder and astonishment, unable to look away from the awe-inspiring sight.

"Our race has reached a level of advancement that humanity aspires to attain," Samuel explained. "We have entered into Level Five of the Spirit on a planetary scale as our Universal Awareness has grown, and we began to experiment and develop our own powers as intelligent spiritual beings. As our knowledge grew, we became aware of your planet and the life that now exists upon it. We began to monitor the advancement of human kind and have been very encouraged."

"But how?" Matthew asked. "How did you do this monitoring?"

"Well, at first our scientists created advanced technological devices sent across the Universe to gather information on life outside our own galaxy," Samuel explained. "Eventually, our intelligence and spiritual powers grew to a point where we could make incredible discoveries by fully tapping into the Fourth Dimension in ways, Matthew, you have only just begun to understand." Samuel paused a moment to search for the words to precisely explain this concept. "We not only tapped into the ULF but found a way that would allow our spiritual selves to be fully submersed within it," Samuel said, hoping his words provided more clarity.

Matthew wasn't sure what to think in terms of how they became submerged within the Fourth Dimension, but he had to find out what that truly meant. "So you've been monitoring us from within the ULF," Matthew repeated. "But what does it mean to submerse yourself in it, and how did you do it exactly?"

"Yes, we have been watching, Matthew, and you will soon know the answer to your question," Samuel replied. "We have been monitoring humanity for a very long time. Then I found my true purpose as The Seeker, and through accessing the Fourth Dimension, I was able to find you."

"But how?" Matthew asked again eager to learn even more.

"Like we talked about before," Samuel replied. "In order to access the Fourth Dimension, it is necessary to be in a place of peace and love. A person in a state of negative discord from things like selfishness, stress, jealousy, greed, vanity and fear is too removed from the very essence of their true, divine spirit to be able to touch the Fourth Dimension. My people, over centuries of growth and evolution, managed to move through the final stage of Universal Awareness to a point where our complete spiritual selves could enter the divine energy of the Fourth Dimension and unlock unimaginable knowledge. Think of it as a temporary out of body experience. We began to learn profound truths not only about our own divinity but understand the nature of divine existence itself. We discovered the existence of entire worlds and civilizations within the infinite expanse of the Universe."

"And that led you to Earth," Matthew finished succinctly, as his glance shifted away from Epoh and back at his guide. "It led you to me."

"Yes, Matthew!" Samuel responded excitedly. "Your spiritual energy was a beacon of light that emitted an incredibly strong signal within the Fourth Dimension. I was drawn to you because of who you truly are, the intended divine purpose you are to fulfill, and the desire to unlock what you felt deep within yourself but couldn't quite fully understand it or know how to access it. Your wonderful dreams were one of the ways I could hone onto your signal because of your desire to reach levels that conventional beliefs on Earth would claim unreachable. I knew you were special, and you had to be The Key. As The Seeker, it was my purpose to find you and guide you."

Matthew looked back at Epoh as he continued to process everything his guide had said up to that point. His spirit was now incredibly uplifted as the clarity he felt deep within himself was expanding his awareness and enhancing his ability to fully comprehend these fundamental, universal truths. It was almost as though he already knew what Samuel had helped him remember. Then a curious question came to mind that he felt his guide needed to address.

"You can actually monitor dreams?" Matthew asked.

"Yes, that's possible in the Fourth Dimension," Samuel replied. "It's usually within that state of consciousness that the human mind will let down its guard and let go of limiting thoughts. Humanity has such wonderful dreams and imagination. The great scientist, Albert Einstein, once said, 'Imagination is more important than knowledge. Knowledge is limited. Imagination encircles the world.' It is the dreams and imagination coupled with the courage to pursue them which has propelled humanity's development so far."

"You said that I asked for this, Samuel," Matthew continued questioning. "What does that mean?"

"Matthew, you came to Earth to fulfill a divine purpose," Samuel explained. "You volunteered for this, as did I."

"I volunteered?" Matthew asked with great confusion. "What are you even talking about?"

"I told you, Matthew, there are those within an Angelic Realm who commission special spirits for specific purposes or missions," Samuel replied. "You are one such being, as am I. You chose to go to Earth, and as such were born into the physical plane to fulfill the purpose of being The Key. You were intended to become a connector and help humanity continue to unlock their true potential."

"And you as The Seeker chose to go to Epoh," Matthew said as he suddenly made the connection to the divine design at play

"Yes," Samuel answered. "It has been done this way for what human kind would consider an eternity. Souls have been traveling across galaxies and planes of existence in order to aid in the development of countless beings spanning worlds across the Universe that only now can you begin to fathom."

A flash of insight came into form within Matthew's mind as he immediately thought about the space-time continuum and the ever growing infinite connections contained within it. Matthew then realized that the continuum is far more vast than he could imagine if it spans worlds.

"Matthew, your true self already knows all of this information, given who you are," Samuel continued. "That's part of my job as The Seeker, to find you and unlock the memories and knowledge within your spirit that you brought with you from the divine plane. It is precisely that reason why you inexplicably had this inner drive and knowing at such a young age. It's because of who you are."

"The Key," Matthew reiterated as he glanced back at the beauty of Epoh once more.

"That's right," Samuel replied with an affirming nod.

Matthew had to ask the next question that came to his mind. "Have I always been a Key?" Matthew inquired.

"No," Samuel answered. "As I've said before, souls range from young to old in their level of evolution. You are a very evolved, old soul who continued to grow in love, truth and God, from which the natural outcome led to your becoming a Key."

"There are others like me then?" Matthew asked with great interest.

"Yes, but not presently on Earth," Samuel replied. "There are others scattered across the Universe for which they have a corresponding Seeker."

"Are they always successful?" Matthew questioned.

"Not always," Samuel answered.

"What happens if The Seeker and The Key cannot find each other?" Matthew asked as he again turned his attention toward Samuel. "What if they cannot connect as you and I did?"

"They both eventually die as they age and return to the Angelic Realm to begin again and to learn from the experience of what they missed in the previous life," Samuel answered. "The bond you and I share Matthew is very special."

Matthew could definitely sense that, but he wasn't sure why it was true.

"How so?" Matthew inquired.

"We both volunteered for the same mission," Samuel stated. "Earth was our target. We came into being on our respective planets, and then I had to move through my journey on Epoh to reach a level of development that would ultimately lead me to you."

"Because you come from the Angelic Realm as well," Matthew said.

"That's right," Samuel replied. "I began to remember through my own evolution and knowledge present within the Fourth Dimension that we have done this numerous times together. We have an incredible, divine bond at a spiritual level."

Matthew somehow not only accepted this as truth but felt this at the core of his being. As his journey unfolded, Matthew felt the connection with Samuel intensify and expand to a level that was beyond rational explanation. It was truly divine in nature. Then Matthew had a flash of recollection, shedding light upon why they shared such an incredibly strong bond.

He and Samuel are spiritual brothers.

They have traveled the expanse of Heaven and the Universe together as spiritual warriors countless times. They have faced unknown challenges and endured great pain to fulfill their intended missions. Sensing Matthew was beginning to unlock more connections contained within his divine being, Samuel raised his right hand and placed his palm gently upon Matthew's forehead. Images immediately began to flood Matthew's consciousness as he instinctively closed his eyes. They were images of past lives, flashes of countless people both young and old raced across his mind. Beings whom he had been connected to over hundreds, maybe even thousands of years. He saw and felt images of parents, siblings, spouses, partners and children. Loved ones whose lives were lost both tragically and others naturally. He saw images of being a protector holding a sword in defense of those who needed protection, and standing at his side was his brother Samuel. Another image came to mind where he stood at the base of a mountain, holding above his head an extraordinary sword radiating a pure, white light. The images continued to stream across his consciousness at a maddening pace.

Anger, hatred, love, betrayal, joys, triumphs, pain both physical and emotional began to take form within him as he continued to remember. Some memories were more explicit than others, but the feelings were very strong and very real. Not only did he see past human lives but incredibly, his own physical existence on other planets.

Somehow through Samuel's touch, these past experiences had been unlocked. God always placed in his path countless beings to further his own growth and evolution. Now, as a Key, it had been his job to help others by forming critical connections and spreading God's love, to help others grow, evolve to become who they were intended to be with the intention of fulfilling their divine purpose by expanding their loving connection to the Divine Field.

Connecting to their true selves and others.

Connecting to love.

Connecting to God.

Matthew suddenly felt an infusion of wisdom and knowingness, not only from connecting to his whole self, but also reconnecting to his eternal self, all of which has led him to this very moment. The young man then remembered something his brother mentioned that he suddenly felt compelled to further understand.

"You mentioned the Divine Code, Samuel," Matthew stated as he opened his deep, brown eyes to gaze upon his mentor.

He then noticed the wind had intensified as Samuel's hair and clothing were being violently whipped about.

"Yes, I did, Matthew, and you already know what that is," Samuel replied.

Matthew closed his eyes again and paused in reflection as he took a deep breath trying to access that which existed within himself. He was accessing the spirit place of knowing within his soul trying to connect to the source of all truth. He was trying to connect to the Fourth Dimension by allowing his mind and spirit to enter that immense pool of knowledge and divine love. He was trying to connect to his own divine spirit. An answer then began to surface surrounding The Code. It is a truth that he swore to uphold and try to live by spanning many lives and levels of existence. The notion of what the Code represents began to formulate.

It is the opposite of vanity and selfishness.

It is the opposite of anger and hatred.

It is the opposite of fear and insecurity.

It does not spawn or condone violent, hurtful acts.

For all those things cause pain. They cause pain within ourselves and sadly, for all of those around us. They suppress our true light and thrust us into darkness. They create a separateness from our true, divine being and an illusionary separateness from God, for He is present in us always. It is about character, integrity and honor. The Divine Code simply captures the one thing that embodies the foundation of all that we truly are.

Love.

The Code embodies the divine love of God, others and oneself, because we all are of the same source.

To live in a manner consistent with The Divine Code, we live in God and He in us. This then spawns compassion, kindness, forgiveness, selflessness and a giving heart. It truly enables us to live in confidence because of the faith that He is always there. He will never abandon us even when our faith may sometimes waiver. There may be times when we doubt His existence or how we may refer to Him but all we need to do is remind ourselves that love is real and love is founded in divinity. We walk with our Divine Protector, and He will always see us through because the true self of the individual is our divine spirit. The One will always guide us when we need it most, especially when we ask for such guidance or help. It may not come in the form of what we think we want, but it will always come in the form of what we need to enable our growth and our tapping into the Fourth Dimension is the key

What a blessing to live by The Divine Code because of the gifts we can bring to others even through the smallest acts of kindness and the ensuing miraculous gifts returned to us. One thousand fold.

"It's time now, Matthew," Samuel commented as he reached out with his left arm and embraced Matthew's shoulder in hopes of bringing him back to the current moment. Samuel knew it was now time for his prodigy to take the next step in his journey.

"What do you mean?' Matthew asked.

Samuel did not answer his pupil but rather raised his right hand, transforming their view to that of the familiar Milky Way Galaxy and the beautiful planet that Matthew called home for eighteen years—beautiful planet Earth. Matthew took a moment to admire the scene as he wanted to appreciate his special connection to the place he has been linked to during this short life within this particular plane of existence.

"Why did we come back here?" Matthew inquired after a few moments.

"Just watch, Matthew," Samuel replied.

Suddenly, Matthew could see a huge, golden beam of light suddenly come into view from an unknown source and connect to Earth. It looked just like the countless ribbons he had seen numerous times within the space-time continuum connecting to a gateway. Within a few seconds, another came into view and merged with his mother planet. Then a third golden ribbon *originating* from Earth shot out into space. It appeared to have a very deliberate path, but Matthew couldn't visually follow it because of the great distance the ribbons stretched across space.

"What's going on?" Matthew asked in a confused voice.

"Maybe this view will help," Samuel replied as he waved his right arm, causing their viewing angle to "zoom" out. The Earth was still visible but much smaller as though they suddenly transported out a great distance. Matthew quickly understood why Samuel changed their vantage point. His mouth dropped open as he saw the three golden ribbons connecting to other worlds. In that very moment, he realized what Samuel was showing him.

"We're in the space-time continuum, aren't we?" Matthew asked with a tone of astonishment.

Samuel smiled. "You see, Matthew, your planet Earth is just another gateway within an even larger grid of the Fourth Dimension," Samuel explained. "The space-time continuum is part of the Unified Life Force binding all living creatures together, not only on your own planet, but to life on other worlds as well."

As has happened countless times on his journey, Matthew's breath was momentarily taken away. His mind began to race as countless possibilities arose. Samuel knew that his prodigy's awareness has been expanding at an exponential rate these past few lesson, and he could continue to reveal further truths and instruct Matthew in his next step.

"This is a part of the intelligent Divine Universe," Samuel continued. "Ever growing and expanding with new connections constantly being formed both within the life of an individual but also on a global and universal scale."

Matthew suddenly noticed that one of the ribbons appeared to have traveled a very short distance and was connected to a planet within his own solar system.

"What is that ribbon connecting to?" Matthew curiously asked as he motioned in the direction of the shortest energy ribbon connecting Earth to the fourth planet from the sun.

Samuel said nothing but rather raised his hand in response and immediately zoomed in their current position in order to more closely study the phenomenon raised by his observant student.

"Don't you recognize this planet in your own solar system?" Samuel asked.

Pausing a moment, Matthew provided a response he thought was the most logical answer.

"It looks like Mars," Matthew replied.

"That's right," Samuel confirmed.

"But why would Earth have a connection to Mars?" Matthew asked completely dumbfounded. "There is no life there. It's a dead planet."

Samuel smiled again for he knew the next revelation of how expansive the Universe truly is would blow his brother away. "Matthew, you have continued to make such incredible strides on your journey," Samuel began encouragingly. "I am immensely proud of you, my spiritual brother. What I am about to tell you is yet another huge step along your path of understanding, as shocking as it might be."

Matthew's gaze shifted away from the energy ribbon which connected Earth and Mars as he looked directly at his teacher.

"This is my home, Matthew," Samuel stated very matter-of-factly.

Matthew was completely taken aback. He looked at his guide with a furrowed brow.

"You showed me your planet Epoh, and that wasn't it!" Matthew said in disbelief. "I saw an incredibly beautiful living planet." Matthew suddenly grew concerned that something had gone terribly wrong on Epoh in the distant past which resulted in the demise of Samuel's people and civilization.

"Yes, you did, Matthew," Samuel confirmed. "But what I have chosen to conceal from you until now is that Mars is my home *within an entirely different dimension of the Universe!*"

Matthew looked back at Mars and then again at his teacher. *How is that even possible?* Matthew thought.

Samuel couldn't wait to reveal the explanation Matthew so desperately sought. "Once my people began to leverage and explore the ULF, we discovered the existence of Earth and the intelligent life upon it," Samuel began to explain. "Initially we believed that Earth's solar system was contained within a galaxy millions of light years away from our own planet. To pinpoint the exact location of Earth, our scientists used the information within the Fourth Dimension in order for us to reach Earth. What they discovered was entirely unexpected and sent a shockwave of spiritual and scientific discovery across Epoh!"

"What was that?" Matthew immediately inquired as he hung on his guide's every word.

"That Earth was actually located here in our own solar system!" Samuel replied. "Given our scientific advancements, we had already explored virtually every planet in the system centuries before and found no evidence of life."

"How did you do such exploring?" Matthew asked.

"At first, we sent probes much like your own," Samuel responded. "Then we progressed to a point where manned interplanetary travel became possible and we actually traveled to these other worlds. As we advanced our spiritual and intellectual selves through accessing the Fourth Dimension, physical travel became unnecessary."

"So, having ruled out that any life exists on Earth when you went there, what did your people do?" Matthew asked. "How did they find out about this other dimension?"

"Our scientists remained perplexed, but by using all Levels of the Spirit, they were able to crack the code," Samuel responded excitedly. "After years of study and development of scientific theories, all of which were aided by our continued interaction with the Fourth Dimension, it was determined that life on Earth existed within a completely previously unknown dimension of space."

Matthew was truly blown away by the notion that life was present on Mars but entirely within a new dimension of existence, a dimension where Mars was alternatively known as Epoh with billions of intelligent, advanced beings living on it.

Samuel knew this would literally short Matthew's proverbial circuits, but he also sensed the immense excitement present within the young lad after learning this truth. "This alone proved an immensely powerful concept," Samuel stated.

Realizing that his breathing was suspended momentarily from the shock of it all, Matthew let out a deep breath as he felt his heart would pound straight through his chest. "Which was what?" he asked once he regained some composure.

"That the Universe is truly formed and changed by thought," Samuel explained. "And its limits are only bound by those thoughts created within the individual and collective mind. In short, the Universe truly is limitless!"

Matthew looked away from Samuel and studied the ribbon connecting the two worlds as he continued to process all of this new information. But interestingly, processing not only entailed the use of his mind but of his own spirit as well to reach deeper understanding. To gain the truth embedded within the eternal intelligence of his spiritual self. Matthew quieted his mind and soul to allow the Fourth Dimension to touch him and he, it.

"How long ago was this, Samuel?" Matthew asked with great interest.

"This all transpired by Earth's standard measure of time over thousands of years," Samuel replied. "But Matthew, you now know that time is merely an illusionary measure created by humanity. Because of the infinite nature of the Universe, time truly does not exist."

Samuel's words resonated true in Matthew. However, the notion that time doesn't exist brought about a dilemma in his mind that needed to be addressed. "If time truly does not exist, then why did you call it the space-time continuum?" Matthew asked.

"Because I wanted to give you a frame of reference that your rational mind could initially comprehend," Samuel replied. "We refer to it simply as the space continuum."

Matthew's awareness and universal intelligence had advanced through his journey to a level where previously illogical possibilities began to make sense. He had moved into a place of knowing. Knowing and understanding more truths about what The One has created within the Universe, and it truly was astounding. It far surpassed any of his wildest dreams, how all life is bound through the Unified Life Force where our thoughts and spiritual energy signatures actively participate within this field, where no boundaries or limitations exist. The Universe is infinitely larger because of all the other dimensions within the space continuum that binds us all together through timeless connections. While his eyes were still fixed upon the image of Earth as a gateway, Matthew needed to ask yet another question.

"You mentioned that humanity's awareness must grow on a global scale," Matthew began. "Why?"

"It's simple really, Matthew," Samuel stated as he joined with Matthew's gaze of the Earth. "Humanity has achieved a great deal in a relatively short period of time and has shown flashes of great potential. But those serving upon the Epoh counsel monitoring Earth have also seen great tragedies and disturbing patterns of life."

Matthew briefly looked away from his home planet and shot Samuel a look which conveyed the concern and confusion he suddenly felt.

"Dark shadows like disease, famine, wars, social unrest, environmental damage and violence continue to exist at disturbing levels on your planet," Samuel continued. "Although there is evidence of past and present teachers who have introduced these universal truths of mankind's potential, they have not yet gained enough wide-spread acceptance to raise global consciousness. We are concerned that if there is not enough momentum in that direction, humanity may very well eventually self-destruct and cause their own extinction! There is so much needless pain and suffering on your planet that can easily be prevented."

Matthew pondered his guide's words. Everything Samuel said seemed so painfully true yet how could *he* be a possible solution to all of these problems?

"So how do you fit into this, Samuel?" Matthew asked. "I know you are The Seeker, but how does that fit within all of this? Within Epoh and Earth?"

Samuel looked at Matthew intensely. "I am a member of this council, Matthew," he replied.

"But coming from the Angelic Realm where we began this journey, why is there even a need for such a council?" Matthew asked.

"Because, Matthew, that was part of my journey and growth as The Seeker," Samuel responded. "Seekers and Keys must find ways to operate within the physical planes into which they are born."

"So the people of Epoh have deemed it necessary to intervene now on Earth's behalf?" Matthew asked.

"Yes, and that was part of my own destiny in this life," Samuel further explained. "As intended by The One and because of the pact you and I made with one another prior to coming into physical form again. Through the Fourth Dimension, I was able to regain my purpose and remember that I was The Seeker in this particular mission. Together, we must help as many people on Earth move into global awareness of these universal truths."

Matthew took a deep breath as he stared into the continuum and the golden energy ribbon that connected their worlds. Even amidst these dark forces in the world, there still is so much beauty and light. Such immense potential for good and God's love to aid in our growth as we connect to our divine goodness. Matthew then immediately thought of The Code and the fulfillment of his mission. He felt an incredible drive to fulfill his destiny in this life. But as he contemplated, another question came to mind.

"If this is God's plan, Samuel, why doesn't He just make it happen?" Matthew asked. "Why the need for you, me or any of this?"

"Ah, yes," Samuel began. "Because God's love is so perfect, Matthew. We are mere children. Just like any parent, he wishes for us to grow and learn, so he bestowed upon us one of the greatest gifts and what some may consider a curse as well."

"What's that?" Matthew inquired with great curiosity.

"Free will," Samuel replied.

Matthew paused for a moment as those two simple words resonated powerfully within him. It made perfect sense.

"Free will, Matthew, is crucial so we can continue to progress and become closer to The One and the divinity within ourselves. Every moment brings choices, and those choices have consequences from which we must accept the outcomes in order for us to progress. Some make choices that they know are wrong or damaging to themselves or others, but they may go down destructive paths anyway."

"Why would they do that?" Matthew asked, well aware that there are countless examples of such individuals and tragic events in Earth's history.

"For many of the reasons you have learned on your own journey, Matthew," Samuel answered. "They have not fully progressed across the Five Levels of the Spirit. They have their own journey to travel, and lessons will present themselves as needed. As the ULF brings forth such lessons, each individual has an opportunity to learn. If they ignore them, though, the lessons may increase in intensity and potentially become more painful until the person finally grasps the truth. It can even take multiple lives and planes of existence before they learn. But when a being does embrace these lessons, especially in spite of any pain they may feel along the way, the rewards and potential for real growth are enormous. You know this all too well, my dear brother."

Matthew took a moment to again reflect how far he had progressed on his own journey. Thankfully not all of his lessons were embedded with painful experiences. His soul immediately recalled the many exciting and uplifting emotions he felt along the way as well. He did have to summon the courage to knowingly face some incredibly painful challenges in order to continue his progression. A journey that he alone chose to embark on in spite of some extremely painful moments. Matthew now realized that each step in his journey brought him closer to his intended purpose. Each step brought him closer to his true self. Each step brought him closer to love, God, and the divine presence within his spirit.

Matthew then felt a sweeping sense of gratitude rush through him. He was grateful for this journey and the courage God helped him summon deep within himself to keep moving through it. He was grateful for learning these truths and the powerful lessons contained therein. He was truly grateful for his free will. Matthew sensed Samuel wanted to move into the next stage, and he now felt ready to do so as well.

"So, what now, Samuel?" Matthew asked eagerly. "How are we, together, intended to help the people of Earth?"

Samuel smiled at his brother, for he knew it was time. Matthew was ready to take on the task at hand. "We plan to introduce an event of global proportions to give a wakeup call to those who walk upon the Earth in a state of lackadaisical awareness," Samuel answered.

"An event of global proportions," Matthew repeated, unsure of how to interpret that statement.

"Yes," Samuel reaffirmed. "We plan on making ourselves known to the inhabitants of Earth and share some of our knowledge and advancements in hopes of positively influencing humanity's evolution. Then we can gradually share some of these truths to further propel the advancement of the human race."

"And how will this happen?" Matthew asked with great anticipation.

"That's where you come in as The Key, my brother!" Samuel said, excitement clearly written on his face.

Matthew, at first, was clueless as to how he was The Key to all of this and what his role could possibly be in this "global event." Then he recalled the event in his own life that started this entire journey. The discovery he made on his grandfather's farm that seemed so long ago.

The Oval.

He had no idea what, if any, passage of time had occurred, but then he remembered that time truly doesn't exist, so why should he be concerned about it? He saw for himself within the continuum the connections that existed spanning this false notion of time across dimensions. He was finally going to unlock the secret and purpose of the object that fell from the sky and set in motion the chain of events that had forever changed his life.

"So, this huge event is linked to The Oval, isn't it?" Matthew asked.

Samuel nodded.

"The Oval will start a chain reaction that has the potential of catapulting your planet into a new renaissance of development," Samuel replied.

"How?" Matthew asked.

"You are going to create a bridge between our worlds by activating The Oval," Samuel answered.

Looking away from Samuel, Matthew studied the energy ribbon which connected Earth to Epoh/Mars more closely. "What kind of bridge?" he asked.

"The Oval was designed to activate a portal between our worlds," Samuel explained. "A bridge connecting the physical dimensions of space between our planets."

"Then our people can travel back and forth between both worlds?" Matthew inquired.

"That's right," Samuel responded. "This journey of self-discovery was intended to allow you to reconnect to your true self. You were to build your own bridge back to the divine in order for you to carry out your mission. You must now activate The Oval in order to open the portal between Earth and Epoh. There is a sister device on Epoh now already activated, waiting to complete the link with the one sent to Earth."

"But how do I do that?" Matthew asked. "There weren't any visible markings or buttons of any kind."

"That's where the secret to The Oval lies, Matthew," Samuel said excitedly.

Having seen that look in Samuel's eyes, Matthew braced himself for the shocking revelation that his teacher was about to impart.

"The switch to activate the device is contained *within* The Oval itself!" Samuel revealed.

"What?!" Matthew shouted.

"You will see, Matthew," Samuel began. "The counsel believed that if humanity could prove it was ready to move to the next level of Universal Awareness, we would reveal ourselves and aide in your development. The activation of this bridge would provide such a test."

"And part of that test involved finding me as The Key," Matthew quickly surmised.

"Exactly," Samuel confirmed.

Matthew was all for taking this next step of the journey and prove himself ready, but he couldn't help but ask the obvious. "How can I activate something internally without any access to it from the outside?" he inquired. Matthew then quickly realized his mind suddenly began to list all the reasons why this task could not be accomplished, how "impossible" it seemed. He took a deep breath in an attempt to control his knee-jerk reaction of negativity to a seemingly impossible quest. He then focused on the truth within his spirit by recalling all that he had learned. He knew he could do it; his limitations were only set by his own thoughts. His spirit knew better. It knew more than his mind, because it was connected to the truth through the Fourth Dimension of existence. Banishing his negative line of thinking, a pathway to activating The Oval came to mind.

"I'm to use the power of my mind and spirit, aren't I?" Matthew realized.

"Yes, you are, brother," Samuel replied.

Matthew paused to let the ideas come to him instead of struggling to conjure up a logical explanation. For some reason, he felt if he let go, release his desire into the Fourth Dimension, his answers would be revealed. *Believing in the solution will pave the way to solution.* Matthew closed his eyes, took a deep breath, and recited the word, "Om," to clear his mind and relax. Upon doing this, a thought emerged almost immediately.

"You mentioned that our thoughts and emotions do, in fact, possess an energy signal of their own," Matthew repeated. "If I can focus with my *mind's eye* on activating The Oval, the energy signal of my thoughts and spirit should match that of the device."

Matthew realized that he was beginning to actively engage in the Fourth Dimension. The key to activating The Oval entailed his entering the ULF at a spiritual level.

"Yes, Matthew!" Samuel confirmed excitedly. "Your spirit will then leverage the power of the Fourth Dimension to access the device's mechanism. You'll be able to immediately establish the link to its sister unit and trigger the opening of the portal. Remember, you have the ability by aligning your mind, body and spirit with the Fourth Dimension, allowing you to manipulate the physical world." Samuel paused a moment watching the confidence grow in Matthew's eyes. "Are you ready?" Samuel asked.

Matthew nodded and tried to completely surrender himself by allowing his brother to guide him once more. He was about to finally complete the quest he started and fulfill his destiny. His divine purpose.

Facing Matthew, Samuel placed both hands on Matthew's shoulders and looked him directly in the eyes once more. "Don't forget where you are, Matthew," Samuel encouraged. "We've been traveling along the continuum and are in the room of infinite possibilities. What does that mean? Anything is possible! Remember what you have learned, brother, and what you have always known. You have made incredible progress, and the key was the desire and receptiveness of your own mind and spirit in having these truths revealed to you." Samuel fully appreciated the strong connection with his fellow spiritual warrior, and an intense pride welled up within him upon seeing the progress Matthew had made.

"Your spirit is so incredibly strong," Samuel said reassuringly. "I love you, brother."

"I love you too, Samuel," Matthew softly replied.

With those parting words, Samuel embraced his brother. Matthew reciprocated, suddenly feeling a surge of emotion. Taking a step back, Samuel could see the tears in Matthew's eyes.

"Matthew, this isn't goodbye," Samuel exclaimed. "It's just the beginning!"

Matthew's ears suddenly detected a faint sound which grew louder and louder with each passing second. It was a steady beeping noise. He looked all around him to locate its source but to no avail.

"What's happening?" Matthew asked.

"It's time to go," Samuel replied.

The wind grew stronger yet again. Matthew saw his guide's hair and clothing begin to ripple about from the sheer force. He felt it move all around him and oddly, even *through* him. Without warning, Samuel suddenly began to fade away with the wind as though the molecules of his physical appearance turned to sand and were gradually blowing away. It started with the red brick path where Samuel stood and slowly progressed up his body.

"Samuel!" Matthew yelled, panicking. He wanted to ask one last question before he disappeared before his eyes. "How can I fully submerse myself within the Fourth Dimension as your people has on Epoh?" Matthew blurted out in hopes he would get a reply before it was too late.

"You already have, Matthew," Samuel responded. "That's what you have been doing throughout your whole journey."

Matthew stared into Samuel's eyes one last time as the final truth embraced him. He realized now, that was exactly what he had been doing this entire time. Somehow he knew. Matthew instantly began missing his guide and spiritual brother, for he could not have made it without him. He felt empty as Samuel continued to quickly disappear with each passing second.

"Remember, brother," Samuel began. "Remember who you really are. We are connected by the ULF. We are connected at our spirit level. I will always be there with you to guide you."

With those final words, Samuel was gone.

Matthew then looked down and noticed the same phenomenon was happening to his portion of the path on which he stood. Matthew instinctively began to back up as the path before him gradually dissolved. Looking behind him, Matthew quickly realized he had backed himself all the way to the edge as his suspended platform of safety was melting away before his eyes. Finally, the last brick dissolved beneath his feet. Having no idea what would happen next, Matthew's heart began to pound. When the last grain of the path disappeared, Matthew began to fall.

"Samuel!!" Matthew yelled as he tumbled through space.

As he was falling, Matthew noticed the stars and planets of the Universe flash in and out of his line of vision. The spectacular site momentarily suspended his thoughts as he briefly found a moment of joy in the experience. His distraction, however, was short-lived, as he noticed the same "fading" effect was occurring now, as all the planets and stars were blowing away.

Having turned downward during his free fall, Matthew saw a single point of light quickly approaching him. His rate of speed did not allow him to determine its source, but he instinctively braced himself for a violent landing. The young man had but a second or two before impact when at the last moment he recognized what was about to break his fall.

His bed.

CHAPTER 18

NEW BEGINNINGS

Matthew gradually opened his eyes, and his ears tuned into the constant beeping sound that so abruptly ended his traveling through the Universe with Samuel. Turning his head in the direction of the noise, Matthew realized it was his alarm clock. As his eyes focused more clearly, he saw the current time of 6:45 a.m., which was the usual time he woke up each morning for school.

Lying face down, Matthew was feeling dazed and confused. He exerted every bit of strength in his right arm to reach over and shut off his alarm. He suddenly became aware feeling "disconnected" with his body. It was as though he had somehow forgotten what it was like to experience the world in the physical realm. Placing both palms on his bed, Matthew attempted to push himself up. Although he struggled at first, Matthew was able to sit upright on the edge of his bed. He began to stretch his back, arms and neck in an attempt to shake off the sluggish feeling. After a minute or two, Matthew noted his physical senses had begun to come alive again.

He stood slowly and took in a deep breath. In doing so, the first thing Matthew noticed was the most wonderful smell from the kitchen downstairs. His dad's pumpkin bread was one of his favorite foods. It was from a recipe that had been passed down several generations to David's mother. Instantly, Matthew felt the hunger in response to the aroma. It was so much more intense than he had ever before experienced.

Matthew then became aware of the wind blowing through the leaves of the oak tree just outside his bedroom window. He turned and walked slowly over to the window, feeling a bit out of shape. It felt as though his body was readjusting to gravity, and his muscles were back in training all over again.

When he reached the window, he saw the beautiful oak tree and its leaves dancing about. Matthew knelt, closed his eyes, and felt the wind blowing on his face and upper body. He took in another deep, cleansing breath, but this time it felt different. He was not only taking in life-sustaining oxygen but felt the energy of the wind enter his body. It felt incredibly invigorating. He felt as though he had absorbed the energy into his cells.

Matthew opened his eyes and gasped at the sight before him. His tree was glowing with its energy signature in all its glory. Every leaf, twig and branch was emitting a golden light. Matthew stood and noticed the energy flowing all about the tree, including the extensive root system *beneath* the ground itself. Barely able to contain himself, Matthew finally let out his breath and a short laugh. He felt a powerful urge to touch the tree.

Removing the screen of his window and setting it aside, he slowly leaned out with his extended right arm. Matthew reached for the closest branch and its small cluster of leaves. He couldn't quite reach it, but for some reason, he knew what he was about to do next. Closing his eyes and taking a deep, relaxing breath, Matthew surrendered his spirit to the task at hand. His body suddenly felt lighter, just as it had throughout his journey with Samuel. Then he felt a surge of energy within himself begin to swell and burst forth. Picturing the cluster of leaves in his mind, he mentally pulled them toward himself. He was using the energy of the United Life Force, an ability he now knew he had. As he tapped into the Fourth Dimension, Matthew felt the tree branch drawing closer, sensing its energy field enter his own. Feeling the surge of energy within and all around him now, he opened his eyes. At that precise moment, he saw the branch bend and stretch toward him. Matthew smiled and began to breathe faster as his heart rate escalated with excitement. The cluster of leaves slowly reached him as the tip of one leaf touched Matthew's right index finger. He felt an intense joy enter his body upon contact. He could feel the energy of the tree itself.

His mind, body, and soul suddenly all came into perfect alignment as the conjoined energies of Matthew and the tree swirled about in divine harmony. Surreal couldn't even begin to express the sensation of the experience he now felt. His elation was interrupted when he heard a familiar voice in the distance.

"Kids, breakfast time! Come and get some pumpkin bread!" It was his father.

Matthew released his hold on the leaf, but it didn't entail the movement of any of his muscles. Rather, he released it with his mind and spirit at which point, the tree complied with his desire by slowly backing away from Matthew's touch. Matthew took a few moments to collect himself and then stood up. A slight dizziness made him pause before walking. Never before had he felt so incredibly alive as when the energy surge vibrated in his body, sending a charge into the physical plane around him.

After the dizziness passed, he walked down the back stairway to the kitchen wearing only his red exercise shorts he typically used for sleeping. His parents were sitting at the table enjoying their morning cup of coffee. As soon as he looked up to gaze upon his folks, Matthew was blown away yet again. The aura of their energy was immense. He felt it right before his eyes detected it. His mom and dad were completely glowing with a purity of divine light coupled with an array of colors swirling around them. Matthew felt the intensity of their love. It penetrated his soul, possessing a powerful energy surge that his body could sense. The divine connection to these two beings was so strong.

Matthew took the last step and stood before them at the bottom of the stairs leading into the kitchen. Matthew's facial expression was unlike anything his father had ever seen upon his son's handsome face.

"Matthew, are you alright?" David asked.

"I couldn't be better!" he said excitedly. "I'm just so happy to see you both."

David and Ann exchanged confused looks with one another.

"I can see the real you," Matthew said.

Ann stood from the table and walked over to him. "Honey, are you feeling alright?" she asked. Ann raised her left arm and placed her hand upon Matthew's forehead, assuming yet again that her son must not be feeling well.

Matthew felt his mother's energy signature approach his own. As soon as her hand touched his forehead, he felt dizzy. The love was so intense. The purity of her concern and need to care for him was overwhelming. Matthew grew a little weak for a few moments. He dared not show it, because he didn't want her to delay the important task he had to complete.

Matthew turned to his mother and embraced her with a love brimming with intensity. A bit surprised at this sudden display of affection, Ann wrapped her arms around her son as she reciprocated the depth of the embrace.

"I love you, Mom," Matthew whispered into her ear.

Immediately, tears welled within Ann's eyes. "I love you too, sweetheart," she replied, her voice thick with unshed tears.

Matthew realized he hadn't said those very words enough over the years. He released Ann from his embrace and looked into his mother's eyes. He could see her. He lifted his hand and gently touched her cheek. He could see and touch her now at a much deeper level. Matthew smiled warmly and then turned to his father. David was clearly befuddled, not knowing what to make of any of this.

Matthew walked slowly over to David sitting at the kitchen table. Matthew reached down with his right hand and grasped David's left arm as he gently pulled upward to coax his dad out of his chair. Once David stood, Matthew repeated the loving gesture by embracing his father. Matthew could feel the paternal love within him—strong, unwavering, and protective. An incredibly good man who loved his family with all his heart and soul. Matthew reflected again how much of his core values and life's lessons came from this strong, noble man.

"I love you, Dad," Matthew said to his father.

David held his son even harder and fought back the tears as best he could. "I love you too, son," he replied.

After a few moments, Matthew released his dad. "Thank you," Matthew said to them both.

"Matthew, really, are you alright?" David asked again.

"I really couldn't be better, Dad," Matthew said with a reassuring smile.

Once again, David and Ann looked at each other with inquisitive expressions. Matthew realized he needed to go back upstairs to meet his destiny.

The Oval.

He didn't know what this would mean for him or his family. Would he even survive? Was his purpose on Earth only to open the gateway and then move onto his next Angelic assignment? Was this goodbye?

Matthew slowly turned and began to walk toward the stairs. Just as his left foot touched the first step, he turned back to look at his parents one last time. Again, he saw the glow of their beautiful spirits filling the entire room as it extended out toward him, embracing him in pure love.

He closed his eyes, took a deep breath and reopened them as he began to walk up the stairs. It was a stairway he probably had walked upon hundreds, maybe even thousands, of times over his short life. It now was leading him to the potential completion of his quest and ultimate divine purpose. As the determined young man took each step, his heart rate increased.

Reaching the top of the stairs, Matthew gazed down the hallway only to be met by his sister, Samantha. Just like his parents, her spiritual energy signature was extremely bright. Matthew always knew his sister was full of life. Now he was appreciating her uniqueness at a completely different level. It surged and pulsed in beautifully bright, varied colors. Samantha was staring down into her hand, holding her music player. She didn't see him at first.

Matthew smiled to himself as he slowly walked over to her. He realized that her spirit was reacting to the music playing through the tiny headphones in her ears. It was truly an amazing sight. She was quietly singing to herself and her feet danced in rhythm with the music. Samantha then caught sight of her brother out of the corner of her eye. She looked at him and saw the smile on his face.

"You goof!" she said. "Why are you staring at me? It's creeping me out!"

Matthew laughed out loud and stopped right in front of her.

"What?" Samantha asked.

"I can see you, Sam," Matthew replied.

Samantha paused the music and removed the headphones. "I would hope so, since I am standing right in front of you," she said sarcastically.

"I had no idea," Matthew stated.

Samantha looked at him with a raised eyebrow. "About what?" she asked in return.

"How incredibly beautiful you are and how brightly you shine," Matthew said with a huge smile.

Sam was completely taken aback. She had no response at first. "Um, I . . . what are you talking about?" she asked, stuttering.

"I'm appreciating you now, Sammy, in a way I never did before," Matthew replied.

Then, another surprise occurred when he proceeded to hug her intensely. After recovering from the shock, Samantha was touched by her brother's inexplicable and rare display of affection. "I guess I'm happy to see you, too," Samantha said as she hugged him back. "You're not trying to sneak into the bathroom ahead of me are you?"

Matthew let out a laugh. "No," he replied while still hugging her. "I love you, sis."

The wall of sibling rivalry that sometimes existed between them suddenly melted away. Sam continued to embrace her brother and uttered the only response she could conjure up. "I love you, too, big brother," she said.

Then Matthew felt their love on a spiritual level on this earthly plane of existence, for his sister and childhood best friend. He thought of the countless hours of playing together and the worlds they created within their imaginations. They became much closer after their mom's mental breakdown and temporary disappearance from their lives. They were there for each other. He always felt this protectiveness toward both his younger sisters. He now sensed within Samantha how safe she felt with him. He could feel how her spirit loved him as a friend, brother, confidant and protector. She knew that he would do anything for her, that he would always be there for her no matter what. Matthew felt tears well up in his eyes as he felt the power of how they touched each other in unspoken ways. An eternal connection. An eternal love.

When they finally released each other after several moments, Samantha noticed the tears in her brother's eyes. "Matthew, what is it?" she asked with a growing concern.

"I'm okay, Sam," he said. "I can't wait to share with you what I've learned."

"What are you talking about?" she inquired, greatly confused.

"You get in the shower first," he said to her.

"Okay," she said, knowing better than to press her brother into something that he wasn't ready to share quite yet.

"Where's our little sis, Katy?" Matthew asked as his thoughts drifted to their younger sister.

"She's still on her end-of-year field trip," replied Samantha. "She'll be home tonight."

"Oh, right," Matthew muttered disappointedly. He wished he could see his youngest sibling now, to truly appreciate and see her as he did with his parents and Sam. Matthew felt comfort in knowing that Katy knew how much he loves her, but he was filled with an undeniable purpose now, and he could no longer wait. He had a destiny to fulfill.

Their shoulders brushed as they passed each other in the hall on their way to their respective rooms. Matthew continued to feel the energy of his sister's spirit with his newly heightened senses.

As Samantha entered the bathroom and flipped the light switch, she found herself pausing just before reaching down for her toothbrush to start her usual morning rituals. Something about Matthew struck her. He seemed different, almost peaceful yet sure of himself.

Just as he stepped through the doorway of his room, Matthew paused and turned back to look at his sister one more time. She was now standing there in the bathroom, preparing her shower as she carried out the mundane task of brushing her teeth. She gave him an inquisitive look just before she smiled.

He continued to admire the glow of his sister's spirit and the energy it emitted. Matthew smiled back at Samantha as she closed the door. Matthew then turned his focus on the task at hand as he entered his room. He saw The Oval resting on his desk where he had left it merely twenty-four hours earlier. This time, however, he could sense its presence. It was powerfully drawing him in. Somehow, he had become in tune with it. Butterflies fluttered in his stomach. The Oval was the catalyst that changed everything. It changed his perspective, his outlook on the future.

It was his purpose. He is The Key.

Closing the door behind him, Matthew slowly walked over to his desk and peered intently down at the object. His job was to activate it as Samuel instructed. He was to apply everything he had learned and awakened to during his journey in order to establish the physical link with Epoh. His job seemed simple yet daunting as he stood there motionless.

Taking a deep breath, Matthew cleared his mind and let go. He released his doubts, his fear, his desire for the Fourth Dimension, his love . . . . everything into the world.

"God," Matthew murmured softly. "Please help me do as you intended. Help me to fulfill my purpose. Help me BE that bridge." Closing his eyes, Matthew slowly reached down with both hands. Just before he made contact with the object, he felt its warmth radiating out. Suddenly, the heat embraced him. The sensation spread across his hands, arms, torso, legs and head. His entire body was now wrapped in a field of heat. Then his hands finally reached The Oval as he touched the surface.

Instantly, Matthew felt a surge of energy course through his body. Within seconds, weightlessness overcame him. He connected with the object on an energy and spiritual level. Although Matthew's eyes remained closed, he could sense a bright light, and then a swirl of wind emerged. The wind's intensity felt like that of a mini cyclone surrounding him. He held his breath, attempting to adjust to the connection. It felt incredible. There was such strength within him. He knew the end of this part of the journey was upon him. He was filled was confidence, peace and love.

The Code. So much hope.

Then an image appeared out of the light, a spiritual view of a being. Matthew knew immediately that it was there to help him. His first thought was of Samuel.

"My brother?!" Matthew said, ecstatic at the prospect of seeing him again. "Samuel?"

The being approached and stopped directly in front of him. It had no detectable facial features, as it appeared only in the form of a beautiful silhouette of light. The spirit shook its head in negative response to Matthew's suspicion. His moment of disappointment was interrupted when the spirit spoke directly into Matthew's mind.

"Matthew, you have done amazingly well," it said in a feminine voice. "I am here to help you continue down the path." Then she reached out and grabbed Matthew's hand. Not the hand of his physical self but of his spiritual self. Their spirits joined. Sheer bliss overcame Matthew as peace melted away any remaining anxieties that haunted him. The hope-filled future was certain. The present was his purpose in carrying out his mission. The purity of love emanating from his next guide filled his soul.

"Come," she said. The being slightly turned to her left while holding Matthew's hand and gently tugged him in an effort to make him follow. The wind intensified even more.

Matthew opened his physical eyes and saw what would have been unbelievable to him before but no longer. His hands were *inside* The Oval. There was no perceivable opening. It was as though his hands were cut off at the wrist as they had disappeared into the device itself.

"Matthew," she spoke again. "Remain with me and focus."

Matthew closed his eyes again and noticed that the white light which had previously surrounded them had given way to a tunnel forming. The end of the tunnel emitted a bright sequence of multicolored lights. She squeezed Matthew's hand firmly in a reassuring manner.

Matthew was not afraid.

They reached the end of the tunnel, and the lights came into focus. They entered a pod shaped room with no corners but rather a ceiling and walls that converged into one round and fluid structure. It seemed he was now somehow within The Oval itself. His new guide released his hand and stood to Matthew's left. In doing so, Matthew could see what was directly in front of them. A control panel floated in mid-air. He walked up to it and saw a circular electronic screen emitting a bright blue light. There were no other buttons, levers or lights. The screen itself was just big enough for his hand to fit precisely within its confines.

Matthew reached down with his right hand and touched the circular screen with his index finger. Much to his surprise, it gave way to the pressure as though it were made of a viscous substance. The contact sent perfect circular ripples throughout the display that extended outward. He pulled his finger away, and the rippling effect stopped.

At that moment, Matthew realized his guide had moved directly behind him. She slowly but gently slid her right hand beneath Matthew's. The palm of his right hand now rested upon the top of hers as she lifted his hand upward until it hovered directly above the circular blue panel. She gently pulled her hand away as Matthew stood there with his hand inches above the panel.

Matthew understood what he must now do. He had to place his hand on the liquid screen to activate the link to its sister device on Epoh, opening the gateway and establishing the bridge between the two worlds.

Matthew began to lower his hand the remaining few inches but paused just before making contact. "Who are you?" he asked. "Was this part of your mission as well?"

"Oh, my dear one," she said tenderly. "I am here because you asked for help." Still standing directly behind Matthew, she placed her right hand on Matthew's shoulder. Her touch infused reassurance into Matthew, who immediately remembered: He had prayed to God just before making contact with The Oval.

"You asked for help, and so I was sent to you," she continued. "All too often, beings on the physical plane wait to pray and ask for help when they are in crisis. But what so few realize, is that you can ask for help and guidance at any time with any task, even when you are not in dire straits."

Matthew gave a slight nod to show his understanding.

"And it will be provided in love, especially when asked from a pure heart and with motives of fulfilling one's higher purpose," she concluded.

Tears of joy filled Matthew's eyes. We do not walk alone—ever. Angels stand at the ready to help when we ask. God's loving design is so perfect. Matthew looked back down at the circular panel and gently placed the palm of his hand upon the soft blue screen with his fingers spread apart. Suddenly, he felt a jolt of energy course through his body which arched his back and threw his head back. The blue panel began to light up, and once again, warmth overtook his body.

A connection was established. Suddenly, the golden walls of the oval room began to flash a white light that pulsated all around him.

Then the voices came.

With each flash of light, more joined in. Matthew could not make out the words as they were interrupted with each flash. Then in one bright explosion, the walls burst and the brightness remained. The golden color had disappeared and was replaced by a steady glow of white light. The voices were now fully audible. They spoke a language that Matthew had not heard before but, somehow, he fully understood their meaning. Then the light began to slowly fade and images appeared on the walls themselves. Matthew could see what was now before him: another control room filled with beings. He could not only see their physical bodies but also their energy signatures, just as he had with his family. He looked all around him as he was immersed within an oval shaped theater. He was surrounded by a similar control room filled with people and instrumentation. They were busily moving about as each one apparently had a job to perform.

He began to notice the Epohnians' physical characteristics. They were very humanoid but with distinctly large eyes and small ripples on the bridge of their nose. Matthew could easily tell which were males and females based upon the contours of their bodies outlined by the tight fitting silver uniforms they wore. The males had short sandy brown hair worn above the ear. The females, however, had long flowing bright red hair extending all the way to their waists. Matthew fully appreciated their stunning beauty. All of them seemed to be in perfect physical condition. Their arms also seemed uncharacteristically long and slender, at least by human standards.

Matthew then took note of one fellow who was standing directly in front of him. Again, in a language foreign to Matthew, the humanoid spoke in his native tongue but Matthew understood every word.

"Everyone!" the Epohnian man said excitedly. "I've got a reading!"

The control room became silent. Matthew could see the hue of a flashing green light reflected on the man's face as he stared intently down at his control panel.

"He's done it!" the man called out. "The device on Earth has been activated!"

All of a sudden there was an eruption within the room. They all let out a collective cheer and a most unusual chirping sound that Matthew could only surmise was a customary excited response. Within moments, the dozen or so beings in the control room quieted down. Matthew noticed the man operating the panel on their end stood motionless. He then looked around the room at all of his comrades.

"It's time," he said softly into the quiet room. The man raised his right hand and held it up for a moment while staring straight ahead. Then he lowered his hand, momentarily hovering over the panel with his fingers spread apart. The room was so quite that the slightest whisper would have sounded thunderous. The panel operator then placed his hand upon the sister unit's blue circular screen. A blinding flash of light in the room caused Matthew to briefly shield his eyes with his left hand but still maintain contact with his right hand on his panel. When the flash subsided, Matthew could not only see them but now deeply felt their presence.

The Epohnian operator looked directly into Matthew's eyes and spoke. "Well done, Matthew!" he said excitedly. "We are so incredibly happy to meet you."

Matthew took in a short breath before his mouth fell wide open in complete shock. The man could see him. Matthew sensed he too could feel his presence. Then out of the corner of his left eye, Matthew noticed a female drop the instrument she was holding onto the floor in shock. She clasped her hand over her mouth as she looked at Matthew. She lowered her hand and walked slowly to their control panel, stopping to the right of the panel operator. As she walked, Matthew noticed her graceful movements as though she glided effortlessly through the air. She now stood directly in front of Matthew.

Matthew noticed her extreme beauty immediately, but far more than her physical attributes, he noticed the perfection of her divine spirit. The colors emitting from her spiritual energy signature had suddenly changed in response to seeing Matthew. They flowed all about her, constantly changing in swirls of red, green, blue, gold and white brilliance. Matthew felt an extremely powerful connection to her. It was like a magnetic pull he could not escape from, nor did he want to.

He knew her. Matthew knew this alien woman standing before him on this oval screen. Without knowing why, his connection with her transcended any sense of time and space.

She also stood there, soaking Matthew in. He felt it. She closed her eyes and took a deep breath. When she opened them, her head slightly tilted to the side. She smiled so lovingly and stepped forward to appear closer and more magnified on the screen Matthew was viewing. She stopped once she had reached the edge of their room. It was evident that Matthew's image must be projected back to them within their control room.

Compelled to follow suit, Matthew lifted his right hand from the blue circular panel, but the connection with Epoh remained, for the bridge was created when the link had been established. Matthew slowly walked to the edge of the oval wall and stared at her. He studied her physical features more closely. Her white skin was smooth but possessed a hint of a sparkle. Her huge eyes were a brilliant blue, a blue deeper than any earthly tone he had ever seen. Nothing could compare to their beauty. Not even on the sunniest days could the color of the Earth's sky ever match what he could see within her gorgeous eyes. He could easily become entranced and lost within them.

Then she took a step closer and raised her right hand. She reached out as though she planned on touching the wall but paused. Matthew sensed a brief flash of fear within her but it quickly dissipated. She extended her right arm and reached *through* the wall and into Matthew's room as her long graceful fingers moved toward him.

He instinctively stepped back but not in fear. He was preparing for what he knew would happen next. The woman then stepped forward and fully emerged through the barrier that had previously separated them. She was now standing directly in front of Matthew.

She was almost exactly his height which was shockingly tall in comparison to that of a normal female of Earth. Matthew stood in awe. Her beauty and the palpable connection between them astounded him. Her arms were at her sides while she stood looking deeply into his brown eyes.

"I know you," Matthew said softly.

She smiled and reached up to place the palm of her left hand upon Matthew's cheek. Her love for him radiated through to embrace him. There was something intensely familiar about it as though they had shared many similar moments before. He then took his left hand and placed it gently upon her cheek. She responded with a quick intake of breath and her eyes closed in response to his touch. He slid his hand across her perfectly smooth skin toward the back of her head feeling every strand of long and silky, brilliant red hair pass through his fingers. Matthew raised his right arm and gently caressed her lower back. He pulled her closer to him and moved his lips to within inches of hers.

She whispered a single word. "Yes."

Matthew kissed her. Their bodies touched while their spirits danced about in a field of electrifying energy that enveloped the two beings in a moment of uninhibited passion. Memories came flooding back of the past. He and this female shared an eternal connection, lives they had shared simultaneously. Some not. But one was always there for the other, spanning numerous planes of existence that corresponded to thousands of Earth years.

They broke from their kiss, and Matthew looked into the huge, beautiful blue eyes that penetrated his soul. "Selena," Matthew whispered.

She smiled in response as a single tear ran down her left cheek. "I've been waiting for you, my love," she replied.

A more powerful and beautiful moment could not have been imagined in Matthew's wildest dreams. He did not want to be anywhere else without her.

She slowly moved her right hand down Matthew's cheek and onto the center of his muscular chest. Selena felt Matthew's strong, pounding heart. She looked down for a moment as though she did not want to say something but knew she must. She then looked back into Matthew's deep brown eyes. "It's time for the next phase," she said.

Matthew knew but didn't want to admit it to her or himself. "But we've finally come together again," he protested.

"My love," she began. "We both know we have an eternity together. We must continue what was started. You are an amazing spirit. It would be selfish of us both to not continue carrying out our mission." Selena paused a moment to look deeper into Matthew's spirit. "You are the bridge, my darling," she said with great purpose.

Matthew looked down as he felt a sinking feeling but didn't say a word. She lifted his chin with her right hand and spoke directly into his mind.

"I'm right here and will be with you the whole time," she stated. "I will be here, Matthew."

Then another strong gust of wind began to blow and form a cyclone around the two intertwined spirits. The next phase was commencing.

Matthew embraced Selena one last time in his arms and his spirit. She fully returned his embrace with her entire body, heart and soul. The brightness and colors of their combined spirits filled the room with a light and intensity that was sheer beauty.

The mission.

The Code.

He knew it was time to let her go once again as he had done so many times before, each one just as painful as the last. Yet, Matthew also knew his purpose, and he knew they would eventually be reunited.

Fear not. Love knows no boundaries.

Matthew released his hold on her body and spirit. She responded by slowly backing away. He held onto her right hand with his left, wanting to extend their moment for as long as possible. As she slowly backed away, Matthew held her hand until both their arms had fully extended, all the while gazing into each other's eyes.

The wind further intensified, and her long, brilliant red hair was now blowing across the right side of her face. Their fingers unclenched from one another, and all that physically connected them was a single finger. She paused just a moment before releasing.

"I love you, Selena," Matthew said trying to gain control of the emotion in his voice. "I will find you again even if I have to search a thousand life times across a thousand worlds."

The wind blew at a heightened pace. Selena pulled away at that very moment, and Matthew felt a sudden drop in energy as a momentary emptiness consumed him.

Then Selena spoke. "I know Matthew because you have already done it. I love you, too, my darling," she said with the most loving and gentle voice directly into his mind. "You, my dear, are The Key as intended. I am so grateful for you and the good which will come from fulfilling your divine purpose." She stepped backwards toward the wall without taking her gaze off Matthew and began to pass through it as she had done upon her initial entry. As the barrier began to engulf her, she spoke one last time.

"I will be waiting for you, my dear, for our reunion," she said. "I will be with you always."

Matthew's left arm was still extended, and his hand reached out one last time longingly for her.

The team of Epohnians in their own room stood and watched silently as they witnessed this tender miracle. The control operator then excitedly yelled out to his comrades triumphantly, "The link is now fully established and the connection complete!"

At that moment, Matthew could hear the cheers and chirps of the souls on the other end of the bridge. He had done it.

The wind was so strong now that it became increasingly difficult to stand as Matthew realized he was leaning significantly to his right to counterbalance the force. Without warning, the wind shifted directions in the room causing Matthew to lose his footing. It was now blowing head on, and Matthew was completely blown backwards off his feet.

Then, a peculiar thing occurred: time slowed and his movements with it. It was as though he was suspended in air momentarily while falling backwards. He noticed that he was exiting the room and had re-entered the tunnel through which he had originally arrived. The screen began shrinking into the distance, and his view of the Epohnians began to fade. A flash of white light again momentarily blinded Matthew, and with one powerful gust of wind, normal time resumed. He then felt the force of impact on his back, completely knocking the air out of him.

Unable to move, Matthew remained still as he looked all around him to gain his bearings. He thought he might have re-entered his bedroom within the comforts of his Earthly home, but instead, Matthew appeared to be in an empty room with no walls. Much like the room of infinite possibilities. Something caught his eye off into the far distance in front of him as he struggled to lift his head high enough to gain a better view.

The silhouette of a figure began to appear, and it walked quickly toward him. He could not make out its physical features as it appeared in the form of pure energy. As soon as it was upon him, the being stopped directly to Matthew's left, bent over slightly, and reached down toward him with its right hand extended. A clear gesture indicating assistance to the young lad.

Then a familiar voice spoke.

"Well done, brother," it said encouragingly. "It's now time for the next phase."

Matthew was relieved that Samuel had returned and felt his strong calming presence. Matthew shifted his body toward Samuel and reached up with his right arm to grasp The Seeker's hand and continue the journey, wherever that may lead. Matthew was ready and willing because he trusted now.

He trusted God.

He trusted Samuel.

He trusted himself in following that inner pull.

He trusted the next steps of this journey to unfold as they should.

For the good of all.

CHAPTER 19

AWAKENING

In a small village outside of Delhi, India, a young boy, no more than nine years of age, practiced soccer, alone in a dirt field behind his modest home in the middle of the day. As he moved about cutting, spinning and practicing his moves, the dust swirled around him. He stopped and rested his right foot on the ball in anticipation of shooting it into the goal when he was suddenly jolted by the sound of thunder. Startled, the boy paused with his right foot still resting upon the ball and immediately looked to the sky. He saw only a few white clouds. The boy took his foot off the ball and was about to resume his shot when he was startled yet again by another thunderous crack. He bent down, picked up his ball, and held it in his right arm against his waist.

The boy looked around again and noticed a peculiar phenomenon in the sky. The few sparse clouds began to move rapidly as a strong wind suddenly appeared. The boy's black hair was randomly blowing all around his brown face as the swirling wind began to intensify, but he barely noticed. The boy was too mesmerized by the scene unfolding before him in the sky.

The clouds began to move toward one another and combine into one. As they shifted to form a circular pattern, they began to swirl in a clockwise direction. Quickly, they had all combined to form a perfect circular cloud. Then another loud crack of thunder shook the boy to his core, and the ball dropped to the ground sending a billow of dust into the air. It bounced a few times as it rolled a few feet before resting silently. The boy noticed some flashing white lights begin to appear inside the large swirling cloud. Even though it was the middle of the day with the sun at its brightest, the white lights were easily visible. Another thunderous crack accompanied by a single flash of light triggered the next event. The cloud disappeared, and in its place, a ring of golden light traced the outline of the vanished cloud.

The wind was blowing even harder now, and it was only then that the boy noticed his soccer ball had rolled away. He turned his attention back to the sky and saw the huge, golden ring hovering high in the afternoon sky. The center of the ring did not contain the white mist of the clouds that previously occupied it. The boy noticed only a strange flowing energy moving about like a large body of water suspended in the sky. White and golden rays flashed with each fluctuating ripple, like those over a lake as the wind blows across it and the water dances to its command.

The boy's heart felt like it was about to pound right through his chest. Instantly, he took off in a full sprint toward his home. "Come!" he yelled out to his parents. "Come see! The sky! The sky is alive!"

The gateway to Epoh had been opened. The next renaissance of humanity was now upon them. A global event to raise the awareness of our true potential where limited beliefs and perceptions will give way to the light of truth.

The spirit can rise above adversity, pain, self-imposed limits, and old, destructive beliefs. It propels us forward and always will, especially when we open up ourselves and allow it to do so.

In the end, the spirit will triumph.

My friends.

I am grateful that you took the time to read this novel.
I am grateful for the goodness and love in this world.
Just the simplest act of kindness will create a positive ripple effect within our home, community and perhaps, even span the globe the likes of which we may not fully fathom in that moment. It can spread like an expansive interconnected web of good.

We all have struggles, scars from the past, and crosses to bear.

We all have times or moments of suffering, losses and pain to endure.

Pick yourself up with that cross, keep breathing and move forward.

And never be afraid to ask for help from others, or in prayerful meditation along the way when needed. It could be as simple as asking for strength and courage to carry on. We do not walk alone in this life.

Try not to succumb to the darkness of past or present pain but rather overcome it by finding your divine light.

And you find your light as you keep fighting the good fight one day at a time, overcome life's challenges, evolve, grow, appreciate the little things, and follow your passions with joy.

Live life to the fullest in spite of past or present hardships.

Then you will unleash your true power.

You will discover your strength.

You will experience healing, peace and a renewed excitement for the path ahead.

You will ultimately find yourself and your light.

I ask you to believe.

Believe in the goodness present in the world.

Believe in others.

Believe in yourself.

Focus on the light within and all around you.

Let the aura of your spirit shine brightly on your journey.

Miraculous things happen when we dare to:

Dream,
Hope,
Believe,
And most of all,
Love.

Love others and yourself for when we do so, we ultimately love God.

We will then connect to our divinity and miracles will unfold.

Let not fear be your guide through life but rather, faith.

And let love be your purpose.